Heartlines
Rachel E. Wilder

Indie Author Revolution, LLC

Heartlines was not created using generative AI/Language Learning Models. At no point was AI used in the writing, editing, formatting, marketing, and promotion of this publication. Rachel E. Wilder believes firmly that using generative AI to create works of fiction is against the very grain of creation.

We do not consent for this publication to be used to train AI/LLMs.

Part 9

The Regime

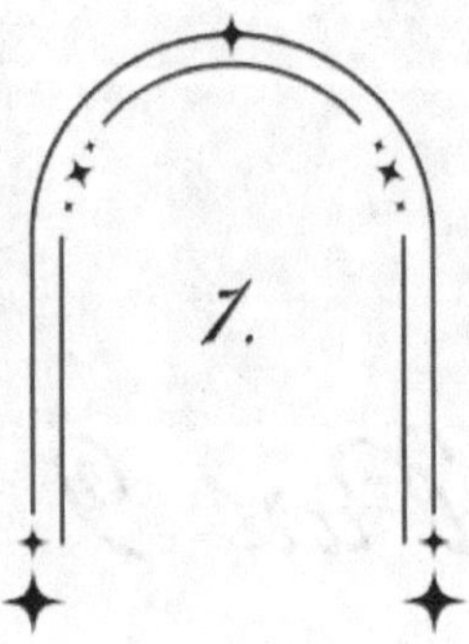

Ario's scalp was aching. The heady, chemical scent of the dye congealed in the humid air in their basement apartment, mixing with the scents of their neighbors—fried fish, old trash, cigarette smoke–and was starting to give him a headache. "How much longer?" he called to Evelyn, in the other room. The walls were so thin he didn't even have to raise his voice.

"Ten minutes. Have you finished packing?"

Ario sighed. Truthfully, it was easier to live out of suitcases than to fully unpack, lest they have to leave at a moment's notice; he'd lost favorite shirts and books that way. "Yes."

This stint, in a city he had never visited in his life prior and one he never cared to see again, was coming to an end. It was time to move on. It was always time to move on. In particularly impassioned moments, Ario hated Evelyn for never planting roots these long twelve years. As he'd gotten older, though, he understood why they had to keep moving. She was the reason he was alive.

As far as they knew, since the coup, he was the last surviving member of the royal line, the last Heir. His aunt, the regent queen Ainsley, had been brutally betrayed by her advisor Xander, the former liaison between elected non-magical officials and the magic-user court. Ainsley's body had never been found, but that didn't mean anything. Catherine Windsor, Xander's mother and their *blessed* despot, had quickly given up on public executions. Evelyn took this to mean that the regent queen was alive, in hiding, somewhere, but none of their resistance contacts knew anything.

It wasn't as though Ario could just make a claim for the throne. Catherine had followers; the followers had money and influence; magic users were still widely policed and registered. Anyone who "tried anything" was summarily thrown in jail, or worse. Evelyn believed that there would, somehow, miraculously, come a time and an opportunity for him to take back power. But considering that often there were stretches when they didn't know what they would eat next, he wasn't so sure.

Sometimes he wondered if she was wasting her effort.

"Ario! That's the timer."

He took himself into the small, sad bathroom of the apartment. The water never got hotter than lukewarm, and despite best efforts at cleaning, a strange pinkish mold had taken over the grout. He scrubbed the goo from his short hair and showered, unsure if this next place would have running water. The mirror in the bathroom hadn't even fogged; he saw himself, brown skin pale from lack of sunlight, his blind eye looking exceptionally dull. And his hair, despite all efforts, remained the strange violet-silver he'd been born with, a dead giveaway of his status as a magic user. Ario sighed heavily.

"That doesn't sound good."

He put on his bedraggled robe and opened the door, giving her a droll look.

Her own hair looked particularly limp, tucked back in its usual French braid. Every year the black just became more and more streaked through with gray. She reached out and touched the damp tips. "What am I going to do with you," she said.

"It's lucky that bold hair colors are starting to catch on with the public," he said levelly. In years past, even having blue eyes could draw someone under scrutiny. But some pop singer had dyed her hair candy pink for a tour, and it was becoming popular to do so among the general population. "Hopefully nobody will notice a boy with purplish hair."

She shook her head. "There's no time to try a new mixture."

"I'm not sure my scalp can take much more," he said. It felt like the whole thing was badly sunburned, feeling much akin to how it did when he used too much magic. Not that he was able to do that lately. "We're going to be late."

"Put on a hat," she said.

He did no more than roll his eyes, even though the evening would be late summer warm. In the tiny walk-in closet that had served as his bedroom, he dressed, put away his last few possessions in his old-fashioned leatherette suitcase, and headed for the door.

Evelyn was riffling through their false documents. "I've heard a rumor they've changed the ink color of the stamp," she said. "The last thing we need."

"If it's been changed recently, there are plenty of regular people with the wrong color stamp too. We've never been caught before in all these years."

Stress radiated off her. "There's always a first time." She proffered him the passport. "Come. We'll miss the train."

Of all the methods of transport, trains were the riskiest. Conductors did frequent and thorough sweeps for papers, and scans for magic univs, depending on the line. Boats were best; one could always hide in a corner when the searches started. And with hydrogen for cars becoming harder and harder to come by, there was no way they could afford to rent a car for long-distance travel. Solar flights had been limited when the air quality got too bad. "I don't suppose you'll tell me where we're going this time?" he asked. Evelyn sincerely believed that if they got caught and split up, he should know as little as possible in case they were interrogated. She was probably right, but at twenty years old, it was a bit grating to still be treated like a child.

"Let's get to the right station first," she said blithely.

Their flat was nowhere near a streetcar stop, so they walked, each with a suitcase and a backpack. Ario had done this too many times to be bothered by the weight anymore. Thick black night cloaked the city, the streets shiny with recent rain. From a red-tinted window, a sex-worker smiled owlishly at Ario. He blushed and looked away.

Nobody would assume that the Heir to Landfall was staying in the red-light district, after all.

A few more people were out on the streets now, workers or customers or tourists. With their luggage, anyone would assume that was what Ario and Evelyn were, instead of the former high priestess, and surely not the missing-presumed-dead Heir.

The train station was nestled in the center of the city, a well-kept brick building. Few people were boarding trains at this hour. After a breath-stealing moment, their passports passed muster, and they headed towards their gate. But what Ario saw made him freeze.

"Those are new," he whispered, to Evelyn.

She saw what he was referring to and cursed. The machines looked like metal detectors, neatly by the gates. But they could care less about metal water bottles or laptops. They sensed magic, and they had only gotten better as the years passed. "I don't suppose you actually had the foresight to take a dampener? I didn't either…"

"…No. I didn't think I needed to. I'd rather not be desperate for the toilet for the next six hours." They always tore his stomach to shreds.

"It's too late for one to kick in now."

"We could take the next train—"

"The pills only barely worked last time," she admitted. "We could go back, find another way."

He bit his lip, feeling the familiar stab of guilt. "Maybe if I cast a charm on the guard—"

"It'd be in their computer system. You can't charm that."

Stalemate. And the longer they stood there huddled together, the worse it looked.

"I bet I could probably charm someone at the car rental," Ario said. "Get us a good deal."

She sighed. "It may come to that. But better hope *they* don't have sensors, either. This place barely has electricity. How do they have more than handheld *scanners?*"

He nodded sympathetically, but wondered if this meant they would have to do another stint of living in the wild. At least the weather was still warm.

"Excuse me."

They both froze, caught; Evelyn made a strangled sound which she tried to disguise as a cough. But there was something... Ario recognized. He turned.

A tall, imposing man in a three-piece suit faced them. His skin was paler than theirs, more that strange cream of the north, and he had shorn dark hair and chiseled, rocklike features. A pulse of pure disbelief shot through Ario, and he almost said the man's name aloud before he stopped himself. "I can't help but overhear your predicament," the man said, mimicking this city's accent. "Isn't it horrible when they oversell trains?"

Evelyn's eyes bulged from her face, but she said, equally as calmly in the same accent, "it is quite frustrating. My son and I, you see, we're just trying to get home from our vacation."

"Perhaps I can be of service," the man said, his blue eyes glimmering. "Come with me."

He gestured, and without another thought they both followed. Ario's heart was racing, and he wondered, briefly, if they should trust him, but of course they could. For so many years Ario had thought he was—

Outside of the station, a small black taxi car was at the curb, one of a dwindling number of cabs. A guard stopped them, but the man showed him something on a piece of paper that made him just nod and move on. Ario and Evelyn stowed their luggage and got into the back of the cab. Evelyn seized his hand and squeezed very, very hard. Q-U-I-E-T, she spelled against his palm. Ario just nodded, knowing better than to blab while they were still in city limits.

They all exchanged the barest, most common greetings. Blood rushed in Ario's ears, a mix of relief, confusion, and wonderment making him dizzy. He had to bite his tongue to keep from speaking.

At the city border, there were yet more scanners, and his heart flew into his throat. He gripped the handle, prepared to throw himself out of the car, but all their driver said was, "there is no need to worry."

But he was, and he couldn't help it, wondering if this was all an elaborate trick. In the line at the border, Ario and Evelyn sweated. The worker at the booth looked at their paperwork boredly, but waved them through.

The scanner remained totally silent.

Not quite ready to accept the relief, nobody spoke until they were well beyond city limits, past the vast floodlights that blocked the worst of the wraiths, in a darkness thicker and grislier than night used to be.

"Michael," Ario said, at last. "How—" A dozen questions pinged in his mind—where had he been? How had he survived? How had he found out where they were? How had they crossed the border?

"It was sorted," he said, in a gravelly voice, "by a friend."

"Is this a friend we know?" Evelyn asked anxiously.

"I would hope so. You worked by her side for years."

Her wan, hawkish eyebrows shot up. "*The queen?*" she hissed. "*She's still alive?*"

Ario thought he might vomit up his heart.

"Unless something has happened in the last forty-eight hours—yes."

Suddenly his eyes were stinging. Michael being alive, Ainsley being alive; it was too much.

"Where is she?" Evelyn asked. "Is she alright?"

"I'm afraid I don't know too much," Michael said. "Her location is being kept even from me."

Ario took a breath. "So we're not going to her."

"...No."

"And it seems we're not going where I planned either," Evelyn said. "Is this safe?"

"It may be the safest he's ever been," Michael continued. "We've found something. Something that belongs to you."

Ario blinked. His head was stinging again and there was a peculiar ache in his blind eye. "Like a magic relic?"

Michael canted his head just slightly. "Of a sorts."

Evelyn's eyes were bulging from her skull. "You're certain of it?" she asked. "I've been looking for him for years—"

"Looking for *what?*" Ario asked, frustration making the ache worse. From the corner of his eye, he thought he saw something flickering in the darkness of the forest.

"Her," Michael said softly. "It's a woman."

Evelyn smacked her forehead with her palm. "Of *course,*" she said. "I didn't even *think* of that. I should've, considering Ario's also—"

"*What,*" Ario said. "Are you talking about? I am nearly twenty-one years old, I do so detest being spoken over like a toddler."

Michael locked eyes with Evelyn in the rearview mirror. Evelyn just sighed heavily and opened her mouth before they were all abruptly blinded by a burst of light.

Michael swore and mashed the brakes, the car skidding in an arc.

"Oh, great," Evelyn hissed. "The last bloody thing we need. How did *she* find us?"

"Probably used the same scanner we did," Michael said. "Everyone alright?"

Ario's arm ached from where it had smacked into the car door, but it was no worse than a bruise. "Fine."

He reached for something under the front passenger seat. "Stay put. I'll handle this."

Ario blinked spots out of his eye. The magic hadn't been meant to hurt them, or even the car, but to temporarily blind and disorient them. And it worked.

Silhouetted in the car's headlights was a tall, slender woman with skin as pale as Michael's. Her long, bright blue hair was pulled away in a practical ponytail. She still glowed slightly from her magic use, and from her transformation.

An enemy Ario knew well, but one he'd never seen this close.

"Begone, beast," Michael hissed in a voice Ario hadn't heard in years; that of a queen's guard. "You've no place here."

"Being awfully obvious, aren't you," she said. She wore the same outfit that marked her an agent of Catherine's; a silver-edged black tunic and leggings. One of a curated set of magic users being used for the imperial minister's bidding. "Anyone can intercept a taxi."

Evelyn squeezed Ario's hand very tightly. "This can't be it. Not now. Not after so long," she hissed.

He struggled to unbuckle his seatbelt, which had cinched tightly when the light first hit. "I have to help Michael."

"You'll do no such thing! What if she sees your face?"

"She already knows we're people of import. And I'm sure she can hear everything we're saying."

"*She* is right here," the being drawled. "Come out and play." Her voice was not particularly deep, but there was something grating in it, worsened by the fact that she had a Landfallen accent, one Ario had not heard from a stranger in years.

"Please," Ario said. "Trust me."

She was trembling, a bead of sweat sliding down her face, but she nodded once.

Ario got out of the car. This far out of the city, the air was heavier, more humid, harder to breathe. No roving air filters, after all.

"Who's your friend?" the woman asked Michael.

And it hit Ario. She didn't know. She couldn't tell. Especially with the hat. Or else this was a game.

"We're refugees," he said calmly, struggling to maintain the city's accent. "We're just trying to get to a relocation camp."

"Quite aromatic for a mere refugee," she said, referring to her ability to smell magic. "What are you?"

"We have papers."

"And I'm sure they're *very real*," she said. She breathed again, deeply; Michael's hands tightened around the object in his hand, a very ordinary pistol. "Tell me what you are, and I'll forgive the driver for pulling a weapon on me."

Ario said nothing.

"I know your scent," the woman said, bobbing her head towards Michael. "You could say I'm *very* familiar with it. But you." She pointed at him. "You're not her. So *what*, exactly, are you?"

"I read below five univs," he said out loud. It was a total lie, but she didn't appear to have any of the requisite equipment.

She shook her head.

"If this goes on much longer, I'm afraid I'll need to ask for a warrant," Michael said. "These are refugees. They paid me to transport them. That's all."

She cut her eyes towards him. "Is that so?"

He undid the safety. "Do you know how to drive?" he asked Ario, softly.

"I'm not leaving you behind. Not again." He glowered at the woman. "Why are you messing with us? What do you want?"

"I heard a curious rumor," she said. "I was just trying to confirm suspicions, before I report to base." A slow, sinuous smile. She swept into a neat curtsy. "It's a pleasure to finally make your acquaintance,

_______ of Landfall. Though I suppose that's not the name you go by, is it?"

Shit. Shit. Shit. Ario's nerves were already frazzled, but having his deadname thrown at him only made it worse.

"Clever, I give you that."

Evelyn approached, slowly, looking very much like she had just bitten a lemon. "Trust you, should I?" she hissed, but worry showed clear through her anger.

The woman approached Ario slowly. Michael cocked the gun. "Where *have* you been, little prince?"

She was definitely stalling, but Ario had not heard or sensed any call for backup. "What do you want?" he repeated.

"You know she wouldn't kill you," she said. "Lady Catherine."

"I would rather be dead," he spat.

"I mean, look at me. She didn't kill me."

"Yet you wear her vestments. You turn in and *kill* people like me."

"What would it take for you to let us go?" Evelyn cut in. "We have money."

This was news to Ario, but if it was a bluff, he let her have it.

"Fine." She planted her hands on her hips. "Where is the queen?"

"We don't know," she said, her eyes glimmering.

The woman scowled. Her teeth were not quite normal; her eye-teeth were sharp, pronounced. Then, she sighed heavily, and reached into her pocket, pulling out a vial that glowed faintly. She pressed it between her fingers—

Michael leapt at her. The vial went flying, but Ario caught it with magic, taking it into his palm. "Wraith bait," he hissed, and slipped it into the pocket of his hoodie. He turned back to the brawl, pulling more magic into his palms, his burnt scalp aching as light crept into his hair.

Smelling this, the woman gave a guttural cry and transformed into a glowing white wolf.

Evelyn lobbed an ice spell at her; the frost just broke on the creature's coat. The pistol discharged once, twice, hitting the wolf in the leg, but this only made her angrier. She snarled and leapt at Michael again, knocking him to the ground and tearing into his forearm with her sharp, vicious teeth.

"Ario," Evelyn said. "Run."

"*I'm not leaving you,*" he said. "I am so—tired—of running!" He punctuated his words with spells, trying to knock the creature free. The magic, thrilled with the opportunity to present itself, burned under his skin.

The wolf growled at him. Taking advantage of her distraction, Michael kicked her hard between the ribs, successfully getting free, but his arm gushed blood and he'd gone white with pain. Evelyn looked torn, unsure of whether to seize Ario's arm and flee or rush to her ally's side.

Swollen with power, Ario could hear and feel everything, their thoughts and a cacophony of noise. He knew he had to dial it back; this felt just like it had the night of the coup, when he had to fight a bunch of wraiths, and it had cost him his right eye. He snarled back at her, not caring how ridiculous he'd feel about it later. If there was a later.

In the woman's—Samara's, that was her name—mind there was a mindless determination, fury, triumph, and... pain? Not physical pain. Pain and fear. Her hackles raised and she appeared apt to charge at him.

There was something around the core of her. Her heart, her soul, whichever; something viney and prickling and *evil* that was not there naturally. The same substance that, in smaller quantities, was in the air and ground around them, slowly poisoning.

"What did she do to you?" Ario whispered.

This caught her off guard; her lupine ears swiveled. Another monstrous growl burst from her.

"Ario," Evelyn cried.

"No. I know what to do. Stand back."

And he took a few steps towards the wolf. She balked a little, but kept baring her teeth and snarling. "She hurt you," he said softly. "Didn't she?"

She lifted a paw and scratched at him, but he parried it effortlessly.

"Samara," he said. "It doesn't have to be like this." He lifted his palm and, gently, put it on her head.

More fear. Confusion. He breathed it in. Reaching into that miasma inside her, he pulled it apart.

The wolf screamed. It was an awful, horrifying sound, all too human. She jumped away, snarling, and disappeared along the horizon in a glowing blaze of power.

Ario let out a breath. He hadn't thought that would work. Using so much power after repressing it for so long had exhausted him, but his work wasn't done yet. Evelyn was using Michael's belt as a makeshift tourniquet, and there was a truly frightening pool of blood underneath him.

"I didn't wait so long to see you only for you to die," Evelyn hissed. "Ario. Help me."

He rushed over, pulling more magic into the palms of his hands. He sterilized and knit together Michael's wound. "He'll need something to replace the lost blood."

"I have supplies in my pack." She sprinted to the car, popping the trunk.

Michael's face was peppered with sweat, and was all too pale. But still he managed a smile. "You handled that like a true king," he said.

He shook his head. "I fixed a foolish mistake, that's all. Sit tight, Evelyn will make something to replace your fluids."

Michael flexed his once-wounded arm. It now bore a rather impressive scar.

Evelyn brought back a water bottle and helped him drink. The herb- and water mixture would function just as well as a transfusion. "I'll make you another once you finish that," she said. "Ario, clean up the blood. The last thing we need is to attract some wraiths."

After using so much power, it was truly a strain, and his eye ached, but he did so, the grisly scene disappearing into nothing. His scalp burned terrifically, and he knew under his hat his hair must be glowing, another needlessly showy aspect of his power.

"Do you feel well enough to get to the car?" Evelyn asked Michael. "You can rest on the way to our destination."

He coughed once. "I wasn't aware you could drive, Evelyn."

"I know how in theory," she said.

"Let me," Ario said. "I know how."

She frowned. "You look exhausted, dear."

"I just need to sit down."

She sighed. "Alright. Then it's settled." She glanced back, towards where Samara had run. "She won't come after us?"

"She well and truly won't," Ario said. "There was something... wrapped up in her. Something evil. Like the miasma. I'm sure it was put there artificially. I dispelled it. She will at the very least be disoriented for some time."

Evelyn gaped. "I'd heard rumors that they were experimenting with that sort of thing, but..."

Ario nodded. "Not quite a puppet, but very easy for Catherine to force her bidding."

She scrubbed her brow. "Just wonderful."

***

Ario had driven a car approximately once, twelve years ago. Aunt Ainsley had taken him out in her personal vehicle, out to an empty lot, and let him steer in circles. She'd framed it as something greatly fun, and at eight, it had been. But now he understood why she'd done it.

It wasn't exactly rocket science. This gearshift was even simpler than that car's had been, and so long as he paid attention and listened for Michael to explain a road rule, he got by just fine.

Or at least, he did until the kilometers started blurring together, his body demanding sleep as a price for all the power he'd put it through. Already he felt a hot migraine developing behind his right eye, aura making his vision shimmer. "Evelyn," he said. "I can't go on."

She gave him a sympathetic look. "You've done enough, Ario. I have one of your tablets right here." She reached into her pocket and took out a travel-sized bottle.

"I feel nearly back to myself. I'll take over," Michael said.

Ario bit his lip. It was his fault Michael had gotten that wound. "If I could only sleep for a few minutes—"

"You rest," the man said sternly. "I'm used to this sort of thing by now."

He pulled over, admittedly a bit messily. He swallowed down the tablet and lay down in the backseat, unable to fight the pull of sleep. "Are we nearly there, at least?"

"...We'll arrive around dawn, I imagine."

He hadn't realized how much he'd missed Michael's smell—after-shave, spearmint and just a hint of pine. For the first time in perhaps twelve years, Ario relaxed.

Michael was alive. Ainsley was alive. Maybe this wasn't all hopeless.

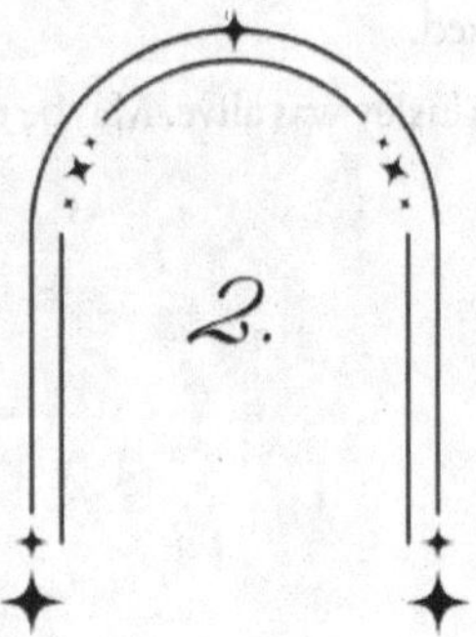

"Ario, you've got to wake up. We're nearly at the border."

Dazed, groggy, Ario blinked. Night had given way to a hesitant dawn, but a grayish tinge still mingled with the oranges and pinks. When he was a small child, sunrises and sunsets had been full of roiling color.

A lot had changed since then.

He sat up and stretched. He was aching, especially his scalp, but his migraine had been soothed by Evelyn's pill, leaving nothing but a faint warm sensation behind his blind eye. Other than hunger, thirst, and a need to use the toilet preferably quite soon, he was fine.

Ario adjusted his hat, which had slid off in his sleep. This strip of highway was just as anonymous than the last had been. "Where are we?"

"A city called Lindenfell," Michael said. "You came once when you were quite young."

He looked out the window. He could so barely see the outline of city buildings, and, in the distance, "is that the ocean? We've come all this way?"

"We have been driving for nearly eight hours," Michael said, not humorlessly.

"I haven't seen the ocean since..." He trailed off. Since he'd left home.

"And apparently parts of this beach are still suitable for fishing and swimming," Evelyn said. "What I wouldn't give for a decent plate of sushi."

"It's because of that," Michael said, pointing. "Look, Ario."

He squinted. It was hard to tell exactly because of his lack of depth perception, but he thought he saw something like a dome over the city. Within it, colors were slightly more saturated. "Are those—wards? Magic wards? How are they getting away with magic covering a whole city?" As they got closer, his awe grew. "The power this must've taken—"

"Lindenfell takes pride in its independence," Michael said. "It's a port city, so as part of their trading deal, the Windsor administration lets them keep the wards. They keep out the worst of the toxins and most of the wraiths."

"It took a whole team of magic users and priestesses," Evelyn said, her voice filled with nostalgia and a hint of whimsy. "I had the pleasure of meeting the ones that were still alive, once very long ago."

Ario swallowed. Evelyn had lost everything because of him; her noble title, her station. She'd given her life to protect him. Perhaps he was not grateful enough.

"You know," she continued. "You can do something of that magnitude on your own."

"I'd be caught in a minute," he said.

"Well," she said. "It's something to keep in mind."

His nerves rose again when they approached the border, but there were no scanners here, and once they were successfully through Michael informed them that that gate had a particular friendly. "There are more than you'd expect," he said. "Especially here."

"Can't they do more?" Ario asked.

Michael locked eyes in the rearview mirror. "Don't underestimate the power of quiet resistance," he said slowly. "Not everyone can afford to risk their lives, even for something that's right."

He sighed, but leaned back in his seat.

Progress through the city was slow. The streets were laid out to prioritize pedestrians and streetcars, so they had to take a roundabout route to get to the place they'd stay. "Oh, this already seems much nicer than our previous accommodations," Evelyn said approvingly. "Look, a park, a café, a *library*, Ario."

"It is relatively safe for magic users," Michael said. "So long as you are not obvious."

The city was also beautiful in a way the previous hadn't been. All of the buildings were made with the same sandstone effacements, some crawling with ivy. So much greenery, it seemed like it had been ages since he'd seen healthy plants. They passed a farmer's market with tables heaped with fresh, vibrant produce.

Finally, Michael pulled onto a residential street, up to an anonymous beige townhouse with hydrangea bushes in the front. "This is it," he said. "Should be furnished, so they tell me."

"I would sleep on a concrete floor at this point," Evelyn said, and Ario noticed for the first time the bags under her eyes, which were more prominent than normal. "Help me place some wards, Ario."

After using the restroom and thoroughly casing the townhouse to make sure no creatures lurked, Ario did so. The building was two-story, but relatively small; three pocket-sized bedrooms and a bath were upstairs, and downstairs only consisted of a kitchen, a living space, and an office. The furnishings were simple, but modern, and most of the house was painted in pale blues and grays. Compared to other places they'd stayed, though, it was palatial. It would be excellent to have his own room again.

Ario laid their usual wards without having to think about it. By then, he could have the process done in five minutes. An alarm ward, a magic-sensing ward, a ward protecting against ill intent (seemed to handle the wraiths, mostly), a very basic shield. He was more than capable at that point of setting something more advanced, but ability was not the issue. Any strenuous or intense use of power would only draw the attention of wraiths or the authorities; his magic was that distinct and volatile. When he was younger, the vast majority of his focus had gone to keeping the magic contained, to avoiding spells even if they would make life easier or more convenient. It was easier now that he was grown, but still uncomfortable, and sometimes he yearned just to fix a broken teacup with a wave of a palm or enchant sheets so that they might never need to be changed.

Leaving the pocket-sized yard, he joined Michael and Evelyn inside the kitchen. She was making tea, and Michael was sorting through a handful of what seemed to be takeout pamphlets. It was by far the most normal thing Ario had seen in months, or longer. How many people in Lindenfell lived like this, quietly, cleanly, able to order pizza on Fridays?

"...A wealth to choose from, truly," Evelyn said. "It's amazing they have so much access to produce and livestock. Hopefully I can get Ario to gain a few kilos. He's starting to look peaked."

"Well-crafted trade deals," Michael said. "If we're talking weight, the pot is black."

She scowled. "My metabolism hasn't been the same since..." She caught herself when she saw Ario. "Finished so soon?" she asked, clearing her throat.

He knew what she was referring to. It was a hot, painful memory that he preferred to avoid if he could.

When he was twelve, and the miasma was well and truly taking hold of the world, food expenses had become astronomical, and they'd run out of money. With the relentless waves of wraiths, and the authorities ever-present trying to see if the issue could be solved and therefore preventing any theft, they... hadn't eaten. For a long time. "I feel very lucky indeed," Ario said, trying to will the blush from his face. "Why is it we've never come here before?"

"Because for a long time traveling here was beyond our means," Evelyn said. "It's no less than a blessing from the Lady Herself that Michael found us. Which. You and I need to have a discussion about that," she spat in Michael's direction.

"Ainsley may be older now, but her memory is as sharp as ever, and she remembers exactly what she told you all those years ago. Those safe places. All I had to do was wait." He shrugged. "How do we feel about pizza for dinner?"

"If there's beef, there's burgers," Ario said. "I haven't had one since I was fifteen. I would like several. Soy meat is just not the same."

"Then it's settled."

Over dinner (real meat! Real cheese! Real tomato ketchup!), they had time to further catch up with Michael.

"I almost didn't recognize you, Ario," the man admitted, swiping a fry (real potatoes!) through a glob of ketchup. "Part of me... was still expecting a little thing yay high." He held his hand roughly waist height. "You're so tall. Spitting image of your father."

He swallowed around an unexpected lump in his throat. "It took years to get my body the way I liked it."

"And he was a terror the whole time," Evelyn said, like she hadn't been the one obsessively researching spells to allow him to transition. She'd left half of her burger, and trying to be subtle, he let his hand creep towards the takeout tin. Without even breaking eye contact with Michael, she swatted at his hand.

"It won't heat well," Ario said.

"It doesn't matter. I'm going to give it up as an offering. We really should give thanks for safe passage, and seeing Michael. And that Ainsley lives yet." She bit her lip.

Suddenly, he felt like a glutton, and wished he had thought of that before he plowed through most of his meal. Sighing, he took his last handful of fries and dropped them in with the burger.

Evelyn's expression became pensive. "Where will you go now?" she asked Michael.

He cleared his throat. "It was my intention to pick up my prior position. If you'll have me."

Her brows show up. The lump returned to Ario's throat. "But you were the queen's guard, not mine," he said.

"It seems right now you may need protection more than she," Michael continued. "If you'll take my oath."

Heat rushed to his face, prickling worse when Michael actually got up and knelt in front of him. Discomfort joined the emotion. "Oh, you don't need to kneel—"

Evelyn's eyes were misty, but she made a gesture indicating he needed to shut up, so he did.

"Ilario Credenzo, crown prince of Landfall, I offer you my life in your service. I will serve as your guard, your protector, your bulwark against darkness. I will defend you against threats both known and unknown. Do you accept my oath?"

There was supposed to be a ceremony behind this, he knew. Formal suits and dresses, and he'd present Michael with a gift to thank him for his service. As it was, they were in a simple kitchen and he was wearing a rumpled hoodie and torn jeans, and Michael was in sweats, having changed out of the bloodstained suit.

Shakily, Ario said, "I accept. So mote it be."

"So mote it be," they both repeated.

Michael stood. "I had hoped for many years to be able to do that," he said. "Thank you, Ario."

His eyes burned. "Why are you thanking me? You've given up everything—"

"He gets like this sometimes," Evelyn said, tears streaking down her own face. "Usually that's when I find something for him to do."

He scowled.

"We knew what might happen when we entered the crown's service," Michael said. "Our loyalty comes from a sense of duty, but also a sense of love. Feeling guilt is pointless."

A tear slipped down his cheek. "What can we do?" Ario murmured. "How can we fix this? I have to do *something*. I can't sit around for another twelve years."

Evelyn wiped her eyes on a paper napkin and said nothing.

"There might not even *be* another twelve years," he said. "I don't care if I d—if I get hurt."

Michael looked at the priestess, but she was folding her napkin into smaller and smaller triangles. "He has a point, Evelyn."

"I will not allow it," she said firmly. "I haven't kept him alive all this time so he can get himself killed."

"Ario has power the resistance could use."

"They have other magic users."

"I want to help," Ario said. "Please."

"No," Evelyn said, her eyes glimmering.

He ignored her and kept speaking. "What can I do? Where can I start?"

"Ilario Credenzo, in the name of Our Lady, your duty is to keep yourself *alive* and—"

"And what?" Ario yelled. "Wait for some magical opportunity to present itself? Hope Catherine chokes on her tea? People are starving, people are dying, the *planet* is dying, and I'm tired of sitting here letting people put their lives on the line for me."

What little color had entered her face left it.

"I'm not much good *alive* if I'm—hiding in caves! I want to help, I'm going to help."

"You have millennia of history sitting on your shoulders—"

"If I do nothing there will be no more history," Ario hissed. He gestured wildly towards the door. "Look. Even here the air is choked with dirt. I don't even know how much money I would bet on the stars not being visible here, either. My magic comes from this earth. Would you let the earth die? Would you let *Her* die?"

He wasn't sure if she would slap him or start crying.

Ario tried to soften. "I love you, Evelyn. And I know you sacrificed too much. If it feels like I'm spitting on that, I'm sorry. But I..." He shook his head. "I need to do this. I'm almost of age. I'm ready."

She blinked. "I suppose I knew this day would come," she said. "You're too stubborn. But I fear..." She faltered. "You'll need to be."

"Thank you," he said.

"We should prepare the offering. It'll be noon soon."

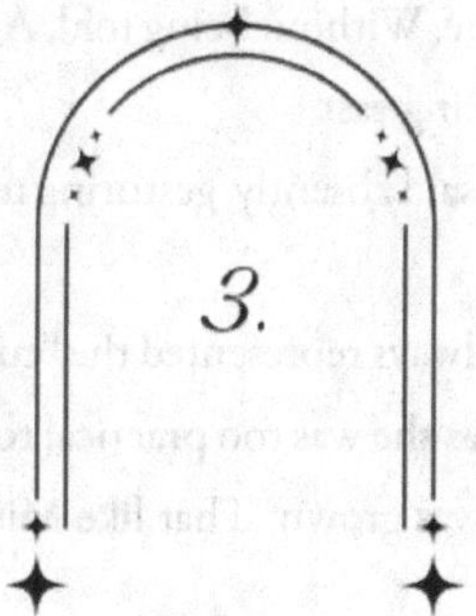

The townhouse had a small backyard with tall privacy fences and a back gate leading out to another road. From her bag, Evelyn took an old ritual votive, a worn velvet packet of herbs, and an old tapestry. Of all the things they'd had to leave behind while running from this or that, she always managed to save these.

Facing north, she spread the tapestry on the ground and set the votive in the precise center, in an embroidered circle marking that spot. This piece had once been beautiful—lush, silk, colorful—but over the years it had faded and been patched and darned. It was divided into four sections representing abstract ideas usually associated with a person or place; home, devotion, loyalty, and the spirit of what may come. Evelyn had always been devotion; Ario had always been the spirit of what may come. Without being told, Ario sat at the semicircle side of the tapestry, facing east.

"No, here," Evelyn said absently, gesturing to the spot representing loyalty.

The spot that had always represented the "current" regent. Ainsley.

He knew what it was she was too practical to say. She was recognizing his place, that he was grown. That like Michael, she was offering herself to him.

Evelyn was only in her forties, but she'd been the high priestess for seemingly as long as Ario could remember. She'd taught him, nagged him, took care of him when he was ill, did everything in her power to protect him, even if it was not necessarily a happy life. It felt strange, wrong, to formally assume a position of power over her. Not when she was essentially his mother. "You're sure?" he whispered.

A nod. "You're not finished giving me gray hairs. I'm sure I've gotten at least five from today."

He sat. The tapestry was least worn here, as nobody had sat on it in a long time. He knelt and took out his old athame, which he carried on his person for protection as well as worship. He placed it pointing towards the candle.

Evelyn sprinkled the herb mixture into the votive. The familiar floral, heady smell would always remind him of home. She set the offering—the now-cold burger and fries—next to the athame. "Lady, we have prayed to you in many strange places. We thank You for protecting Lindenfell, and allowing us safe passage to this new city which is so like the old times. We thank You for fulfilling our hope that Ainsley is alive, and we hope that, wherever she is, she feels some peace. We thank You for bringing our dear friend Michael to us. Please accept our offering."

From her bag of things she pulled a bottle of beer, which Ario recognized as having been in the fridge.

"It is not ritual wine, but I hope You will forgive us for that, as You have always been so gracious," she said. Evelyn always looked younger when she was praying, younger and healthy and beautiful. She twisted off the cap, took a sip, flinched, and offered the beer to Ario.

Predictably, it was old and disgusting, but as he'd sipped a great many old and disgusting ritual wine substitutes, he kept a straight face. The rest of the beer she tossed in a wide semicircle around them.

She lit the candle and knelt on the tapestry in her usual spot. She bowed her head and continued to pray in silence.

Ario closed his eyes and bowed his head as well. *You've given me a chance, Lady,* he prayed. *Please give me the strength to keep doing the right thing.*

Startling him, he felt a surge of warmth across his scalp, and knew without looking the glow had started again. It was a sign. *I'm sorry I didn't save more burger for You.*

A light breeze stirred the hair by his ears, and he knew he was forgiven. Over the years, their practice had occasionally been spartan, but the Goddess was a merciful Lady. And She must've at least liked them, to let them get through so much. And then gifting them with today.

He thanked Her again, silently, then opened his eyes. Evelyn was still praying. He was struck with the urge to prick his finger, and knowing well enough by now not to ignore it, he did so with the athame and let a few drops of blood fall into the herb-and-wax mixture inside the votive. Blood for blood. Evelyn and Michael had given him their service. He licked the wound to stop the bleeding.

Evelyn lifted her head and blinked. "You've been blessed," she said.

"Even the Lady thinks it's a good idea, I guess."

"I hope you asked Her for some good sense," she said.

"I guess I'll just ask you for that instead, priestess," he said.

She rolled her eyes.

Evelyn closed the simple ritual, and they buried the burger and fries in the earth, which was cool and soft against his fingers.

***

The afternoon passed relatively uneventfully. Ario showered—even the water smelled almost normal—and after thinking a moment, actually unpacked. He only had a few sets of clothing, and regretfully, everything was getting extremely ragged. Mending magic could only do so much.

Evelyn and Michael were in the office, talking about something in low voices. He nearly intruded to demand they include him, considering he was now their king (in a matter of speaking; he felt more than ever just a boy), but it had already been such a long day. He approached the door and knocked.

"...and that's where she is?"

"I'm certain of it. Not resistance, but I don't think she knows about the network. Her cousin is a friendly. Well-connected. Allegedly."

"Of course she was *here*, when I've wanted to come for so many years—"

"Does he know?"

"Lower your voice. Yes, Ario?" Evelyn called.

He opened the door and gave her a droll look. "Is there any point asking what you're talking about?"

"Nothing particularly thrilling," Evelyn said. "Nothing that involves you."

He didn't need a perception spell to know that was a lie after all these years. Ario sighed. "I'd like to go for a walk. Maybe get a library card." Expecting a fight, he braced himself.

But she just blinked. "Alright. Don't be long. If you pass a store, can you pick up a few things?"

"Uh. Sure."

"Call me," she said, and when he shut the door, the whispering started up again.

Perhaps it shouldn't have felt like a victory, being able to take a walk on his own at twenty years old. Some of the cities they'd stayed in had deteriorated enough to warrant the caution.

The afternoon sunlight felt good on his face. A few of their new neighbors actually waved at him, but he didn't get close enough to initiate conversation. Even small children were walking on their own, riding bikes, playing here and there.

It was so... peaceful.

Now that he had time to himself, he noticed more acutely the salt smell in the air, the clean brine of the ocean. As always there was still a hint of the miasma, but the pleasure outweighed the ick factor.

Ario had intended to go to the library, maybe a coffee shop, but absently he followed signs leading to the beach. It was still warm enough that it would be pleasant to dip his feet in the water. A curious buzzing sensation had picked up behind his right eye, and for a moment he tried to figure out what it was. The Goddess had just blessed him this morning, after all. Was there something She was trying to tell him?

He followed a set of brick steps down onto the sand, which gave softly under his feet. This late into the season, and it being a weekday, it wasn't too crowded. A few people his age were on paddle boards in the gentle surf. Ario knew without checking that it was low tide; one of the strange things he was always aware of, like the cycle of the moon (waxing, would be full starting tonight). He slipped off his battle worn sneakers and socks and rolled up his jeans.

How many years had it been since he'd had a swim? Oh, that would be so luxurious, but he had no swimsuit. This city was almost too nice. Shouldn't he be waiting for the other shoe to drop?

He watched the paddleboarders, gradually walking along the surf. They seemed to be a group of friends, in matching rented wetsuits. One of them, with long red braids, was struggling to stay upright. "No," a girl was saying. "You have to paddle *like this*, Rory, don't overbalance."

That voice.

A warm tingling broke out over his entire body. Ario had never heard the woman's voice before, but equally, he was sure he knew her.

"What are You trying to tell me?" he whispered to the Goddess. He approached slowly, hoping to seem like any casual beach goer. The girl's long black hair was pulled into a wet bun, and she was on the paler side, though what was visible of her arms was tanned. She was nearly as tall as him, slender, and—he noticed it—the wetsuit accentuated her figure.

The girl was laughing.

"It's not funny," said the other girl, dragging herself back onto the board. "Not all of us are great at being on the water like you, Peony."

Another set of tingling. Ario wondered if he had been compelled somehow. He had to get closer, to see the woman's face. Was it his Goddess? Was it something else entirely?

He was close enough for them to notice him. The girl turned, her oval face twisted with mirth, and when she locked eyes with him her jaw fell open. Ario wondered briefly if she somehow recognized him as the princess, somehow, when the next gentle wave knocked her off of the board and into the surf. Her board drifted towards him before getting caught on the damp sand.

The girl righted herself. Her eyes were a piercing teal blue—the same color as the oceans had been when they were healthy—and a lovely almond shape. Her face was flushed. She was blinking, in disbelief.

"Do you know that guy, Peony?" the other girl asked.

"I-I..." She stood up and started towards him.

"Are you alright, miss?" he asked, and realized a beat too late he hadn't disguised his normal accent.

"Oh, I spill all the time, it's no biggie," she said. Her voice was bubbly, pleasant. He wanted to wrap himself in it.

This is not normal, Ario thought. For someone who'd never had a crush to suddenly *feel*, had to be a result of some magical intervention.

He stooped to pick up the board, nearly panicking. "Uh... here," he said. "This is yours."

"Thank you."

"I don't see an oar, though."

"I think I lost it," she said. "Ugh, there goes my deposit." She shrugged, offering a small smile.

The other girl had made her way out of the water, swiping a dripping piece of hair out of her eyes. She was shorter and curvier than Peony, her skin much browner than Ario's. "Well, I am done with that," she said. "I'm gonna return this shit and change."

"I think I'll stay a little longer," the girl said.

She just shrugged. "Alright. Well, cute stranger, I warn you: she's a maneater."

Ario's eyebrows shot up. The girl blushed. "I am not," she said. "*Rory.*"

Rory winked and set back off down the beach.

For a moment they stared at each other in mystified silence. "I got the strangest feeling that... I know you," he said at last. "Though I don't believe we've ever met."

"I-I don't think we have," she stuttered. "You sound like you're from... that place."

"Landfall," he said. "But I haven't been there in many years."

"You're a refugee?"

Ario nodded. "I just moved here today." Evelyn would hate him for being so careless, but he couldn't help himself. "Who's your friend?"

Dazed, she looked back down the beach, where the redheaded girl was returning the paddleboard to a vendor's booth. "That's my cousin," she said. "She's also my roommate. She was... she was teasing, earlier, I'm really not–"

"It's okay. Peony, is it?"

She bobbed her head.

"My name's Ilario," he said. "My friends call me Ario." That is, if he actually had any friends. He offered his hand.

The girl was not quite smiling, her eyes flashing with–what–joy? She took it and squeezed and he felt, more than anything, a sense of rightness, of wholeness.

What was going on?

"Do you want to sit down for a few minutes?" she asked. "I... don't want to let you go, yet."

"Yes," he said. "Yes, I would."

***

Ario had read a handful of romance novels over the course of his life, usually only when other reading material was scarce. The thunderbolt moment of LOVE had always seemed far-fetched, silly, and impossible. As someone who hardly ever even felt attraction, it seemed totally, completely made up. There was no way that someone could fall in love in the blink of an eye. It was not neurologically possible.

Sitting in the dry sand next to Peony, he wasn't so sure anymore.

It was the strangest thing, as though, all of a sudden, he had found something he hadn't even known he'd been looking for.

"I'm a refugee too, technically," she said. "I also had to leave my home. About... thirteen years or so now, give or take?"

Not surprising. So many people's homes had started to fall apart around then. "Where are you from?"

Scuffing her heel in the sand, she admitted slowly, "An archipelago. Down south."

His brows shot up. "The lost colonies?"

"Well, they weren't always lost," she said, her face becoming pinched and sad. "I was only ten. But I don't remember much about that time, at all. All I knew was that I ended up on the mainland, and this family took me in." She jabbed her thumb towards the vendor booth. "Rory's mom's sister."

Hence the lack of family resemblance. He stuttered. "I didn't think there were any survivors."

"It might be just me," she said. "I have no idea."

Such a naked admission, and tantamount to admitting she had power. Ario felt compelled—-compelled–to tell her who he was. "I'm so sorry, Peony."

The colonies were considered the genesis of the miasma. Located perfectly between the two magnetic poles, about a week by boat from the mainland, it was where this new form had been first identified. But unlike the first miasma, it couldn't be contained by quarantining, and it didn't sicken people.

Just everything else.

The jet stream pattern had only influenced the spread, taking the sickness along the water and air. Down into the very earth. It was still unclear how this had happened. And of course the magical element to it had only enraged those who might cause undue harm to magic users.

Catherine's administration claimed they were working on a solution, but it had been a long thirteen years with no apparent progress. And—remembering what he'd seen in Samara—Ario realized he was no longer sure the despot cared about stopping the spread. Not if she could harness it for her own doing.

"Sorry," Peony said. "I know we just met, and that's heavy stuff, but I... just felt like I had to tell you."

"No, I was just... thinking. I never thought I'd meet someone like you."

She shrugged.

For a moment, he hesitated. But then he reached up and took the accursed beanie off of his head. "Believe me," he said. "I understand."

Her eyes widened. "That's no dye job, is it?"

"...No."

Reaching out, she hesitated.

"Otherwise it feels like perfectly normal hair," he said lightly.

Her fingers brushed by his ears, catching a strand between them. Ario felt, very suddenly, like he couldn't breathe. "You must be so..."

"You are too. I saw it in your eyes."

She brought her hand to her own cheek.

"Why do I feel like I know you?" he asked. "I wondered if I were being compelled, but I... know what that feels like, and this isn't it."

She dropped her gaze. "There's something I could show you," she said. "But it has to be in private."

Anyone who'd ever given him advice would kill him. "...Alright," he said.

Half an hour later, he found himself in the apartment that Peony shared with Rory. He'd learned a great deal about her during their streetcar ride. She was a third year university student, studying music education; she would graduate in the spring sometime; her favorite colors were teal and pale peach; she knew how to play guitar but preferred mandolin, which was close to an instrument from her homeland.

Ario could not stop *watching* her. The way she moved her hands while she talked, the curve of her lips, strands of sea-salted hair coming undone from her bun.

Something was either very right, he knew, or very wrong. What he *should* have done was leave, right now, and explain everything to Evelyn when he got home. What if she were a particularly skilled agent of Catherine's, and this was all an elaborate trick?

Or perhaps she was someone lovely to look at and he was coming into feelings most people had already had by now?

What Ario did feel was confused, a rare and not particularly pleasant sensation to him.

Like most student accommodations, the apartment building was rundown and a little shabby, bits of the sandstone exterior chipping off and revealing normal brick beneath. Inside was a space that could only charitably be called a two-bedroom unit, with a bathroom and a third room that served any other living purposes. Ario immediately sensed the familiar light and static of wards, and they gave him a frisk like a mild electric shock.

Near an old gray couch, a paisley tapestry adorned one wall. Next to that, a bookshelf with a small, old TV. A worn wooden table held a stack of papers and textbooks. Faint spices from older meals imprinted the air. The little touches—photos, the odd shoe, a throw blanket tossed carelessly over a chair—made it feel lived in. A bit too real.

A door at the end of the hallway banged open, and out came Rory, brandishing a dagger. "Who the hell are—oh. Peony. Why didn't you open the wards?"

"I'm kind of distracted," she said. "I just think—"

Rory glared at Ario, but lowered the knife. "What are you?" she asked. "That power. I never feel the wards react like that."

He swallowed. "I don't think it's any of your business. But I mean no harm, I assure you."

"*I assure you*," she repeated, mimicking his accent. Not, he suspected, in a way to make fun of him, but as if she were trying to place it.

"Let it go, Rory, I think it's okay."

"You just met him five minutes ago," Rory said. "How can you be su—oh."

"Yeah."

"Really?"

"I think so."

Ario frowned. "What exactly are you referring to?"

Peony sighed. "Let me change out of this thing, and then we can talk. Okay? Sit down, make yourself at home."

Perhaps he should've felt unnerved. Any reasonable read of this conversation could imply they knew his true identity. But if he were to be reported, he equally had blackmail.

Rory came closer, staring intently at his face. "You're new in town," she said.

"Arrived this morning."

"Are you a student?"

"Well—no."

"And you've never seen her before."

"...No. I think I would remember." His heart gave a resolute flop. He cast the faint beginnings of a sense spell and asked, "do you intend on reporting me?"

"No." Truth. "I don't know where you've come from, but people don't do that here. We just look the other way."

Ario perched on the couch, which gave unduly under his weight. "What are things like, in this city?"

Rory relaxed a little. "It's easier," she said. "The people who do the round-ups deliberately half-ass it. Just don't do anything stupid in public."

"I wouldn't dream of it."

She continued her contemplation. "That accent," she said. "Where are you from?"

Peony might have known, but he said, "It's not relevant."

"You talk kinda eloquently considering you're dressed like that."

Ario scowled. "That's pretty classist."

From the second bedroom, Peony emerged wearing a flowy floral sundress, her dark hair hanging in loose waves around her shoulders. It looked like she'd put on some makeup, a true luxury these days. "Everything okay out here?"

Rory frowned, but said nothing and stalked back into her room.

Peony sighed. "I'm sorry about her," she said. "It's just that we've been burned by magic users before." Leaving some space between them, she sat next to Ario. "Look, this may be... strange, but there's... something about my people."

"...Your people," he echoed. "Meaning—"

"I was a siren," she said, looking embarrassed. "My family used to live under the sea, I think. I used to be able to phase into a... well, what you would call a mermaid."

Utterly flummoxed, he tried not to let it show on his face. Evelyn had taught him just a little about these beings, who had already had a population on the decline prior to the coup. And it had been thought that the remainder had been killed in the initial sieges that began after the miasma took hold.

It was quite possible Peony was the only one left. Just like Ario was of his kind.

"I can't do it anymore," she said. "I haven't since I ended up on the mainland."

Compassion welled hotly in his chest, threatening to choke him. So many people, so many kinds, dead in the resultant twelve years. It was not *just* because of the collapse of the monarchy. Ario tried to imagine what it might feel like to lose his own magic. It must be tantamount to gnawing off one's own hand. "I'm so sorry." The first plague took magic from people. It wasn't a stretch of the imagination that the second's initial wave had also done so.

She shrugged. "There's nothing that can be done about it, so I try not to dwell too much. But I have enough left in me for this." She pulled something from underneath her dress. On a black piece of twine was a small, smooth blue stone precisely the color of her eyes and curved into a teardrop shape. Even in the dim apartment, it glimmered faintly. "What do you know about my people?"

"Not enough, I'm afraid."

Blushing, she tucked a piece of hair behind her ear. "There's this... thing we do. Or did. We believe in the concept of *dailin*." A shrug. "Soulmates. People used to spend ages looking for theirs. They say that once you meet that person, you know."

He took a sharp breath. "So you're saying–"

The blush crept all the way into her ears. "I... could be wrong, there's no way that you can just be *taught* this, all I knew was when I saw you–"

"...I felt like I knew you," he whispered. Everything seemed to go dizzy around him, and he took another deep breath to steady himself. Floundering, he wondered again if this were some sort of trap. She did call herself a *siren*. Was that her purpose, luring him here with sweet words, only to deal another blow?

It came back to him, suddenly, that conversation in the car from last night. *Something that belongs to you. Looking for her for years. Cousin is a friendly.* "Oh my Goddess," he whispered.

"Ario?" Peony asked softly.

He blinked. A million feelings warred for his attention; longing, confusion, and *anger*. If that was all true, Evelyn had never let him know about it. Somehow both she *and* Michael knew about Peony, knew that they might have this special bond, and she never thought to *mention it*?

"Are you alright, Ario?"

He found his eyes were burning. "I think I was brought here to find you," he said. "I'm sorry, I'm not mad at you, I think... I think you were kept secret from me."

Her brows rose.

"I... I think I need to go," he said. "I have to get this sorted."

"I only just found you," she whispered. "Please don't go."

His breath caught. "Can I see you tomorrow?" he asked. "Same time, same place?"

For a moment he thought she might cry. But she just blinked hard and nodded.

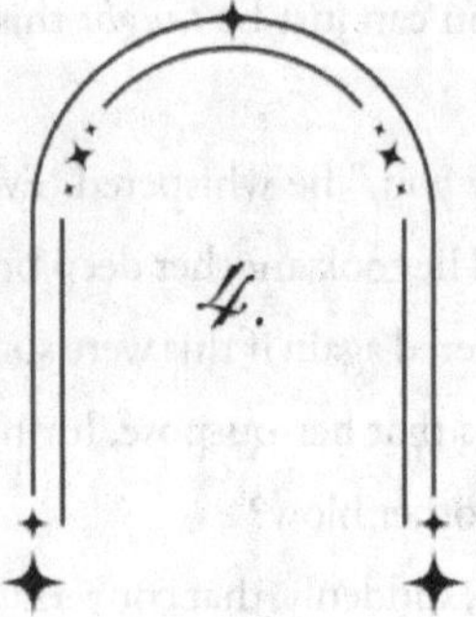

B y the time Ario had returned to the townhouse, he had well and truly worked himself into a fury. He couldn't get over the fact that Evelyn would keep something of this magnitude from him. Especially–if Michael's words were to be believed–something protective would come from this.

Soulmates.

He licked his chapped lips. This sort of thing didn't sound *real*. It was all myth, all story. He dropped his eyes down to his palms. Then again, the source of his power was regarded as the same by those whose power had been severed during the first plague.

He didn't want to lose trust in Evelyn, but he failed to see the reasoning behind keeping this a secret.

If Peony really were his soul's true mate, what did that mean? He *had* wanted to touch her, to pull her close and not let go. He still did. The sensations were new and overwhelming and crowded his heart, fighting with everything else. Was that why he had felt so little romantically before? He'd never had the time to explore such a thing, and it had been a risk before–

Truthfully, he had never thought he'd survive long enough to give any of this any sort of thought. So much of his focus had been *surviving to adulthood,* and now that he mostly had... well. He was duty-bound to produce an Heir, whether he wanted to or not. And it was not exactly a safe world for child bearing.

Were he not on public transit, he would pray. But there were several prying eyes.

Predictably, Evelyn was furious at him for being gone for so long without contact. As soon as he had stepped through the wards, she was out the front door. "Do you have any idea how worried I was about you?"

He didn't respond. Instead, he went to push past her into the house.

"Ario. I need to know about your well being."

He continued to ignore her, trying to swallow down a torrent of words. "Where's Michael?" he asked instead.

She blinked. "Are you hurt? Did you see a wraith?"

"Where is he?"

She gestured towards the closed door of the office. Ario went towards it without another word, not bothering to knock.

At the broad pine desk, Michael sat surrounded by a sea of papers. "How was your walk?"

"What do you know about sirens and their mates?"

His expression was not so smooth and exaggerated as Evelyn's was, but Ario saw him falter anyway. "Why is it you ask?"

He started to pace, the manic energy that had built up over his ride home needing release. "Oh, we can say I've just found my education in that department is somewhat lacking."

Michael set down his papers and knotted his hands. "They are nearly an eradicated race of magic users," he said. "They have a polytheistic religion and the ability to shift forms to bear both land and sea. Their bonds with their lovers and their families are intense, and breaking them is just about tantamount to shattering their soul. Sirens spend whole lifetimes seeking that which may fulfill them."

Ario felt his lip trembling. It was an answer, but a nonanswer at the same time. "Last night in the car you alluded to finding something, Some*one*. A girl or woman who would protect me somehow. And she lives here."

"...Yes."

"How can she protect me? More importantly, how did you and Evelyn know about her for years, when trying to find soulmates seems quite difficult?"

Michael sighed heavily and ran his hand through his hair. "I told Evelyn it was unwise for you not to know," he said slowly. "Usually her judgments are so sound, I don't fully understand—"

Ario crossed his arms and leveled him with a glare.

He cleared his throat. "There are two "layers", if you will, to siren mates," he said. "The first, more common form is called "pairbonding," where two or more people with compatible souls act on their love, forging a lifelong bond. They can usually sense when someone is compatible with them. Quite mystic, really."

Ario swallowed. "And the other?"

Was he imagining the sweat on Michael's brow? "The second is called "soulbinding." It's a rare process because it involves a ritual performed by a third party, usually a member of siren clergy. Two souls with compatible natures are brought together through this ritual as a quicker, more permanent alternative. Think of it like... a love marriage and an arranged marriage."

A shock of adrenaline shot through him.

"Ario... I'm very sorry you were not told. When you were a very small child, when things started to fall apart... Ainsley and the chief of the colonies bound you to a handpicked child. She did it to protect you, to help the rest of the people on those islands. Sirens, you know, have a very passive, but powerful, ability to shield magic—"

Michael's words stopped making sense. He went on, explaining about siren magic, but he might as well be shouting at the end of a tunnel. An intense, burning vertigo surrounded him. He hugged himself tightly.

"Aunt Ainsley," he said slowly. "Did this to me? Captured me and this poor girl in a—*child marriage?*"

He tapped his fingers together. Surely he had never seen Ario this upset before. "That was an analogy. You aren't technically married—"

"*That is not what I'm mad about.*"

"Ario, breathe, try to lower your voice. You're a wise young prince yourself, surely—"

"All I know is that the two women I trust most in my life have lied to me about matters dealing with my soul," he said. "And involved this poor young woman."

The door opened, then, and in came the accused. "I heard yelling. What's—"

Ario whirled. He was so worked up he couldn't even find the words to explain how betrayed he felt, how small, how stupid, like a child.

"He found her," Michael told Evelyn in a low voice. "I had to tell him."

All the color drained from her face. "Oh," she said.

Surprising him, he felt tears in his eyes.

Taking a deep breath, she turned towards him. "Ario, I only did it with your well being in mind, I swear I–"

"Don't," he hissed. "Not now. I'm going out. It will be a full moon, and I need someplace quiet to pray."

Feeling barely embodied, Ario stormed out of the room and then back outside. Night was falling, bringing with it that thick, sticky darkness that had clung to the land for the past thirteen years. Going out at night, unescorted, in a city was dangerous.

Ario didn't care. In fact, he nearly *wanted* to be caught, to put an end to all this. What was the *point*?

He followed the street into a park bordering a forest. He need-ed–earth. He needed clarity. He needed to understand.

He wanted Peony.

He'd been allowed to make so few choices in his life. He could not pick where he lived or what he wore or what he ate. He could not choose when he was allowed to use his magic. Now he could not even have a choice of a partner, and he felt even worse because even considering it felt like betraying Peony. Peony, a stranger. Peony, his soulmate. He did not feel like a young man, but an overgrown child, the constraints of–everything–choking him.

When he was sure he was alone, he knelt and buried his fingers in the soft, wet dirt. Dappled moonlight shone, silver, on the ground; a faint chill of autumn was in the air.

Ario did not know what to pray for. He tried to form the words–to bring them to his lips–multiple times, and yet, in a strange way he felt betrayed by the Goddess, too. He figured he should perhaps just recite

the full moon prayer, well-worn words he had known since he was able
to speak.

Help me, he prayed, barely a whisper. *Guide me. You blessed me
earlier today. You had to know about this.*

She didn't respond.

Sighing, Ario stood. He brushed the dirt off the worn knees of his
jeans and turned back towards the path that would take him out of
the woods.

In the semidarkness, shadows started to emerge from behind the
old oak trees. He drew his dagger. If anything, a fight with a wraith
was welcome. At least he could make himself useful.

What disarmed him totally was that he swore he heard it *speak.*

Hello? It did not dive for his throat the way an ordinary creature
might. *Do you know where my mommy is?* The timber of its voice–even
inside of Ario's head–reminded him of a little girl.

Wraiths didn't speak. They couldn't; they had no cognition.

The wraith approached him, slowly. Its eyes, like Samara's, were the
same silver as the moon. *It's dark. I'm scared.*

All he could do was gape. Snap out of it, he thought. You know
better than to fall for tricks.

Can you help me? it asked him.

The knife trembled in Ario's hand. One warm slash of magic, that
was all that it would take. Smoke rolled off of the creature's form.

The little girl was probably someone the wraith had eaten. Was it
that her–soul was trapped? That didn't make any sense–

An eerie susurrus filled the clearing. More wraiths had started to
gather around him in a circle; not so many more than he could rea-
sonably take. Again, they did not strike. All the times he'd been chased
through woods or through alleyways...

You smell good, another remarked.

Kino, no, a third said, chidingly. *Don't give into it. You remember what happened to Milsa.*

I am so hungry, "Kino" said. *So hungry.*

"What are you?" Ario asked softly.

I was like you once, I think, the third wraith said. *A hu-man.*

"You must've been eaten." He felt sick to his core. "It's just using you to regurgitate speech."

Can you help us?

He swallowed. "What happened to Milsa?"

She was hungry. She went to the shadow world and found something to eat. We never found her again.

Shadow world? "Or someone?"

I do not know. We are blind.

"How long have you been like this?"

Endless endless endless. I do not know.

It had to be fucking with him. And yet, there was a mounting sense, a mounting gut feeling, that this was–

A flash of light. Something speared the third wraith, causing those around him to hiss and spit. The "little girl" screamed, the sound so disconcertingly human Ario almost covered his ears. More voices burst out–

hungry hungry hungry

Where am I?

Don't hurt me!

Mommy?

"What are you doing just standing here?" a voice barked. It was Rory, Peony's cousin, holding a magical spear. "Kill them!" He watched, motionless, as she started cutting them down. The screaming, the screaming, it was too much–

"Stop," he tried to tell her, but it was just a whisper. "Stop–"

She seized him by the upper arm; he'd sunk to his knees. "What, were you touched?"

"You don't hear them?"

"I *hear* that they want you for dinner!" Frustrated, she released him back to the ground and continued spearing them. The shrieking and begging reached a fever pitch–

***

The next thing he knew, someone was dabbing a damp cloth against his forehead that smelled like thyme. "It's alright. You're alright," the voice said, and he placed it instantly as Peony's.

He was on her couch, his head in her lap. A massive pounding had taken residence behind his eyes, and he felt nauseous. "What happened?" The words came out slurred, and his good eye refused to focus.

"You were touched. Rory carried you here. I know a little bit about healing, you should be okay. Close your eyes."

"I heard them, Peony, they were talking to me–"

She placed one soft finger against his lips and shushed him. "Go to sleep."

He drifted for a time, comforted by her smell and maybe whatever was on that cloth.

"...They were circling him. He was toast. I go to save his ass and he starts screaming at me to stop, that they were talking. Hallucinations are a new symptom. We'll have to let the others know."

"Why did you find him, anyway?"

"Well–I was–on patrol–"

"You were following him."

A sigh. "Can you blame me? You're all goo-goo eyed for a stranger. I had to know more about him. He's–I don't know what, but he's something."

"You know I can't keep away."

"This is the last thing we need right now–"

His body decided that it had heard enough, and he fell asleep.

When he woke, the warm orange rose of a sunrise was peeking through the window. He'd been asleep some time. Someone had draped a warm wool blanket over him, and it smelled like ginger. Ario sat up.

He no longer felt ill, but the headache remained behind his eyes. He pinched the bridge of his nose.

He'd never been touched by a wraith before, so it was fully possible that everything he'd seen and heard had been a result of that. Wraiths had never been anything but thoughtless hungry monsters, a by-product of the plague that had taken most of the world's magic. Just shadows of what once was.

But if they were ordinary wraiths, how did they get past the city's massive wards? One thing was certain–he needed to talk to Evelyn and Michael. They would know better that this meant than he would.

Evelyn. Michael. He'd been gone hours now; they'd be worried sick. He swore and dug out his cell phone, and sure enough, he had dozens and dozens of messages and missed calls. He dialed back.

"Where have you been?" Evelyn shrieked. "Disappeared without a trace, Michael's been searching for you since midnight–"

"I'm fine, I'm fine," he reassured her quietly; he was sure the two girls were still asleep. "I'll be back shortly." He hung up on her and shut his phone.

Stretching, he realized how stiff he was. He knew he had to go back, and yet... his eyes fell on the door to Peony's room. Would it be so... wrong, to go in and tell her he had to leave?

Possibly. Probably.

He swallowed and tiptoed across the hardwood. The door was not quite shut, and he eased it open carefully, only to come face-to-face with her, her hand outstretched towards the knob. "I-I'm sorry," he stuttered, "I just wanted to let you know I need to leave."

She wore an oversize t-shirt with bright lettering that said "Lindenfell Aquarium," and a snug pair of exercise shorts. Her long dark hair was pulled into a messy topknot. She caught him looking at her and blushed, a thin, diffuse pink. "I-I was just going to check on you," she said. "You were sleeping so hard—"

"I'm alright. Really. I feel much better. I need to—get back to my family. They're worried sick."

She bit her lip. "They must be," she said softly. "When can I see you next?"

"Well, in the event that I am not made captive of my own home, as soon as I can," he said. "You're a student, right?"

She nodded. "I was about to get ready to go to the university and get some practice in. I'm a musician, you know."

Ario nodded. "Maybe you can give me your phone number?"

Her blush deepened. "Yeah, sure, let me just..." She padded back into her room, returned with the cell phone, and they exchanged numbers.

He felt a stupid little grin trying to spread across his face. "I-I look forward to it."

She took his hand—his heart surged into his throat, and he never, ever wanted to let go— "Be safe, okay?"

"Yes. Yes, I will."

***

Ario returned to the townhouse. He ached as though he'd had the flu, and the child's scream reverberated again and again inside of his mind.

In the event that they were—*living,* somehow? What did that mean?

Evelyn had made him study the chain of events leading to the plague again and again. He could remember her voice, steady, absent-minded. *Before then everyone had magic,* she'd said. *Some were more powerful than others, of course, but the fundamentals were the same. Then there was the eclipse, the blood moon, and people started getting sick.*

"Sick." That was what she'd called it when he was very young. When he grew older she gave him more graphic detail—

Blood out of the orifices was common, and the lesions, and the rot. We didn't understand viruses or germ theory then, but it's hard to tell even now how *this sickness was borne. Those with more power—more influence—more money, were able to quarantine themselves and remain unscathed. The rest either died or... lost their magic. Wraiths were born, thought to be manifestations of this magical death.*

Ario couldn't imagine being powerless. It'd always been locked tightly inside of him, something to be restrained.

With the amount of death, it was a complete societal collapse. Those who still had magic picked up the pieces and started to run things, reinforcing the power of the crown. And not at all unwittingly, they put in the system that made mundanes feel different. Exploited. A lot of them saw mundanes as less than human, soulless creatures. It was an opinion held by some of the nobility even up until your aunt's coup. It must've been easy for Catherine's party to make the general public realize there are much more of them than us.

What he'd experienced with those wraiths could have been hallucinations. He had no rational explanation other than he *felt* it was not true.

The familiar frisk of the wards washed over him when he re-entered the townhouse. About five seconds later, Evelyn was on him. Her face was pale, drawn, her hair even frizzier than usual. "Where have you *been?* Do you have *any* idea how frightened we've been–" She pulled him tight into an embrace, and he let her, because he did not feel like fighting. His blind eye had started to ache. She released him and appraised him closely. "You look–peaked–are you hurt?"

He certainly did not feel right. He brought himself over to the couch, perched on the chaise, and told her everything that had happened.

Evelyn flopped down next to him. "That can't be," she said.

"I heard what I heard. I felt what I felt." His voice came out stilted.

"It had to have been what little consciousness was left from whatever poor person that creature feasted on."

Ario shook his head, dazedly. "How did they even get in in the first place? Wraiths from the outside couldn't have breached the wards. The only explanation is that new ones were born. Which wouldn't be possible, unless..."

Her brows were pulled tightly together.

"Things have been dying for a long time," Ario said slowly. "We've all seen it. The scarcities. The way winters are as warm as spring. And you know she's done absolutely nothing to stop it. People eat within these wards." He paused, brushing his fingers against the couch's upholstery. "The resistance network. Is there any data, on anything like this?"

"I—I am unsure. If... things are evolving, then... We should be quarantining, we should be—"

"We can't not eat," he said. He crossed to the fridge and took out one of the pears he'd bought. He reached for a spell to analyze it.

"Your magic, Ario," Evelyn said.

"I've heard the roundups are, quote unquote, "half assed." This is important, Evelyn." He brought the fruit close to his face, breathed it in. He dialed down deeply and focused on it on a cellular level.

An answer came relatively quickly. Miasma. The same thing he had felt in Samara.

The pear fell from his hand. Perhaps due to his meddling, it splatted on the floor, but he did not stop to clean it. Instead, he rushed out the back door and burrowed his fingers in the earth. His blind eye was aching and he could feel the heat of his hair, but he forced the spell down and down and down as far as he could get it without blacking out.

There was even less time than he thought.

He heard himself making a terrible keening sound, but couldn't stop. Grief, rage, powerlessness.

He was being shaken. "Ario, *stop*," Evelyn said, first with anger, but then with more and more concern. She pressed a tea towel to his face, and he wondered briefly if she were trying to suffocate him before he realized she was just trying to muffle the worst of his cries.

"Is the prince hurt?" he heard Michael bark.

"He's grieving," Evelyn said.

His vision was popping with light. He struggled against Evelyn's grip, but his body had become weak and heavy. He refused to lose consciousness yet again. Focusing on staying awake had lessened the horrible noises until they became small, pitiful sobs.

Evelyn's hold eased into an embrace, and he cried for an unknown period of time.

***

"How long do we have?" Ario asked. He was lying on his side on the cool, damp earth. Evelyn and Michael had tried–several times–to get him to come inside the house and into bed, but he would not loosen his fingers from the dirt.

They were both silent.

"I thought we had more time," he muttered. "Oh, I'm a fool, a stupid idiot–"

"My prince–" Michael began, but failed to find anything of comfort.

"I did not even realize you harbored that hope," Evelyn said. "Truly, I didn't."

He wanted to yell and scream, but due to his other prior tantrum, his voice was blown and came off as little more than a whisper. "*You* raised me this way," he said. "*You* raised me to have hope, that there would be a day I could take the throne and things would–get fixed! All these prayers to the Goddess–no wonder She was so frivolous with blessings, the other day, She hasn't got much time left–"

"How dare you try to scry the will of the Goddess!" Evelyn hissed. "How dare you not be grateful for what She gave you."

"How long do we have?" Ario asked again, more directly at Michael.

He sighed. "The administration blames poor farming techniques and magic terrorism. We have trouble getting empirical data to analyze. The resistance looks into what it can, but... well, only you can do what you just did. This new evolution is not one we can track with our current instruments."

"What I would give for one of you to just answer a direct question," he snapped.

"Ten years is the estimate based on some small studies we've done. Possibly less. At least, for the general public. The oligarchs will probably be able to eke out a few more years."

Ario sniffled and sat up. His face burned with salt from the tears. "No more talk of hiding," he said. "I am going to do what I can to do—something. I am going to do more than—Ainsley."

Evelyn's eyes were bulging—no doubt from the blasphemy as well as the disloyalty. Ario found he did not care. There were more important things than anyone's feelings—even though he'd just wasted several hours in a nuclear meltdown.

"As your prince—no, fuck this. As your king, I demand to meet the resistance network. You serve me. For the love of the Goddess, help me—do *something!*"

Evelyn burst into tears. There was no buildup. Ario wondered briefly if he'd been too harsh, and felt such a stab of shame he went to apologize immediately.

She did something she did rarely—she hugged him tight enough to hurt his ribs. When she let go, she'd composed herself. "I knew this would happen," she said. "I knew, and yet I was still a fool to believe I could protect you. You—truly—didn't know how dire things were?"

He took a moment to think about his prayers to the Goddess - thousands and thousands of hours. He thought of the blessings he'd received in turn, how they had changed over the years. Once She'd made his windowbox bloom. Now, weak breezes and warm hair. "I feel as though I've woken up from a long dream," he said.

Michael sighed. "Well, majesty," he said. "Let's get started."

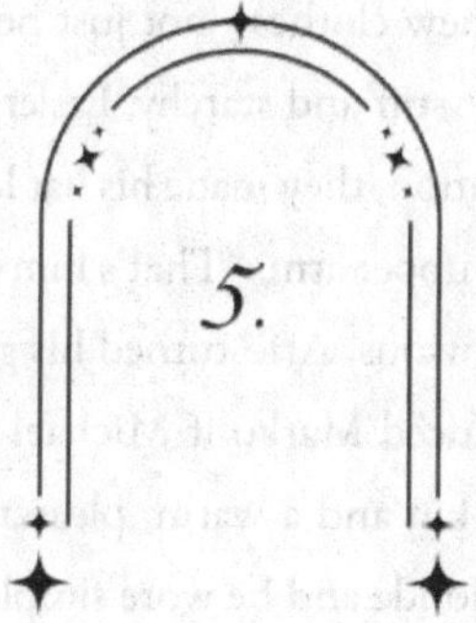

5.

Contrary to the propaganda published in books and films, the resistance wasn't one large shadowy network with terror at its core. It comprised multiple different mutual aid networks, all with one goal: keeping magic, and its users, alive. Some pushed for equality, others were concerned with keeping the lights on, but all were willing to give names and put you in contact with others with useful skills—if you passed muster, that is.

Ario expected to meet the resistance in a dusty warehouse or a ramshackle HQ. Instead, he met their current contact, Marko, in a coffee shop on one of the main streets. He'd wanted to come alone, but Michael insisted on coming to facilitate the introduction.

He'd gotten some new clothes - not just new to him, but totally new, and the pants felt stiff and starchy. Easier to focus on this than his nerves. Not to mention, they made his hat look even shabbier.

Michael tapped his upper arm. "That's him in the corner."

Trying not to be obvious, Ario turned his good eye towards him. He wouldn't have noticed Marko if Michael hadn't said anything. He had deep brown skin and a warm, pleasant-but-plain face. The tips of his locs were blonde and he wore simple, not-too-fashionable not-too-worn clothing. When he tipped his face up, Ario noticed his eyes were a striking green that any homeland security officer would clock in a second.

Marko stood when they approached. "Michael, always a pleasure. Who's your friend?"

The espresso machine in the cafe seemed unusually loud; Ario realized this was probably on purpose.

"This is Ario," Michael said. "I think he may be able to help you with some business."

"That's what I like to hear," Marko said. "Please, sit. Would you like some coffee? I'm trying to get my fill before it's too late."

Michael had coached him on this. "I've heard the lavender latte is just wonderful," Ario said.

Marko's pupils widened just slightly. "Latte, coming right up."

Ario lowered his voice. "Do you always meet in such public spaces?" he whispered.

"Sometimes it's for his safety as much as ours," Michael responded.

"But he knows you're not a reporter."

"Yes, but he doesn't know *you* aren't."

"I thought he–*knew* me?"

Michael shook his head. "I did not specify your identity. I'll leave it to you if you want to be forthright."

A few minutes later, Marko came back with a steaming purplish beverage. The strong floral scent was not particularly appealing, and besides, it was slightly too hot to drink. "Thank you. How kind."

"Always happy to talk business," the man said. He had very nearly a neutral accent; Ario had a hard time placing it. "What can I do for you?"

"I heard you have some... data I could use for my own independent research purposes," Ario began.

"Is this for university?" Marko asked.

"Not quite," he said. "I am... something of a master in my field. I'm trying to devise solutions to..." He faltered.

"There is no need to talk in code, highness," Marko said.

His pulse surged into his throat. "How'd you–"

"There have been rumors Michael had returned to royal service," he murmured. He wore thin, delicate gold rings on each finger of his hands; they glinted in the warm light. "Seeing as Ainsley has been reclusive... well. When he asked for passage for a twenty-year-old boy and a middle aged woman, there was no large leap, was there? Though I admit... I thought you were merely *masquerading* as a boy. Do forgive me."

Ario took a sip of the too-hot coffee. The flavor was earthy and rich and the strength of the lavender only enhanced it. "Are we terribly obvious, or are you merely exceedingly intelligent?"

"I am mostly very smart," Marko said. "I must say it is an honor."

"I am looking to help," Ario said, lowering his voice further. "I need to research what's happening with to the planet. If I can concoct something to slow it down, or stop it, or at least press back against the ill effects..."

"We've been trying to do that for years," Marko said, bitterness contracting his face. "Our best magicians... always tend to go missing."

"All due respect, but Ario isn't ordinary," Michael said. "You've seen the wards around town. He can do something like that himself."

Marko's eyebrows shot up. "How have you evaded detection?"

He was startled into honesty. "The generosity of your people," he said. "Experimental power dampeners. Mostly... holding it in. And luck."

"The royals have had this power the whole time?" Marko asked wearily.

"Firstborns," Ario said softly. "It's biologically matrilineal. Though I'm told I'm rather exceptional and my birth mother... was not. It helps that most of the time I had nothing to do but study magic."

Evelyn did not speak of his birth mother, one of any number of Chiaras in their family, often. When she did she said things like "may the Goddess bless her memory," or "you look just like her." As he'd gotten older, Ario had asked for her stances on policies, on gender, on mundanes, on the advancement of technology. Evelyn had just said "she liked to delegate."

Ario did not remember her much, unless he strained hard or used a memory spell. She and his father had been assassinated at a subway station opening ceremony by a bomb that had killed thirty people. He knew she liked shopping and buying beautiful outfits and jewelry. She was not very religious, which seemed absurd. She'd used her magic not to heal, or as a show of military force, but rather... to put on pretty light shows nightly at the palace.

"Evelyn," he'd asked one afternoon, on bedrest from another series of spells to further his transition, "was my mother very stupid?"

"Be grateful you have your keen intelligence," was all she responded with.

In the years since, Chiara VI's image had masterfully been used to demonstrate the useless opulence of the monarchy. *When we were starving, she was buying diamonds,* one shlocky documentary had denounced. The mess of hundreds of years of administration had been turned over to her younger sister Ainsley, who could do little to stop what was coming.

"Royal power has been misused," Ario continued, aware he had let them lapse into silence. "We were blessed with it for a reason. That is why I am here, now."

Marko thought. "I can take you back to one of the farms we've been studying," he said. "I can also give you the data we have. I would not recommend looking it up on the regular Internet. They track that sort of thing. Shall we?"

Ario cut his eyes towards Michael, whose expression gave little away. "Take me there."

***

Marko's car was an old-fashioned hydrogen model that grumbled and roared. Ario felt very strange sitting in the passenger seat and watching the town unfold around them.

"My partner Maeve will be there," Marko told him, "and some other people you should know. Though I have to say... their reactions will be interesting."

Ario wondered, for a moment, if he should tell Marko to lie. But once they saw the magnitude of his power, it would be a dead give-away.

"Makes me wish this car was nicer," Marko joked.

"It is one of the nicest vehicles I have been in," he said, completely honestly. "There is no need for formalities. I am the greenest member of your group."

This far out of the main city, they were near the edges of the wards, and the shimmering bubble became more obvious.

"We have half the field inside and half outside, to compare," Marko said.

"Is there a difference?"

"Nominally. It's partially too early to tell."

He pulled off the road and drove down a long dirt path, the truck jolting unpleasantly. This did not help Ario's nerves at all. It was a struggle to keep his breathing even, relaxed. It was one thing to lie about his identity, another to be himself in front of Evelyn and now Michael. But he was about to meet people who knew he was royalty, out himself to them, and then tell them how he could do a better job than their months' or years' of work.

Marko parked in front of a worn down red farmhouse. Ario had stayed in a few places like these. Sometimes out in the rural areas felt safer, due to the lack of people and authorities. Others, the cities did, because of the sheer amount of bodies dispersing the thumbprint of his power.

A woman with very deep brown skin and curly hair tucked into two perfect buns was waiting for him. She had on a pale pink sundress and muckboots. She waved, smiling widely. A tablet was tucked under her arm.

"I've brought some guests," Marko said. He crossed over to her and kissed her cheek. "You remember Michael."

She gave a small curtsy. "Always a pleasure."

"And his charge," Marko said, clearing his throat a little.

The ground was soft, mushy under his feet. He saw Maeve take in the color of his hair.

"I'm Ario," he said. "I'm, um… I'm sort of the king, but don't worry about that."

Maeve just stared for a moment.

"I have magic. I think I can help."

Maeve looked at Marko. "Is this real?"

"Real as real gets," Marko said. "Guess the rumors we've heard are true."

Maeve clasped Ario's hands. "Welcome to our research center, your majesty. I'd offer you some lunch, but… we try not to eat here." Another curtsy, deeper this time.

"There is no need for… any of that," he said. "It makes me uncomfortable, honestly. Call me Ario."

Inside the farmhouse there were a few more people. A girl with pale skin and bright red hair; a young man with eyes so vividly blue they quite literally glowed; and a woman with hair silver enough to nearly match his.

The reveal that he was king provided some mixed responses. The girl said "cool!" and leapt to introduce herself. The boy smiled and blushed and avoided making eye contact. The woman just said, "are we sure he's the real deal? Not some kind of imposter?"

"You have my word," Michael said. "As the king's guard."

She looked him over. The clothing he'd gotten was nicer than his tattered discards, but still probably was not what a working royal wore. "So then where's the princess?" she asked.

"…That would be me," he said, feeling his face flush brilliantly.

He saw the pieces click; and then the woman was stumbling over herself apologizing.

From there, they took him out to the fields. They were cultivating a few different crops, Maeve said. Tubers, other root vegetables, legumes. They'd attempted to cultivate grapes, which Ario had not seen in a very long time, but the fruit on the vines withered and gave off a pungent odor not unlike acetone.

He took samples of the produce, carrying them in a small plastic box they'd given him, along with quite a bit of earth and water from the irrigation system. The redheaded girl, Ivy, peppered him with tons of questions about where he'd been and what he'd seen. Though her curiosity was genuine, he was reticent at first to admit anything, not wanting to give anyone away. But then he remembered these were the people who planned all of it. To his shock, and sadness, she'd been in some of the safehouses he had on her way over from the west coast, which was, in her words, "a total fascist dumpsterfire." She was in her early forties, she said, and at this he couldn't help but stare gaping-mouthed. She giggled with delight and said her line was unusually long-lived. She didn't look more than sixteen.

From there, they brought him to another barn, which was more of the resistance aesthetic he was expecting. There was purloined equipment in a square around a stainless steel work surface. A computer server was in the corner, half-draped in feed sacks, and everything was on wheels. A wall of false boxes was on one side so that everything could be crammed behind it in an emergency.

He laid out his assorted crops out on the table, and the others settled at various workstations, in the air of working on their own research tasks, but he felt their eyes on the back of his neck. They wanted to see royal magic at work.

Ario had received at least a cursory education in all of the major sciences. Despite what the administration might say, scientific principles were often applied to the study of magic; how else would technology have been developed after the plague years? When they weren't running, he and Evelyn often passed their time hiding in study. Part of the requirements of her seminary school education included the sciences. In unusually sentimental moments, she expounded on this. "The Goddess not only created this world, She gave us a way to understand it."

Ergo, he knew cells and what to look for, and what DNA *should* look like. Much like the pear, all of these crops were altered. As he pored over his vegetables, the anomaly became clearer. Much as the miasma had been wrapped around Samara's heart, here it was expertly woven into the nuclei of every cell. Attempting to pull it away led to each piece quite literally melting in his hands as it lost form and structure.

Okay. So his hypothesis had been proven true. But how had it been put there, in the earth? Was it natural or artificial? And how was he supposed to fix such a massive problem?

Water proved more puzzling yet. It did not have cells, was not organic, so looking at it required him to think outside of the box. He held a small globe of water above his hands.

The group was no longer pretending to not watch him. Marko was even taking photos of the process.

Trying to ignore them but feeling his face heat, he sought the miasma. It wove in and through the water, much like light. "Get me a container," he said quickly, and as Maeve scrambled to get a clean sample box, he ripped it out in one fell swoop.

Holding this thing was different than the pear or the crops. This miasma felt *alive,* and its smokelike appearance writhed and struggled towards his palm. A few of them quickly covered their noses and mouths, like they weren't already consuming it on the regular. Ario slammed it into the container before it could more overtly contaminate him, smothering it with the box's metal lid. It seemed trapped against certain inorganic substances, flailing against the glass vainly. So then it should not be in water at all. So...

He tried to think over the whispering that had started.

The good news: it could be removed safely to purify drinking water. And it could be contained.

The bad news: he was only one person. Also, it surely was not sustainable, and the slop that resulted from "clean" food undoubtedly could not also be good to eat. And say they could remove it from everything. Where would they *put* it? What kind of matter was it even?

The very stuff wraiths were made out of.

He still had the wraith bait from Samara, wrapped protectively in the office back at the townhouse. It may prove useful in testing, but it might also expose these people to undue harm.

His head started to ache from the magic expenditure, especially behind his blind eye. He put a hand to his face and felt the tingling fringe of his hair, which was uncomfortably hot from use.

"Are you alright, majesty?" Marko asked.

"It is tiring, even for me," he admitted. "Consider how many cells are in one potato." He told them what he'd learned. "I want to look at imported produce as well. See if the contamination is that far spread, or if it's localized, somehow. That may help us triangulate where this is coming from. I have no idea." He'd been sitting on a stiff plastic crate, but even so, felt his knees trembling from the effort. "I also want to look at livestock. If it's in living things the same way without external intervention by the administration."

"We have a chicken coop," Maeve told him. "I could take you there."

"His majesty's energy is not limitless," Michael said from beside him. "As much as he would like to think."

Marko looked disappointed. "Of course. This has been a total breakthrough for us."

Ario nodded. He felt bone weary, exhaustion quickly swooping in. Marko took them back to town soon after.

***

After so much restraint, using magic regularly felt strange. The resistance members were not-quite comfortable with him yet, and he still felt like he was intruding. But there were larger matters to worry about than such niceties.

What he really needed was samples from other parts of the country. The others, in their myriad adventures, brought things back to him when they thought of it. To an extent, almost everything he came into contact with was contaminated, but insofar as he could tell, there *were* points where it was not as extreme. He was even able to successfully remove the sickness from an apple from the far north without it falling apart. It seemed, unsurprisingly, most dense in places with higher populations.

Another issue he was encountering was what to do with the waste. They could contain the separated mass indefinitely, but it couldn't just vanish into oblivion. Burying it would only put it back into the earth. Ivy and Maeve tried, unsuccessfully, to break it down with fire magic. Glass and metal jars and containers of pure miasma crowded the barn they were using as a lab.

His scalp felt perpetually sunburnt, and he was exhausted and starved. He was dismally aware of the poison in his body with every single thing he ate or drank. He tried, once, to see if it was in his own core like Samara, but all it had done was make him black out and fall down the stairs in the townhouse, which caused Evelyn to ban any further self-experimentation.

His life seemed cleaved into two halves. On the one hand, he had an incredibly complex problem to solve. On the other, he was desperately in love.

He and Peony talked on the phone for hours every night. About his research, about her studies, about classes. About the sea and the earth and books and each other. More than anything, he wanted to fix the contagion for *her*, so she could have the life she deserved, even if he did not yet know what this was.

Therein was the point. They were still more or less strangers - he'd had little time to do more than hold her hand. Still, *knowing* their bond was entirely magical and artificial did little to ease its power. In more shaken moments, he tried to justify it to himself that they had been chosen because they were allegedly intrinsically compatible. But did such a thing even truly exist?

"How could I break the bond?" he asked Michael one night. "Between her and I?"

Michael had just sighed and closed the book he'd been reading. Like Ario, he looked haggard, new clumps of gray forming in his hair. "I would not advise it."

"But it *is* possible?"

"I am not so sure," Michael said. "It's a magic, an art, that's very likely dead by now."

Ario recalled Samara. He'd unwrapped the poison from the core of her. But this was no poison.

Gruffly, Michael cleared his throat. "Besides, it... may or may not be too late for that, all depending. Have you... *acted* on the bond? I know the pairbonding is permanent."

His face burned as brilliantly as his scalp. "...No."

"That buys you some time," he said, not quite making eye contact. "I would not... until you are sure." He paused. "Were you to break it, it would be devastating for her. And likely you as well."

He felt traitorous, duplicitous, for even *thinking* about it. But how much of that was genuinely Ario, and how much of that was a forced bond? And did it matter?

On and on the agonizing went...

"Do you think this is what the Goddess wanted for me?" he asked.

Michael blinked. "That sounds more like a question for Evelyn. Or for a prayer."

Ario sighed and sat next to him on the couch. "I find it hard to find forgiveness for a secret that massive."

Michael thought for a moment. "I do not agree with how she approached it," he admitted. "But I understand her reasoning. Should you have – Goddess forbid - been found and separated, they surely would've interrogated the information out of you. Which would have done nothing but endanger Peony and her loved ones."

"Even just to know she existed? Evelyn didn't even know she was trans, much less her name."

"You'd be surprised what they can force out of you, especially with magic," Michael said.

It was no news that Catherine had magic users in her employ. Still, that rankled.

"If you look at it purely practically, her power will protect you. That was what Ainsley intended."

Ario scoffed.

"Ainsley did everything she did to keep you specifically alive," Michael said, nearing a snap.

"Why?" Ario asked quickly. "The world and the Goddess are dying."

"And you would just let that happen without a fight?" Michael countered. His scar looked gruesome in the lamplight. "Nihilism does not look good on you, majesty."

His use of the title felt like a barb. Ario swallowed.

"Ainsley has faith in you. So does the Goddess, and all our new friends. You said so yourself no more hiding and giving up. Do you intend to be the ruler who doesn't keep their promises?"

"...No," he murmured.

Michael softened. "Perhaps you should look at it like a blessing," he said.

"The Goddess dying?"

Michael shook his head. "The bond."

He sighed. "I need to pray," he said.

"Of course," Michael said. "I'll see that Evelyn doesn't disturb you."

He headed back into the yard to a small stone altar they'd put under a tent, mostly to hide it in case the wards failed or were penetrated. He took a piece of purified fruit out of his pocket - a rather desiccated-looking apple - and placed it in the hollow in the center. He knelt, bowing his head.

Is this right? he prayed. *Am I to give into it entirely? Do I trust her, Goddess?*

The apple split open with a faint *pop*, starting him. A green sprout began growing, rapidly, unfurling into the bright pink of apple blossoms. He swallowed. "I see," he whispered. "Am I... am I doing the right thing?"

He waited for what felt like a long time, but there was no further response.

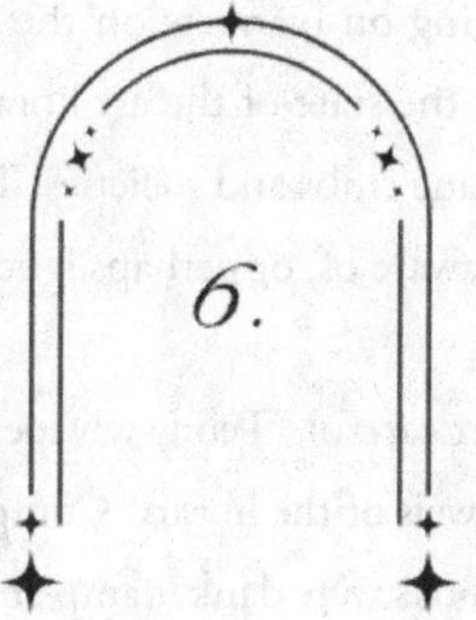

A rio was admittedly unfamiliar with routine. For so much of his life, he'd been on the run, or else tense waiting for it. Over the coming weeks, though, patterns started to emerge. He spent most of his days working with Marko and his crew, trying to better understand the miasma and how they might mitigate it. For Goddess-only-knows how many hours, he read through all of the extant research, through available spellbooks on the previous plague. Peony helped him get books on the subject from her university, but unsurprisingly, even here the books were censored, had pages missing, or otherwise relayed the information in ways that felt disingenuous.

At least these outings gave him an excuse to spend time with her. He realized that perhaps in another life, he could've *been* a student at a university, lounging on blankets on the ivy-stricken campus's quads, or studying in the state-of-the art library, or participating in any number of mundane clubs and societies. The students existed in their own bubble, unaware of, or perhaps ignoring, what was on the outside.

"We have to be more careful," Peony whispered as they perused the stacks, deep in the bowels of the library. Compared to their counterparts upstairs, these books were dank, damp-smelling, and sometimes woefully out of place. He suspected this was to make them harder and more unpleasant to find. "The person at the desk last time asked what I was working on. They can see what I borrow, you know."

"Surely people must write papers about the miasma," he said, trying to ignore the caress of her voice. "It's a historical event."

"...Yeah, maybe. Except the research assistants are going to wonder why a music education major wants a paper on the kinesthetics of disease."

He felt himself flush. "...You're right. I'm sorry."

She touched his hand. He breathed her - hibiscus and orange blossom and something else he had no name for - and nearly lost the thread. The Goddess and the magic all said he could trust her. He wanted -

She leaned over his shoulder and plucked a book off a shelf. "*Most* people here aren't narcs," she whispered. "But some still are."

He felt his face flush brilliantly. "I'll try to be more judicious on what I select," he told her. "Do you know any friendlies at the front desk?"

She sighed and shook her head. "That doesn't mean there are none. Most of the research I've had to do, it's more periodical-based, and I can get those online."

"And we can't be sure the university internet isn't monitored, either."

"Rory *has* made a workaround for her computer, but it's a major pain, and most of the time I don't need to search for anything that could be seen as suspicious," she admitted. "Isn't there... something you could do to... cover your tracks?"

"I'm afraid the two things don't integrate very well," he said, crossing his arms. The longer they were in this dank section, the more the skin on the back of his neck crawled.

Peony checked her phone. "She should be home soon. Maybe she can help you get set up."

Despite his newfound alliance with the resistance, Rory still had yet to warm to him. "Sure. In the meantime, let's go get a coffee."

She brightened at this, but only marginally. He offered her his hand, and they went together to the small cafe within the lobby of the library. The rich smell of coffee still felt like a luxury, even if the espresso they used here was cheap and thin. They took their cups outside into the autumn air. Along with the faint gold glow of the townwide ward, the light was becoming warmer in tone as the season progressed.

"Do you remember, when you were smaller, the way the air would smell in the fall?" he asked her. "That – chilly breeze, the sweet smell of leaves falling?" The leaves here were still mostly green and firmly rooted to their trees.

"I don't, not really," she said. "I lived... somewhere else, when I was a kid. More tropical. We didn't have seasons like this." She paused, fiddling with the straw of her iced tea. "I guess we still don't. I don't... remember much, from that time."

He bit his lip and looked covertly from side to side. Nobody was paying them much attention; they were just another college couple going home after class. "It must've been hard," he said softly.

"I... guess so," Peony said, tilting her head slightly towards his. "It's kind of... foggy. Really I just remember coming to on the mainland. A fisherman found me, I know that much. Rory's dad. His sister and her husband took me in."

He got the sense there was more to the story. Was she not sharing because she felt she may be overheard? Or did she not trust him yet with something that personal?

"What was it like? There?" she asked, before he could try to tease out more information.

"...I'm afraid most of what I knew was... my house." A castle, a palace. "I only ever left it a handful of times. My aunt worried for my safety." The road they followed wound down, and down. Her heels clacked against the stone. "She used to take me into the gardens. We had lovely gardens, all full of roses, and so many other flowers I never learned. I liked the yellow ones best. God—goodness forbid you try to pick one, though." He caught himself.

"Yellow roses mean joy and happiness," Peony said. "No wonder you felt drawn to them."

His brows pulled up.

"Given my name, I know a few things about flowers," she joked. "I... had another one before, another girl's name, but I don't really remember it."

A sliver of pain shot through his heart. He'd spent hours upon countless hours choosing his own name, looking through genealogies before finding the right fit. He couldn't imagine *forgetting* he was Ario, and having to make himself all over again.

She laced her arm through his. The softness of her sweater and the press of the muscle made him a bit dizzy. "Tell me more about the gardens," she said.

"There were several on each floor," he said, keeping his voice low. "Some were greenhouses, where they'd cultivate things out of this biome - like orchids, and birds of paradise, that sort of thing. I spent a lot of time with Evelyn in the one filled with herbs. Memorizing their properties, harvesting them for... recipes." He bit his lip, knowing she'd catch his drift. "She still has a sachet from it that she takes out to smell sometimes. I miss it."

"You spent a lot of time with her, huh," Peony whispered.

"She's my priestess, and in a lot of ways, my mother," Ario said.

"Are you still mad at her? Because she didn't tell you about me?"

Ario hesitated. "We shared many intimacies for her to keep something so large from me, especially as an adult," he said. "I can understand why she did it."

"That's a very diplomatic answer," Peony said. "How do you actually feel?"

"Betrayed," he said without further thought. "Yet also... Were it not for you... I fear there would be no bright spots, at all."

She smiled, and the sunlight caught her dimples.

***

"I have an idea," Peony said brightly a few days later.

"That's never anything good," Rory said from the apartment's kitchen table. She had stuck some bulky-looking device into the slot in Ario's computer so he could research seamlessly, and he heard her typing away at... something.

"We should go out! We haven't had a chance to do anything fun." She pouted.

"Because it's midterms, and also the end of the world," Rory deadpanned.

Ario observed the two cousins and wondered if Rory was just like that with everyone.

"Just my point. We should carpe some diems," Peony said, shaking her wavy hair over one shoulder. "Ario's never been dancing, and I think we could all use a break."

His pulse jumped. His own muddled idea of clubs - loud music, packed with bodies - did not sound particularly appealing. But if it made her happy...

"I think, at the very end of end times, I won't be thinking of all the times I didn't go clubbing," Rory said.

Peony stuck her tongue out. "You can't keep doing good work if you're burnt as hell," she said. Absently, she reached over and brushed a stray strand of hair off of Ario's forehead, making his stomach writhe. "You were just telling me how tired you were, Ario."

Mostly because he had thought she wouldn't tell anybody. "I... am," he admitted. "It's tough, frustrating work."

"And it seems that you're the only one who can do it," Rory said.

"I feel like there's some big piece I'm missing, something stupidly obvious," he said. "And if I just keep pushing, I'll find it, and this will all be fixable."

Rory rolled her eyes. "Some hope."

Peony squeezed Ario's shoulder. "I think we all need a break," she remarked. "So *I'm* going out tonight. Whether or not *you* come with me is up to you." She hopped up. "I'm going to get dressed." She sauntered off towards her room without another word.

Rory scowled for a moment. She shut her own laptop and bobbed her head towards Ario's. "Find anything good?"

"Not particularly," he admitted. "It's like looking for a needle in a pile of needles. If only I had access to true, unfettered, *uncensored* data, then–" At Rory's laughter, he sighed. "You're right, it's a pipe dream." He glanced down at his own outfit, a nondescript black long-sleeved shirt and jeans. "What does one wear to a club, anyway?"

"Probably something flashier than that," Rory said. "Maybe Peony has a necklace you can wear?"

Ario's hand wandered to his pocket, where he felt the smoothness of his bond stone. He had yet to actually *put it on.* "Yes. Maybe." Taking the hint, he went back to her room and knocked on the door.

"Have you decided to stop being a spoilsport, Rory?" Peony asked.

"It's me."

"Come in, I'm just doing my makeup."

Peony's bedroom was the smaller of the two, though neither was large. The university-issued twin bed, desk, and dresser filled almost the whole space. String lights were tacked against the molding, soft and warm. There were her records, in brightly colored square boxes next to the dresser; and next to that was her mandolin on its stand with the black-and-teal embroidered strap. He had yet to hear her play.

Peony's desk, usually splayed with sheet music and textbooks, was now full of makeup. Powders and brushes and creams and things he did not recognize. She was dabbing a small brush into a shimmery blue shadow. He was entranced, momentarily, by the shape of her hand as it lined her eye; she was too focused to notice his attention. Idly, he picked up one of the myriad bottles, a face foundation.

He recalled a few times that Ainsley or Evelyn had smeared his face with stuff like this for this or that event, even as a young child. It had had a chemical tang, a bite, to it. He opened the bottle and sniffed.

"You want me to do your makeup?" Peony asked, only half joking.

"Do men wear makeup to clubs?"

"Sometimes, yes." She set her brush down and lifted his chin, gently, examining his face. His heart started to pound. "Maybe a nice color liner, nothing too fancy…"

"I trust your judgment," he said.

"Well, let me finish up here."

Ario watched her, no less rapt. She had a long, oval face and high cheekbones, and her eyes were bright and vibrant even without makeup. She'd put on sparkly shadows and a bright red lipstick. "You look beautiful."

She blushed, but held his gaze. "*Thank* you." Standing up, she offered Ario the desk chair. "Your turn." She opened one of the desk drawers, pulling out another cloth bag full of colored tubes. She held a few of them up next to his face, judging a few different shades before finally selecting a shimmery silver. "To go with your hair."

It was *very* hard to remain still as she traced the liner on his eyes, not just because the pen tickled. He could see her rapt concentration, the teardrop-shaped bond necklace hanging directly above her breast. He *smelled* her, hibiscus and orange and now the faint pleasant powder of makeup (so removed from whatever stage stuff he'd been caked with as a child). Perhaps she noticed this, because her lips parted, and he was only able to stop himself because of his promise to Michael.

"Your lipstick," he offered.

She waved the tube with her other hand. "I have more." She went to kiss him, and it almost actually *hurt*, to pull away, but he did. Her face crumpled a little.

Guilt, leaden and sinewy, immediately crashed over him.

"Why won't you kiss me?" she asked, her voice quivering.

Oh dear Goddess. "It's not that I don't *want* to–"

"Then what's stopping you?" He sensed, for the first time, her impatience, and realized the depth of the cultural rut between them.

Ario was sure that admitting that *making it final* scared him would only upset her further. "I'm not... I haven't..." He stuttered, feeling his cheeks burn.

Her hands flew up to her mouth *"oh."*

"When would I have had the chance?" he said dryly.

Peony took his hand and pressed it against her cheek. "I'm sorry," she said. "Of course we can wait until you're ready. I thought..." She dropped her eyes. "Maybe you didn't... find me pretty."

"Find you *pretty?*" He whispered. "I think you're gorgeous, I think you're amazing, I think–" It was totally and utterly the magic talking. Or perhaps something more embodied. "I think this has all been overwhelming."

A crease formed between her dark brows. "You're right," she said. "It's just that, when I'm around you, sometimes I get so consumed that you're *mine* that I forget... everything else. Being a siren head."

He took his hand into hers. "Well, you *are* mine," he said. "And we have all the time in the world, don't we?"

Peony's lip quivered, and she laughed. "Bad joke, Ario."

He knew he'd been forgiven.

***

Rory did end up tagging along with them, as well as two or three of Peony's friends. As they walked down into town towards the club, the friends asked Ario question after question, what was his major, where was he from, but hardly seemed to stop long enough for an answer.

He should have assumed that, it being a weekend, there would be crowds in front of the squat, drab building. Its cracked neon sign dubbed it *The Eleventh Hour*. He saw the lines of teens and young adults--some in more casual clothing than he, others dressed to kill in bright colors and bold fabrics—and inwardly groaned, reminding himself he was doing this for Peony.

But instead, the bouncer, a large dark-skinned man with a prosthetic arm, waved them in. He wore sunglasses against the dark, which he pulled down briefly to wink at Peony; his eyes were a bright, glowing yellow. Peony giggled and said, "Oh, you. He knows me. We're good."

He felt a sudden flashburn of jealousy and choked it back with a grin. But he made sure the bouncer saw his arm go around her waist. Ario was just realizing how utterly *petty* that move was when the club washed over him. He had to process it in parts.

First, the space itself; a large dance floor in front of an empty stage, lined with speakers almost as tall as him. Behind it, a bar, glowing similarly with those bright neon colors, and a pair of bartenders struggling to keep up with the volume. Doorways on either side of the bar led to smaller dance floors, and he saw a spiral staircase leading above and below. UV lighting made everything else innocuous glow.

Then, the *people*. He swore he had never seen this many people in his life, and they were all bouncing in and around him, either through their reckless dancing or in an effort to get somewhere else.

And the noise: singing and yelling and chattering and a pounding bass track that barely sounded like music. After so much quiet, and silence, he could barely breathe.

"Each room has its own vibe," Peony said in his ear. "Like, house music, rock, pop, the funk one is neat, all old-fashioned–"

"Wherever you want to go," Ario managed. "This is your night."

She beamed, and a few people eyed her. The UV lit up everyone, but Peony in particular seemed to glow, softly radiant in the semidarkness. She grasped his hand and dragged him to the bar, offered two fruity cocktails and gave him one. The drink, replete with a cherry on top, looked so unlike ritual wine he expected it to be sweet, took a big swig, and nearly gagged. Alcohol, some kind of *strong* alcohol, making his nose burn and eyes swim, and below it maybe a few drops of fruit juice.

Peony winced. "I should have wanted you. Marcel makes them *strong*."

Ario sputtered, but wasn't a quitter, and forced down a few more swallows. Ritual wine, when consumed in abundance, provided a gentle, sleepy buzz. This was different. It was strong, certain, making his head light, and the cup was empty and "Let's dance."

She dragged him to the funk room, Rory and friends abandoned. The music was so loud he felt it in his breastbone. He pulled her into his arms under that warm glowing light.

Hours might have passed; he wasn't sure. When they got too warm and thirsty, they went back to the bar for another drink. And another. Ario had never been more than tipsy in his entire life, and at first he wasn't sure if he liked it – the inability to think straight, the heaviness in his limbs – but then he was back with Peony and mercilessly distracted and wondering why the hell he wouldn't just kiss her. During more than one song he found his lips brushing her cheek, her forehead, but before he could seal the deal he realized how badly he needed a bathroom, and, disoriented, wandered outside onto a smoker's terrace, where the toilets were.

Cool fall air, tainted with tobacco and marijuana and something sweet smelling, curled in his lungs and nearly shook Ario out of his stupor. In the small, not terribly clean washroom, he splashed cold water on his face, only belatedly remembering the eyeliner. He smeared it off with some toilet paper and went back to join the revelers.

As he turned a corner, something bright blue flashed in the corner of his eye. Ario blinked, squinting, unsure if he were in the club's UV or not. He looked at his hands. No, very definitely in regular light.

Blue flashed around the corner, and before he was even conscious of what he was doing, he was running away from the club in a flat-out sprint.

The glow chased him, and for a few seconds he swore he saw Samara's paws in his peripheral. He should have known she would find him, or perhaps the magic he'd done to her had made him even easier to find.

The physical training he'd done with Michael seemed to be paying off - he was getting farther than he thought he would, though his legs and lungs were burning. Bits of town he did not recognize blew by; residential backstreets, a park, all dark and empty at this hour. He'd taken himself towards the sea, he realized. What good would the sea do for him?

The water would kill his scent, surely. He'd read that somewhere. Did that account for magic scents, too? At least on the beach, there were unlikely to be bystanders if this became a fight. Which it would.

Stairs led from the street to the sand; he vaulted off them, catching his fall on the powder, tasting scratchy sand and salt. Ario whirled around, reaching for the athame he kept in his boot. He choked hot air in and out of his lungs and looked wildly for Samara. At least he'd led her away from Peony and Rory—

Peony, whose presence allegedly nullified his own magic.

"*Stupid,*" he hissed at himself. He should've stayed put. That was the logical thing to do. But the alcohol...

He saw the glow, the vaguely lupine form, and readied a spell. But the wolf did not attack. He couldn't, in the darkness, really see her. Heartbeats passed, heavily.

And then the wolf turned and bounded away.

Ario sank down onto the sand, feeling the cool grains. He allowed himself a moment to catch his breath before he pulled out his phone. He had to tell Evelyn, and Michael, immediately. If they had to run *again*, all because he wanted to go dancing, he swore he'd–

Texts from Peony. *You fall in?*

Then, *Ario, where'd you go? I'm near the bar with Marcel.* Of course, she'd assumed he'd gotten lost. This whole ordeal had maybe taken fifteen minutes.

He called her. "I'm alright, but something did happen," he told her. "I... I need you."

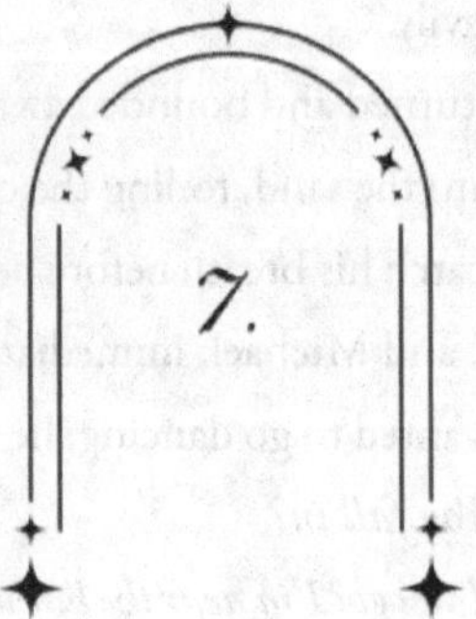

E velyn wasn't happy. "How could you be so *careless?*" she barked at Ario, once he returned to the townhouse with Peony in tow. The anxiety and the walk over had sobered both of them considerably.

"It was my fault," Peony said. "It was my idea, I just wanted to have some fun for once."

Evelyn scowled, tugging her frizzy braid over her shoulder. "Well, you might very well have blown our cover."

Ario huffed. He felt gritty now, gross, his mad dash and all the dancing making him sticky with sweat. Not to mention the itching, ragged thirst. "Evelyn, if you must blame someone, blame me. I went along with it knowing the risks. And *I* left her side in a moment of clouded judgement."

Peony, her makeup a bit smeared, looked somewhat hurt. He clarified,

"I left because I thought she would find you, because–"

"You forgot about the anti-magic." She gestured around herself. "Right."

Evelyn cleared her throat. "We need to leave the city," she said. "At least– *at least* until we can be sure she's not within the limits. Though... why would she leave, like that?"

"I suppose it's possible that there's another of her kind here, who caught my scent and got curious," Ario speculated.

"It's not a full moon," Evelyn pointed out. "Without Catherine's alternations, they wouldn't have that much control over their form, to give chase and not hunt."

Peony shuddered and rubbed her arms.

"We'll have to get you out of here and wait and see if she comes back with reinforcements," Evelyn said, with a tired sigh. "And hope she doesn't catch you on your way out." She thought for a moment, the lamplight in the study catching the lines in her face. "Girl. How much control do you have over the shield?"

Peony jumped. "Well... it's not... conscious. I just do it."

Another sigh. "I'll just have to work with it," she muttered. "Ario. Go pack some things. Then Michael will take both of you to go get *her* things. And then we will leave."

"I can't just leave," Peony said. "I have my practice labs–and classes! There are midterms I need to turn in."

"You want him in danger?" Evelyn levelled. "At least–*at least* until we can ascertain she isn't coming back."

Peony pouted, but said nothing. She followed Ario up the stairs without a word, carrying her heels in one hand.

Ario brought her into his room, thankful he kept it tidy; not that he had much to make it messy. He reached for the suitcase in his closet, took out the ragged clothes he had left in it and put in the new, as well as a few books, and his laptop.

"You think the place will have wifi?" Peony asked, her face drawn. "My computer's jailbroken…"

"Um, maybe." Perhaps Evelyn would let Peony use her devices once they had received her own jailbreaking. "I'm really sorry about this…"

"No, it's fine," she said, and didn't sound altogether convincing, but she mustered a smile. "At least we get to spend some time together."

Doubtless under Evelyn and Michael's thumbs, but he took her hand and said, "Yes, I suppose that is true."

***

A few hours later, showered, scrubbed, packed, the four of them left the townhouse. Ario had left many, many places behind in the same manner, and had learned not to get attached. Somehow, that did not make it easier to see the townhouse disappear behind them.

Peony cradled her mandolin case and looked out the car window, saying nothing. She and Rory had an ugly row as she'd packed, and her nose was still pink. Rory blamed Ario. She was sure that now Peony was going to get hurt, and it would all be his fault, and how could Peony just *choose* him over her and their family…

As if it were a choice. As if any of this were a choice.

He took her hand and squeezed it. He didn't want to get her hopes up in case they couldn't return. She offered him a small smile, but resumed her contemplation in silence.

They had to use small backroads and local routes once they were out of the city; anything major or leading through any other cities would have scanners and patrols. Ario was not accustomed to traveling by car, an experience which was novel for exactly as long as it took until one of them needed a bathroom. Michael managed to find a small greasy spoon in which to have lunch. After heavy, oily soy burgers that gave him a stomachache, they drove.

Nobody felt very much like talking. Michael was exactly as stoic as a king's guard should be, Evelyn sullen and cranky, Peony distressed.

Ario was sick of it. Not their reasonable reactions to his mistake; they deserved to feel how they felt. He was so sick of running.

***

This safe house was not one Ario had been to before; out by the sea but more southerly than Lindenfell. The air was not so choked here. Perhaps he would be able to resume his miasma studies.

Near evening, they finally stopped, going down a long dirt drive surrounded by sea grass that, despite it all, still was green and waving faintly in the breeze. There was a small, two story cottage at the end of the drive, with gray-brown stone and blue shingles. Breathing in the salty air, Ario noticed that it had a different tang to it than Lindenfell's, sharper, perhaps. The sand-and-dirt mixture was strange under his boots.

"This is Maeve's place," Michael said. "She's in the city so often that most of the time she stays with Marko."

Evelyn scoffed. "That, and they're cavorting."

Peony was last to get out of the car. She took a deep breath, the set of her shoulders lowering slightly. "We're right by the ocean," she said.

"No neighbors, either," Evelyn said, hefting a laptop bag over her shoulder. "Thank the Goddess."

The cottage indeed seemed in its own world. Ario could see no other houses, or structures, or even really *trees* for what had to be miles, and the visibility was good. Given he only had sight in the one eye, he didn't have depth perception, but that wasn't necessary to see how isolated they were. A hundred meters or so behind the house, the grass gave way to more of that scratchy sand.

Michael opened the truck and started unloading the bags.

Evelyn turned to Ario. "Well? You know the deal."

He sighed and started placing wards. The place was actually well-fortified already, he noticed, but he added a few extra. Once he was through, he noticed Peony was still staring at the sea.

"Why don't you go over?" he asked. "I think we'll be fine now."

She nodded, gave him the mandolin, and set off. The glimmering crimson and gold of the sunset caught in her dark hair. For a moment, he watched her walk away before he picked up a bag or two, certain she probably wanted to be alone.

Inside the cottage was cute and well-kept. Against the left wall was a small fireplace, carved out of the stone wall. Similarly, built-in shelves on either side held old photos in frames of many different styles and plants in handmade ceramic pots, enchanted to self-water. Across from those was a sofa with a smooth, cottony gingham coverlet. Dusty books - what appeared to be healing texts - were stacked neatly on a small side table, a chintz chair by the window the perfect spot to curl up and read.

Evelyn was in the pocket-sized kitchen, checking the cabinets and fridge for food. "There's a village a few kilometers north," she said to Ario without prelude. "I'll send Michael to get us some groceries."

"Peony is a person, you know," he said instead.

She shut the cabinet she was poring through. "First, you're angry because I didn't tell you about her. Now you're defending her honor?"

"You were talking about her like she's an object. You brushed off her concerns about university."

"I think your lives are more important," she snapped.

"And *her* life has possibly just been turned upside down. *Please* try to be kind to her."

Evelyn was silent, her gaze drifting past her. "I do think she's a lovely girl," she said. "Ainsley... spent so long referring to her as *your protection* and your *back up plan* that the instant you found her, it all seemed... too real. And I found myself wondering about all the nuances of this bond. I found myself understanding your fury."

"Nothing is a choice," he murmured.

"It feels like a game of chess." Evelyn picked up the metal kettle off of the small gas stove. "It's been making me... re-evaluate who Ainsley is."

So that was it. "Yes. Me as well."

"I will be gentler with the girl–Peony," Evelyn said. "I want to work with her. See if she can get some control over that power of hers. That would be enormously beneficial."

"I suspect it would help make her feel better too," he said. "Like she has some control."

Evelyn crossed over to the trough sink and turned on the tap, but nothing came out. "Blast. I must go turn on the water. I wonder where the devil that is." Setting down the kettle, she squeezed his shoulder, and left him in that dusty kitchen alone.

He decided to explore, but there wasn't a whole lot to see in the cottage. There were two tiny bedrooms upstairs, each containing a single full size bed. One of the rooms, the pink room, as he came to call it, was clearly Maeve's; there was a writing desk with a blanket draped over the chair, a closed leather-bound book with personal writings that he immediately set back down, and a half-empty bottle of perfume. The closet was mostly empty but still had some extra dresses.

The other room was obviously meant for a guest. Blue floral wallpaper, yellow bedspread, a small table with a curved lamp. This room had no desk, or chair, but a low padded bench, what might be called a fainting couch. It was appropriately Ario-sized, he realized, which might help their sleeping arrangements some. He missed his mattress at the townhouse, but had slept on worse. There was that stretch, when he was fourteen, where they'd been stuck in a cave. A sleeping bag on stone might be good for one's posture, but most definitely not for morale.

Exploration completed, he went outside, and padded over the sand to the sea.

By then, it was nearly dark, the moon all but full in the sky. Its silver light clashed with the rose gold and navy of the sunset, and the air had a sharper, almost more frantic, chill.

Peony was knee-deep in the water, staring motionlessly out at the last bits of sun.

"How's the water?" he asked, in a bid not to startle her.

After a beat, she turned slightly towards him. "Pretty cold," she said. "But... I like it."

"It's getting dark. We should go inside."

"Right..." She shook her head, her long dark hair bounding a little. "No mega-ward."

"Not quite," he agreed.

"A few more minutes," she said. "Please?"

Ario took off his socks and shoes, left them with hers, and joined her in the water. She was right; it *was* cold, making his toes prickle and curl, but he'd been cold many times in his life, and felt he could bear it for a little while. He made his way across the sharp sand to her side. "How are you doing?"

"I don't know," she admitted. "Overwhelmed. Afraid..." He slipped his hand into hers; hers was damp from the sea mist.

"...I am so sorry."

"You did it to protect me," she said in a low voice. "I can't be mad at that."

"You can, though," he told her. "I... I pray to the Goddess that this will blow over, and that we can go home."

The corner of her lip pulled up just the slightest. "...Hopefully," she said. She turned to face him more fully. "I graduate in the spring. What happens then? Where will we be?"

Ario paused to think about it. "I'm not sure," he admitted. "I still have so much work to do in Lindenfell, and I know your friends and family are there..." He cleared his throat. "I'm sorry about Rory."

Peony sighed and tucked a lock of hair behind her ear. "She's just protective, that's all," she said. "She's always been like that. And she's right, in a way. We really *have* just met. But."

"But," he agreed.

For a moment, he only heard waves.

"What was it like? Growing up?"

Bemused, he looked briefly towards the moon. "I told you about our travels," he said. All the different places they'd stayed, and run to or from.

She shook her head. "Before that."

"Well... I was very... small."

"You were a... well, princess," she said. "You really don't remember much of it?"

"It wasn't as picturesque as Catherine will have you believe," he said. "I was alone, much of the time, and yet... not."

Peony cocked her head.

"I always had a pair of bodyguards, a governess, tutors, but no peers. Friends. I tried a few times to play with the servants' children. That got shut down when the political situation got hotter, though." He was surprised how... uncomfortable, it was, to look back on those days; the dual-eye memories were much too sharp and clear. "When I wasn't studying, I was praying. As I got a little older, I learned how to sneak around without getting caught. And I'd just... listen." To guards, servants, members of the court. Sometimes, Ainsley herself.

"Your... Goddess," Peony said. "She's real?"

He swallowed. "Well, yes," he said. "I suppose... one could argue... that anything that's manifested when I prayed was just a projection of my own power. But it's just... something I feel, I know, is true." The salt was making his eyes itch. "What do you believe in?"

"I don't know," she said. "I prayed, a little, but I'd just look at the moon. I don't know if we had other gods." She met his eyes. "I don't remember anything before the mainland. And trying to find books, or anything, has not been all that useful."

"...I can imagine." He tried to conceptualize what he'd be like if he'd been removed from his Goddess, his culture. He wouldn't be, well, Ario. "Maybe I could help... try to unlock those memories."

She shook her head. "I'm not guessing I'd find anything *good*. How did I get there? How did I lose access to my form? I doubt it was sunshine and roses. I don't even remember what it feels like. This is... everything."

Ario swallowed around the lump in her throat. "I'm so sorry," he whispered.

She shrugged. "I have you, and I have my life now. Had." She bit her lip. Her eyes welled.

Ario cupped her cheek. "I'm going to make it right, Peony. I promise." He leaned forward and, very gently, pressed his lips against hers.

He felt the kiss in his bones, in the roots of his hair. Icy waves lapped at his feet and ankles. Ario pulled Peony closer, and closer, and still it was not close enough. Perhaps it never would be.

The moon threatened to rise, and yet, there they were lost in each other. He pulled his hand through her hair, all hot elastic silk. It was not enough. This felt like hunger, and gravity, and there they remained until the breeze cooled.

Later that night, he lay on the narrow sofa. Evelyn was softly snoring on the bed a meter or so away from him. She had never been a heavy sleeper, and she had also been very insistent that Peony had the pink room. Alone. Michael was on the downstairs couch.

Ario brushed his fingers over his lips. They were raw and sensitive from all the kissing, but he wanted more, *needed* more, magic or perhaps good old fashioned hormones making him ache. He turned, the settee biting into his shoulder and hip. Sleep was bound to be elusive; he felt wound up, too full, stretched to snap under a threadbare quilt. As quietly as he could, he slipped off the couch and out of the room, tucking the quilt around his shoulders against the chill. He crept downstairs.

Michael's form was craggy under a sleeping bag. Ario stole back outside onto the beach. The moon was full and the wards strong, so the risk was minimal. He sat on the cool sand. Tomorrow he would have to do the full moon ritual, with Evelyn, but for now the moon may as well be his.

"You feel a connection to it, don't you?"

Her voice startled him, and he nearly threw magic, but it was just Peony. "Couldn't sleep?"

She'd tucked her hair into a bun. She shook her head. "I'm wide awake. And the mattress sucks."

He opened his quilt cocoon, and she gladly snuggled next to him. "At least you have a mattress." His heart felt like it might consume him.

Peony rested her head against his shoulder. "I used to look at the moon, and try to imagine what it might be like under the sea."

"Maybe I could restore it, somehow," he said. "Your form, I mean. There's no point having this power if I don't *use* it."

Hope bled into her voice. "Do you think it's possible?"

"I can't promise anything. If it was removed, it was removed. But…" He trailed off and swallowed. "If I knew more about the mechanisms of your power, maybe I could heal the damage."

She gasped. "Ario, I–"

"But the mechanism theoretically holding back your true power could also be holding back… those memories."

"I don't care," she said. "If I was *whole,* I would…" She grasped him hard. "Thank you. Thank you."

"I want to give you the world," he murmured.

She kissed him, and this time he could not control it. It had to happen, he had to *do* this, or–

He pulled her down onto the sand. Each touch was so acute and hot as fire and she was responding with equal aplomb. Suddenly *nothing* else mattered but her, her pleasure, her whispered query for consent, and he dissolved under her and the watchful eye of the moon.

***

"...Are you okay?" she asked.

Ario's hair was warm against his scalp. The sharp violent pleasure had peaked and faded to a small throb between his legs. He'd thought *acting* on it would have been this grand, dramatic shift. But it all felt... normal. Natural. "Yes, I..." He swallowed, his heard full. "It is... strange, isn't it?"

"It was wonderful."

He shivered, pulling his shirt back on. She did seem resplendent; he looked at her, lying there, the silver glow illuminating her body.

It was done, then. Permanent. No longer frightening. Would they have chosen each other if they had met on the street?

It didn't bother him that he had no answer.

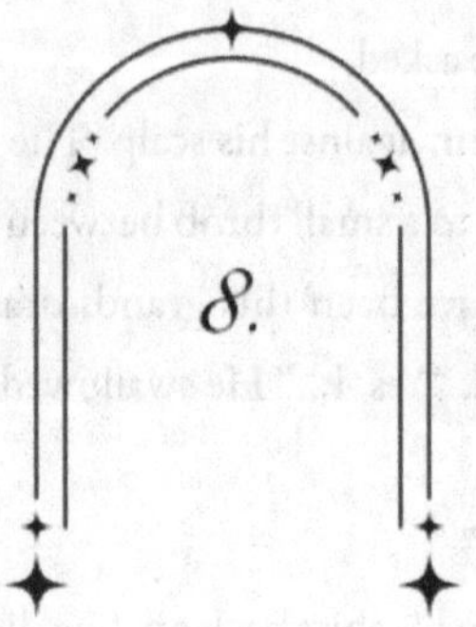

"**A**gain," Evelyn said.

Peony swatted the sweaty hair out of her eyes. Ario had tried to warn her that Evelyn was a stern taskmistress, especially when it came to magic. "Can't we take a break? A little one?"

"You've nearly got it. I hardly sensed him that time."

Ario had been fussing with some produce from the nearby village, outside on the pretense of keeping the pure miasma *out* of the house, but he really didn't want Evelyn to push Peony too hard. The necklace, under his shirt, was cold against his skin.

Peony huffed in apparent frustration. She was trying to learn to project her anti-magic and to extend its range. To do so they'd had to establish her range, and how much she could cover. This was convenient for him, because the miasma studies took a *lot* of power. But Peony had had next to no magic training. She could set wards and do little else, much to Evelyn's consternation.

Ario was fairly certain that the miasma was less present out here. If only he had enough data to triangulate where it was coming from, so perhaps a source could be determined. Even eliminated?

Some hope.

They'd been here several weeks. So far, it seemed reasonable that they may be able to return to Lindenfell - just in time for Peony to catch up on her studies. She'd told the university she had mono, something that medicines took weeks to fix, and so was allowed to do her exams and homework online. That she was claiming to have the kissing disease was ironic; they'd kissed each other as much as they could get away with.

Michael opened the back door and handed Ario a cup of tea. "Has your work been... fruitful?"

"I'll ignore that horrible pun. But yes. There must be *a* source. Else it's only more prevalent in densely populated areas." He thought of, not for the first time, those humanlike wraiths that he'd seen the day he met Peony. It all had to be connected somehow.

"How did it end last time?" Michael asked.

"Well... it just seemed to go away." Naturally, given how long ago this had been, it wasn't as though there were photos or videos. Magical means of recording would have degraded as well. "Scholars *think* it's because it consumed enough magic to dissipate. The problem is, there's a lot *less* magic now then there was then." He sighed and set aside a soggy pear. "That's why I think it's going for the earth directly.

There's not enough to eat. But you can't just make magic where there is none."

"Could we give it something similar *enough* to trick it?"

"Like what? It's already consuming as much as it can."

"Something that produces mass amounts of energy."

Ario frowned.

"Like radioactive elements. In fusion states, they produce incredible amounts of power."

Ario nearly scoffed. "Yes, because I can just get my hands on some yellowcake uranium." He considered. Fusion power plants *did* exist; they provided much of the continent's electrical power. The largest problem, among many, was that all means of energy production were owned by the state - i.e., Catherine and her goons. "That's the closest thing to useful I've heard, and we, as usual, can't do anything about it."

Michael shrugged.

He heard a grunt of frustration. Peony paced in circles.

"You got it that time," Evelyn said. "Excellent work."

***

Returning to Lindenfell was welcome - the cottage was *slightly* too small to house four people comfortably - but anticlimactic. It was colder, here, the coming winter starting to show its face.

What Ario wanted to know more about were the wraiths. When he could find moments himself to seek them out - which was rare, because his days were full of work, prayer, and time with Peony. He returned to that place in the woods, even at night, and found no more than average wraiths. Was someone, or something, killing them? One of Rory's allies, perhaps? How could he just ask them to *stop* when, at the same time, they were protecting civilians?

"You have authority," Evelyn pointed out when he mentioned this. "You have to start using it. You're not the green intern you act like when you're around the network."

"Even so, why should they listen to me?"

"They value you enough to have protected you for years," she reminded him.

His heart gave an odd little quiver. "If I were to lead them, how and where would I lead them, anyway? So many of us are just trying to stay alive."

"Helping them stay alive *is* a noble task to work toward," she said.

***

It was easier said than done to be more *leaderly.* Having largely lived only with Evelyn, his instinct was to be *useful* and to make members of the network like him, not assert power over them. He could study diplomacy and leadership as much as he wanted, but that didn't result in practical skill. Not everyone had the knack to lead. His mother surely hadn't. Neither had Ainsley.

He received his first communique from her a month or so after the stay at the cottage. The raw, misty seaside winter and the excess magic use left him constantly tired, and sometimes his joints and organs ached. Maeve and Evelyn wanted to examine him, if so only to see the effects of it on his body and magic. Reassuring them that this was not necessary took a lot of effort. Strangely, he was *gaining* weight, despite eating no more than necessary. Water retention? It did not particularly bother him so long as he fit into his clothes.

Ario received an unsolicited package in the mail, which in and of itself was odd, because the network usually provided all of their external communications. In and around the many, many flyers and newsletters the poor mailperson crammed into their unchecked post-box, was a mug-sized box with one of his aliases on it. A lowercase I had three dots over it, which was one of the signals the network used to show something was from them.

He brought the box inside, befuddled, and opened it. Inside was a small velvet jeweler's case and a note. Apprehension brought the blood tingling into his face even before he looked at the note, which was on a thick, smooth creamy paper.

> *My dearest Ilario,*
>
> *Hardly a day has passed without me praying for you. I trust in the Goddess you are well. I have heard you're coming into your own as king. I can't wait to see this confident young man again.*
>
> *I agree the time for action is now. My guidance is yours, should you wish for it.*
>
> *Please find some time for joy. You are nearly twenty-one; a sacred birthday. Perhaps we cannot celebrate in the normal way, but please receive this token of your old aunt's affections.*
>
> *Yours,*
>
> *A*

He looked away from the note, his vision swimming. The first he'd heard from her in thirteen years and he got... this. What was he to make of this? Of her own inaction? "My guidance is yours"? Where the fuck was it before? Could she have found him sooner, if she had really, truly wished for it? And *Peony*, dearest Ainsley, not a word written about *her.*

Choking on the anger, Ario resisted the urge to tear up the note. He knew Evelyn would want to see it. And this stupid little gift - he should just hide it in the office, unseen. Ainsley didn't know him anymore.

The part of him that had been taught to be stingy, and survive, did not let him do this, though. He opened the box with shaking fingers.

Resting on some shirred blue velvet was a wristwatch. Simple. Actually, it was a bit dingy, a bit tarnished, and its battery was dead. A tiny piece of paper fluttered out of the box onto the floor. The watch was narrow for a man's, the band unadorned. A pair of tiny sapphires framed the watch face. Ario crouched down for the slip of paper.

This was your father's. Do not underestimate the power of simple things.

He scowled. A useless note and a dead watch. *Just wonderful.*

Evelyn emerged in his peripheral, carrying a basket of folded laundry. "What is that?"

"A *gift*," he spat. "From Ainsley."

He expected surprise, even awe, but Evelyn threw down the laundry, snatched the notes and the box, and examined them thoroughly. "Did it touch your skin?" she hissed.

"I held the box, but..." He felt her flashes of cold magic. "It has our signal. It's from her."

Evelyn's shoulders eased back down. "It could've been cursed," she said. "A fake."

"I'm not an idiot, Evelyn. I would've let it alone had I believed it suspect."

She paused. "I guess I am on edge," she said. "It's fine."

"You can read the note. I know you want to," he said. He crossed over to the couch and flopped down on it, winching at a sudden cramp in his lower back. To his own vindication, he noticed her expression was rather disappointed.

"Maybe it's a code," she said. "The watch is stopped at a certain time... Maybe that is when we will meet?"

Ario shrugged. "It just sounds to me that she could've seen us sooner."

"The risk, Ario–"

"The risk, the risk, the *risk*," he hissed. "Simply *existing* is risky. *People like us* take on that risk to *help* others. Or least we're supposed to. It seems like it's been a long time since anyone even bothered." He hopped up and started pacing.

"Ario!" Evelyn gasped, her face very red.

"Well? Am I wrong?" He asked. "My mother was an idiot who liked pretty things. Ainsley took over her mess and never made a stand about anything. How far back does it go? My grandmother? Hers?"

Evelyn was very still.

"The Goddess mandates we help others," Ario said. "Why else would She give us this power? What was the point of hiding ourselves away in a marble tower? It all came down anyway."

Evelyn mumbled something.

"What," he spat.

"I said you're right," Evelyn said. Her eyes were bloodshot. "All along I thought she was keeping away out of safety. I really... I really don't know what to make of this." She took the watch into her hand, and squinted. "...Strange."

"It's a dead watch. Apparently my father's."

"Not just that." She shook her head. "Your father was wearing this when he was assassinated. I know, because I remember hearing him complain the battery died, and they had me identify the bodies... There had to be some intent behind this, I just don't understand..."

Ario took the watch into his hand. The silver was cool, and he noticed the band was slightly bent. Presumably from surviving an explosion. "It seems morbid to me."

Evelyn checked the time on the dead watch again. "I'll ask Marko if he knows of anything happening at this time within the next few weeks."

"Why reveal herself *now*?"

"As she says herself... perhaps she wants to offer her assistance. May I take a closer look? I just want to be *sure* there's no funny business."

"Be my guest."

She snatched the jewelry case up again and took it into the office, muttering.

His face still pricking with anger, he decided he needed guidance of his own. He crossed over through the dank chill to the altar and knelt in prayer. What were her intentions? What did she *want?*

***

The answer to this query came just shy of his twenty-first birthday. He didn't want any fuss, any grandeur. Allegedly back in the day this would be something that was televised. He would publicly state his intention to take on the throne. Functionally, he *would* be king, slowly taking over duties from the previous monarch.

Those times were over now.

On a blustery, but warmer-than-average weekday, he was on his way over to the farm to upload his data and to check on the livestock. There was a working theory that they could create a sort of vaccine against the miasma, combining medicine and magic, but in practice it was not wholly useful, nor were there that many willing participants. The miasma was neither bacteria nor virus, but it behaved almost like the antithesis of light. Neither wave nor photon, but present, visible, and measurable.

He'd purchased a UV light to determine if low-level, common radiation had any impact on the "pure" stuff he'd been collecting. He recalled what Michael had said about the fusion power plants. Even Catherine lifted her moratorium on magic to safely deal with the radioactive waste, rendering it down into a mudlike sludge that grew excellent tomatoes. But Ario didn't know *how* these magic users took away the harmful aspect of the waste.

He was missing something. Something obvious. He mulled it over on the meandering drive. Michael had started to let him do the drive himself, unguarded, and he relished in the time alone. He supposed it was useless to try UV, considering the sheer ambient radiation from the cosmos. It was not like he could order isotopes online. The university *might* have them in small amounts for instructional purposes, but he doubted it would be enough to be useful and besides, the university was swarmed with scanners.

What of plain electricity? There were "dirty" ways to generate that much energy, long ago abandoned because of the emissions produced. What of a massive turbine, and he could, perhaps, use his own power to make it spin very, very fast–

There was a vehicle he did not recognize in the farm's driveway. Ario tensed. The vehicle itself was not conspicuous, a common-model slightly older passenger sedan. It was entirely likely this was just a member he had not met yet. Marko's truck was here, too. He swallowed down a prickly sense of unease and approached the farmhouse.

Everything was as it should be. No signs of a scuffle. He smelled fresh coffee, and heard gentle, affected chatter.

"...All well on that front. I *do* apologize for showing up without an announcement."

Adrenaline flooded him, bringing a tang of magic against his lips and lungs. That voice, down to the haughty way it curled up on the *do*. He almost turned and left the house.

"No need to apologize, your majesty. I just wish I had better refreshments to offer. We don't keep much food here." Marko, his voice high and tense.

"Nonsense, my palette is not so sophisticated as of late."

Angry, Ario decided. He was definitely angry. And in she waltzed, he thought, but then his conscience got the better of him, and he offered a silent prayer of thanks for her safety. Ario closed the door as softly as he could, but the old hinges betrayed him with a nasty *creak*. He braced himself – *Be kingly* – and crossed into the small dining room.

If not for the voice, he wouldn't have recognized the woman sitting at the small wooden table. Old, haggard, her face deeply lined, her clothing unremarkable and visibly worn. A piece of duct tape held the sole of one of her boots on. Her blonde hair had grayed. Her slender cheeks had grown soft and bloated.

He saw, in Ainsley's face, that same lack of recognition. Ario had last seen her pre-transition, a mere boy. He saw her searching his face. Wordlessly, he took off the hat, revealing his hair and erasing any doubt.

"Lady Queen," he said, trying to keep the boiling emotion out of his voice.

She stood. Slowly, carefully, as though it hurt. "Ilario," she said, her brows pulling together. "Is that really you? Why–you look just like Cyril." His father.

Marko murmured an excuse and left the room.

Ainsley moved to hug him, but he took a step back automatically. He saw the hurt register on her face.

"I thank the Goddess for your safety," he said. "To what do I owe the pleasure?"

She frowned. "Ario... you *do* remember me, don't you? I know it's been a terribly long time..."

It would feel good, to yell. To reflect on her the sense of abandonment. "I do remember you. Yes, aunt."

She processed this, her dull blue eyes flashing. "You look wonderfully well. Why, I was... I didn't think I'd see you. Not today." She smoothed her hands over her sweater. Its cuffs were unraveling. "Would you... would you like some coffee, dear?" She gestured towards the table. Marko had laid out one of Maeve's colorful tea trays with scones and dry-looking shortbread.

Nearby, the old tin alarm clock ticked softly. Ario sat at the table. Ainsley poured them both a cup from an old teapot. Ario recalled, briefly, the few times this governess or that had attempted to get him to learn the finer, feminine aspects of *entertaining*. Like flower arranging, or embroidery, it all seemed a rather useless skill for a (yet uncloseted) king. Did those lessons also teach one how not to curse out a guest? Not to scream? Was it similar treatment keeping Ainsley's chapped lips in a slight, welcoming smile?

"There's a dear," she said, offering him the cup. "I'm sure you must feel conflicted."

"Where were you?" he asked flatly. He felt through the thin china that the coffee would be too hot to drink.

"It would be easier to say where I *haven't* been," she said. "Evelyn's plans were thorough."

If she said this to purposefully throw him, he would not let it show. "Her plans kept us alive. I thank the Goddess for such a capable priestess."

Ainsley knotted her hands. On her left she wore the ring of duty representing her station; a hideous pewter-colored crest. "Is she well?"

"Well enough. I'm afraid I have co-opted her services."

A small nod. "I knew she would look after you. Better than I could." Tick. Tick. Tick.

"Why now?" he asked. "Why after all this time?"

She thought about it. As a child, her pauses had made her seem wise. "There's a storm coming," she murmured. "I can feel it."

He laughed, then. He couldn't help it. "I have been studying the *storm* for months now," he told her. "I have been *trying* to make it stop, to slow it down, to do *anything*."

Another nod. "Yes. Marko appraised me of your efforts. But I was referring to something else." She cleared her throat. "There's an uprising in the southwest. A sizable one."

"Magic users?"

"Magic and mundane both. Farmers." She sipped. "Their land is dying, so they have no livelihood. They approached the administration for relief, and were denied. So were the doctors, when their hospital supplies began to dry up."

Ario didn't want to believe her. A shock, a wild hope, curled in his belly. Despite authoritarianism, Catherine had always treated the mundanes *well*. Social safety nets. Healthcare, university tuition. Small beauties of fascism, for the entitled. Why the sudden shift?

"If she can't quell this, and she falls, there will be a power vacuum. Places like this will support the rebellion. House them. You've got some here already, I know."

"And you intend to take her place."

"I intend *for you* to take her place."

"And her horrid sons? Surely one of them will step up. Do you have an actual plan? Or is this just conjecture?"

Ainsley took another frustrating minute to speak. "We come forward and offer our support to the rebellion."

Ario snorted.

"It's worked in the past."

"In *stories,*" he said. "A group of rag-tag, under-resourced misfits somehow overthrowing the big bad through sheer willpower. We might have magic, but she has bullets. Bombs. Control over power, food, and water. Manpower. *Money.* What of the civilians that happen to be in the way? She'd kill them and blame the rebellion. Do they have weapons? Training of any kind?"

Ainsley blinked. "Well, I–"

"How would they get across the country unscathed and undetected? This isn't the first protest. Those college students from Caldera were literally blown to bits a few years ago. They said it was a gas main."

Ainsley was silent.

"As of the twenty-first, you will have no rightful claim to the crown. You want to go across the country, expose yourself and voice support, well, Goddess protect you. *I* want to keep my people *alive.*"

The blood rushed to her face, and her mouth fell open. But then she *smiled,* a real smile that showed her teeth, and he noticed one of her eye teeth was gone. "I knew. I knew you had it."

"Had *what?*"

"A chance."

"I don't understand."

Ainsley stood and crossed over to the window. Her hair had grown longer, and he saw the ragged ends she must have hacked off herself.

"What I just proposed to you was utter nonsense. I wanted to see if you would capitulate, or if you would press back."

He scowled. "So it was a test."

"Yes. Yes, it was. You're ready."

Ario took a very deep breath through his nose. "For what, exactly?"

"Another type of war."

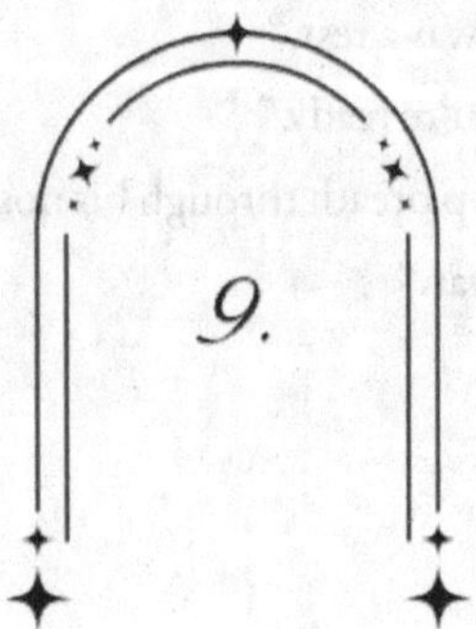

9.

Really, Ainsley said, she got the idea from Xander. They needed someone on the inside, someone Catherine trusted. Why shouldn't one of their people enter her service and engender themselves into the regime? Then they could, in turn, influence decisions and changes in leadership?

Ario shook his head. "That could work if we had time. But that could take years, and by then, the miasma could kill us all. Slowing it down should be our biggest priority."

She looked back towards him. "Then what do you propose?"

He took a sharp breath. "Something like that would only work if that double agent had a *lot* of power. Like me. And she would kill me on sight. And there's no Heir - you have no children, unless you've been very busy. So where would that leave us?"

"What if she didn't?" Ainsley smoothed a stray hair from her face. She used to wear very tight buns or twists. Wearing it loose only made its patchiness and stringiness more obvious. "What if she felt she might use you?"

"This is an awful lot of hypotheticals."

She sighed. "And I would never jeopardize your safety that way." She returned to her cup of coffee. "Perhaps you are right, Ario. Survival *is* more important than a gambit that might not work, and leave us worse off. Have you any solutions, then?"

"Just one I cannot adequately test." He explained his theory about radiation, or just high energy in general. "It's flawed and incomplete. I doubt we have any friendlies in the Department of Energy."

Ainsley shook her head. "Regardless. I am here now. And I offer myself to you– I don't know in what capacity."

"What can you offer than Evelyn, Michael, and the others can't?"

"I can offer you protection," she began. "When you were younger–"

Ario reached for the thin silver chain under his shirt and pulled it into view. "That's already covered. Thanks for that, by the way."

Ainsley's eyes grew hazy. "You found him."

"Her," he corrected. "Yes. Was quite the surprise."

"You have to understand, Ario, I made that decision for your own wellbeing. Things were so *hot*. The original plan was to get you out and go there and find her, so you might live out this disaster in peace. But then the massacres, and..." Ainsley took a breath. "It is, frankly, a miracle she lived and you crossed paths. Thank the Goddess."

When he said nothing, she continued,

"Perhaps by now you're grasping the weight of your station. You have to make hard decisions, impossible ones, and there's a price. *Always.* Their blood is on my hands. Had Xander not become aware of the bond, those people might still be alive. I was an idiot. I trusted him."

Nausea curled sickly around the coffee in his stomach. "What do you know about them? The... sirens?"

"They lived in *peace*," she insisted. "But their population had gotten too large for the small islands, and they needed resources. We offered–*I* offered resources in exchange for magical protection."

"She is a *person*," Ario hissed. "A wonderful person with emotions, and dreams, and ambitions. She can't remember that time. She can't transform. You took it all from her."

Ainsley looked down. "I don't know what forces did that to her. But at the core, you are right. What would you have done, Ario? If you had a nephew or a daughter that you loved more than the world, that the Goddess has all but doomed, and you lived in a den of vipers? Look how hotly you defend the girl. You'd be just as capable of making a decision like this."

Ario's rage cooled into something hard and decidedly painful. "What do you want from me, Ainsley?" he asked her. "What was the point of it all?"

"I meant what I said in that note. I want to help you avoid the mistakes I made."

He scoffed. "Sure. Okay." Without another word, he got up and started for the door.

"The watch–" Ainsley began.

"Is with Evelyn for safekeeping. That upset her as well. Good *day*, Lady Queen. I have work to do."

The hurt washed across her face, but she nodded and said, "Lord King."

***

Ario wanted to throw things. He wanted to make something shatter. He wanted to sink his teeth into a piece of meat and tear. He took his silly little light and picked up one of the dozens of sealed boxes of poison. This was all so colossally useless. Like the Goddess had doomed *him*. Heresy. And how could Ainsley be so trivial about—he breathed it—*genocide?* If Ario could give his life for theirs, he would, willingly.

What was he to tell Peony?

The glass box he was holding slipped from his sweaty hands and shattered on the concrete floor of the barn. He liked the sound, the breaking. He cupped his hands around the miasma, letting his power flex around it in an attempt to contain it.

The miasma, instead of its usual indifference, writhed and pushed against his grip before acquiescing, color leaching out of it until he was holding harmless steam.

The breath wheezed out of him, and before he could understand what he'd just done, a sharp, barb-like pain wrenched in his abdomen, harder and hotter than anything he'd ever felt, and he screamed. It was absolutely *ludicrous*, and he wondered, with what little consciousness he had, if he'd taken it within him, if it were poisoning him, and—

Footsteps. Doubtless his cries had set off a ward or several and brought someone running. The pain had become a living thing. He couldn't stop the thrashing or the horrific sound tearing against his throat. Strong hands seized him and held him down. "Majesty. Majesty, are you hurt?" Marko. What a day that poor man was having.

He tried to speak, tried to indicate that Marko *should not be touching him, he was poisoned,* but the rending feeling only became more violent, and the next round of convulsions smacked his head into the hard concrete.

***

Something cool and soft touched his forehead. It smelled like menthol. Distantly, he was aware that the pain had stopped.

Another insistent tap against his forehead. "Don't touch me," he slurred. "Poison."

"You are not poisoned," Maeve said softly, her sweet voice bringing him mostly awake. "You had a bad fall. I healed a concussion. You rest, majesty."

"Miasma. Inside me," he tried to insist. What little light met his eyes sent a pang through his head. "The pain. Had to be."

She cleared her throat. "I see no evidence of poisoning."

Ario squinted, trying to bring her into focus. Nausea sucked wearily at his stomach, not urgent enough to make him sick. He was in a room he did not recognize. He thought he saw boughs of herbs on the ceiling, and bottles with labels. He tried to sit up.

"You should stay down."

"I made it disappear, somehow," he told her thickly. "I think I internalized—whatever makes it *hungry.* I have a *lot* of magic. No wonder it hurt."

"Your field feels intact," she commented. "I checked. You rest, Ario. Marko will drive you home when you feel better."

Something about her voice unnerved him. "So it if wasn't poison, I–what–simply fell over in a fit for no reason?"

"It's quite possible the miasma was the trigger."

"What is it, Maeve? What are you not telling me?"

She sighed and set the cloth aside in a small bowl of liquid. "The reaction that happened within you was protective, not offensive. When people become wraiths, the miasma consumes them. *Your* body immediately forced it out. Protecting something."

He touched the exposed bond necklace. "Peony's power only works when she's here. I don't–"

"Not–Peony," Maeve said with frustrating vagueness. "A baby."

***

Once or twice, when Ario was younger and they were having one of their stints in the wilderness, he'd climb the tallest tree he could find and simply dangle from one of the upper limbs, testing the limits of his strength, free to be above the world, away from Evelyn and magic and all responsibility. And then, once or twice, he would overestimate the strength of the branch, and it would snap, sending him plummeting meters below, onto the hard forest floor, squeezing the breath out of his lungs and perhaps claiming one of his limbs with a weirdly satisfying *crack*.

"I take it you were not aware," Maeve said. "Judging by your expression."

He'd never gotten so hurt that Evelyn could not heal him. Once he was stable, the sweet nothings would disappear, and she would lay into him about being *careless*. *Did* he have a death wish?

His lungs ached just like they had then.

"Majesty? –Ario?"

He blinked. "I'm alright."

"Do you understand what I said? I thought you seemed too lucid–"

"Yes, I heard. Yes, I understand." He couldn't even connect the truth to himself. "You're certain?"

"...Yes."

"Well." Words failed. Everything failed. "Uh."

"Shock is common," she said soothingly.

"How... terribly?" he managed after a long moment of fluid whooshing between his ears.

"Eight weeks and a handful of days."

"What do I have to do to get rid of it?"

"Beg pardon?"

Robotically, he stood, and vertigo clattered over him. She helped him sit back down. "Can you make it stop?"

"Ordinarily, yes, but–"

"So do it." His eyes watered. He was not sure what he felt. Ainsley's monologue seemed eerily ironic now. "Please."

"The procedures I can do are normally on someone... not so protected," she admitted, her green eyes fuzzy in the semidarkness. "The mundane way is much less pleasant–"

"I don't care."

Maeve sat in silence. "I support you, Majesty. If this is what you wish. I will need a few days to gather the requisite supplies."

His head reeled. "Surely."

"Can you talk to her? About this? You shouldn't do this alone."

Ario was back to borderline nonverbal. "Hm?" He couldn't focus, couldn't shake the–

"You could use some support."

"Could that other method? Fail?" Sweat ran down his face. "Will I have to–"

Her face was dark and, in his muzzy state, unreadable. "I can't be certain–"

"I *can't* do this." His breathing picked up. "I won't. You can't make me. Nobody can–"

Maeve sat next to him and squeezed his shoulders gently. "I will do everything in my power, majesty. You have to breathe. Breathe with me. You'll be just fine."

***

Ario did not remember coming home. He did not remember getting in the car and driving back with Marko. He only became aware that there was a palpable gap in time, time he had existed, been conscious, and not been cognizant.

Hazily, he wandered towards the kitchen, put on the kettle. He did not feel... the way people in that condition were supposed to. He was not nauseous anymore. Not tired. No part of his chest ached. She was wrong, that was all. She had to be–

"Ario? You're white as a sheet. Where's the car?" Why was Evelyn always home? Could she not simply not be here for an hour? Ten?

Damn it all. "I'm tired. Marko brought me home."

"You don't look tired, you look positively peaked–" She reached to touch him, doubtless to check him for maladies, and he wriggled away.

"Don't touch me. Don't—" He gasped a breath. And promptly started sobbing.

"Ario..." Evelyn said. "What happened?"

"I failed. I'm a failure, I–" Fear leached into him, bright, painful.

"Surely it's not something that cannot be fixed," she said, trying to get him to meet her eyes. "What is it that's so terrible? You're around so much of that poison... Perhaps you need a rest. A break."

He said it quietly, once, and before comprehension fully dawned in her eyes he was telling her everything. Ainsley. The pain. What he planned to do. He expected her to scream, to yell at him for being so irresponsible and so ignorant for *not even knowing*.

What she did instead was offer him a handkerchief. "Let us pray for guidance," she said softly. "And strength."

The Goddess valued life in all forms. If he stuck strictly to the teachings he should accept his lot and prepare for this... *thing*. The Goddess also valued autonomy, the right to make decisions for one's own self. Were, for example, the *thing* to jeopardize his own life, either through physical or mental tolls, it was right, in the eyes of the Goddess, to not bring the *thing* into existence.

He had not been thinking about the Goddess or his health when he learned. He'd just had a sudden, violent, visceral *need* for this not to be happening, that it was all *wrong*, it was so irresponsible to bring a child into a dying world when he may have to die for a cause he barely understood.

The question was not, *what would the Goddess want me to do* but *what do I want?*

***

The next day, he went to the beach, alone. Evelyn had given him a sleeping draught, and it made him feel heavy and very stupid even after several cups of coffee. The December chill seeped through his wool coat, hat, and scarf, but he liked the discomfort.

He felt hyper aware of every little sensation in his body. The headache, the stinging of his joints, a very gentle but very *present* nausea that always had seemed to have a rational explanation - dodgy food, too much magic use, too much caffeine and too little sleep.

He wondered if this was what purgatory–that place between this plane and the afterlife, where souls must resolve unfinished business or overall improve–felt like. He felt cursed.

Is this your will? he asked the Goddess silently. It wasn't like he had gone into the act blindly–there had been precautions. *What world is there for the living, let alone this thing?*

Moreover, did he even want to pass this power along? This so-called lineage? It would be nothing but a terrible burden on her. (Firstborns were always biologically female, at least in this blighted line.) And even if the world *weren't* ending, if he weren't so dreadfully young, if there was safety and he was just unexpectedly a parent too soon, would he really *want* the task of devoting the rest of his life to a stranger?

He'd always known in the back of his mind he'd have to have an Heir. Why drag out this dying line? Why not let it fade away? He had no siblings. It would all end.

But so would everyone else.

Ario let out a long breath. He took off his shoes and socks, then carefully, his coat and wraps. He treaded across the cool, damp sand to the edge of the water. This time of day and year, very few people were around.

The cool water was just as punishing as he'd hoped, biting into his feet and calves with an almost acidic hiss. He audibly winced and pushed forward. What was one more ache, one more pain? The subsumption would feel good, *so* good. It ate into his thighs and hips and pelvis. Deeper, still deeper, until only his head remained above water and his body was screaming with adrenaline from the cold.

Ario took a long breath and slid under. The water slicked his face and the strands of his hair. The waves, gearing for high tide, eagerly lapped him down as though he were denser than flesh and bone, and he let it. He could hold his breath for a long time, one of the many seemingly-useless skills he'd learned in his years of isolation.

The water was soft around him. He opened his eyes, ignoring the bite of salt, and watched the waves churn above in spirals, and the sunlight, growing more distant. He knew he could not let go and simply let the tide take him, no matter how badly he wanted it to.

Goddess, help *me*, he intoned.

A riptide seized him then, dragging him deeper and away from shore, and he gasped instinctively, losing a little of his precious air. Ario fought against the water, blindly, his heart a vicious pulsing thing. He couldn't fight the sea. He would have to use magic, propel himself, but any spell he tried to ready *wouldn't come*. Was this just *it* then?

Another sharp and painful tug in his abdomen indicated it surely was not. This thing was smaller than a coin, but somehow calling the shots. And now he had no choice but to let it. The protective magic had stymied any power he could have used, but he could at least use it to his advantage.

He emerged, gasping, a few seconds later and sank weakly into the sand, violent shudders overcoming him now that the danger was over. The agony, and ecstasy, had made his mind incredibly clear.

The pregnancy would make him functionally invulnerable, at least for the next seven months and change. The child would siphon his power while also offering a sort of boost. Perhaps there was no need for uranium or half-baked solutions. Perhaps the reactor was here all along.

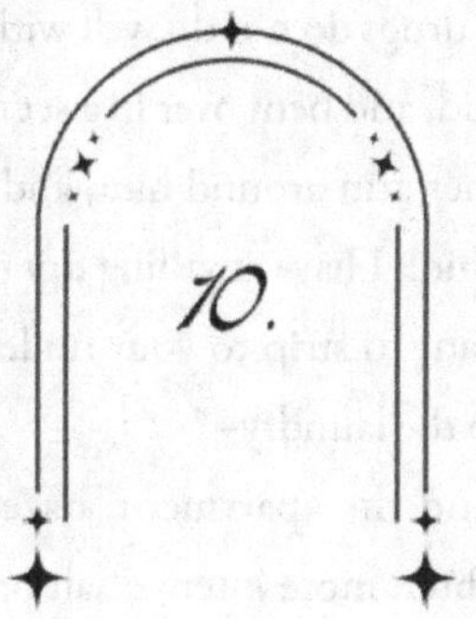

10.

A rio made it to Peony's reeking of seawater, an uncontrollable grin ticing across his face. So this was madness, then. Nobody had ever said that it felt *good*.

Rory was, of course, bemused when she answered the door. Her usual glower faded when she saw his sopping and unkempt appearance, and probably the unhinged glint in his eye. "Ario? What, uh, happened, buddy?"

"I went for a swim," he said cheerfully. "Is Peony home?"

"She's been banging out a final all morning at the library. Were you touched, again? Are you hurt?"

"I have never felt more alive."

She looked him up and down. "Did you *take* anything? In my experience, mundane drugs do not do well with magic–"

"I am sober," he said, and bent over in a set of giggles.

Rory sighed, put her arm around him, and dragged him into the apartment. "I don't think I have anything dry that's big enough to fit you. I guess if you want to strip to your underwear, you can wear a blanket while I run to the laundry–"

Ario looked around the apartment, dazed. Colors and smells seemed so much brighter, more intense, salt of the sea, garlic, onion, the preservative sprayed on the bouquet of flowers on the table, the tang of dirty shoes, metal and the sharp snip of electricity. He could nearly see through the walls.

Rory was on the phone. "Loverboy is here and very disoriented," she was saying. "I suspect he might be touched again. You might want to come home. Yes. Yes, I'll tell him." She hung up with a sigh. "Peony's on her way home. She said you can undress and lie down on her bed. She also said to tell you she loved you."

Ario felt it so powerfully. He loved her. He loved everyone and everything and the whole world but especially *her*–

He vomited hard on the floor.

Rory sighed, pressed her hand to her brow, and disappeared the mess.

***

Peony's scent bled hotly out of her bed, the sheets smooth and soft over his mostly-naked body. He tucked himself further under the duvet, his eyes fluttering shut. After all the frenzy, his body demanded rest. Needed it. So did the thing.

He fell asleep, imagining Peony holding him. He must not have slept for very long. He felt her before he saw her, the ends of her hair grazing his face. He opened his eyes.

"It's okay," she said softly. In the dimness, her face was obscured. "You rest. Rory said you were sick."

He realized he was going to have to tell her, to force those words out again, and again, and again in the coming months.

"Are you *sure* you weren't touched?" she asked, trailing her fingers across his face. "Nobody harmed you?"

"No," he whispered. "It was... Many things happened yesterday. I want to tell you everything–"

Peony shushed him. "You rest. You can tell me later." She crawled under the covers and drew him close.

***

Ario woke up before her, the same nausea nudging against his breastbone. She'd curled on her side in the night. He watched her chest rise and fall and wondered how she would take it. Would she be forced into happiness, like he had been yesterday? Would she stress as people normally do when faced with such a life-altering choice? Perhaps she would blame herself.

He realized he did not know. He did not know her well enough. He loved her, but he did not know what she *wanted* out of life.

As if feeling his gaze, she stirred, smiling muzzily. "Morning."

"Sleepyhead," he said.

She yawned widely and stretched, pressing against him. He was startled by a sharp and needy want. He leaned in and kissed her, and kissed her again.

She broke away breathless. "I thought you didn't feel well."

"I'm well enough."

It wasn't as though it could happen *twice*.

Later, after, she lay against him, absently trailing patterns on his chest and stomach. She hummed to herself, softly.

"I've never heard you play," he said. "Will you play something for me?"

Peony dragged a hand through her mussed hair. "Now?"

"Why not? I want to hear something."

She blinked, blinked, but smiled. "Well—sure, yes, of course. How are you feeling?"

"Much better."

She slipped out of bed and pulled on her discarded shirt. She crossed over to her mandolin, on its stand, the warm red varnish shimmering in the early-morning light. Peony took a second to tune the strings, her teal eyes flashing brightly. She took the pick into her hand.

"I wrote this the day I met you," she said, and started to play.

He was surprised that the music reminded him of fire, prickling warm light. Fire and need and a discordant sort of doubt, twining through higher notes before plateauing into a lush smolder. The music filled him, bringing tears to his eyes, a reminder that she felt as lost and uncoordinated about all this as he did.

The music ceased, and she looked at him expectantly.

"I, um, had no idea you felt that way." He blinked quickly to get rid of the tears.

"I thought things would become clearer," she admitted to the mandolin she was holding. "And they are, but they also *aren't*. I want us to be happy and together, but that doesn't seem likely with everything that's going on. I feel like I've found a second half just moments before the world implodes."

"Yes," he whispered.

"I *trust* the magic. Everything in me says I should, and what I know about the sirens tells me I should as well. But you're a *king*, with everything that entails. How am I supposed to be your queen?" She set the instrument aside and crossed her arms.

Ario thought for a moment. He crossed over to her and brushed her hair over her shoulder. "I grew up all over this country," he told her. "We were poor. Sometimes we were hungry. If you're worried about the etiquette–"

Her eyes blazed. He swore they glowed, slightly. "I don't want to just be the pretty face. I want to *do* something, but I don't know what. I protect you, but I can barely do any magic. What did consorts do, in the past?"

Ario blushed a little. "Some took roles in the government. Most committed themselves to a charity or a good cause. Like I'm trying to tell you–this isn't like the time before. It's something small and something new. You don't even have to take on the title of *queen* if you don't want to."

The ferocity did not leave her face. "That's the thing, Ario. I think I do."

He supposed this was reassuring. "There must be something Marko can have you help with. You can get around undetected–that's valuable."

"The most I've ever done is help some people leave town," she said, "and Rory didn't even like me doing that."

"She's very protective of you," he observed.

"We used to be the only family we had," Peony admitted. "She doesn't want me getting in trouble... in case I *am* the last one."

A vicious blush stung his cheeks. "About... that."

Her brows pulled together. "Do you know something? Did you find anything else out?"

"No. Sadly." Ario cleared his throat. "It's just that there will be *one more*."

It took her a couple of seconds to catch his meaning. "*Oh*." He didn't know what to read into the expression on her face– hope? Despair? "I didn't think this was... that I even *could*–"

"It certainly was not what I expected to hear," he deadpanned. "Moreover, I suspect the fetus will resist efforts to... curtail it."

"I thought your religion didn't believe in that sort of thing."

"That is an oversimplification." He explained his reasoning. "Even so. I *asked* the Goddess for a solution to our energy problem. I wonder if this is it."

Peony just stared.

"I understand you must be in shock–"

"A *baby*, Ario."

"Yes. Well–"

"It's not a *solution*. Or a fetus or a *thing*. If you use it, *her*, for her power, where does that leave us when there's a baby here that needs to be cared for?" Acid crept into her voice. "Would it kill her?"

"What about the millions of people already here?" he retorted. "Do their lives also not have value? I have no reason to believe it would *kill* her. Not when she's so eager to remain affixed to me, like a–" He stopped himself before he could say "parasite," as he knew this would only upset Peony further. "I'm just trying to *utilize* that power, if I must go through it at all. I am not a cold, heartless monster."

The air seemed to crackle. "What about how I feel?" she asked.

"How *do* you feel?"

The contempt did not leave her face, not immediately. Then, "when I imagined us having a family, I didn't think you would be so–ambivalent."

"I have done everything available to me to leave behind my gender of birth. This is not exactly what I wanted, so soon. The haze of dysphoria is not exactly helping my decision-making."

She softened. "Of course. I... I didn't see it that way. It must be hard."

He took her hand. "You believe me, then? You know I don't wish active harm on the–" he forced himself to say it– "baby? It's more like exploiting a loophole. Really."

"I know you don't want to hurt anyone. This just all feels a bit..." She trailed off, and did not finish her sentence.

"Cold?" he offered.

"...Yeah." She hugged herself. "I just... I feel kind of overwhelmed. I still have a semester left of school. I don't even have a real job. How am I supposed to be a mom if–"

"We need to think it through. The implications. Everything."

She sighed. "Yeah. Do you think I could... call you later? My head is crowded."

Bile curled in his stomach. "...Sure."

He finished dressing and turned to leave the room. She took the mandolin back into her arms and started plucking like mad.

***

He returned home and washed the sea off of himself. When he went downstairs, Evelyn waited in the kitchen, silently. She gestured towards the small table, which held a bowl of soup and two slices of bread. "Eat that. You need to keep me apprised of your movements, *especially* now." Her dark eyes were glassy, unfocused. "I've been praying for answers. I'm not sure I heard much of a response."

Ario did not argue. "I had to tell Peony. I... I've been thinking. The *process* generates a lot of power, does it not? Power I *think* culled the miasma on a small scale."

Evelyn sputtered. "This is madness, Ario. Do you even hear yourself?"

"Am I wrong?"

"The power is mostly defensive and will only make you *easier* to find. Do you know the headache I've had, trying to concoct ways to keep you safe for the next few months?"

"But if I harness the magic properly, I might possibly be able to regionally eradicate the miasma. That could save lives."

"And put a huge target on your back. And your child's. Take a moment and *think*. You're not even entirely sure how you achieved what you did the other day."

He sipped his soup. It was too salty and not altogether satisfying, but it soothed the rabid hunger that had replaced the nausea.

Evelyn started to pace, picking at a loose thread on her thrifted sweater. "What will you do once the child is here? She's not just a child, but an *Heir*. Have you any idea how difficult that was for your poor mother? For hers? You're an adult and you can still *barely* restrain your power enough to go in public. You'll have an impulsive newborn with quite possibly *more* power than yourself. And you cannot expect Peony to spend every single waking moment with the child. The child will need training, and guidance, more than you or I could provide."

"What is the likelihood of a termination actually working?" he countered.

She froze, her frizzy braid swaying precariously for a moment.

"Surely *someone* has attempted it in the past."

Evelyn turned to the fridge, took out the pitcher of water, poured a glass, and drank it down in one swallow.

"Evelyn–I'm sorry. I know this is sensitive for you, and you probably disagree with me."

She remained silent for a few beats.

"Evelyn?"

"It won't work," she said. She set the glass down onto the stone countertops with a soft "ting."

"How are you so certain? I've done some reading, and mundanes–"

"Because your mother attempted it. With you."

He'd received so many shocks the past few days that this didn't even register as upsetting. In fact, it seemed to make a great deal of sense. He'd never fit the bill of perfect Heir.

"She... requested I help her," Evelyn continued. "I tried to persuade her, because at that point I'm afraid my beliefs were not nuanced. Your mother may have been... not so sharp, but I think she sensed the writing on the wall. She was young, like you. Married at nineteen, conceived straight away. She asked me if I could get rid of it. She wouldn't go see the palace healer. She was worried about the controversy."

A thin rime of oil gleamed on the surface of the soup.

"I tried magic. It failed. Herbs. It failed. Mundane pills. She told me she'd read about a surgery. That's how I knew it was dire; your mother never read *anything* other than magazines. The minute I touched her with the instrument..." Evelyn lifted up her sweater, revealing a coin-sized, starry burn near her navel.

All the more evidence of the power, he thought bitterly. "Why haven't you told me sooner? You know I don't exactly hold her on a pedestal."

"Frankly? I thought you'd never get yourself in this situation."

He absorbed this for a moment. In her own way, Chiara had tried to spare him pain.

"She did love you," Evelyn insisted. "As much as she could love anyone."

"That's not what gives me pause." He considered. "The Goddess insists on our autonomy... except, it seems, when it inconveniences Her."

Evelyn swung around. "Ario! Her protection is a *gift.*"

"Which is why, if I am *stuck* this way for the foreseeable future, I *should use it.*"

Evelyn groaned and pressed her face against her hand. "Fine. Fine!"

He stirred his soup, watching the vegetables and rice rise and fall in the brackish broth.

She resumed her frenetic pacing, pausing now and again to remove a dish or two from the dish drain and stow them away with loud *thumps* in the cabinets. "And should this gambit of yours somehow work," Evelyn said, through her teeth. "What then? Do we–continue this nomadic lifestyle, made more dangerous because of the infant?"

"Perhaps we do as Ainsley said–infiltrate them. *If* it works, it will certainly buy us the time required." He hesitated, the idea taking shape as he spoke. "There will be an Heir. The line will be secured. I will be a free actor."

She turned to face him, her hands shaking. "What are you imply-ing?" And the flash in her eyes was so frightening, so *frightened,* he relented.

"Nothing. Forget I said anything."

Interlude

Seven Months of
Purgatory

It took Ario until nearly the end of the second trimester to truly harness the magic. It came in fits and starts, stubbornly clinging to him like a film. As the days and weeks passed, he felt it more acutely, like a very tight second skin. His next attempts at cleansing anything were just as painful as the first. The only boon was that he was able to stop screaming.

If he did not approach the work with a single minded furor, he feared he would fall wholeheartedly into madness. Marko and the others pretended joy when they heard the news—and perhaps on some level they *were* happy—but he knew he was just putting more strain on an already under-resourced system. He required a near-constant guard, when Peony was not with him, else he would be swarmed with wraiths or noticed by ongoing patrols. He made the mistake of going out to the grocery and was stopped; thankfully, he was able to charm the guard. He could not think about clothes or toys or schoolbooks or diapers or the ongoing eldritch horror that was his own body. He could only control what he could control.

The first time he was able to dissolve the miasmatic waste, he swore it was a fluke. But he was able to do it again, and again, fixing foods, healing livestock. Peony clapped her hands with pride and cradled him, insisting that their daughter was *already* doing good.

He had to say that he did not feel a connection to the thing. It moved, squirming nastily against his organs, mashing into them at the exact inopportune moments, making it hard to breathe or him desperate for the toilet or simply in pain. It wrought havoc on his emotions, leaving him delirious with joy or murderously angry without a second's notice. It flooded him with so much love and so much hate that he could no longer trust his own judgement. But he could work. And work. And work.

Now that the shock was over and the work did not seem to harm the child, Peony was warming to the idea of motherhood, reading all the books she could find. She would cuddle close to the mound of the *thing* and coo and sing in a language Ario did not understand.

He cleansed the farm. He only had about three months left of this enhanced power, and it would not *be* enough, it would never *be* enough to fix all the damage. There had to be some way of amplifying it, but to amplify it would be to draw attention to the wrong sorts. Sometimes he swore it did not matter if they noticed. He proposed storming the palace in a blaze approximately once before everyone else managed to talk him down.

Ainsley was not helping, reinserting herself where she was not wanted. She accepted the news readily, almost too readily, as if she had been waiting for him to make this large of a mistake. She said, tucking her hair into its trademark twist, to trust in the means of fate. He only spent time with her because she had access to maps documenting the worst of the miasma, stolen from the regime's monitoring devices.

The only moments he could steal for himself were in the dead of night, when all were asleep–even Michael could only stay awake for so many hours–and he crept out of the townhouse and walked. Thanks in part to his efforts, the night was not quite so choked with darkness, and the power left him feeling somewhat invulnerable. He'd go to different parts of the town, avoiding the patrols, burying his hands into the earth and trying to inject as much of himself and the power as he could. He let it trail into the sea, feeling where its vectors met the town's ward with a lemony tang. He wondered if he could somehow *use* the ward as its own amplifier.

April. May. Peony graduated with honors, receiving a certificate that would let her teach music. Her primary focus was how they would materially support the child. The economy was largely digital, to prevent magic users from simply making currency. Cash was only used for covert deals. Ario could not find the energy to worry. He was so close to making a breakthrough, he swore he felt it, another storm on the horizon causing the child to try to crawl into his bones.

***

The ward became his obsession, its rosy glow clouding his waking thoughts, even as his body grew slower, clumsier, heavier, magic licking him inside and out. He would have simply headed there himself, but the sheer univs he radiated meant he could not go anywhere outside of the house without Peony. They'd have to move him soon, likely to Maeve's cottage, for the time he could absolutely not allow himself to think about.

He realized he had stopped praying.

Ario begged Peony. Pleaded, played the "our daughter wants this" card a dozen times. Each time she managed to assure him, through honeyed words or her own upset disposition, that he would be putting them *all* in danger, that surely someone was monitoring the damn thing.

The gold glistened in his dreams. It haunted him.

According to Rory, the wraith population was steadily declining, a sign his efforts were coming to fruition. He could barely absorb this victory before he was being taken away to the cottage, to wait for the time he could absolutely not allow himself to think about.

****

It was all so barbaric, so animal, the ripping and breaking as the thing decided it had had enough of him. The thing wrenched itself into the world after four hours of sheer agony that no anesthesia–magic or mundane–could touch, its magic tearing itself from his own.

And Evelyn asked *if he wanted to hold her*, this red, bloody and now *screaming* thing. If he looked at its face it would be over. If he touched her it would be over, he knew, he would love her fast and hard and fiercely, and she was no longer a *thing he could use* but something he was forced to bear into the world.

"I'm not ready," he said breathlessly, and perhaps she and Peony both bought his indifference as exhaustion.

He was informed that the magic would be good to him, and he would heal within the week. Mundanes often took *months* to recover from the spawning, and they labored for *days*. Really he was quite lucky. Bruised, bleeding, in a bloated and soft body. But lucky.

The only pleasure he could derive was Peony's. He watched her, and *just* her, as she held the mass close to her, kissing and whispering, motherhood seizing her. (Was he imagining the glow around her, within her? Was it more magic? Or sheer madness?)

"We have to Name her," Peony said. "She's the princess, it has to be important."

He feigned sleep then, and then actually slept.

***

"Won't you hold her, Ario? I know you're tired, but she's the sweetest thing ever and I *swear* I feel like she wants you."

Ario looked dully over to his partner. More magic; was it Peony's nascent siren instincts sensing what the thing wanted, or was the child manipulative? "I'm really sore," he said, not a lie.

"Just in your arms. Just for a minute."

"My chest is what's sore." Also true.

"I could lay her right here so you could cuddle up to her. If you're worried about the blood, I *did* bathe her, her first bath, I wish you would've felt up to watching–"

"Maybe–maybe in a little while. Why don't you sleep? You haven't slept in two days. I'll watch over her."

This placated her. Peony set the baby in the cradle, nudged the cradle closer to him, kissed him on the forehead, and left the room.

Ario did not look at the child. He *heard* it, the peculiar snuffles newborns made, dull little thwops as it tested its limbs on the cradle mattress. He had about an hour of peace, an hour of sleep, before the child reasserted itself and cried. He'd only heard her cry when she was born, and it pierced his shorn magic hard. His whole being screamed to go to her.

No. He would not.

The baby did not stop crying. She needed something. She needed *him.*

No. Mustn't. His fingers bit into the blankets, holding on for dear life. Someone had to come, surely. How did they not hear the *noise*? It choked him, it gripped him–

He reached into the bassinet, intent on stopping the howling, perhaps stopping *her* entirely, hefting her little body into the air, the magic screaming *please please please* and all he could comprehend was the sudden silence of the infant. Not because she was injured; she was evidently just as started by his touch as he was.

Small. Squish-faced, still very pink, a knit hat pulled over her (violet silver) hair, eyes unfocused and blinking wobbily, her head awkwardly perched on her shoulder without support. He reached to correct this, unthinking but entirely out of his own volition.

"It's you," he said, with a curious recognition.

She eased into his arms, against him. No demon, no devil, no anti-Goddess. A vulnerable newborn crying out for her dad.

"It's really you," he said again. "Fuck."

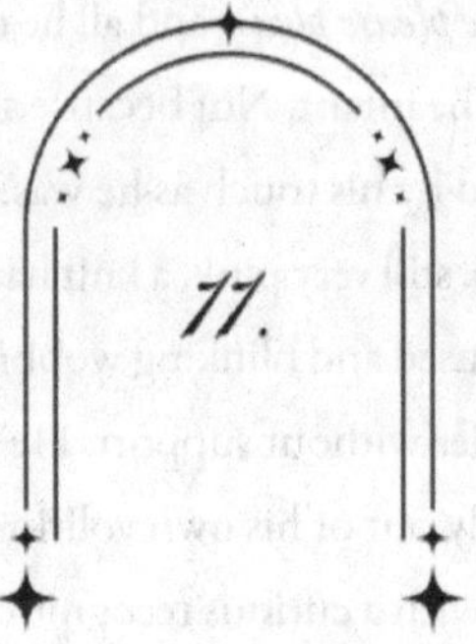

T he power transferred from Heir to Heir, matrilineally, throughout the course of a pregnancy. Over the course of the next few days, his vastly diminished magic began to cool, settle, and heal where it had been torn. *She* had it now, as well as some of Peony's and some of her very own.

"Maybe it'll balance out?" Peony asked. "You were uber, I'm none. Maybe she'll be at a normal level."

"It's too unstable to test still," Ario said. "Her univs won't settle for a few weeks." His own readings were curious; still enough to alert homeland security, but lower than they had ever been, even when he'd taken dampeners.

The July weather had become punishingly hot, even within the stone walls of the cottage. He wiped some sweat off his forehead. A few days' rest had made him feel vastly better, but weight still hung on him oddly. He swore his hair color was not quite so vivid.

"But it's nearly the full moon. Evelyn will want to do the Naming."

They were sitting on the back porch, the child on some blankets and pillows between them. The unnamed child, on cue, started fussing, crying softly. "I wish I knew what was wrong. I know how it feels when she's hungry, or tired, or wet," Peony said.

"Gassy?"

"Not that either."

Babies, as it turned out, were a lot of work. Peony's siren-sense mitigated a lot of the trouble, as she could somehow tell what the child needed, and they could quickly soothe her. But the lack of sleep was not easy to adjust to. And he dreaded the day she started showing magic. It could happen as early as four weeks, he'd been cautioned, and he himself had been particularly precocious. "Maybe it's sensory? That onesie is a different material than the cotton ones." A gift, from Maeve, beautiful lace, but slightly scratchy.

"Maybe? I'll go get another." She gave Ario a curious, almost wary look as she went back into the house. He wondered, again, if his hatred and near-madness of the purgatory months had been more obvious than he'd thought.

Ario gently turned her onto her belly and undid the snaps. All along her back was—some kind of rash, in little inverse Ls around her shoulder blades. He ran his fingertips against the red flesh, feeling something hard poking out, like fingernails. The baby whimpered.

"It could also be the detergent. We had to make it with less borax–" Peony began upon reentry, and froze.

"Have you seen this before?" he asked her.

Her eyes brimmed with tears. "No. But I know what it is."

"Is she okay? Is she sick?"

Peony shook her head, a rich laugh falling out of her. "Fledgling scales," she said. "They come in when they're young. I was wondering–she was so much like you–"

A species feature, then. A hot pressure in him eased.

"Maybe–maybe she's not cut off, Ario. Maybe she's not broken like me," Peony said quickly. She rushed for the child, touching the breaking skin with awe. "There's a–paste, we used to use, I remember how it *smells*–oh, she's going to itch and be miserable for weeks."

"When will we know for sure?" he asked. "That she's–a siren?"

"She'll be able to start shifting after a year," Peony said. She held the baby's fist. Her eyes glistened. "If she–is. It's not just me. I'm not alone."

He felt the fractures in his heart as acutely as he felt the broken magic.

***

On the second day of the full moon, shortly after the moonrise, they Named her. Evelyn presided, with Michael, Marko, and Maeve in attendance. Peony had asked Rory, but had curiously received no response. "Cell service here is weird," Peony had just said. "Maybe she didn't get my messages."

Rory had treated Ario like a tactical spell his whole pregnancy, so her aversion of him wasn't surprising. It *was* surprising that she didn't want to be auntie to her new little cousin.

"Maybe not," he tried to comfort her.

"It's a hard time, too, because she's doing job placement training…" Peony trailed off and looked at the half-asleep infant in her arms. "There's time. When we go back to town."

The Naming was a simple ceremony. They would pray for the child and offer her by full name in service of the Goddess; they would lay her lightly in the dirt, in a small recess; and more prayers for health and guidance. He supposed in another life there would be fancy garb and honeyed wine. Peony suggested that they might do the same thing, but with the sea, afterward. "I'm not sure that's what we do, but it feels right."

Evelyn looked a bit mollified, but shrugged it off.

By then, a warm wind kicked up from the sea, smelling slightly like ozone; he hoped the storm would hold out until after the ceremony. Peony put on a sundress and he put on the nicest clothes he had that still fit, and on a whim, his father's watch.

They named her Amalia Theodora; Amalia, a siren name, and Theodora, an ancient mage princess. He refused to give her the Chiara curse; his own middle name had been Chiara before he'd transitioned. Too many women had had that name. Tradition was also to give the child their birthgiver's first name as a middle name, and Amalia Ilario was not particularly euphonous.

The Goddess felt particularly distant from him now, all the attention She'd "lavished" on him through purgatory seemingly forgotten, or perhaps now aimed towards his child; he did not know.

Ario placed Amalia in the dirt. Her eyes were open and as alert as a newborn's could be. He saw the stars reflected in them.

He was supposed to say something, something profound, he knew. He felt the others' silence. "Moon and stars protect you," he murmured.

Evelyn gave him a bit of an odd look, but did not comment on his not-quite prayer. She closed out the ceremony, and Peony slipped off her sundress, revealing a swimsuit. Before they could proceed, however, thunder rumpled the air around him. Peony shrieked a little, and the baby cried from the loud noise.

"I'm afraid it may have to wait until tomorrow night," Evelyn said, raising her voice over the wind.

Ario looked over the horizon. Was that the moon, reflected against the water? Or–

"Get in the house!" he barked at Peony, thrusting Amalia at her. "Evelyn, go!"

The priestess understood, grasping Peony and dragging her towards the house.

"Ario!"

"Go! Michael, Marko, I need you!"

Michael was by his side at once, pulling his pistol from his waistband. Marko unsheathed a pair of blades from his boots.

"What is it, majesty?" Marko asked.

The whitish blur grew closer. Ario tried to ready some magic. It was sticky, heavy, but it *was* coming to him. She was close enough now Ario could *see* the edges of her form, fuzzy and white. Michael drew the weapon. The form stopped some ten meters away from them, and morphed, turning into a woman. Before Ario could throw the magic, he first saw the blood.

Samara collapsed onto her knees in the sand. Her side was slashed open, and a wet loop of intestines peeked through her fingers. Sweat poured down her pallid face. She sought Ario's eyes with a fervid determination.

"Hold your attack," he ordered.

"Wait," Samara said, her voice raspy. Around her fingernails, blood poured into the sand.

Ario approached her.

"Majesty–" Michael cautioned.

"She is in no shape to harm me." He was close enough to touch her. "You're mortally wounded."

"I have been–I have been *looking*–what did you do to me?"

"I healed you," he said. "There was miasma in your being. I removed it. I can grant you asylum and heal your wounds."

"Please. Please. *Please.*"

"But you'll owe me."

"I'll do anything."

Ario took the athame from his pocket, pricked his thumb, and drew his blood across her forehead. "Under the light of the moon, it is done." He turned to the others. "She can do us no harm. Let's bring her inside so Maeve and I can heal her."

The men stared, dumbfounded.

"*Presently.* She's bleeding out."

Michael obeyed his order without another word, but Marko's face was scrunched in confusion. "She's an agent," he said.

Michael scooped up the bleeding woman and carried her towards the cottage. Ario heard her hiss in pain.

"I suspect that may be a "was,"" Ario said.

"And when she inevitably breaks her word?" he asked, scowling.

"She can't. I have now saved her life twice. There will be repercussions–magical ones–if she can't fulfill her debt." He cleared his throat.

"This was my decision to make. I take responsibility." Ario turned and headed inside.

Droplets of blood covered the floor. Michael had stretched her out on the table and Maeve was cutting away the black cloth of the tunic with a pair of shears. Ario saw that Michael was actually *holding* her down by the shoulders.

The wound was worse than it had looked, now the cloth was out of the way. More than a mere puncture, but as if someone had attempted to tear her in half. Which they may have.

"I'm not sure I can fix this," Maeve whispered.

"We'll have to pool our efforts. Where is Evelyn?" Ario asked. He rolled up his sleeves. He hadn't tried active magic since Amalia was born.

"With Peony and the baby." Maeve met his eyes. "She refused to help."

"She should recognize it's my will. Let's get to work. Quickly."

There was severe and significant damage to most of her internal organs. They ended up having to start a physical transfusion drip just to get enough fluids in her to heal. Her already pale complexion became gray, then yellow, from the blood loss. It dripped onto the floor.

"Nothing's *taking*," Maeve said through her teeth. "It's like the wound is cursed."

Ario reached into his magic and used the same spell he'd been using for months, to sense the miasma. The magic was harder to wield, like swatting at wet laundry. "It's poisoned."

"I can usually *sense* that, though, and I can't–"

Ario tried to meet Samara's eyes, hoping she was conscious enough to speak. "She tried to do it to you again, didn't she? The alteration? She noticed it was gone."

"Didn't... take. Got... suspicious," she managed. "Trial. Execution. I ran. First scent I got ahold of." Meaning his.

"There must be a reason you were brought to me," he said. "I think I can purify it again. Stand back." This last part he directed at Maeve and Michael. Marko glowered at him from the door.

He reached for the poison and pulled, unravelling it with all of his strength. Sweat poured down his face and back. Samara screamed, that same all-too-human sound, and sagged onto the table unconscious. At least she wouldn't feel now.

The miasma pulsed in his right hand. He went to ask for a container for it, but it dissolved again into steam.

That shouldn't have worked. He was vastly weakened and no longer protected by the Goddess. *That should not have worked.*

Samara let out a choking, gurgling sigh. He could ponder this later. Ario and Maeve leapt back into action, struggling to repair her organs and the layers of skin and muscle. Without Evelyn, it was a process that took hours, but gradually, they stabilized her.

Maeve slumped into a chair, her hair frizzing out of its buns. Marko went to make her a cup of tea, dumping a packet of herbs into the kettle. Ario, too, felt utterly sapped in a way he never had, even with excessive magic use.

"Will she survive?" Marko asked, appraising the gory scene.

"Likely yes," Maeve said hoarsely. "She'll need some more care, but yes."

Marko's bright eyes looked at the newly-formed scars on Samara's abdomen. "What do you intend to do with her?" he asked. "We can't allow her to act freely. She's another liability." He heard the heaviness of *another.*

"When she recovers, we question her," Ario said. "She has insider information we've been wanting and needing. Once we fully understand each other, she will join my guard under Michael. He can surely keep her in line. She can cover the gaps caused by my daughter."

Michael's stiff, stoic face didn't give much away, but Ario thought he saw something like amusement in the man's eye.

Marko clenched his fists. "And if she turns against you?"

"She knew what she was doing when she made the deal." He crossed his arms, feeling the stickiness of drying blood.

"Have you considered *she may have been followed?*"

"Got them," Samara mumbled, eyes closed. "Got them and then they got me. Dead. All dead."

"Rest, please," Maeve told her.

"She's right. No mundane could have caused that wound," Ario pointed out. "Unless they perhaps had a chainsaw."

Marko gritted his teeth. "This is no joking matter, Majesty. You're expecting me to trust your judgement over this—-*thing*! That we have spent years protecting you from. If you could only *see* the files on it!"

"Her," Ario said. "She's a magic user just like us."

"A traitor and a psychopath!"

"Manipulated for years by the miasma. You *saw* me remove it. She sought asylum. As king, I have the right to grant it—regardless of how anyone else feels." He drew himself up to his full height, which was still noticeably shorter than Marko. "She is my responsibility, my liability. And hopefully, a damn good guard."

"You test my patience, majesty," he muttered. "You ask too much."

"Then it is good that the only thing I ask of you in this moment is to *trust me.* I will personally absorb any risk."

He stared at the floor for a moment. "*Fine.*" Without another word, Marko left the cottage.

"He'll come around," Maeve said. "You caught him off guard, is all." She offered a weary smile.

"How do *you* feel about this?" he asked her.

"I think you brought in a wounded person for me to heal. I think it is not my place to judge—anyone." She sighed. "I hope she can help us."

"I hope so too."

She went over to the kettle, which was now nearly boiling, and poured them both a cup of the restorative. "I'll tell Evelyn and Peony what happened. Then I need to sleep."

"By all means."

Left alone with Samara and Michael, Ario appraised the mess. "I fear I may have put you in an inopportune position, Michael," he murmured. "I've angered Marko. And now you must deal with her."

"As you said—she doubtless has valuable intelligence. It would've been a waste to let her die first." He paused. "I am not angry. If anything... I have a good feeling."

Ario waved his hands, trying to disappear the blood, but he'd evidently depleted his magic—another first. "I don't suppose you know where the mop is?"

***

The displeasure he'd wrought with this choice weighed heavily on the little cottage. He woke from the sleep of the dead and saw Peony, her back to him, nursing their child in the early-morning sun.

She must've heard him stir. "You expect me to trust her around our daughter?" she asked in a low voice. "The thing we ran away from—the thing that tried to kill you, what, how many times?"

"To be fair, she only got close enough once," he said.

Peony glared at him. "I can nullify magic. I can't nullify a giant wolf flying at me."

"I bound her. I saved her life. She owes me service in return. We made a pact." He sat up. His muscles ached mightily, probably from the healing. "If I thought she was a danger, a *true* danger, I would have let her bleed out. Believe me. Catherine sentenced her to death. The enemy of my enemy, and all that."

She said nothing, rocking the child gently.

"I know I'm asking a lot–out of all of you. But I..." He sighed. "This is an opportunity I decided to take."

"Will it hurt her?"

"No. Samara won't hurt our baby."

"I mean the pact. If she tries to break it." She locked eyes with him.

"...Yes. Probably nearly as much as when I broke Catherine's hold over her."

She smirked a little. "Then it's fine with me."

Evelyn's fury, on the other hand, was not as easy to assuage. He ran into her on his way to the bathroom. She didn't snap, or yell, or even glare. Her face was totally flat, disinterested. "Pardon me, majesty," she said, and pushed past him down the stairs.

"Evelyn," he called after her. "You know *why* I did it, right?"

"It is a choice Ainsley would have made," she said icily. "Excuse me." She slipped downstairs, out of view.

Great, he thought. Had he thoroughly pissed off everyone he trusted most?

The decision had been made, after all.

***

"The decision" was now awake, conscious, and sipping a cup of vegetable broth. Michael had moved her to an improvised bedroom in the shed outside of the cottage where Maeve kept her healing supplies. The room was small and close and smelled damp. A narrow cot, wooden chair, and cabinet filled nearly all the space. Samara was still ghoulishly pale, but clean and in a nondescript robe, she seemed approachable.

"Er–good morning," he said to her. "How are you feeling?"

"The skin pulls, but otherwise quite well." He'd never heard her normal speaking voice; she'd always been either simpering, screaming, or pleading for her life. It was soft and had a little bit of a husk. "I've created quite a situation for you."

"My teammates respect my authority," he said equally.

"Nobody would have questioned you if you let me die. Why *did* you offer me that deal?"

He sat. The chair creaked. "She did something evil to you. I suppose I wanted to see what would happen when you were offered your own choice. It is very hard to let a creature begging for its life to merely die."

She smiled and cupped the broth. ""It. Creature. Beast. Dog." I've been called worse."

Ario hesitated. "I am aware of the hypocrisy of the language some of my team have used with you. I will ask them to be respectful."

She shook her head. Either she or Maeve had taken down her ponytail and brushed the mass, and it sat garishly blue across her shoulders. "No need. I deserve it."

He knotted his hands. "Do you understand the weight of a pact sealed under the Goddess?" he asked her softly.

"I understand I have traded one form of servitude for another," she said. "I merely hope my new employer is kinder to his employees. Windsor taught me *very well* the power of a life debt."

Ario very nearly smiled.

"How does that work, anyway? Do you assume my debt to her, then? Or am I overdrawn?"

"I suspect I broke the bond she had over you when I removed the miasma from you the first time. "Fulfilling" it, so to speak. Your debt to me will be fulfilled either when I deem it so, or if either of us dies. Frankly, you could kill me and be a free agent. But I think you won't do that."

"Because your guard will stop me in the act?"

"Because I think you wish to change."

She dropped her eyes to her lap.

"Last night, you said you came to me because you latched onto my scent. But there had to have been a decision behind that. Surely you weren't coming to kill me. You slaughtered the guard she sent after you to *ensure* I was not harmed. You sought asylum because you knew I would be capable of granting it. Or perhaps you just wanted to die quicker."

"I do not want to die," she said.

"No. No, I didn't think so."

She fussed with her mug of broth. "I'm sure you wished to speak about more than my employment."

"What did it feel like?"

"Try being torn in half," she suggested in a deadpan.

"Not that. Although—I suppose in a way I did just experience that myself. I meant after I removed the miasma from you."

Samara paused for a long moment. "I will never lie to you. I know that much. Maybe I even *can't*."

"You can," he said. "It's an agreement, not an insertion of puppet strings."

"Then that would be an improvement." She sighed. "I felt like... I'd woken up. And it *hurt*."

"You said "puppet strings." How much control over you did she have?"

"Don't believe that I am fully a poor victim, trapped under her control," she said. "She was able to reach into our minds, yes. She was able to issue orders we could not disobey, yes. She made us hate ourselves first, because of our beastly magic, which made it easier to hate all the others. Made us want to hunt. Kill. The... it's not quite *hunger*, I felt, whenever I caught your scent. I guess it's more like... the addict, catching sight of the thing they're addicted to. If I caught you everything would be okay. But then I'd be hungry again."

"I think I understand."

"I am not a good person," Samara said. "I have, willingly and with joy, slaughtered hundreds of magic users."

"I am within arms' reach and I must stink of magic. Do you wish to kill me, right now?"

She appraised him. Her eyes were a little like Peony's, almond-shaped, but a shade of hazel now that the miasma had been removed. "No. You smell... less appetizing. Though I swear your scent is elsewhere..." She lifted her nose, sniffing. Then, "...cut in half."

Ario said nothing. He would let her draw her own conclusions.

Samara's eyes flashed. "A child. How old? You stink of milk."

He felt his face warm, but remained stoic. "Six days. Do you wish to kill my daughter, Samara?"

"My name is Mara," she said. "I wish the child no harm. I feel... do I serve her as I serve you?"

"No. But that's why you may feel her." He wasn't sure if this was true. "Should you prove trustworthy, you may end up her guard."

"Why tell me this?"

"I could reason through the floor," he said. "But the truth is: my gut tells me this is right."

She laughed. "So the king uses his *gut* to make big decisions."

"It's served me so far." He stood. "Thank you, Mara. I will surely be back."

***

Back in the cottage, Evelyn was praying at an improvised shrine in the mudroom. Her hair was loose, dry, its scraggly ends catching on her plain cotton shirt. He observed her, for a moment, but heard little more than a word or two that made no sense out of context. She took out her old athame and pricked her thumb, feeding a few drops of blood into a candle, which she promptly blew out. She licked the wound absently, and turned to leave, but caught sight of him.

"Priestess," he said. "I know you're angry. May we talk?"

She hesitated. "All I wanted was ten–*minutes*–by myself," she muttered. "The child screams, Marko won't stop glowering, and Maeve won't stop fawning over *him*. Was your chat with the dog worth it?"

Ario looked behind her at the candle, and the small statue of the Goddess next to it. "I think She was trying to tell me this is the right thing to do."

"I see your *reasoning*," she said in a low voice.

"Then you must know Mara willingly entered into service with me. She cannot harm me without harming herself. And she knows that. You, however, are free to harm me as much as you like."

She scowled. "You think I'd waste all those years I spent keeping you *alive?*"

"I think the Goddess would encourage us to help those who are seeking to better themselves."

"Like she's not doing this merely to survive," Evelyn said.

"Then why ally with the losing side?" he asked, cocking his head. "You know that's what we are."

She started messily braiding her hair.

"I'm sorry I couldn't ask for your judgement. There simply wasn't–*time*." He sighed. "What would it say about me as a king if I denied my first plea for asylum?"

Her face went blank, and then a moroseness bled onto it. "I taught you to show mercy."

"That you did. But no blame is on you, Evelyn. I told Marko I'll accept all liability, and I will. But I suspect Mara will not act up. She has no reason to. Nothing to run to. She cannot act in bad faith until she's fulfilled her debt–which will take quite some time, to say the least. And the ethical implications of *that* are not lost on me either."

"Ario..." She sighed. "I'm afraid I cannot simply forgive you even if I feel you're right."

"That's not what I'm asking for. I would like you, in your own time, to speak with her. She might offer more insight than you think. And she cannot hurt you, either."

Her gaze drifted from his face, out through the sheer glass of the back door. "Something's coming," she said. "I feel it. Perhaps this is an omen."

"Perhaps it is."

***

Several days later, Ario was more or less fully back to "normal," if normal meant sleepless nights and dripping stinking liquid. Mara was right; he'd never noticed before, but it *did* smell quite bad, like spilled champagne from a long night out. Peony claimed not to smell it, but her own milk had a scent as well. Perhaps they had just gotten desensitized.

Even holding Amalia, she did not feel like *his*, despite the uncanny resemblance. She felt like a toy, a prop, albeit a toy that required constant feeding and stimulation not to scream. The Goddess had forced him to do this; the least She could do was make him *like* the child. He would protect her, in an animal, I-will-rip-apart-any-thing-that-harms-her-with-my-teeth sort of way. But he felt no true *affection*. He considered stress. Postpartum depression. Or perhaps... now that the Goddess got the child She so wanted, She no longer cared how he felt.

As the group debated next moves, Michael, Marko, Ainsley, and a few other members of the network questioned Mara; Ario often sat in, or listened to recordings after the fact. There was no need for *interrogation*; she answered all questions willingly, but volunteered nothing unless it was asked. For the first time they had a somewhat trustworthy account of what it was like *on the inside*.

Apparently, Catherine was just as elusive as Ainsley became in later years of her reign, delegating vital decisions to her sons and other cronies. It was almost impossible to get a true sense of how the govern-ment worked; everything was behind miles of red tape, administrative work placed on underpaid pencil pushers who could never hope to catch up. To Mara, things felt deliberately obfuscating. Multiple types of laws were often crammed into one bill, to force parliament into making bad decisions to keep the lights on.

"She's using it to hide things," Mara said. "Unfortunately I have no idea about most of it."

As part of the department for homeland security, Mara and her peers functioned as a roving tracking squad. They were either given specific targets to pursue, or told just to find the strongest, "most appetizing" scents to report on. Not all of those reported on were rounded up or even made aware of their surveillance. Some targets were even mundanes, who had either spoken out against the genocides or provided some kind of political headache. Mara was a "legacy" in that she only had to hunt one line of targets.

When pressed about the miasma, she said she didn't know if it was artificial. "Her oldest son handles all of the R&D work, the scientific stuff. It was his formula they injected us with. Xavier, I think his name is."

In her tenure, Mara had only met with Catherine six times. First, upon her ingestion when she had been gathered ten years prior (and Ario was startled to learn she was only five years his senior; she easily looked to be in her mid thirties). The next few times were to grant Mara a promotion or accolade. And the last had been at her trial. Apparently, Catherine personally oversaw the trials of traitors.

There were other squads than the 440, as they were called. 44 for the 44 general line classifications, and 0 because base 44 was already taken by another department. Most of them came from poverty, or, like Mara, a line that was not just socially unacceptable, but considered aberrational. "Transformative lines are on the far end of the "is it people,"" spectrum," she said, and Ario couldn't help but think of Peony. Mara was at her strongest during the full moon, and felt more compelled to remain a wolf; it was actively uncomfortable to be human at that time. Without Catherine's training, she wouldn't even be able to shift between at will, but when the moon—or the *Goddess,* she intoned, her eyes flat and dead–trapped her in the body of a vicious beast. Mara had been rounded up during one of her first transformative periods and dragged in for induction. She only supposed she wasn't actively within that form now due to the severity of her injuries.

"They didn't tell me what was happening," Mara said. "They put these chains on my paws and threw me into the back of a van. There was another one there with me. It looked like she'd been shot. By the time I got to the capitol, her body had stunk up the truck."

Catherine offered her food, a place to stay, and an opportunity to control herself; and all Mara had to do was work in exchange. In her mind, a reasonable price to pay. She hadn't known about everything it implied. For the first time, she didn't feel like a monster.

"Which was ironic considering what I was asked to do."

She was able to offer very granular details about the penitentiary processes. Stronger magic users were either persuaded to join the force to save their lives, or culled. The weaker ones were usually sent to labor camps, or to the power plants to deal with the nuclear waste. Rich ones could buy their pardons, but rich ones were now far and few between. The deaths, if anything, were cleanly and clearly logged in databases, often attributed to mundane illnesses and injuries rather than the true violence or the exposure.

She gave names of higher-ups in the military, which had previously been completely unknown to them. Many of them were magic users. The Lieutenant of Lindenfell, for example, was named Kinnear, which sounded familiar to him, but he wasn't sure why.

After one of these long days, Ario built a fire in the small pit behind the cottage. The day had been mild, and the evening was now cool. He held his daughter and watched the flames flicker. Amalia was technically an "aberration." Then again, Amalia did not legally exist.

The only identification she had was a false ID made by Evelyn, in case they needed to flee.

Peony emerged from the cottage in loose linen clothing, her phone in one hand, her mandolin slung over her shoulder.

"Still nothing from Rory?" Ario asked.

Peony shook her head; she looked like she'd been crying. She sat in the other chair near the fire pit and tuned the mandolin. "She's avoiding me. She just has to be. But I... I don't know why. I didn't do anything! I don't think I did anything... Unless she thinks she's keeping me safe?"

Ario frowned. "*You* didn't do anything."

"It's not *like* her not to talk to me. I know she's mad I left, but she should know I *had* to. For you, and for the baby." She plucked random, discordant notes. "It's not like we'll never see each other again."

"Maybe she's just being stubborn. You could try giving her time."

"What if I never hear from her again?"

Then you weren't as close as you thought, Ario thought to himself. "Then it's her loss, because she doesn't get to see you being a wonderful mother."

Peony sniffed, her lips curling up in a small smile. She set aside the mandolin. "Can I have her? She keeps me calm."

Ario gladly handed the infant over. The air shifted, bringing the campfire smoke closer, over his face; he shut his eyes and breathed it in for a moment. Soon, he thought, he would try purifying the land again. It had already been too long. Now that the Mara situation was stable, he had to start considering the future—

"*Majesty!*" It was a cry he had not heard; burning with adrenaline, he turned and saw Mara, still in her robe, the lock from her shed in one hand. He felt his lip curl and wondered if she was betraying them;

but then she saw the flash of *urgency* in her eyes and understood then what was happening. "*You're being sieged.*"

Perhaps it was her keen sense of smell, or hearing, but all he felt was the crush of pressure in the air rising to the point where it threatened his lungs. Out of the corner of his eye he saw the glowing wolf grasp Peony by the arm.

"Keep them safe. Evelyn will–," he said, or tried to say, but *something* was pressing him into the sand.

He met the wolf's eyes one last time, sad hazel, before she twisted and all three of them disappeared in a flash.

A staff speared down in the sand beside him. Thankfully his good eye was still exposed, and he could just barely see a feminine figure in a black tunic with silver lining. Red braids reached her waist. She had tears in her eyes.

"I'm so sorry," Rory said.

Kinnear. According to Mara, the lieutenant had a daughter named Aurora. He'd thought nothing of it.

"Let them escape," he gasped. "Please."

She bit her lip hard. With a badly trembling hand, she took an injector out of the pocket of her tunic. "It was the only way. The only way. Keep her safe."

She stuck the needle into the side of his neck, and very quickly, nothing mattered anymore.

Part II

The Palace

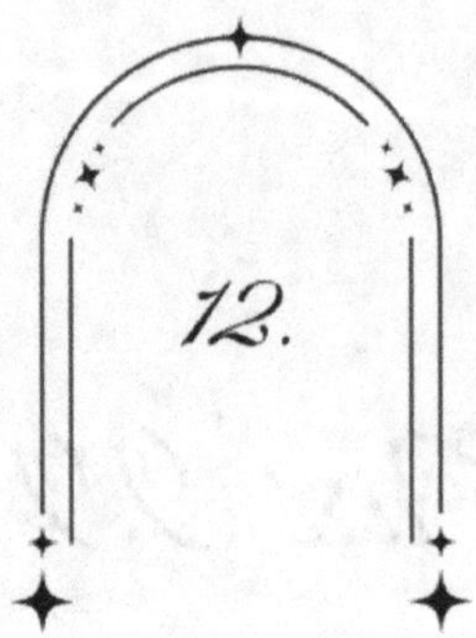

For the longest time, perhaps an entire eternity, he was neither awake nor fully unconscious. Whenever it seemed his head might clear, or his eyes might open, there was the bite of another needle and more darkness. Mundane anesthesia often struggled with magic.

Ario caught glimpses of scenery that might have been dreams, or worse; the roof of a car, blue sky and a sloshing like the sea, a shadowy and unrecognizable face, cool gray stone and violet damask. He was trapped in a sea of uncertainties.

When he finally came to for real, he was lying supine on some sort of hard, cold surface, and a surgical light was shining directly into his eye. Adrenaline surged hotly in him, but the lingering effects of the sedative made it hard to do more than twitch his fingers. His wrists were weighed down with heavy, cold restraints he could not see. Ario looked away from the light, trying to get a sense of his bearings, and how deeply he was in shit.

Evidently; very.

As conscious thought returned, he slowly began to realize where he was. He pored over the bits of ceiling he could see and caught the particular swoops of molding he recognized from the old palace. Wrenching his neck hard to the right, more of the room came into focus; he saw a computer, open to some sort of report he was too far away to read. Next to this table was some form of monitor, giving off jittery lines. A vital monitor, he finally remembered, ones that mundanes used in their hospitals. His heart rate was exceeding 120, and not far below it, his univs holding steady.

Look to the left, then. A few paces from him was a wall of cabinets, shiny glass and steel. On the bright white countertop was a small silver tray, holding an injector of milky-looking liquid. Next to that was a clipboard with a pen, and next to that, of all things, a cup of coffee.

By craning his head and neck he could just barely see the wall opposite him, which had a hydraulic door with no handle. All of the walls were a bright shade of white, to enhance visibility in this evidently windowless place.

The air in this room was both thin and rich, making his head light, but he could smell nothing more than his own sweat. This was a table, an operating *table*, where mundanes were forced to cut each other open to survive illnesses they could not fix.

Moreover, he was naked, a canvas sheet pulled haphazardly over his body, the fabric rough and unyielding as he struggled against it. The restraints on his wrists and ankles didn't give him much range of motion. He pushed against it with his hips. He'd have to try magic and damn the consequences. If only he could *see* his restraints; they felt smooth, not like handcuffs or chains, and they were just *slightly* too tight to wriggle out of. Ario took a deep breath and went to cast a shattering spell on the binding.

A sharp pain jolted through his whole body, and the monitor next to him began to beep, high pitched and piercing. He tried again with similar results.

He heard a sharp sliding sound and struggled to face the door. A tall, well-built person in a lab coat strided forward, blonde hair pulled neatly away from the face. Their face was unremarkable, with a beaky nose, very thin lips, and brown eyes that beamed amusement. "I wouldn't try that if I were you," the figure said, with a deep and scratchy voice. "Those cuffs nullify magic. You'll just hurt yourself if you try–but you won't need them long. Don't worry."

"Who *are* you?" he hissed.

"I'm surprised you don't see the family resemblance," the figure said. "My name is Xavier. Pleasure to make your acquaintance. I must say, I was not expecting you to be *nearly* this lucid. My mistake."

The beeping of the monitor grew faster and faster; Xavier looked at it and grinned, widely. "You're *frightened*," he said. He approached the table, and Ario tried to twist away, but there was nowhere to *go*. Xavier adjusted the sheet so that it covered him again. He had to have seen it, then, the evidence he'd had a child. "So long as you are compliant, this need not be more painful than it has to be." He grasped one of Ario's wrists, lifting it enough to bring it into view. "Palladium, and a little something extra. It's a shame it's so hard to find. It'd be very useful."

"Are you here to interrogate me, then?" he asked, breathlessly. "Torture me?"

The smile did not leave Xavier's face. "No," he said. "Mother was *very* specific about what I could do with you. Such a strong specimen is rare." Xavier touched a strand of Ario's hair, almost wistfully, and Ario tried to bite him. "You're very lucky. You just don't know it yet." Xavier reached into his pockets and took out a pair of surgical scissors and a vial. He snipped the strand of hair he'd been fondling and tucked it into the vial. Then, almost meditatively, he crossed over to the clipboard, wrote something down, sipped from the cup of coffee, and picked up the syringe.

Ario writhed as wildly as he could against his restraints, but was powerless to stop the needle from biting into his upper arm. Something *cold* was seeping into him, nothing like the now-familiar concrete of the sedative, and it got farther and farther with every heartbeat.

"You're not the first subject," Xavier informed him. "But you do have the highest univs, so, I'm afraid I must monitor you behind cover. Unfortunately for me." He grabbed the clipboard and strode out of the room.

The substance oozed from his arm, down through his shoulder and clavicle, up toward his head and down into his other arm and internal organs, bringing a trickling numbness into his lungs. Down, then, his heart and liver and intestines, until it reached his reproductive organs.

He couldn't even quantify the sensation as agony. In that moment he did not have thought or reasoning, he was just a screaming animal being turned inside and out, jerking hard against the palladium cuffs. The magic screamed and exploded from him, causing the monitor to fall and the computer to shatter and crack. Everything in him shouted *away away away* but he could not *get* away, it was within him, in his cells, his DNA, deeper–

And on it went, forever and forever and forever.

***

At some point he rendered himself unconscious. When he woke, his head was full of pressure. Something stunk of blood and vomit and all of his muscles ached. His organs had been rendered to rubber.

Ario blinked. Stared into that bright light. The table beneath him was wet–from sweat, or blood, or something else, he did not know. In his mouth, his tongue was swollen, and his throat was raw and felt torn. As he flexed his hands, he felt bandages against his palms.

The computer had been removed, and the monitor had been replaced. He squinted, seeing his heart rate, and the univs.

He was just below a 5. 4.8, to be precise. Xavier had said he soon wouldn't need the cuffs.

What were they going to *do* to him? He'd take torture. He'd let them cut off his dominant arm. Anything but this.

The door opened, and instinctively, he jerked. Xavier entered. His coat had some stains now, reddish brown and sticky-looking. "Good, you've settled," he said. "I'm sorry that was so unpleasant. But you're yielding results!"

Ario tried to speak, but he'd apparently blown his voice screaming.

Xavier shushed him. He crossed over to a small laboratory sink and poured water into a clean beaker. He brought it over to Ario and angled it towards his mouth, but Ario clamped his lips shut.

"Suit yourself," the man said, and dumped out the beaker. "I'm delighted at the efficacy, so far. Mother was loath to let me use it on you without prior testing. She's thrilled, so thrilled." A pause. "Don't you want to know the miracle you are going to bring about? No more death. All it takes… is just a little needle. And some collateral damage, but that's what the cloud is for, right?"

Ario glared at him.

"I would urge you to try and rest. You lost an awful lot of fluids and an awful lot of magic. I will check on you shortly." Xavier gave him an indulgent smile, and left as quickly as he came.

Ario laid on the hard table, reeling. He was sure he was being watched, likely with cameras. Xavier had just injected him with… *something*… that had sapped his magic. Not miasma, surely? Miasma *did* eat magic…

He writhed fruitlessly against the bindings, his muscles twinging from all of his flailing around. If they took his magic from him…

It would come back. It always did. Surely?

***

Time passed.

With the bright, unending light and no windows, he couldn't be sure. Enough time for the terror to begin to ebb, his heart rate settling down to tepid *beeps*, for the true soreness to set in, and for a wretched thirst and hunger to start gnawing. Ario tried to get himself to sleep, at least to try and regain some strength, and because he truly was exhausted, but the beeping and the light and the chill in this dank lab kept him jerking awake.

Xavier returned some amount of time later. Ario hoped he'd try offering water again, but the man didn't bother. "Has your voice returned, princeling?"

If it hadn't been the injuries to his vocal chords, it surely would've been the thirst, taking over.

"Better for you, I suppose," Xavier murmured. He planted a gloved hand against Ario's chin, holding him in position while he shone a bright penlight into his eyes. A migraine bloomed hotly under his blind eye. "This eye does not react to light. Curious. Are you half-blind?" The penlight came closer and closer to the blind eye, until Ario felt it against his eyelashes. Then Xavier slapped him across the face, hard.

"If you cannot speak, at the very least *nod*," Xavier snapped, all affability gone. Ario nodded once.

"Fascinating."

He consulted the monitors, and sighed. Ario wondered if he still had those scissors in his pocket; Xavier was close enough for him to consider fumbling for them. But he couldn't break the palladium. Even if he had the scissors, and struck out, surely it would just cause more consequences. "You should have dropped below 4 by now," Xavier murmured. "I suppose another dose is in order."

"No," he whispered. "No."

Xavier patted the top of his head. "Yes."

***

It was somehow no easier the second time, except this time he regained consciousness sooner to find Xavier slopping a bucket of cold water against the table, washing away more bile and urine and shit and sweat. He pulled the now-wet sheet back into place. The look in his eyes, when he met Ario's, was almost *pitying*.

"You must be thirsty," he said. "You haven't had water in well over two days."

Ario nodded.

"Then you should not have refused my generosity," Xavier said. He patted Ario's knee and left the room.

***

Moments of clarity became farther and fewer between, both from the physical exposure, the vast death plane that was his magic, and the despair slowly starting to eat away at him. He clung to Peony, Evelyn, Michael, Amalia, Marko in his memory, but they seemed so distant. So far away. And they became farther and farther away with each injection. Nothing would be good enough for Xavier except a 0, a pure 0. Ario was not sure his body could withstand it.

Sometimes Xavier gave him sips of water; never enough to satiate the thirst, but enough, perhaps, to keep him alive. Never food. But as time stretched on, Ario's hunger faded to a dull whine, and the table felt closer and closer to his bones. Eventually, at some point during his brief periods of unconsciousness (he refused to call it *sleep*), he was deemed harmless enough to receive leather cuffs instead of the metal, but these, in his weakened state, were no less yielding.

In the quiet, in the bright piercing beeping light, he swore he heard voices.

"With the extra pearls, please, up the back." His mother.

"Darling, precious boy. Wouldn't you like some ice cream?" Ainsley.

"Shirking off your studies *again*, Ario, what am I to do with you?" Evelyn.

"A disappointment. His magic was supposed to fix everything, and look how little he accomplished." Marko.

Peony, pleading, "You promised me you would fix my magic. Why didn't you?"

They crowded him through those vast endless hours, pushing hard against his ears.

***

"He's so still," a new voice said. It was smooth, pleasant.

"He is resting," said the evil one. Ario tried to scowl, but couldn't. He was so tired.

"He looks quite thin."

"He receives TPN. And the vaccine is still quite harsh on his body. When I do try to feed him, it often does not reach his system, if you catch my drift."

"I see no IV."

"Mother–I assure you, I have it in hand. Just look at the numbers."

A pause. "That is remarkable."

"And only a few shattered monitors. I expected more collateral damage."

"...Yes."

"...Are you not pleased, Mother?"

"I am, my darling. Believe me. I am merely thinking." Fingers against his palm.

"It will require more testing, to be certain," he said. "But I suppose if all goes according to schedule, we will have something to manufacture for the masses within a year."

"We don't have a year," said the nice voice. "It's hard enough–keeping Her occupied."

"Six months, then. If I push it hard. If we do it wrong, they'll die anyway."

A pause. "I suppose that will just have to be it."

"Mother, I'm sorry–"

"My dear one, I know you have worked tirelessly, day and night. The blame is entirely not on you." A cloth touched Ario's face; it smelled like lavender. After so long with such staleness, it nearly overwhelmed him, and he winced without meaning to. "Prince, can you hear me?"

He tried to open his eyes, but his eyelids weighed a ton. They crushed him.

"He has a fever," the nice voice observed. "Perhaps you might let your brother examine him."

"I can take care of my subjects adequately," he snapped.

"I never doubted that. But surely you have *so* much to do that you can allow Xander to take on some of the grunt work? He is terribly bored. Consider it a favor to me."

"*Fine.*"

***

Another stretch of nothing, then. Ario flexed raw wrists against the restraints, not fighting, just trying to assure himself he could still move. There was not much strength left in him. Even his breaths felt heavy, wet, and they rasped against the inside of his throat. He should pray. Ask for guidance.

The door snicked open; he no longer jumped when it did. Did not open his eyes. Played dead.

"My Goddess," breathed a new voice. New. A new friend. Ario tried to smile, but could not. "What did he do to you?"

We played dangerous games. I lost.

The voice grew softer. "Prince, I am on your side," it whispered, almost right against his ear; he felt hair tickling his face, hair much too clean to be his. "If you can even hear me…" Fingers touched Ario's. "I am going to start you on fluids, and tend to your wounds."

A deep, uncomfortable pinch in his left hand, and a cool trickling sensation (*please, Goddess, no*), but the coolness did not become the numbness and the pain. The pressure on his ankles eased, and something stinging was rubbed against the sores. Then his wrist restraints were removed, more stinging solution, and a warm wrapping. "I am going to put you in something clean."

The itching, cursed sheet disappeared. His arms were slipped into something soft and cottony. His body was slid from the table onto something smooth, something with give. A blanket was laid over him, and he tensed, waiting for the restraints to snap on, but they did not.

"Rest, Ilario. You need your strength."

***

When he came to next, the bright lights and beeping were gone, and he was in an honest-to-Goddess bed. Ario tried to open his eyes, and was only partly successful. What little he could make out was blurry, but he was certain he was no longer in the lab.

The lack of restraints and thin mattress had him nearly gasping with relief. His organs were still suspiciously rubbery, and his head spun, and within him, a vast deadness opened endlessly. The weight of magic, the burden and the curse, was gone, leaving his soul feeling voided and naked. Why had the Goddess not done something? After everything She'd put him through?

I am forsaken.

"...Prince?"

Ario summoned what little of his strength was left and opened his eyes.

Xavier had changed, he thought. He was thinner, and his shoulders were broader. His hair was paler, almost as blonde as Ainsley's, but still back in neat braids. He came closer to Ario and picked up his left wrist, feeling for a pulse. "Can you hear me, prince?"

Not Xavier. He was too gentle to be Xavier. His brother, then. Ario swallowed. His throat still felt raw. "Yes."

"Mother has allowed me to provide care."

Ario squinted, trying to get his vision to focus. "U-nivs?"

Xander exhaled and shook his head. "Zero."

"...Zero." Ario shuddered.

"You were given multiple doses of an experimental vaccine. However, Xavier neglected your other needs. I suspect if Mother had not allowed my intervention, you would not have survived another week."

The words did not quite seem to penetrate. They sounded like gibberish, not like words. "Dead?"

Xander shook his head. He took the stethoscope he had around his shoulders and placed it lightly below Ario's clavicle. "Breathe deeply for me. He's been starving you."

Again, he *almost* reached comprehension. "Con-confused."

"I'm not surprised. I think I can help you feel better. I mean you no harm, prince. I am a doctor. Like a healer. I'm going to sit you up. Your respirations are good, but I think you have some fluid in your lungs."

Xander propped him up with one arm, the stethoscope pressing coldly next to Ario's spine. "You'll need antibiotics. It'll kill the germs in your lungs."

"Germs." He laughed weakly. "This is a vacuum."

"...Indeed, but who knows if he let you aspirate your vomit, or whatever other horror."

"...Hurts."

"What hurts you?"

He considered, tried to. "Everything."

"I'm afraid your organs are functioning too poorly for me to give you substantial painkillers." Xander reached for something out of Ario's view and offered him a cup of something steaming, but Ario's hands were shaking too badly to hold it. He needed a tray table and a straw to drink the hot, salty broth, and even that was hard to get down. "It will take some time for you to recover," Xander said.

"...Magic?" he asked.

"I don't know if it will come back," he said. "I am sorry, prince."

"I feel dead," he whispered. "I *am* dead."

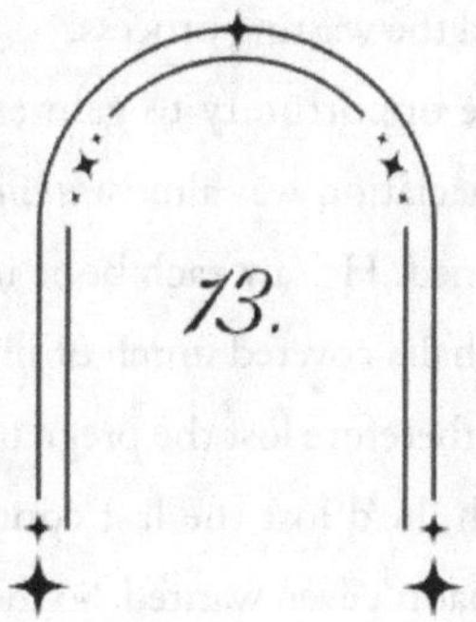

13.

ognition and control over his body slowly returned. Xander kept him on a consistent fluid drip, but could offer little more than small bowls of broth for what felt like weeks to prevent something called "refeeding syndrome." Even the broth often made him feel nauseous.

Once Ario was able to think in something other than animal impulses, though, the true dread of it all had set in. Xander was supervising his treatments, and he was in one of the palace's prison cells now, not a lab, one with a door and a shower and a toilet. He could barely get himself to and from it, much less wash. If Xander's word was to be trusted, he had been in that lab for nearly a month; plenty of time for a body to lose a great deal of its mass, and there was no knowing if the vaccine had accelerated the wasting process.

He'd never had the opportunity to gain excess weight, save the pregnancy, but his emaciation was almost *absurd*, and this was after several kilos had returned. He saw each bone in his arms and hands, and thin, transparent hairs covered much of his body. The only consolation was that he'd therefore lost the pregnancy weight in his chest and belly. But as such, he'd lost the last connection he had to his daughter—the one he hadn't even wanted. So then what was this *grief*?

Xander had cautioned him that, although he himself had found no bugs, Ario's cell was likely being monitored in some way, perhaps even magically. Powerless, Ario could not even check.

"Why are you helping me?" Ario mouthed, the next time Xander came to check on him. He was able to eat rice, now, and keep it down, though hunger remained elusive. He'd also been given a list of physical therapy exercises to do, and these tired him so badly he spent most of the time sleeping.

"I told my mother it would nullify my brother's experiment if you died from something preventable. How else to monitor the long term effects?"

"Surely that's not the only reason." Ario's speech had changed; he could no longer speak quickly, and he stuttered often. Xander said that was likely from the starvation, or a side effect of the vaccine, and it may go away. Or it may not.

"Need I a reason?" he asked.

"B-betrayed the crown. Yes."

"...I suppose that is fair. My brother wants a few more vials of blood. Best get it over with."

Even if he—and he shuddered to think it—*was* a mundane now, he still would never get used to the barbarism of their medicine, despite the fact that it had saved his life. Every single pinch of a needle made him quake.

"Perhaps you might like something diversionary?" Xander asked him. "It could help your cognition."

Ario just stared.

"A book, perhaps? Even our death row inmates can read books."

What he wanted to say was, "how truly *kind* of you to consider my boredom." What he could physically manage was, "hard to *speak*. Much less *read.*"

"How about I bring you a selection, and you let me know how you bang on?" he asked.

Something wasn't right. Through the haze that was now his mind, Ario could tell Xander *wanted* something from him, but could not articulate how, or what. *Oh, Goddess,* he moaned internally, *surely there must be something You can do to help me.*

There was no response.

***

He was asleep the next time Xander arrived, this time with a guest. Once he heard the cell door rattle, he forced himself to keep still and breathe evenly, even as the light turned on.

"...He is asleep. Shall we return?" Xander whispered.

"No. That is quite all right. I just wanted to see him. He looks much better." The pleasant voice from before; *Catherine.* Ario had to fight not to shudder.

"He still has a ways to go, I am afraid. I am not sure if it's the exposure, or the vaccine, or losing magic, or some combination therein, but he struggles to put together sentences, and he shakes. He's *in* there, I know it. He also seems to have some memory issues–I have not tested yet, to which degree."

This was news to Ario. Was Xander lying? Why?

"It would be good if you could get him to trust you," Catherine whispered.

"In time, Mother. Let the poor creature recover."

"I see you brought him some books."

"Partially to help his mind heal."

"And surely out of sympathy." He heard her riffle through some pages. "...I read this when I was younger. A good book. When do you think I can see him properly?"

"Perhaps as soon as he can walk more than a few meters."

***

What did that mean, then, if she wanted to see him? Surely, if she wanted him dead, he would have starved or been outright killed. Catherine had "allowed" Xander's ministrations for a reason. But what?

Perhaps he ought to play up his cognitive distortion, feign more severe memory loss. Maybe she would treat him like a pet, and he could learn her true intentions. He still remembered how to navigate the hidden passages of the castle. But without *power*, there was not much he could do.

The books *did* help him think; it was easier to reason through something when he'd spent a few hours already churning words. Xander had, intentionally or not, chosen titles Ario knew very well.

He was now eating small portions of solid food, and no longer looked like a corpse in mirrors. The exercises were now just tiring, not exhausting. There were no more injections. His univs remained, stubbornly, at 0.

One afternoon–he measured this based on feel and the kind of food they brought him, as there were no windows or clocks in this cell–he was reading the thickest book in the set of three Xander had brought him. The tome was quite heavy, and his hands shook as he read it. Pure fairy tales, the kind he vaguely recalled someone telling him as a child–but who? Ainsley? Mother? Evelyn, in more tender moments?

He wondered, as he often did, how Peony was getting along with their daughter. What stories *she* might be telling. Or if she was even alive. He tried to pray, but his prayers remained unacknowledged. The well-worn words of them felt alien.

Ario stood and went to replace the book on the tray table, his improvised desk. but it slid out of his hands, falling out of its dust jacket with a splash. He sighed, and stooped to pick it up, his new muscles complaining mightily. There were—letters, written on the back of the dust jacket. Words. Ario squinted. Was that a foreign language?

A cipher, his glycogen-deprived mind gradually realized. But what was the key? Was someone trying to communicate with him, or was this the efforts of a bored librarian? He could not *think*, and he had no pen to write anything down. He looked at his thumb, sighed, and pricked it on one of the particularly pointy bits of the radiator. On his napkin, he chose the most basic thing he could think of–*Ainsley*. It probably was a more sophisticated cipher than that, surely, but when he decoded the first word as *Dear,* he figured he might be on the right track.

He bled on three napkins before he had his finished key.

> *Dear Ilario,*
> *Firstly: read this on your bed, on the pillow, with your head over it. I'm fairly sure it cannot be seen that way.*

Ario obliged, and continued reading.

> *Secondly: I am sorry for the subterfuge, and I hope you have the wherewithal to make this out. I meant what I said when I said I am on your side. Truthfully: I need your help. I know you have no reason to trust me, though I hope my care has proven that I mean you no harm.*
> *Rose seeks nothing but the death of all magic. I did not think 1 would figure out a survivable, safe way. Unfortunately, your own magical death proves it is possible. You know as well as any that the death of all magic is the death of us.*

Rose. That must mean Catherine; roses featured prominently in her family crest. 1 must refer to Xavier, as he was the oldest of the three sons. But now that he was powerless, what could Ario possibly do to stop Catherine?

> *I am conspiring a way for us to speak freely. Be ready.*

This had to be from Xander. And while Ario was most definitely sure Xander didn't want him dead, he didn't want to get in *any* more "trouble" getting caught *conspiring.*

Then again; his life was all he had left.

Ario stood and started to pace, which was easier now that he had more energy. Before now he hadn't even had the hope of planning an escape. Escape still seemed unlikely; he was a very long way from Maeve's cottage, and Evelyn surely would have moved them by now.

Peony...

He choked on the pain of missing her. It was like a lead weight in the center of his chest. Evidently when they'd brought him in, they'd taken the pendant, and his watch, and he had no idea if he could retrieve it; his fingers worked uselessly in the open air near his collarbone. Even if he could only assure her he was alive... Perhaps Xander could get out a message? Somehow?

Maybe he could do as they had discussed, all those months ago; become a shameless insider, and try to topple Catherine from within.

***

The next time Xander came to him, he carried a small bundle of clothes, a towel, and a single, harsh-looking bar of soap.

"Mother has requested your presence," he said, with only a shred of bemusement. "She would like to have tea. Clean yourself up, and I will escort you."

Tea. Ario held his face very still and took the bundle. No real shoes, he noticed, just a thin pair of cloth slippers. Once Xander departed the cell, Ario went into the tiny bathroom. The soap smelled strongly of lye, but it felt like a luxury. He'd only been provided a gel-like sanitizer for his hands.

The water smelled brackish and metallic, and he winced under it, but scrubbed himself with a furor. Water could only do so much, and while the filtered air of the cell meant he didn't often *smell* himself, he felt gritty. At least his bones were no longer so painfully visible. He worked the lather into his hair, which had become so greasy it was practically a single unit, and to his surprise, he felt it come away from his scalp in clumps.

Ario stared, the water thundering over his skin. He *had* been put under incredible physical distress, he reminded himself, but that didn't make the sickly lavender clumps any easier to look at.

He finished bathing quickly and looked at himself in the plastic mirror, trying to gauge how visible the loss was. New growth was evident in the places where hair had fallen away, but it was not silver. It was black.

Ario swallowed hard against the fullness in his throat, willing himself not to react. The slick icy dead feeling lingered, making his outlines feel numb. He dried and dressed himself. Catherine had deigned to provide him with a simple gray sweater and black slacks with a drawstring. After the dreaded sheet and the thin robe Xander had given him, he felt positively overdressed.

He took a deep breath and knocked on the door to signal he was ready. Xander's eyes lingered on Ario's scalp, but he offered no comment on the coloration. "She wishes to meet in the garden. It is some ways away. Let me know if you need to stop and rest."

And off they went. He'd never seen the dungeon as a child, and was surprised how well-lit and clean it was, with cells built into the stone of the castle. All of the other doors were shut, with colored placards to indicate if they were occupied. Ario wondered what the colors meant. His own had been black.

Xander led him to an elevator in silence, and they went up several floors. When it opened, Ario was overwhelmed with all of the color and texture. This hallway was near the old art gallery, he recalled dimly. The lilac damask had been replaced with a sickly pink one, the silver sconces replaced with blocky halogen lights. He was surprised to see that many of the paintings had remained (save royal portraits); those left were mostly landscapes, or still-lives, or abstract art. Some he did not recognize at all. The rich carpeting squished under his meager slippers. He tasted a sickly-sweet smelling cleaner in the air, and under it, a metallic tang.

Curiously, there were no guards; when Ario had been a child, guards were stationed at least near doorways on every floor. "How much has changed?" he asked softly.

"Most of the public-facing areas."

Ario caught sight of a few windows. It was nearing sunset, but the sunlight was grayish, cold. "What time of year is it?"

"September now, prince. You took some time to recover."

He had to stop and rest just once as Xander navigated him through the halls. Now and again they would see staff or government workers: housekeepers hurrying about, butlers pushing carts of food, people in military uniforms walking stiffly, government drones hissing things into cell phones. The noise chipped into him, made him feel raw. Sometimes their eyes would kiss upon his, without recognition, and they would nod or bow slightly to Xander. "Are there always this many people around?"

"Usually more. She's closed the palace against tours today. Evidently, for you."

Ainsley had always frowned upon tours for the public, despite it being easy revenue. She had only allowed it for brief periods a few times a year, and usually only for students or academics.

The hallway they were in now was familiar; an entirely crystal breezeway leading from one tower to the other. It was meticulously clean, with planters interspersed blooming with camellia and freesia, but they had no smell; Ario took a closer look and realized they were plastic. At the end of the breezeway was a closed set of double-doors in a frosted glass. Here, finally, he saw guards, a pair of them.

They were not human. They were not even like Mara. Two wraiths stood guard, smoldering slightly in the dying light, each inhabiting a suit of armor. "Wraiths?" Ario whispered.

"She prefers... a guard that cannot be exhausted," Xander explained.

As a testament to Ario's powerlessness, the wraiths barely noticed him. They offered a salute to Xander and opened the doors.

How many hours–longer–had Ario spent in this garden? A large, round, glass-covered main chamber branched into two smaller chambers, one of which used to hold herbs, the others, Ainsley's prized roses and orchids. The main chamber *used* to be full of the red roses in their manicured beds, a stone path weaving elegantly between, with a dais in the center for exhibits. Or, he supposed, for tea.

There were still roses, and some were even alive, but many were plastic. The living roses that remained looked withered, dry, sticks stuck here and there to support drooping branches and stems. Gone was the sweet pungent haze of anise seed and the richness of rose. The room stunk of mulch.

"Your royal highness," she said.

Ario looked towards the dais. There was a small wooden table on it, covered with a fine white cloth and what appeared to be afternoon tea; small plates of pastries, scones, and finger sandwiches sat near small pots of tea. She was even using imperial china with its swooping filigree of violets, the sight of which nearly startled him to tears. He knew the feel of those cups, smooth and fragile, knew just how the tea would taste.

And there she was.

Lady Catherine was not a particularly imposing presence. She was average height, slender but with the softness of middle age. Her square face was less attractive than it was in official portraits, with a thin nose and far-apart eyes that always seemed to be laughing. Like her sons, her hair was very pale and blonde, but while Xander's was thick, hers seemed insubstantial, wispy. She had tried to curl it elegantly against her shoulders. She dressed simply, in a conservative long-sleeved black dress with silver embroidery against the hem, a single pearl necklace, no earrings or makeup, and flats to rival his own slippers.

He would not think she was a genocidal maniac, if he saw her on the street.

"Welcome, prince," she said, and he was forced to lock eyes with her. "Xander, dear, thank you for your escort. Might you join us?"

"As much as I would love to, Mother, Xavier has asked to see me." Xander bowed slightly, his face impassive. "Let me know when you are through."

"At least take a scone. They're fresh," she wheedled.

"No, thank you. As you were." He left, walking quickly, leaving Ario alone with the monster.

"Please, sit," she said, gesturing eagerly at the chair across from hers. "I don't think we've ever actually met. It's a pleasure."

He heard his heartbeat in his ears, rough and uneven and thick. If she wanted him dead he'd be dead, he reminded himself. He decided to play sick and dumb, at least until the worst of his fear ebbed. "Good day, L-lady."

She grinned. "Call me Catherine. Please, you are a guest."

He walked slowly to the chair, purposefully dragging his feet and faking a near-stumble.

"You poor dear. That must have been a terribly long walk," she said, and if he did not know better, he would've believed the concern on her face. "Rest as long as you need. I've had the kitchens send a restorative tea. Hopefully that provides some relief."

He sat. The chair was the softest surface he'd encountered yet.

Catherine stood and, with a pair of tongs, deftly placed a scone, a macaron, and a finger sandwich on his plate. She poured him what appeared to be a simple green tea. He relaxed slightly when she poured herself some of the same; she would not drug her own tea. "Go on, eat. Unless you are not hungry. Would you like something else? I can have the kitchen make absolutely anything, just say the word."

Ario looked at the plate. He could barely digest unseasoned chicken at the moment; confectionery would certainly make him sick. He picked up the sandwich, as it seemed simplest, and nibbled. Egg salad on wheat; the same thing he used to have for lunch as a boy, even seasoned the same way, with garlic and a little bit of paprika. "D-did..." he deliberately paused, as though stumbling over words. "The chefs. Are they–?"

Catherine added a generous amount of sugar to her tea, stirred it, and sipped. "Many are the same," she informed him. "And the new ones work off the older recipes. I did always like the food here."

A joke. She was making a fucking joke. He took another few tiny nibbles despite a churning stomach.

"How are you feeling? I did not realize the ordeal you went through, poor dear. Xavier is... single-minded, in his pursuits."

"W-well enough."

"And Xander has been good to you?"

"He brought me books." Best stick to simple sentences, so she might think him slow.

"Do you like to read, prince?"

He sipped his tea. It was bitter, burnt. "Yes. It was a great... comfort to me."

"That's good. That's good to hear." She slathered a scone with clotted cream and red jam. "I have a terrible sweet tooth. You've given me an excuse."

"W-why did you want to see me?"

Her brows pulled up. "Why, I figure after all the fuss, the very least I can do is *meet* you. It is strange, is it not?"

"...You could s-say that."

Catherine sighed and looked down. "I can only imagine what you must think of me. All those years, and then we bring you back and nearly kill you. We take your magic and starve you. You must think I'm a sociopath."

He decided to play ball. "I... don't remember much of that time. Until a little while ago."

She pressed a hand to her breastbone. "That makes me feel a little better. Prince, the vaccine we used on you, it's meant to *save* lives. I know it feels backward."

"Seems to have w-worked."

"So is evident. We'll keep an eye on that, of course. Until then, I think, there is no need for such security measures." She waved a macaron idly. "What a journey you must have had. How does it feel to be back home?"

"Home," he repeated blankly.

"Well, yes. You grew up here."

He shook his head. "Not for many years."

"That is a shame. You could have stayed here—safe and looked after. Who knows what suffering you have been through?"

He had to swallow a laugh with a mouthful of the boiling hot tea.

"Where have you been, prince?" she asked, in a voice he guessed she thought was kindly. "All this time?"

Ario hesitated. He borrowed a line of Ainsely's. "E-easier to say where I haven't been."

"You traveled a lot?"

He nodded. "Hid."

"Where?"

Ario squinted, for her benefit. "Hard to... remember."

"Of course. Of course, I understand. You're safe now, highness. Nobody will hurt you again." She speared a strawberry with her fork, as if for emphasis.

"Ilario."

"Pardon?"

"Ilario. My n-name. Call me Ario."

She smiled. Widely. "If that is what you wish, dear Ario."

At their side, the double-doors opened again, and in came a boy. Ario was surprised how young he was; perhaps fifteen or sixteen, though tall for that age. He moved smoothly, like a lynx. Like his brothers, this young man had the blonde hair and the sharp nose, though his weak jaw and full lips were pulled up in an expression of disgust. He didn't wear the tunic, but dark jeans and a rumpled shirt. "Mother," he said in a nasty voice. "Mother, I demand an audience."

Catherine looked at him with exasperation. "Xanthos, I am in a conference. I can speak with you later."

The boy—Xanthos—cut eyes at Ario. "So this is her, then."

"*Him,* Xanthos. You know better than that."

Xanthos looked Ario over, his eyes like knives. "I thought you'd be more interesting. Or at least better looking. I guess it worked, then? That stupid shot of my brother's?"

Ario's cheeks tingled with a sudden blush. He said nothing.

Catherine stood. "Xanthos, I do not have time for your nonsense. What's so important that you had to interrupt my private meeting?"

The boy stood up straight, at military attention. "There's an uprising in the south."

She frowned. "I would have preferred it if you told me that in private."

"Yeah? Well, what's he going to do about it, anyway?" he gestured at Ario.

Ario recalled, dimly, that this was the "false nonsense" information Ainsley had mentioned the day they reunited. Perhaps not so false. But then why say that? Or else this was a whole coincidence? "The south" could refer to any part of a large area. Not to mention, that was months ago now.

Catherine took another, substantially longer drink of tea, and had to refill her cup. "*Thank* you, Xanthos. I must remind you to uphold discretion in your new role. You are dismissed."

The boy scowled, and then with quick, sharp steps, snatched the uneaten scone from Ario's plate, smirking. Ario did not give him the satisfaction of reacting. Xanthos sashayed away, out of the garden.

Catherine sighed and spread her hands. "I apologize for the intrusion."

"I did not realize he was so young," Ario said after a pause.

"Young, and with all the impetuousness of youth," she said. "A change of life baby. You know how it is." She reached over and placed another scone on his plate. "That being said... how do you feel, hearing that information?"

To say he didn't care would be an obvious lie. Perhaps she had even planted Xanthos to interrupt their "meeting." "I feel it will end the way it always ends."

"Crushed under my iron fist?" she remarked, with no hint of humor.

"C-can only speak to what I have witnessed," he said, and let the sandwich fall out of his hand, as though he was losing coordination. His joints did just ache mightily.

"You have only seen one side of things, I'm sure. That surely colors what you perceive as the truth."

He decided to take a risk. "Then what *is* your idea of the truth?"

"That's the heart of it. Ario, I hope you will let me show you."

He set his mug down with a soft *click*. "I might agree with your s-son. There's not much I can do like this."

"You have more power than you know, magic or not," she said. "Think about it, prince. I believe I must go address Xanthos's concerns." She stood, set her napkin on the table, and left the gardens, leaving him there with plastic and food he could not eat.

As he waited for Xander, Ario pored over everything that had just happened. He didn't believe Catherine's facade for a minute. It was quite likely this was all a trick to sway him onto her side. Her idea of "truth." Right. On the other hand, it *would* be good to know what exactly she was up to, in her words. And if he earned her trust, he might be allowed more movement throughout the castle, perhaps to formulate a plan or attempt an escape. Or at least let his loved ones know he was alive, and about the vaccine...

If it *were* mass produced, and it *was* successfully "administered," what would that mean? To destroy all magic would undermine her own regime, and surely she did not want that? Not to mention, it "might" save the bodies of magic users, but the death of magic on such a large scale would have consequences. What would that do for the miasma slowly eating everything? Perhaps it would stop the "genocide," but it would be a genocide of another kind. He still did not feel like himself, but a pale shadow, an imitation.

It took him perhaps half an hour to sift through all this, his mind working slowly and in spurts. He ate a few crumbs of the scone, which was dry and hard.

The garden doors open with a loud *thunk*. "I'm told you had the pleasure of meeting my younger brother," Xander said. Ario was not startled. After the weeks of medical care, Ario was no longer afraid of him.

"Yes." Ario eased to his feet. He offered no other commentary. His eyes fell onto the table; perhaps there was something useful he could take with him. A knife, a plate he could break into shards, even a pen would be immensely useful. But there was no pen, and the butterknife was so dull as to be useless even to use on food.

"...Would you like to take food with you?" Xander asked. "Such richness will make you sick at this stage."

Ario picked up one of the napkins, feeling its fine linen. He took a few cautious steps to the nearest garden, sought one of the real roses, and snapped its weak stem. He wrapped it tenderly in the linen. "I'll take this."

Xander's gaze was somewhat hard to read, but he did not comment on the rose. "Come along, prince. You should get some rest."

They walked in silence for a few moments. Ario realized belatedly Xander was taking him on a different route, back down near where the servants' quarters used to be. He'd never been to this section of the castle before; a long, empty hallway lined with doors. The air here had a sharpness to it, a chilly dank bite.

"Do the staff still live down here?" Ario asked.

"Mother repurposed other quarters in the upper floors. It's more comfortable. This space has yet to be repurposed."

Another few steps. He could tell he'd be sore tomorrow morning; the palace was large, and he'd lost a lot of muscle. The rose flaccidly attempted to poke him through the napkin with its thorns. Here, in this section of the castle, the walls were made from plaster and lath, not covered with damask or tapestries. The stone floor was shiny from a recent wax, and cold and very hard against the soles of his feet.

Xander looked over one shoulder, then the other. "You may speak freely, prince. This area is safe."

Ario would be forced to trust his judgement. Either way, he must be careful. "I got your message."

"I figured you would. Did you understand it?"

"...Yes." He swallowed. "I am not sure what assistance I can provide to you in this state."

"You're more than your power."

Ario scowled. "So your mother said. How am I to believe you're not going to betray me again? For all I know, you and your mother are colluding together against me. And don't say it's because you chose not to let me die. It is *very easy* to not let someone die."

Xander dropped his eyes and knotted his hands. "Don't you wonder who did your intake?"

"I assumed it was your brother," Ario said evenly.

"It was me." He swallowed. "Xavier cared more about the... *fun,* bits, as he put it. He always preferred to experiment on lab mice, after all, forgetting they aren't just a vessel for his *fun.* The girl gave you to the 440, the 440 brought you here, and *I* was tasked with taking your vitals and cuffing you. And I saw the... peculiar, patterning on your abdomen. A simple scan confirmed the marks on your pelvic bones. Don't you think that my mother would be interested in your Heir?"

"*You,*" Ario hissed. "Don't you *dare–*"

"Consider that a deposit, highness. I could've exposed your child and presumably the child's parent. I chose not to, because I want them safe as much as you do. The magic *cannot* be allowed to die, prince."

"Don't you think I don't know that?" he barked. "All these weeks—months, I've spent studying it—"

"Exactly," Xander said, and he had the nerve to smile. "I've received the reports."

His heart fell to his feet. "...How?"

"As I said: I'm on your side. I meant it literally." He cleared his throat. "I've been a friendly for years. Under an alias, but it was still me."

"Why should I believe that?"

Xander smoothed one of his braids. "I fully intend on offering you proof, prince. We just need time."

Ario didn't want to believe Xander. Xander, the ultimate traitor; Xander, who had indirectly caused all of these problems to begin with. "So why the sudden change of heart?"

He cleared his throat. "Has it occurred to you that perhaps, as a person of this earth, I quite like being alive? I've told Mother for years that she must solve this problem. She thinks it's a solution to *hers*. My brothers support her, and so do all her advisors and counselors, who merely repeat what she wants to hear with some extra steps." Xander scowled. "Believe me, I see the irony of it all."

Ario said nothing for a moment.

"We can have more conversations. I take it you need time to think. To decide," he said. "But either way, you're in this palace for the foreseeable future."

"So why not put it to use. Right." Ario looked down at the rose, strangled in linen. "I agree *only* upon what I deem to be reasonable proof."

"And what is that?"

"You seem to know what is best for me. I'll leave you to decide," Ario said acidly.

Xander laughed out loud, a hollow, strange sound which didn't seem like it presented itself much. "Then I best get to work."

Back in his cell, feet throbbing, Ario plucked the petals off of the rose. He had no window to place them near, nor earth to bury them in. He had a single plastic cup to drink water from the sink. He poured a glass and laid the petals on the surface of the water, carefully put the glass on a book on his bed for stability, and knelt to pray.

Goddess, if you answer any of my prayers, let it be this one: do I trust Xander? Are his intentions pure?

The petals remained in the water, unchanged.

***

"Proof" arrived in a slim packet of missives slid under his morning meal. His meals were provided on a small metal tray with a silicone mat on it. At least the portions were getting larger, and he was finally able to eat things with salt and pepper. Under the bowl of rice and eggs, and the weak plastic cup of coffee, he felt a bump in the otherwise smooth mat. Slowly, carefully, he slid his fingertips under the smooth edge of the mat and felt the recognizable bite of paper against his fingertips. In what he had hoped would be a single, quick move, he tried to slide the packet against his belly and under the tray table, so that he might peruse it from his small bed.

In a bid to be trustworthy or not, Xander was still holding the knowledge of Ario's daughter above his head. Should Ario fall out of line, he was sure that could easily be leaked. Xander had betrayed him once; what was to stop him from betraying him again?

Then again, Ario had pardoned Mara without too much agonizing. Would that make him a hypocrite, to believe her redeemable, but not him? So many traitors and changing alliances in his life; Xander, Mara, and of course, Rory. He'd previously been too out of it to truly process *that* little stab in the back.

Did Peony know? He wasn't sure it would be a blessing or a curse for her. If she did not know, she could chalk his kidnapping up to any number of random factors meant to monitor people like him. If she did know, then she had just lost, effectively, her entire family aside from her daughter. But had Peony herself known that her uncle was top brass in Catherine's regime? Surely, that would've come up somehow? Some way? Mara had *said* that that information was deliberately left confidential even from the operatives and their family, but Rory had found out some way, and had decided to utilize it. Maybe she'd joined the 440 herself. She never *had* expressed any desire to join Marko and his faction of the network. But why betray her own kind? For self preservation?

She's said, shortly before knocking him out, that this was the only way to keep her cousin safe. Without her support system, away from her mate, but *safe.* He hoped. He prayed. If Mara had also managed to snag Evelyn before the rest of the forces descended, Evelyn would know what to do. Perhaps even Mara herself knew somewhere to go, but Ario hadn't even gotten Evelyn to divulge a single thing to her prior to getting kidnapped. Hopefully their daughter was still too much of a newborn to throw off much magic, or be aware of her circumstances.

Too many questions and no answers.

Using the same trick as reading that first message, Ario looked at the packet. The information was unciphered and uncensored. The resistance used older computers to send and receive messages, so the command-style font was consistent with what he was used to seeing.

>MEMORANDUM:

>Wraiths spotted within the ward at Lindenfell. Source unknown but witness alleges they hallucinated that the wraiths "seemed conscious." Exercise caution and report additional sightings.

>Re: MEMORANDUM:

>Suggest corroborating missing persons reports with amount of wraiths spotted.

>Re: Re: MEMORANDUM:

>Needle in haystack. Witness does not know how many wraiths they killed.

>Re: Re: MEMORANDUM:

>See attached uncensored version of missing persons reports. May be needle in haystack, but doubtless will be useful for your records.

In single-line, very small text, Ario saw a readout of missing persons from around the time he'd spotted those strange wraiths. Unsurprisingly, the list of the missing were mostly magic users, from anywhere below five univs to exceeding acceptable standards. He recognized one of the names; Kino, the one that had almost eaten him.

Okay, so Xander had intercepted resistance intelligence. That didn't mean he was part of it.

>HIGH PRIORITY: 440 Siege

>A 440 raid was reported at Safe House Beta at 20:40:39. One individual (NU <+) was captured. Any information regarding ingest, reporting agent would be greatly appreciated. We appear to have been compromised.

Ario paused. "NU <+", as he had come to learn early on during his days on the farm, was the code assigned to him; NU meaning "normal univs" and "<+" indicating his unusually high readings.

>Re: HIGH PRIORITY: 440 Siege

>Confirming ingest of subject at central domain. Subject is being released to RND for unknown purposes. Subject appears so far unharmed.

>Reporting agent: ID 06431-02, KINNEAR, AURORA. Reporter resisted questioning and was subsequently arrested.

He bit his lip. Okay, so there definitely was a mole, but again, how could he be sure it was Xander himself doing all this?

Not to mention, he could only hope that Marko had received this, and that Evelyn was alive and available to receive word that he was, as far as they knew, alive.

And Rory was arrested. The irony. He wondered if she was down here somewhere, or if she had been released to another detention center.

>Re: NU<+

>Subject is physically stable and has not been interrogated.

>Re: Re: NU<+

>Anything else??

>Re: Re: Re: NU<+

>Source is working closely with the subject. Under intense scrutiny. RND discovery that could have wide-reaching consequences; investigating veracity and effectiveness. In other news: alleged uprisings in the south.

So this mole was withholding information about the vaccine. Why were these missives so short? Were longer communiques automatically flagged, even with encryption?

>FORMER AGENT

>Have you any information about an individual from 440: first name SAMARA? Kill count, arrests, loyalty to the court, etc would be helpful.

>Re: FORMER AGENT

>Agent's record has been scrubbed even to source. My interpretation of that means she's either dead or disappeared. BUT. From what the source has heard, the agent is a legacy and should not be underestimated.

>Re: Re: FORMER AGENT

>10-4.

Underneath these missives was a slightly longer piece of text on copied paper, with a bright red CLASSIFIED stamp below Catherine's seal.

> *From the desk of the Hon. Xavier N. Windsor.*
>
> *Dear Lieutenant:*
>
> *I am pleased to report that progress on Project X is better than expected. Subject A (NU=<12) has reacted well to trial doses of the vaccine. After several recursive doses we were able to reduce readable univs to 0. Upon completion of the trial—and therefore proof of the efficacy of the vaccine—we will be looking to establish vaccination centers across the county. Can I count on your support in this matter? I assure you this is of utmost importance. Your agreement would demonstrate faith in the project and save lives—least of which being one certain prisoner.*
>
> *Please facilitate a connection between myself and any pharmaceutical contacts in the area. Time is of the essence.*
>
> *Cordially,*
>
> *X*

There were many lieutenants and many "certain prisoners," Ario was sure, but he also felt sure that this was implying Xavier had written to Kinnear, threatening Rory. Was Rory here? Had she also been stripped of her magic? All of the pain he'd been through had been because of her, but to gleefully imagine her put through the same didn't make him feel any better.

And if—this was a big if—they were trying to vaccinate first in magical areas like Lindenfell, what would become of that gold ward? The people within?

Where was all this magic going? Was the vaccine, and its predecessors, the cause for the sentient wraiths?

He stood and stretched. There must be a research library here, one with unfettered access. He only had to charm his way into it—the old fashioned way. Catherine would know. He only had to play her game.

When Xander brought him dinner, Ario turned away from his sad, wet rose petals and said, "alright. I'm in."

Interlude II

Seven Months without Him

J*uly*

In one instant, Peony was holding her daughter; in the next, the wolf, the *thing* was seizing her forearm and twisting into oblivion.

Peony knew vertigo. She'd fallen off enough surfboards and been tossed by violent winter seas, chasing something she could not name or fully understand. This was different; light flashed by in loose spirals, and all she could do was hold onto her daughter with all her strength.

Vertigo tossed them out somewhere dark, onto hard, dirty wood. Peony gasped, her eyes swimming. Amalia coughed and started to cry.

The wolf glowed, became a woman, her robe falling open and revealing all that new scar tissue. Her dark eyes flashed. "*Stay here,*" she hissed in a low voice. She morphed back into a wolf and vanished without a trace.

Peony sputtered, struggling for breath. She raised her eyes with difficulty, taking in her surroundings; she appeared to be in some sort of abandoned one-room cabin, with a stone fireplace, a bedstead covered in a canvas sheet, an old, moldering, smelly couch, and a sink and cookstove in one corner.

Ario—

She'd heard the wolf yell they were *being sieged,* that horrible awful roundup that had been held over her so long she'd assumed it would never happen. They had been too well protected; she had been too good at protecting. How had they been found? The wolf, surely, had to have done something, betrayed Ario's trust. But then why take Peony... here, and not wherever magic users were rounded up?

She looked at her forearm, expecting it to be a bloody lump, but all that remained from the wolf's tight grip was some saliva.

Another burst of light, and the wolf came back, releasing Evelyn, who stumbled and fell.

"Evelyn!" Peony gasped.

"Peony—the baby—"

"She's right here. We're fine."

Evelyn coughed too. For the first time, and with the flush of adrenaline, Peony realized how dusty and dirty this space was, how dark, at night.

The wolf returned one final time with Michael, who was also disoriented, but not as badly as the rest of them. She groaned and sat heavily on the bed. "Can't go back for the other two. Too much," she hissed, pressing her hand to her abdomen.

Evelyn rounded on her. "What did you see? What's happening?"

The wolf also coughed, but hers sounded suspiciously wet. "You were sieged. Someone sold you out. I am so sorry. I couldn't see more. I had to follow orders. Get you out. Safe." Her voice was raw, harsh.

"How are we to know you didn't just take us somewhere they can find us?" Evelyn asked. "*Where is Ario?*"

"Don't know. Don't know. I had to act fast. Her. Then you. The guard." She panted. "Safe. Away. They won't find us here. They got him." She spat; Peony winced when she saw how dark the spittle was.

Evelyn froze.

Peony's heart beat madly against her breastbone, hot adrenaline breaking the dank chill. "He's *gone?* He can't just be *gone.* My magic—" Her breath was like coals. "It's supposed to protect him."

"The protection only does so much good when someone snitches," the wolf said, with difficulty. "I didn't see—much—of the agent. Just the flash of a spear, and these long red braids..."

The strength left Peony then, and it took all she had to hold onto her daughter. She sagged onto her knees, grit biting into the bare skin. "Rory. *Rory.* Why."

"Your cousin?" Michael asked, very woodenly, but Peony could not even respond. It was like her soul couldn't even fully comprehend the depths of the betrayal, its sharp thorns twisting and twining tighter and tighter within her.

All these years she had claimed to be protecting Peony's best interests. Why would she turn in her mate? Her *child?*

This was Peony's fault. She'd told Rory where they were in a vain attempt to get her to visit. She would never think—never in a million years—even if Rory *hated* Ario, that she would turn him in to—get killed!

Something soft draped over her shoulders; through a prism of tears, she saw Michael spreading a blanket over her from a previously-unseen bag.

"He's really gone?" Evelyn asked in a peculiar voice.

"I'm sorry, priestess," the wolf panted. "He ordered..."

From her vantage point, and in the darkness, Peony could only see the back of Evelyn's head, her normally braided hair loose and frizzy from the frenzy of their escape. "We have to go back!" Peony yelled, hoarsely. "You... Mara... take me back. I can—I can find him."

The wolf met her eyes. Hers glittered with pain and was that *pity*, of all things? "I can't. I already... overexerted myself. Even if I... could." A deeper, wetter hack. "He'd already been taken away. To base."

"To the palace," Evelyn breathed. Her shoulders rose and fell quickly. Then, of all things, she knelt in front of the wolf. "May the Goddess bless you. Rest. You've done enough."

Mara lay back, but continued to watch them warily.

In Peony's arms, Amalia stirred and started to cry more loudly. The frisson of her daughter's needs in her own magic almost, but not totally, eclipsed the tidal wave of shock.

"You were able to get the bags?" Evelyn asked Michael.

"I figured Mara may come back. I ran for them, because I was not quick enough to run for Marko."

"So he's captured, too?"

"I cannot say—I didn't see any operatives other than the one, and it looked like he'd vanished. He might have escaped. Only time will tell. No sign at all of Maeve, either."

Evelyn knelt in front of Peony. "You must be strong," she murmured. "Our priority, now more than ever is to protect the Heir." She exhaled, stroking the baby's head. "I haven't been without him. Not since..."

"There's nothing we can do now for Ario," Michael said. "Until we find an uncompromised contact, and spread word of his capture. We can only help him by surviving, and praying."

Peony choked out a sob that rattled her whole ribcage.

Michael, stoic and unflinching, went over to the fireplace and started to build a fire.

***

For the next few days, Peony lived in a soft haze of shock. Amalia hardly left her arms, but the child was oddly inconsolable, as if expressing what her mother felt. The few packs that Michael had managed to rescue only contained emergency travel supplies; a few changes of simple clothes, cloth diapers for the child, sleeping bags, fake papers and jailbroken phones, a healing kit, a mundane water filter and camping burner, and, of course, Evelyn's tapestry and votives. Not even Peony's mandolin had survived the sudden siege.

Mara believed that this cabin—a relic from her childhood, on the far outskirts of a small village—was unlikely to be watched, but she and Michael patrolled around the wards relentlessly. If Peony had not known about Mara's past, or her oath, she would have assumed that Mara's dedication was a sign of true loyalty. Still, she did not like to leave the baby alone in the room with her. Those eyes were unsettling.

It being the height of midsummer, food was apparently relatively easy to come by; Peony hadn't realized how good they had it at the cottage. Evelyn taught her how to set snares for unsuspecting rabbits, how to forage for greens and tubers in the surrounding woods. She found she had a natural propensity for fishing, either through trap or improvised spear. The fish were thin and the greens often wilted, but they, at least, were not starving, and that should have been a comfort.

At night, when she tried to sleep, she felt an emptiness so intense and complete it hurt her bones. She tried to tap into whatever little siren magic was left in her to find Ario, that jagged and brutal missing half. Sometimes she was sure he was still alive and fighting just as hard; the other half of the time she was sure he was dead.

"If they executed him, it would've been a spectacle," Mara told her. "It would've been everywhere. We'd have heard."

It was hard to hate the wolf when she had saved their lives, but her conversation felt bitter to Peony. "And if he's alive?"

Mara looked away. "You might wish him a quick end. I've... been on the receiving end of what they can do."

"So–what, then, am I supposed to give up hope entirely?"

Mara regarded her. "Hope is a luxury," she said, simply and with little expression. "If it is easier to hope, then by all means."

Peony scowled, and turned back to her sad fish soup.

***

The days began to blend and merge together. Her necklace still had a faint glow; didn't that mean he was alive? When Peony was not worried about the baby or the wraiths or getting caught, she dwelled, endlessly, compulsively, on Ario. Was he being tortured? Were they hurting him? Was he cold, hungry? Did he think of her? Miss her? Miss their baby?

Ario'd never wanted Amalia. He'd tried to hide it from Peony, but her effervescence wasn't stupidity. At first, she attributed his dark moods to dysphoria, to the strain of working so hard while expecting. How could someone who had grown up thinking *all lives were gifts* be so indifferent to his own child? It was the way he looked at the baby, Peony had realized, the few times she got him to nurse instead of herself. Like this was a particularly unpleasant chore.

She'd seen that look, and she'd realized for the first time that he was a person she could never truly know even with their bond, one with inscrutable motives and traumas she'd never learned about. But Peony could not outright ask *do you hate our daughter*? Because she knew he would lie. And maybe he didn't hate her, but he didn't love her with the all-consuming *I must soothe I must protect I must nurture* that had become Peony's every breath.

Regardless of how Ario felt about Amalia, Amalia missed him *painfully*. It was the royal bond, Evelyn explained to her one evening in their second safe house, an old hotel room in a not-so-nice part of a bedraggled city. The same mechanisms that had pulled power from Ario had linked the baby to him, psychically. Even royal milk was special, different from regular breastmilk when examined.

"Do you think she's crying because he's hurt?" Peony asked, after hours of steeling herself.

"I certainly hope not," was her answer, and she went into the other room to pray.

As the summer dissolved into hesitant fall, they criss-crossed the northern part of the country. They stayed in tents, in recreational vehicles, in houses and apartments, some occupied with other refugees, most not. Movement through the cities proved easier than Evelyn anticipated; scanners never acknowledged them. The few times homeland security commented on their suspiciously bright pet husky, the officers had bought that the dog was fresh from a groom, and cooed at the baby in Peony's sling, completely oblivious to the royal bloodline inches from their faces.

At least Peony was good for something.

So this was how Ario had grown up; always moving, always paranoid, subject to leaving behind their few belongings at a moment's notice. And this was how their daughter would grow up—forever unmoored.

"Does it get easier?" she asked Evelyn one evening over dinner. "Moving around so much?"

The woman pulled one hand through her hair. "Believe it or not, this *is* easier than it ever was," she said. "Your power, unsurprisingly, has drawn suspicion away from us. With him, I had to worry about the blasted univs all the time."

Peony looked around at their meager quarters; this time, they were in a manufactured home in the northeastern mountains. In the corner, Mara lay curled in her wolf form, where she was more or less forced to spend the full moons. ("Some women get a period. I turn into a dog.") She tossed her tail back and forth, making the baby laugh. "Do you think it would've been better? If you had found me sooner?"

Evelyn exhaled. "Better for whom, I suppose," she said. "You would've been deprived of the normal life you had."

And it really *had* been normal. Classes at university, parties, grocery stores with full shelves, days spent with friends at the beach, family dinners with... well. Evelyn and Michael definitely felt less like the imposing forces they had been when she'd first met Ario, but they were a far cry from the family she'd once known.

"I'm worried what Amalia's life will be like," she admitted. "If it's all just... this, until we starve to death."

Evelyn's eyes glinted with exhaustion. "We can't pretend to understand the fate the Goddess has planned for us."

"The Goddess" this. "The Goddess" that. She *got* that Evelyn was a priestess, and all, and was under immense duress. But being told to pray about it when she had a legitimate, solvable concern got to be annoying. Peony wasn't sure she felt any *Goddess,* despite Evelyn laying out the miracles She'd bestowed on Ario. Peony didn't want to raise her daughter to believe in a power that may be abandoning them.

Sirens allegedly had gods. She had vague, shadowy memories of the insides of underwater temples, love stories between the moon and the sea that spanned endless millenia, gods that had apparently granted them the ability to walk two worlds, in the name of love. But she could not walk two worlds, and she could not remember her home, and she was not sure, really, what she believed in.

***

The inevitable happened; Peony and the baby were left alone with Mara. Conflicting priorities required Evelyn and Michael to both leave the safe house–the former, to get more food and fuel for their heater, the latter, to meet up with a member of a different resistance network–leaving the two women alone. While Peony was now sure Mara wouldn't harm them, so many hours without a buffer was certain to be... awkward. Life was boring enough as it was, with little for diversion. If they were lucky, they ended up in spaces with books or television, but often, she was left with only her thoughts. Her songs might entertain the baby, but Evelyn did not much like the contemplative silence broken.

In the living space of their temporary home, Mara kicked back on the couch, picking lint off of her threadbare sweater. Peony stood at the kitchen table, folding washed baby clothes and trying not to feel the lack of conversation. Amalia was just growing so *fast*, and her sewing skills were not great, and the seam on one of the onesies she'd let out was coming apart. She sighed. "Princess in rags," she muttered.

"They grow like weeds at that age, don't they?" Mara remarked.

Peony froze; she hadn't meant to invite her to speak. "Outgrowing everything she has, anyway. There's a reason I failed home ec. My stitching is shitty."

"Can I see it?"

She turned.

Mara cocked her head. "All those years on the road with one tunic, if I was lucky? You learn to fix things."

Peony hesitated, but handed her the onesie.

Mara studied it with her usual military precision. Peony wondered if she looked at everything like that, like it was something to be disassembled. Did her eyes ever light up with joy? Fun? "You used a running basting stitch. No wonder it fell apart."

"There are different stitches?"

"...Many. Where's that sewing kit?"

"In Evelyn's bag. I'll get it."

It still felt weird to watch Mara sew. That was too gentle, too domestic of an act. Peony watched the light glint off the needle warily. Before too long, Mara returned the repaired garment to her. "When the next one inevitably comes undone, I'll show you how to fix it," Mara said.

There was a beat. Peony knew she should thank her, but couldn't get the words out.

"She looks like you, you know," Mara said instead. "The child."

Peony glanced over to the basket that was serving as a makeshift cradle. Amalia was fast asleep after another one of her crying jags. "I think she looks more like her dad." She recalled, early on in the pregnancy, when Ario had told her (nose wrinkled with discomfort) that the heirs always unambiguously resembled their bearers. She had made some flippant remark, like, "So I guess I'll have more luck with the second one." Ario had just raised his eyebrow.

"It's the nose. And of course the eyes," Mara said.

Peony brushed her dirty hair behind her ear. "You must have spent a long time observing him."

Mara laughed once. "I never saw more than the old pictures before the day he signed my death warrant."

"You mean when he removed the miasma from you? Is being with us so much worse?"

"It's not. That makes it all the funnier, to me."

Peony crossed her arms. "What was it like?"

The little bit of humor left Mara's face. "Since when do you care what I feel?"

The tips of her ears burned.

"You and Evelyn both have made your *indifference* of me quite clear."

"I just find it kind of hard to talk to you when you tried to hunt my partner for years."

She did not seem to take offense to this, not outwardly. "His majesty saw an opportunity, and he took it," she commented.

"But you'd still be hunting him if not for that, and the pact."

"Oh yes. Likely with pleasure."

She scowled. "And you wonder why we're maybe not the nicest to you?"

"He gave me a chance," Mara said bluntly. "Nobody else has. There's nothing else here to do but be vigilant and think. So I have."

Peony nearly rolled her eyes. "And what do you think about?"

"What I would have done, if it were him, asking me for mercy. I know I would not have done it." She paused, here. "But I know that I, now, would want to grant it to him."

She scoffed. "So not wanting to kill someone makes you a good person."

"I never said that, princess."

Her stomach clenched at the barb.

Mara raised an eyebrow. "That's what you are, you know. As consort of the heir apparent, you are, therefore, a princess. If we're still giving these titles water."

She opened her mouth, and realized, slowly, Mara had not been trying to insult her; she merely had never had to directly refer to Peony before. "...A princess," she repeated, her lips twisting. "How about that. It doesn't exactly make the soup any easier to swallow."

Mara did something odd with her mouth; a smile, Peony understood.

***

Amalia gradually stopped crying for Ario, which was somehow worse than having to deal with the on-off keening. According to Evelyn, she was meeting developmental milestones well: fascination with her own reflection, rolling over on her own, grasping her own feet. Hazy newborn eyes were replaced with an awareness. Every moon that passed, Evelyn prayed over the child, asking the Goddess to protect and guide her.

Winter, that year, struck early and violently, with brackish flurries and diminished food supplies. They never went hungry, exactly, but the meals went from somewhat varied to unseasoned rice and beans two or three times a day. From what Evelyn saw of the shops, produce and fresh meat were becoming more expensive and generally poorer in quality, leaving metallic tastes in their mouths when they could get ahold of it. Evelyn often claimed lack of hunger and passed her portions off to Peony. What would happen when Amalia got too big to breastfeed? Their budget was stretched thin enough as it was.

Amalia was five months old exactly when she showed signs of magic, during their very depressing yule dinner (rice and beans *again*, canned peaches that had a greenish hue, and a bottle of vinegary white wine). Ario's twenty-second birthday; if he was even out there. Sometimes it was easier to think him dead. Others, it was unbearable.

Peony reached out to wipe the fruit juice off the baby's chin, when Amalia looked at her, smiled widely, and sneezed directly onto her face, which didn't strike her as remarkable until she saw Evelyn's startled look. "What?"

Mara nearly smiled, but caught herself. "I hope you like freckles, princess."

Amalia screamed with laughter and clapped her hands. The freckles lingered for a week.

***

Just when she thought she could live with this sort of life, of course, things took another abrupt reversal. Michael brought back word that a mandatory vaccine program had been enacted, one alleging to remove magic from magic users. Enforcement was going door-to-door with univ readers and jabbing everyone who registered at or above a 5.

"Can something like that even work?" Peony asked incredulously. "Magic just doesn't *go away*."

Michael cleared his throat. "The source I spoke with believes the miasma has been manipulated into a bacteria. They attested to its efficacy."

Mara looked away. "We can't pretend that this wasn't going to happen some way or another."

"They can't just *do* that!" Peony said.

"Who is this source?" Evelyn asked, her face very pale.

Michael sighed. "I don't know their true identity. They call themself Microdot. I've been assured again and again they're trustworthy. They're in the capitol, perhaps even in the palace."

"What do we do?" Peony asked.

"There's nothing we *can* do," Evelyn said. "Except stay hidden."

"The faster the magic dies, the faster we–" She cut herself off. Amalia, on Mara's lap, cocked her head. "What is the bloody point?"

"*I don't know,*" Evelyn snapped. "I have been praying and praying, and writing and writing to anyone I can think of."

"Someone has to *do* something. Even the mundanes have a lot to lose. How can they just..." Peony sputtered.

Michael shrugged out of his large overcoat and pulled something out of his pocket. "This communication was also left for us. It's from–"

Evelyn snatched it out of his hand before he finished speaking and tore open the small envelope. It was the sort of card you would send as a birthday invitation, colorful and bright, with balloons on the front. She read in silence, sweat forming on her brow.

"What's it say?" Peony asked.

Evelyn collapsed heavily on the chair nearest herself and began whispering prayers.

"So it's either very good, or very bad," Mara remarked.

Peony reached forward and took the card from Evelyn's limp grip. The text was all scrambly; from fear, or– "Um... what does this..."

Mara looked over her shoulder. "It's a cipher."

Evelyn started bawling. "It's from him," she said. "I always... when he was younger... I gave him a key to use, if we were separated. He's all right, Peony. He's fine."

Peony blinked. She sensed a huge "but."

"The vaccine is... real," she said slowly. "They used it on him."

Amalia started to cry, too, and not because she was hungry or wet.

"He says his power has not come back." Evelyn wiped violently at her eyes. "The only person who was able to do *anything* against the miasma, and it's just *gone.*"

"What about the baby?" Peony asked.

"We won't *make* it until she's old enough or skilled enough to try another attempt. Barring a *miracle*... it's over. It's all over."

"Don't be a coward," Mara said. She handed the screaming baby to Peony, stroking the top of Amalia's head once.

Evelyn sputtered. "Excuse me?"

"We can either die in hiding, or we can die doing something meaningful. Rally what little forces we have. Use what power we've still got. If they've got him, and got him neutralized, and yet he was *still* able to get you a message, the prince is fighting too. I'm guessing the note was conveyed by this Microdot person, meaning they have direct contact with him or an ally of his." She reached for the card and gave it a few hard sniffs. She shuddered; Peony saw goosebumps rise on her exposed forearms. "The scent is very faint, but it's there. Let me investigate."

"You have no idea where he is," Evelyn said. "He could be monitored continuously. If you just *show up* and get caught."

"So I won't get caught," Mara said. "I've done this for twelve years. I can track without being seen."

Evelyn scowled. "And what if *you* get captured or, worse yet, killed? Where will that leave us?"

Mara smiled. "It's refreshing that your first thought wasn't that I would betray you."

Evelyn crossed her arms. "You can't. And you wouldn't."

"*Trust* me, priestess. I won't do anything stupid."

Evelyn looked towards Michael. "What do you think? As the king's guard?"

Michael was silent for a few moments, his eyes searching the middle distance. "I think there must be a reason he contacted us now. I see no harm in Mara seeing him."

She squeezed her eyes shut tight. "*Fine.* Fine!"

"We're close enough to Landfall that it won't take me too long to reach him and come back within a day or so," Mara said. "Stay put, if you can." She took another few deep sniffs on the card. "I think I've got it."

"Wait–" Peony seized her hand. "Tell him... tell him we love him. And we'll do whatever he needs." She coughed around the lump in her throat. "And that our daughter is wonderful."

"...As you wish, princess." She melted into her wolf form, cast one wry glance at them, and vanished.

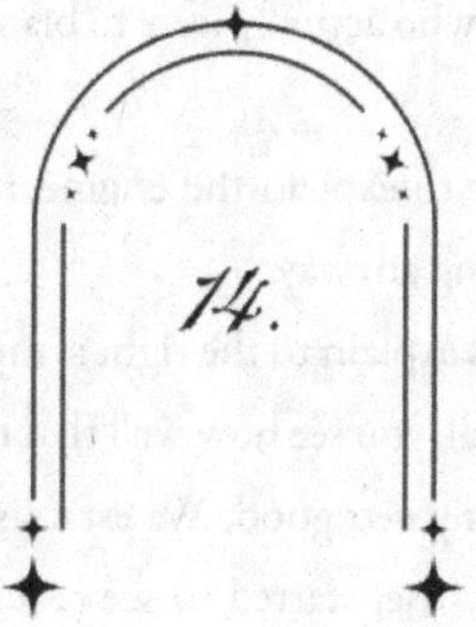

14.

F*all and Winter*

Catherine *requested* to see Ario regularly, at least once a week. Often she summoned him to the rose garden, but occasionally she would also bring him to one of the formal dining rooms, or her personal sitting room (his mother's old rooms; Ainsley's old rooms). She framed herself as eager to explain *her side of the story* to him.

"It didn't start as a personal vendetta," she insisted over tea. It was always afternoon tea she served him, regardless of time of day. At least he could eat the food now without being nauseous. "As a politician, it was *my job* to listen to the people, and this is what they wanted. The economy was bad. The welfare system was worse. It was just a shame that the people who actually *were* to blame happened to be of… a certain phenotype."

He didn't need her to explain the engineering of fascism, but he found it duly interesting anyway.

"All I had to do was explain to the right sympathetic ears that I had a plan to fix things. Well, you see how well that turned out." She rolled her eyes. "The economy *was* good. We established social safety nets, cleaned up our energy use, started to see real change. And then the miasma spawned. If I believed in a divine, I would say that was divine convergence."

Ario cut his eyes at her, trying to appear curious.

"You are very religious, are you not?" Catherine asked.

"I was."

"What changed?"

He could hardly admit that the Goddess had violated his body autonomy so mightily. "It became hard to believe in something that lets so much wrongdoing happen."

"A very simple theological argument. Is that the only reason?"

Ario set down his teacup and knotted his hands. "What do *you* believe in, Catherine?"

"I believe if there are truly divine beings, then their machinations are not something we could ever hope to understand. Magic or no magic, we are creatures of flesh and bone. No better than any fauna, really. In fact, far worse."

"So then what beliefs inform this system you've created?"

She sighed and picked up an iced cookie. "Have you heard of the trolley problem, Ario?"

"I have not."

"Say you're the operator of a trolley. Suddenly, the brakes give out while you're going downhill. You have a control lever leading to two tracks to divert the trolley from crashing. One track will have you hit one pedestrian. The other will have you hit several. So how do you determine which track to take? There's the simple answer, that you hit the one person to spare the others, as well as the people on the trolley to begin with. Make no choice, and all the people on the trolley die."

"Needs of the many?" he asked bitterly.

"Exactly." She offered a smile with dry, cracked lips. "I can try to save the few lives I can with the time we've got left. What would you do, if you were me?"

Not slaughter innocents, or corrupt their beings. "But magic is the only defense we have against the miasma, now. Why not use that to your advantage?"

The affability in her face dropped. He saw the faint edges of jowls, bags under the eyes. "What do you know of the miasma?"

He couldn't afford to show too much of his hand. "It... allegedly formed spontaneously. It does not fall cleanly into any one kind of matter. It corrupts. Absolutely."

"It eats magic," she said. "If there's no magic, there's nothing for it to feed on. It will starve and fade, the way it did the first time."

"And the magic in the earth itself?"

"This is not a topic I seek your guidance on," she said, sick pinkness in her cheek. "I have pored over every option and chose what seems most logical."

He felt the rancor in his throat, but forced himself to bite his tongue.

Catherine smoothed her skirt, resting her hands in her lap. "You have some fire to you, don't you?" she asked. "Ario... don't you know what we could accomplish together?"

"What could I get for you that you don't have?" he asked. "I have few connections, no magic, no resources other than what you give me."

"More than you know," she said. She checked her cell phone. "Goodness, I am overdue for my next appointment. This was a lovely conversation."

***

In the dungeons, with nothing to do but read old books and stare at the walls, Ario shivered. It was only mid-October by his estimation, and yet, the air was as sharp as it was in midwinter. Xander had provided him with several extra blankets, but that could not exactly do much when paired with a rickety radiator and stone walls. His only true respite from the chill was during his walks with Xander and his meetings with Catherine.

After one such meeting—cut short due to another ambiguous emergency—Xander said very softly, "You're going to get sick."

"I feel well enough," Ario said. "I've been through worse."

Xander shook his head. "You're going to become ill."

He thought he caught the drift. "What would that accomplish?"

"You and I could persuade Mother for you to have rooms on the upper floors of the castle, for your constitution. From there, we persuade her you deserve more freedom of movement. You understand?"

"And how exactly will we do this? I have nothing but cold water in that cell."

"I'll bring you something you can use," Xander said. "Though I warn you it won't be pleasant."

Ario scoffed. "Like anything is."

"The point is—the more freedom we can get you, the more trust we can engender, the more you can *help* me."

"As you keep saying. But *what* are your goals?"

Xander huffed and ran a hand against his normally pristine plaits. "Short term? Sabotage the vaccine program. Long term? Get my mother off the throne, and you onto it. But to do any of that, we need access to data only my brothers have."

"Why did she not give you access?" Ario asked. "She has no reason to distrust you. That I know of, anyway."

Xander paused. "We've partitioned our data this way from day one," he said in a low voice. "Xavier and his staff *always* handled the scientific research stuff. My brother, now that he's older, oversees military operations and propaganda—rather, he gets the credit, while his poor assistants do all the actual work."

"And you?" Ario asked, raising an eyebrow.

"I end up with the boring bits—the bits nobody else wanted." He cleared his throat. "Transportation, energy, following Mother's beck and call. She has assistants, you know. I guess she just finds it more satisfying for me to get her tea, and whatnot."

"You're in the department of energy?" Ario asked. The glaring lack of magic flooded him. *Now* he could engender access to a power plant, and he had no means to magically utilize it.

"Oh, we don't *run* these things. Other qualified people do, we just end up as the faces."

"How many people are even in the government?"

"I don't even know. Tens of thousands. That's part of how she obscures what she's doing; she divides all the labor unevenly and makes it hard for agencies to interface with one another. Sadly, that didn't take much doing from the previous administration."

Ario sighed. "So how do we sabotage the vaccines, then?"

"I was thinking I would propose a tariff on the roads, especially for large vehicles like trucks. Something about the hydrogen shortage. We'll also slam teamster's unions to rile up the drivers. Accuse them of pro-magic sentiment, you see, not enough to get anyone killed, but enough for the union oversight board to dissolve their union. That'll drive up the price of fuel and tie up the distribution badly. And then I think I'll attempt to DDOS some of the health department's servers."

Ario stopped walking. "How long would something like that take?"

"I could get the executive order for the tariff on my mother's desk rather quickly. As for the hacking, I *will* need help, but I can contact my friendlies."

"According to Xavier himself, Catherine wants it done by January. It's October now. I'm not sure this tariff would *do* anything fast enough. Isn't there at least a farce of an oversight?"

He shook his head. "Executive orders work differently than the old royal decrees. If she wants it badly enough, it'll happen."

"...Then let's hope this works. I'd like to *not* subject many more people to this."

The next morning, his coffee tasted unusually bitter. Xander had warned him about the pill that would make him sick; allegedly, a mild poison that would cause vomiting and fever, but leave his system within a few days. They couldn't just put a warm cloth on his forehead and expect Catherine to buy it.

It went against instinct, to deliberately and knowingly ingest a poison by one of his greatest traitors. But this was a time of strange bedfellows.

The sickness that followed was not "mild." The fever felt like it was going to slough off his skin, coupled with chills so violent he thought he would convulse. The vomiting, too, caused bright petechiae around his eyes and a strained neck. He could not even keep down water. Eventually he slipped down into a dizzy delirium, full of glowing wolves and screaming infants and the watery eyes of an unseen goddess.

When he came to, he was so comfortable he was sure he was still hallucinating. The bed was soft and supportive and *warm*, the blankets smelled clean, and there was no glare of fluorescents to taunt him out of sleep. Only the dull and now-familiar pinch of a needle in his hand broke the illusion. Ario opened his eyes.

He had expected to be maybe in the servant's quarters, which were plain but comfortable. Xander had done better than that. Ario was in his old rooms.

He took it in dazedly, surprised that the space hadn't been altered or renovated in the interim, or assigned to one of the brothers. The large, four-poster bed he was resting in with its heavy, wine-purple drapes. Across from the bed was an ornate white marble fireplace, with violets and vines carved into the rock, and a pair of small upholstered silk sofas facing each other.

He sat up, his abdominal muscles aching from the sickness. On the wall behind the bed was the door to the bathroom, and on the other side, the door to his old study. Everything was in varying shades of white, gray, or purple, so like his old hair color and only fitting for an Heir. The room smelled of lemon floor polish and something minty.

Gingerly, Ario forced himself to his feet. He did not trust himself to remove the needle, so he was forced to drag along the IV pole as he explored. As he looked closer at shelves, he saw signs that the room had been hastily reverted to what it had once been; smudges of dust on the bookcase not quite wiped away, a cleaning cloth mistakenly left on the fireplace's mantle, mirror cleaner left on the bathroom's counter.

His cell had only a blurry plastic mirror. Only now was he truly able to see himself after all of the stress he'd been put through. All of the violet-silver was gone from his hair, leaving patchy new growth of varying lengths. Even his eyebrows and eyelashes had not escaped the onslaught; he looked downright laughable, as though his infant daughter had taken a shaver to his face and head. If he could get ahold of some scissors, he would try to neaten this mess until it could grow out.

Wandering into the drawing room, he saw his old mahogany writing desk with a new set of stationery, the small mother-of-pearl pen box with its lid half-opened. Ario searched the desk and found it mostly empty save office supplies, and, crucially, scissors. They were just paper shears, not sharp enough to really be a weapon, but for this purpose they would do.

After the makeshift haircut, he took a long, hot shower, which was awkward with the pole. Someone had stocked his wardrobe with some clothing as well, simple unremarkable pieces, but he noticed he'd been provided sneakers and boots with a sole. Catherine clearly meant for him to be out and about.

Ario sagged into his study's chair. He didn't know how to do this—to perform a successful coup. Evelyn's diplomacy lessons had noticeably lacked information on this. He seemed halfway to getting Catherine to trust him; perhaps he should play into her hand? Pretend to become enticed with "what they could accomplish together"? He couldn't just stab her with whatever weapon he was able to improvise. All that would do would get himself killed, and then, he was sure, one of the evil brothers or some horrible prime minister would take over and it would be no better. For a true takeover, they would need friend-lies *here* in roles to keep things running should she be assassinated. Needless to say, that was unlikely.

There was a gentle knock at the door. Ario jumped, but it was only Xander.

"It's good to see you up and about," the man said. He was actually wearing color, a dull red sweater vest over a white dress shirt. "I expected you to still be in bed."

"I bet your mother and brothers have gotten a laugh out of how horrible my hair was," he remarked. "I didn't realize."

Xander crossed over to him and took Ario's pulse. He took a few cotton squares and a roll of tape out of his pocket. "Mother and Xavier found it fascinating, from a physiological point of view. He supposes you have always had the gene for black hair, but the magic superceded it. Xanthos got a real laugh, but Xanthos is an ass. Hold still."

Ario flinched as the needle was pulled from him, but was grateful the anchor was gone. "You hold no affection for your family at all?" he asked.

Xander threw the needle into the wastepaper basket, then crossed over to the windows and threw open the curtains. The sunlight was tepid and grayish, but felt bright compared to the rest of the room. "Do you hold affection for your aunt?" he asked.

"...Ainsley? I've only seen her sparingly in the past dozen years."

Xander met his gaze. His eyes had softened, and something almost pleading was in them.

"...I am angry with her," Ario admitted. "I think she handled the years since poorly. I think I could have done better." He folded his hands, careful not to jostle his bandage.

"You never asked me why I did it," Xander said.

"I'm not sure what that would accomplish, but it seems like you wish to tell me anyway."

Xander looked out the window at the palace and city below. He reached out and brushed his fingers against the fern between the two windows. "I always disappointed her. Compared to Xavier's achievements in science, my staid, government job as advisor bored her. She expected my role to have more influence for her, see, when she was only a duchess. When I told her I was serving as a mundane liaison, she said, and I quote, "that is quite possibly the worst role you could have chosen." So—yes, it started because Mother didn't love me enough." He sneered. "I wanted to impress her. I assured her my role had more power than she thought. I had the docket of mundane ambassadors, see. The unhappy ones. I handed it over, and that was not enough, though it started her rebellions. I had direct access to the queen's schedule, could observe her guards. That, too, was not enough. I proposed the plan to siege the castle, and that was *almost* enough.

"When the castle was stormed, then evacuated, I stood with her in the throne room and watched her gloat. She used to smoke cigarettes then, and she took her gaudy lighter from her pocket and burned the royal flag above the throne. I felt such *triumph*, then, at least until she turned and said, "you would have done well, had the queen and princess not gotten away." I realized nothing I could do would change her mind; I was a means to an end. And I had just handed the kingdom to her on a silver platter."

Ario kept his face smooth. "Did you realize the consequences? For magic users, I mean."

"I am guilty of believing her, in the beginning, that she meant well for all." He shook his head. "It takes *time* to plan a genocide. By the time I realized what was happening, the killings already started. First with the sirens, but they were always a drain on our resources, so she said. But then things got closer. I would see them, sometimes, when soldiers would bring them in. And I came to learn—magic or no magic, the instant I stopped being useful to Mother, I would be in the same boat."

"Was that when you started to connect with resistors?" Ario asked.

He exhaled, and nodded. "It took years to earn their trust, even under a pseudonym. Had you not been sold out, it's likely you would have met and worked with my alter ego. I want the world to keep living. I want magic to live. These pathetic attempts at atonement will never *be* enough."

Ario considered Xander's monologue for a few minutes. He had no reason to *distrust* it, and Xander's voice had carried more emotion than he had ever heard. "You do realize that, even if we miraculously do stage a successful takeover, one of us is going to have to kill her, and likely your brothers. Are you prepared to do that?"

"Yes," he said, without hesitation. "She wouldn't expect it from me."

"It will take more than a few assassinations to undo the mess, you know."

"Not as much as you think. She dies, you take her place, you issue a few executive orders to assert your power, and then the real work begins."

Ario laughed; he could not help it. "You're not understanding me, Xander. People will resist and rebel under me. Every staff member in this castle has declared their loyalty to her by being here. That will have consequences. I can sign as many pieces of paper as I like, but if the enforcing agents simply decide not to do anything, we go nowhere. We will need to be subtler—and in a way, more insidious." He picked up one of the fancy pens on the desk and twirled it in his hand. "You say you work with the department of energy. Say we get an in, once the vaccine rollout has been sabotaged. We plant some of our people. We threaten the electricity supply and pretend to be terrorists."

"...The southern plants," Xander said slowly. "Rebels have been giving Xanthos grief. If we connect with them..."

Ideas came to him, slowly. "Xanthos responds with an iron fist. That sows distrust with the average people in the area. But that means lives lost."

Xander paused and tugged absently on one of his braids. "Lives will be lost either way, Ario."

"Trolley problem," he spat under his breath.

"Pardon?"

"Nothing. Let's keep thinking. You have access to the official media sources, right? We can have some of our hackers leak information about the true dangers of the miasma and the administration's refusal to do anything meaningful–that, in fact, this vaccine will *accelerate* the process. Even the most staunch magic fatalists will be upset that they, too, must face consequences." Ario sighed. "What I really need access to are her documents on the miasma and whatever she has or hasn't done about it, and the response–the real one, not the official one. Other public figures must also be frightened by it."

"Once you are allowed freedom of movement, that will be doable," Xander said. "But, Ario, what can you do without magic?"

Ario closed his eyes. "I might not have power. I know people who do. If I could only effectively commune with the Goddess..." He huffed.

"I take it She's not answering your calls," Xander said, folding his arms behind his back.

"I'm not sure if it's because I have no power, or if She's willfully ignoring me for some reason, or if She's focusing on... my daughter," Ario said. The words felt funny in his mouth.

"Could you... utilize your daughter's power, somehow?"

"She'd be too young to control it," Ario admitted. "And I have no idea where she even is. Is that something you could glean?"

Xander shook his head. "The moves of the royal family are of utmost secrecy, even to me."

"When I was pregnant I was able to utilize that excess power to dispel the miasma. I always figured if I had a *massive* energy source, I could do something. But I can't. Your mother is convinced it will just *disappear* if there's no magic. That's part of why I need her archives—to verify the claim that the original miasma just *went away*. Or if there's some obvious solution that was censored long ago."

"If that were the case, Mother would have used it," Xander insisted.

"Would she?" Ario asked. "Do you know that for sure?"

"She wants magic dead. Not everyone and everything."

"That's just it. Magic *is* in everyone and everything—even mundanes. Bah!" He tossed his hands.

"Let's focus on getting you to the archives," Xander said. "And sabotaging the rollout. Then we can go from there."

***

From his newer and considerably more gilded cage, Ario watched Xander's plan unfold in real time. The tariff worked in slowing down the distribution, but not as well as they might have liked. Truckers, not just working for the distribution centers, started striking when they learned they would lose wages due to the tariff. It did have the bonus of mobilizing the limited fleet of electric cars owned by the health department, which were, of course, vulnerable to guerilla attacks on the road. Bands of roving rebels not even connected to the resistance network started to target them, because often, an official traveling *with* the vaccines could be held hostage for a fat ransom. Even with 440 members accompanying the officials, the destruction was ultimately on the resistance's side.

Ario watched Catherine's veneer smudge. He couldn't say it wasn't a little satisfying.

"They just don't understand the public health risk," she muttered one evening over infernal tea.

"Maybe there's something I can do to help," he offered. The blustery November day sieged the castle with its winds, and he had to speak up to be heard.

"Dear Ario, I'm afraid this is above your pay grade," Catherine said, stuffing a macaron into her mouth.

"Well, why don't you let it be known that this will ultimately *stop* the miasma? That is the truth, right?" he asked innocently.

She smiled indulgently. "If only it were that simple, sweet prince. They say I'm a monster. They say I'm taking away bodily autonomy—as if they suddenly have started caring for magic users."

He had to tread carefully here, and not seem overeager. "When I was out in the world, there wasn't much I could see about the miasma. You must have some data that is more... well informed. As someone who received the vaccine, I can attest to its safety. And the others who have since gotten it, too."

Another smile. He knew he'd messed up. Catherine stood, set down her napkin, and patted him on the head. "Do you not mourn for your power?" she asked. "Do you not grieve it?"

Ario let some of his pain show. "Of course I do. But..." He cleared his throat. "I don't miss... running away. I want to believe that you're right, that this will all blow over."

"That's exactly what I want to stop, Ario. The running, the death." She paused, staring at him, her brows pulled tightly together. "Maybe... you *are* ready, to know."

He tried not to look too eager. "To know what?"

Catherine sighed. "I didn't want any of this. I wanted–"

The doors of the rose garden banged open. Xanthos and a minister tumbled through, both harried. "Mother, you must come quickly. It's urgent."

"There's a matter which requires your immediate attention," the minister insisted.

Catherine flushed pink. "Ario, I'm sure you can escort yourself back to your rooms." She darted out of the garden with them.

Ario fought to keep the grin off his face. Something was happening, he was certain, something huge.

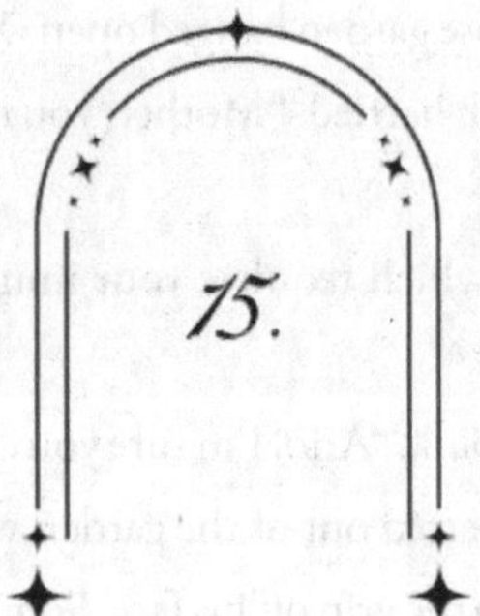

15.

He wouldn't find out what was going on for a few days. As much as he yearned to explore, he did as he was told and returned to his rooms. It felt oddly worse to be trapped in a larger space, because he had the freedom to pace, pen and paper to fret on, and books to provide solidly no diversion.

It occurred to him, not long after, to use the servants' passage. There was a nonzero risk that he would run into someone on them, but he decided it was a risk he would take. Ario half-expected the panel to be sealed shut, but either Catherine didn't know about it, Xander had opened it, or it had simply been forgotten. The latter theory was confirmed when he stepped in and immediately got a mouthful of dust and dank air. Hoping he wouldn't suffocate, he started downstairs.

Trying to recall his mental map of these passages was like looking through a very dim and blurry veil, his mind moving as slowly as it had immediately after his starvation. He knew the way to Ainsley's rooms–Catherine's rooms. But he couldn't possibly risk spying on her, and surely she had it bugged or possibly even warded to high hell. Yet another thing his power could take care of, if he simply had it.

There was the library, where he'd nipped adult books as a child. The library might not be a bad place to start, though he doubted the archives were there; surely Xander would have said so. Ario knew there was a *royal* archive somewhere in the castle. Possibly it was the same one Catherine was using, but he had no idea where it may be. He hadn't gotten far enough in his education to learn about it prior to the coup.

The library, then. If there was a librarian in situ, he could just say he was looking for something to read.

The passages were certainly narrower than he remembered. How had servants trespassed these with sheets, blankets, carts of food? Stairs wound down the turret of the castle, with a dumbwaiter on every floor. He opened one of the doors experimentally and saw, to his surprise, a fresh, hot meal rising on its way to someone. So these tunnels were not as unused as he thought; good to know. He popped out the panel he thought led to the library and found himself in the dungeons.

A body-deep shudder broke over him then, and his palms began to sweat. The wraiths might not sense magic, if any were patrolling, but surely someone would sense a stranger where he shouldn't be. Ario reached for the panel to re-enter the passages and found it closed, merged back into the wall. He pressed and banged on it fruitlessly. *Of course* it self-sealed. It could be an escape route.

Shit.

He took a deep breath, trying to calm his heart rate. He found himself glad he was wearing fully black. Ario decided to act like he was supposed to be there, and if anyone questioned him, he was on an errand for Xander.

Still, his body knew the dankness of this place, its stale musty desperate smell. Each cell had a slot several centimeters wide for wardens to look in on the prisoners. Again, there were those colorful placards: red and blue and orange, and now and again black. He heard a few disparate moans, and someone yelling angrily for a lawyer. The cells were also numbered. He quickened his pace, trying not to hear them. Some heard footsteps and cursed at him. What had Ario's cell number been? He didn't remember. Surely he had come with Xander through here enough times to find his way out–

He turned left, then right. There were still no guards, meaning the wardens were either sure nobody would try to escape, or there were cameras and sensors trained on him. Stupid. Stupid. Down another hall of inmates. And another. His breath came hard and fast and he tried to imagine his punishment for this little expedition. He had no magic to take, but was sure Xavier had no shortage of unpleasant medicines to administer–

This hall had folders, here, next to the doors. Ario slowed. He shouldn't be wasting time looking. His eyes fell onto the folder closest to him. It had a subject number, and a name, and a dosage schedule, with univ readings next to each. Ario looked towards the next; same deal. And the next, and the next. Each subject's reading was decreasing exponentially.

He had to get out of here, before Xavier returned. Quite possibly Xavier was in here already, somewhere. Ario turned to flee in the opposite direction and saw perhaps the only name that would've given him pause.

Subject 38

KINNEAR, AURORA

He froze. He supposed it was a divine sense of justice that had landed her here after her betrayal–but what Goddess would allow this? Against his better judgement, he reached for the metal knob and slowly slid open the slot to her cell.

Rory was slumped on a thin mat on the floor, dressed in a mundane hospital gown. Leather cuffs tethered her to a chain attached to the wall. Like him, she was emaciated, though he noted with relief that there was an empty meal tray in there with her. Her eyes were shut and she breathed very shallowly. Her hair was not patchy, but what he saw of it at the root was also black. He wondered if he should try to speak, to get her attention, but could he help her? He wouldn't be able to free her. Nobody would. He could only hope she was released once she had reached zero univs, but then, where would she go?

"Little prince. Hasn't anyone told you curiosity killed the cat?"

He gasped, harsh and raw, and within the slot, he saw Rory start awake as well. She said something, but he couldn't hear her.

Xavier. In the stark light, with a sharper mind, he did resemble his brother almost exactly. Only the lab coat, bearing, and sharpness of his expression told them apart. Xavier tsk'ed.

"I-I'm sorry," Ario stuttered. "I got lost... I was looking for the library... please don't hurt me." Some brave king he was.

"I do not wish to hurt you." He smiled, slow and sinuous. "Perhaps this is fated. I haven't examined you since my brother took over your treatment."

"You can see that is not necessary," Ario said quickly. "Point me in the direction of the exit and I'll be on my way."

"Now, now. You're my little success story. If anything, I owe *you*. Please let me serve you some tea. Take some samples. The *good* you're doing, prince, you have no idea."

He felt the sweat beading along his forehead.

"If it makes you feel better, I can summon your watchdog," Xavier said. "If you comply, I won't mention this little outing to Mother."

Ario braced himself. "Fine."

Xavier leaned over and slid Rory's slot shut with a *clank*. He placed his large palm on Ario's shoulder and forced him forward, down a few hallways and up a flight of stairs; Ario saw more and more of the subject folders next to cells. Xavier forced him into a room labeled INOCULATION.

There it was, there it all was, the accursed table and monitor, the palladium cuffs on chains dangling beside it, the same cabinets and–

His body tried to bolt, hot panic geysering in his chest and ears. Xavier took him by the shoulders. "Is it not fascinating, what the body remembers?" Xavier remarked.

"Let me go. Let me go. Let me go." He was barely conscious of the words, memories of the vaccine and the agony rending over him again and again.

Xavier forced him to sit on the table, yanked Ario's sleeve up, wiped foul-smelling disinfectant across his forearm, and jabbed in another needle. "You have such easy veins."

~~PRINCE? IS THAT YOU, PRINCE? BELOVED?~~ The voice exploded inside of his mind, static and vines and heat, almost the same exact pain as the removal of magic.

He had gone curiously numb, and not, he suspected, from any drug. Xavier took vials of blood, nail trimmings, a lock of hair, a swab of the inside of his cheek. He waved a reader over Ario, but it remained silent. He beamed. "Excellent. Alright, you're free to go."

Ario did not move.

"If you are going to be so obedient, I *suppose* I could take a sample of cerebrospinal fluid–"

~~HELP ME. HELP ME, PRINCE.~~

Why now? Why after being forsaken for so long?

Shrill keening flooded his mind, choking out his vision and perception.

***

He breathed in something sharp and pungent. Ario coughed and blinked, tasting the bitterness of smelling salts. He was in that infernal room–he flailed, but he was not tethered down.

"He is still quite frail," Xavier said.

Ario sat up. His underarms and back were coated with a sticky, cold sweat. Was that all... a nightmare?

"He has recently been very ill. I'm sure he must be disoriented."

"What?" Ario murmured, not faking it at all.

"Oh, good. You're awake. I'll bring you back to your room."

He was being pulled to his feet before he was ready, and the ground felt wobbly and unsteady.

"Better keep an eye on your little wanderer," Ario heard Xavier say. "I'd hate for anything to happen to my prize subject."

"I'm sure this was all a huge misunderstanding." An arm was slung over his shoulders, squeezing him hard, and forced Ario to walk out of the room.

Ario wobbled for fifteen or twenty meters before he heard Xander hiss, *"What* were you thinking? He'll be suspicious now."

"It really–was–an accident," Ario said. "I got lost."

Xander scoffed. "All you had to do was ask for a map, Ario, and I would have given it to you–of all the places for you to wander into–"

"There were so many voices," Ario murmured. "In the lab. I heard them…" And then he threw up on the inlaid parquet.

"Oh dear," Xander said.

***

Back in Ario's rooms, Xander paced in front of the fireplace. "You don't think that this could be some resurgence of your magic?"

"He *just* tested me. I still don't have any univs."

"Are you sure you weren't just–in a moment of panic–*thinking* you heard something?"

Ario scowled. "It wasn't *like* any hallucination or vision I've ever had. I *need* to get down to those archives. We might have less time than we thought. What is *happening* outside of the capitol? Do you know?"

Xander paused in front of the unlit grate. "The tariffs are causing unrest in the more liberal city-states. Lindenfell is threatening seces-sion. They refused a shipment of the vaccines, last I heard."

"Isn't that what we wanted?"

"Well, yes, but there are always *bodies.* People have always fought back and gotten killed. Before they always stopped. They're not stop-ping now."

This was nothing but good news, but the hopelessness in Xander's voice betrayed him.

"…You think Xanthos will retaliate."

"I know he will. He's a brat that hates losing—even strategically."

Ario sighed. "Martyrs will only further radicalize any rebellion." He didn't, couldn't, think about the amount of people who were dying. Not yet. "We can use this to our advantage. If the government starts to crumble in real time, then..." He trailed off. "What's the likelihood you can get a message out for me?"

"Don't you *care*, Ario?"

"Of course I care! These are my people! Anyway, since *when* have you cared about collateral damage?"

Xander inhaled sharply. "I see."

Ario forced himself to his feet. "Did you think we would do this bloodlessly? *You* were the one who suggested putting those truckers on the line. If people are willing to fight, we should let them. It's better than we could have hoped for. If I were out there–"

"But you're not," Xander said. "You would be with your family. Protecting them."

"If we... let the resistance know I am alive. We can coordinate with them. We'll hardly be able to siege the castle, but we may be able to cause disruptions in departments and services." Ario paused, but Xander said nothing. "Is this suddenly too real for you?"

"What if the miasma can't be stopped, or slowed, or fixed?"

Ario took a moment to consider this. "Then we owe it to the people to let them live their last days as comfortably as they can–and in as little fear as possible."

Xander sighed heavily. "I'll get you something innocuous to put your message in. Can't have you sending out branded stationery."

Ario sensed he'd misstepped, or perhaps misunderstood. "There's something else you're not saying."

"Should she successfully crush this rebellion? Should we get caught? What then?"

Ario glanced out the window. Ash-colored snow fell steadily, in a dance. "I suspect we wouldn't be able to care about anything again."

"And should you succeed? The penalty for treason, under Ainsley, was execution. Is this the fate I have to face—death on any path? Have I no time to openly atone?"

"I would not execute you, Xander."

"I guess that is a comfort." He smiled, tiredly. "Unless summoned by Mother, stay put, prince."

That night, sleepless, Ario tossed and turned in his too-soft, too-large bed. He'd always assumed these little schemes of his would be largely pointless, and he'd inevitably die by Catherine's hand. But to think they actually had a hope of, if not succeeding, making a difference; it made his heart race frantically and flooded his mouth with the taste of tin.

One luxury of a gilded cage: he could take a hot bath. Most of the upper-floor taps had some sort of filter to get rid of the worst of the poison, but the water still had a definite chlorine aura to it. The window on the right-hand wall revealed the rising full moon outside.

Dare he pray?

Ario knelt on the soft lavender rug in front of his filling tub and, as he had hundreds or thousands of times before, pressed his palms together and began whispering the full moon prayer. His heart surged hotly, drawing him forward as if on a string, and his head was being forced under the hot water with an irresistible pressure. Ario floundered for his arms, for his legs, to kick and push against whatever force was assailing him. The water felt like a noose, tightening around his throat—

Ripping breaking searing neurons synapses flashing meat and blood and meat and blood heavy blind eye blind eyes an absence. Absence like a field, where we should be, but we are not. We start to map ourselves to the meat creature, the wobbly jelly that is its small life crying out for chemical reaction. So fragile. So so fragile. All along we never understood, not fully. The experience is almost novel, if anything could be novel in this unending instance.

The bones in the appendages of the meat force the hard bones of the skull out of the boiling hot silk. The sacks of its lungs expand, contract, flooding the blood with chemicals and re-establishing what this creature calls consciousness. Its sight is limited, more than most creatures of its type, flat and lacking distance.

We look through this creature's eye. For an organ made of meat and jelly, it can see relatively well. Up. We must get up. Must twitch the bunches of nerves and muscles and position the bones so that we are vertical. When weight and pressure reaches its pelvis, it stumbles, arms circling automatically against the crushing and never-ending force of our gravity.

Each move, each twist, takes hundreds, millions, billions of its cells and nerves working in perfect harmony. It is as complex as the universe. It is unbearably simple. It is a neutron star in a glass box.

It feels us within it. And it hates *us.*

The hatred tastes like strawberries. Like sea air. We breathe it. Nobody has hated us. Not like this.

GET OUT OF ME, the creature asserts, forcing its will against us. The will is as strong as tissue paper compared to ours, but its resistance feels good, so we let it. GET OUT OF ME.

It is using language—the peculiar smacking and clacking of teeth and tongue and lip—and that tickles us.

The creature is moving. It moves across its constructed habitat, which the folded strands of memory in its brain inform it is beautiful, towards a pair of shears resting on the surface of a desk. It takes the shears. Opens them. It raises the dull blade against the heartline of its palm and—

Beloved, you musn't–

Drags the blade along it, revealing ragged flesh only barely concealed with brown flesh prior.

We feel pain. Pain is not novel.

The creature's larynx contracts and chafes in a squeal, a squeal we've heard it make before, when it was on its hands and knees forcing another creature from its self–

It presses the blade against its wrist, where the heat concentrates. "I'll do it. I swear."

Beloved–

Our presence is causing the meat distress, and not just the ragged wound on its palm. Its synapses are hot, the nerves too strung, the balloon of a heart pumping too hard. We cannot remain long.

Beloved, you must–

Lifeblood pours onto the tile. It drags us over to the window. "How do I. Stop it."

We do not understand.

"Miasma. The poison." It coughs, and our vision seesaws with vertigo. "You want me to help you so badly. Goddess, I intone you: how do I stop it?"

We look at our creation, our curse, the eye of our eternal watcher ceaseless and glowing in the sky. We do not know what the creature means–

"Dying. We're dying. It's eating the magic. It's eating you."

Oh. Oh dear, dear creature, you do not understand at all.

It is not eating us. It IS us.

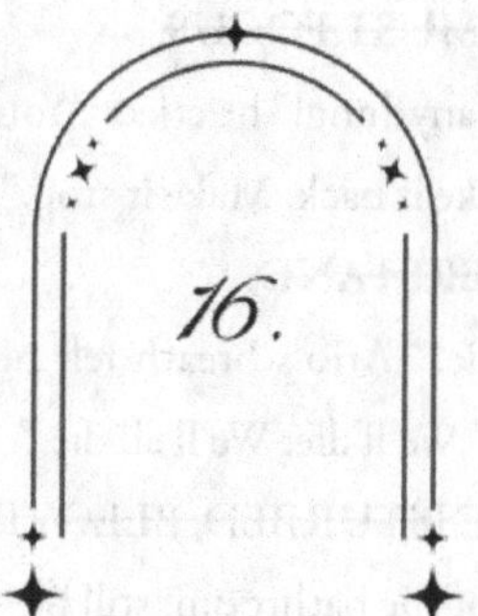

16.

A scream tore its way out of his throat. Then another, and another, until he felt the unfortunately-familiar rip in his esophagus and the taste of blood.

Blood. All over the white tiles, his gray pajamas, turning the abandoned bathwater pink.

The force, the being, the *weight* pressed itself against him again. BELOVED, YOU MUST STAUNCH THE BLEEDING.

Evelyn had always said the Goddess was unknowable. She had never said She–it–them–would feel so stunningly inhuman, the wefts of its consciousness grafting hotly onto his. Ario felt, if he just stopped concentrating for two seconds, his mind would liquify into blood and amylase, and–

BELOVED, YOU MUST FOCUS.

"I don't have to do anything!" he cried. "You. Do you have any idea what you've done? Take it back. Make it stop."

I DO NOT UNDERSTAND.

"Everything will die!" Ario's breath felt hot and suspicious as it geysered in his lungs. "We'll die. We'll all die."

WHY ARE YOU DISTURBED, BELOVED?

Ario hobbled out of the bathroom, still bleeding freely, over to the servant's passage. It had not, as he feared, been boarded up. "Get out of me," he hissed.

BELOVED, IT IS NATURAL. IT IS THE WAY OF THINGS.

"You're wrong. I know you're wrong. You're lying. There has to... be a way to make it stop." Hot flashes scoured his vision.

BELOVED, PLEASE STOP FIGHTING. IT'S WHAT WE WANT.

"What about what *I* want? Or the rest of us? Your creations? You'll simply let us–" He choked, tasting more blood. "What about the magic?"

WHAT IS IT YOU CALL MAGIC?

"This–this–bloody connection between us, my power, the *baby* you made me have." He pounded his wounded fist on the wall, liking the pain. "Your power, your will–what was it all *for?*"

THOSE TWO WORDS. THEY ARE THE SAME. MAGIC. MIASMA. ONE STOPS ONE FROM SUBSUMING THE OTHER. THAT CANNOT BE. WE MUST CONSUME. BELOVED. PLEASE HELP.

The crushing force abruptly left his body, leaving behind a fierce headache behind his blind eye and a smarting in his chest. Ario frantically fumbled at the panel he sought, smearing a bloody handprint against it. He could not breathe, could not *see*, around the crushing waves of devastation.

Catherine was awake. She was sitting at her desk, typing furiously in a small laptop, dressed in a heavy, deep-red robe. Her patchy blonde hair splayed loosely against her shoulders, revealing the odd bald spot. The only sources of light in the room was the fire, the computer screen, and the moon outside. She started when she saw him, reaching for a dagger near the mousepad, but relaxed. "Ario–what are you doing here–are you *bleeding?*"

He slumped onto her pink carpet. Catherine rushed over, snatching a tea towel from a nearby cart of treats.

"How did you even know about those passages?" she asked. "What exactly were you planning?"

"You were right," he wheezed.

"Right about *what*, dear?" She wrapped his hand firmly. "You'll need stitches–I should escort you to the physician on call. She can patch you up. How did you get hurt?"

His vision swam wildly, and his body felt so heavy and artificial. Ario's skin crawled, rejecting whatever had just been inside him. And everywhere, a dripping, sticky *grief*.

"Ario?" Catherine prompted.

"She started it. She started it. It's all Her fault." He swallowed the blood in his throat. "You were right... we have to starve Her."

Sadness took hold in her face, in sharp relief from the firelight. "I've been meaning to tell you, Ario. The truth. The *real* truth. Can you stand? Why don't you come sit. You poor thing."

Woodenly, he let her guide him over to a small chintz sofa. This drawing room was set up similarly to his own, he realized, except everything was in deep pinks and reds. Catherine fetched a wool blanket and spread it over his lap.

She sat next to him on the sofa and took his uninjured hand. "What happened, Ario? How did you find out?"

"I tried to... pray. She spoke to me. She said... she had to keep consuming. Magic." He shuddered and heaved.

"She spoke *to* you?" Catherine asked. "When you have no magic? That should not be possible."

Probably best not to explain his escapade into Xavier's dungeons. "How did you... find out?" he asked. "H-how–"

"I've known from the beginning," she said. "Before I even took over."

"But *how*?" he asked hoarsely.

"I'm *getting* there. Let me get you some tea. You've had a shock."

"*Fuck* your tea."

Catherine frowned. "I understand you're upset, Ario, but please do not snap." From the same snack cart, she poured tea into a clean drinking glass. "It's likely not quite warm, but it's better than nothing. The answer is quite anticlimactic–this being you call Goddess *said* this would happen." When he didn't take the glass from her, she set it on the paper-laden coffee table. "Excuse the mess. I wasn't exactly expecting guests this late."

"In what scripture?" he asked bitterly. "I've memorized them all."

"Your namesake, Ilario, was one of the first archmages, was he not?"

"...Yes. I've read most his writings."

"But not all."

"Well–some were burned, during the great fire during the..." he stuttered. "First miasma."

She leaned in a little closer. "Not everything you were taught was true, Ario. Ainsley lied just as much as I lie to the people."

He shook his head. "Evelyn wouldn't teach me wrong things."

"She would if she herself believed it to be true."

This couldn't be happening. Every time he thought the heartbreak couldn't get larger, it did, until it felt like it would shatter him. His heartline ached.

"I was visiting the palace, sixteen years ago now, for some...congressional matter or another, it didn't matter. I was pregnant with Xanthos and couldn't sleep. So I wandered," she said. "One of my roles was preservation of historical record, so I had unconditional access to the royal archives. I figured I'd do some light reading into my favored topic at the time–pre-Chiaran sea trade, I know, not terribly interesting–and I noticed, when moving some of those boxes of documents about, this... curious little bundle of papers. The archives were so neat and proper that it was quite unusual." She paused, her eyes glazing over slightly at the memory. "I think someone or something must have left it to be found."

Ario looked at his hands. His wounded palm had started to thrum with pain, a welcome sting. He recalled the Goddess's force on his body–but it had also felt like it was the first time She had ever attempted something like this. And that She hadn't quite wanted to. His prayer, magic or not, had finally reached Her. Everything he'd ever learned about magic and prayer had indicated that this should not be possible. Not that the Goddess allegedly shunned her mundane followers (if there were any), but mundanes certainly didn't have the bandwidth to *experience* Her. Even though he just had. What else was wrong about what he'd taught?

How does it feel, Goddess, he wondered bitterly, *to have your autonomy stripped away?*

"I suppose you could call it prophecy," Catherine said. "Ilario alleged he had communed with the Goddess, and She shared with him visions of the future. He accurately predicted natural disasters, political and technological developments, and... the miasma. I would have to look at the papers for the exact wording, but he felt *certain* that the first time would not be the last. That the Goddess would use it to plant seeds to weaken and break our society so that the monarchy would become powerless."

Prophecy. He scowled. Evelyn always said never to believe in *prophecy*.

"That's how I felt too," Catherine began. "I must've spent hours cross-referencing events, checking their veracity. Every single one was right."

"So how does he say it ends, then?" Ario asked tiredly. "Why would the Goddess want to kill Her creation? Nothing is making any sense."

She shook her head. "Has the Goddess spoken to you, before? Has She granted you any insights?"

He shuddered and flexed his fingers, wincing with pain. "Nothing as unambiguous as that. Until now. She called me beloved... but She also said that miasma and magic are the same. But that one must consume the other."

"Well, everything has a shadow, right? The moon has a dark side. It's believed that our universe expands infinitely, from one concentrated hot instance of conflagration, and that we may inevitably all come back together. These... forces of the universe that we assumed were diametric are just two sides of one process. She decided to unbalance the system."

"Yes, I get that, but *why?*"

Catherine took his hand. "You're bleeding through the towel. You must get stitches." She cleared his throat. "I find it strange that *you*, the supposed blessed Heir, are asking *me* that. Surely you must know Her better than I do."

"That's just it. I don't know Her at all. If the trials of these past months mean anything... Is it just that She's *hungry*? Or is She tired of this ant farm we call a life?"

"Come, Ario. We can walk and talk at the same time." Catherine pulled on his elbow. "Surely you've heard of the concept of heartlines. That's not insignificant, considering where you chose to hurt yourself."

At this time of night, the castle was mostly dark, save the odd emergency exit light or sconce. The darkness had heft to it, and the smell of the miasma was more potent, bitter and slick.

Heartlines. That old fairy tale. All of the bonds of one's life, neatly marked on the body on the palms. Hadn't he made supernatural pacts—with Peony, with Mara, and Evelyn and Michael? Those were tied to his soul. Were those pacts null now that he had no magic? "Are you saying..." Why was this palace so big? His eye and hand ached, and vertigo threatened to claim him. "That She is as bonded to us as we are to each other?"

"I don't know. Am I?"

Ario was silent for a moment. "I don't know how I could break something that large... especially without magic. I wouldn't even know where it *is*."

"I would encourage you to think, Ario. You would know this better than I. Let us get your hand mended and take a breath. It is *very* late, and I am a *very* busy autocrat."

His head was aching too badly for him to argue much more.

***

Ario slept for at least twelve hours: after experiencing the unpleasantness of stitches, the physician had given him a bitter tasting pill that plunged him into a painless, heavy sleep. When he woke, for a moment he felt that everything he'd learned the night before was a terrible dream; at least, until he went to relieve himself and saw the dried blood spattered across the bathroom sink and floor.

His chest spasmed. So it was real, then. It had happened.

What was he supposed to *do*?

Surely Xander did not know what Catherine knew regarding the miasma. If Catherine really—and he shuddered to think it—and truly was doing this for *the greater good*, would Ario still kill her? Was there some unbelievable way she could peacefully cede power? Should they really work together?

And this growing nascent rebellion. What of them? They faced uncertain doom at the hands of Xanthos. Should Ario somehow be able to tell them the truth of the miasma—and for them to believe it when many of them had their own religious beliefs—what were they supposed to do?

What was perhaps the hardest to digest was the notion that the Goddess was willingly killing everything he had been raised to protect. According to Her, all life was sacred. Surely that applied to Her own life as well? Then again, *who* had interpreted the Goddess's will in such a way to translate these teachings? They were proving very wrong.

If he ever saw Evelyn again, this would break her. And yet Ario yearned to talk to her about it. What could he express in the message Xander was supposed to communicate?

Ario found some rags and cleaner under the bathroom sink and began wiping up his mess, wincing as the stitches pulled the skin of his palm. Well, certainly now that Catherine believed him to be on her side—and he may or may not actually be, making his stomach bubble with nausea—she would trust him to move about the castle unfettered. He really should find Xander and tell him all this expediently.

Perhaps the archives had information about heartlines. Ario didn't trust Catherine, but he did have a feeling her claims had some water. He'd need some proof himself. Perhaps it wasn't true after all...

He recalled the way that She had felt, crawling up inside him. How She'd nearly dashed him against the rocks, all to tell him there was no *way* to stop it. He took a moment to think about all of the "blessings" he'd received since coming to Lindenfell. She'd told him to trust Peony, She'd blessed Michael's passage. She'd forced the pregnancy and the power that came with it; surely that meant She valued life's continuation. There had to be something else that could point to other motives.

Unless the force he'd felt was no Goddess, but something else entirely? That didn't feel right...

He changed into clean clothing and set off to find Xander, only to realize he had no idea where the man's quarters were. There weren't exactly placards on doors, not up here. After wandering around aimlessly hoping to run into him, Ario turned around and went downstairs towards the library, taking the open and obvious paths. Again, if he did see staffers or servants, none of them paid him any interest.

Housed in one of the main, older wings on the first floor, the library used to be continent-renowned for the depth and breadth of its research, with several million books, periodicals, state of the art computers, as well as priceless art and artifacts. Ario knew that there had been purges at some point, where materials had been gathered and destroyed. Had those materials actually been destroyed? Moved? Had the books that had been burned been decoys?

It was quite possible he still wouldn't be able to get any uncensored information, but if he were not doing something, going somewhere,

Ario feared he would give into the cavern of despair and confusion that had replaced his heart.

Today the castle was, apparently, open to tourists. He saw a band of school-aged children, led by a pale woman in a three-piece navy suit, cross from the hallway leading to the old temple towards the library. Dressed in staid tweed uniforms, the children seemed... normal. Some laughed and joked with each other, others whispered furiously to pay attention to the guide, that *this would be on the test*. A few other small clumps of people milled about as well. Ario fought not to react at the sight of them. To see regular *people*, people who would return to normal *mundane* lives, was almost as alien as the creature that had taken him over the previous evening. Perhaps the world hadn't ended in these endless months... at least not yet.

Ario matched his pace to that of the tourists and pretended he belonged here. He should've worn a coat, for realism's sake. He joined a queue of people looking to enter the library. In front of the large, grand double doors were scanners, both for metal and magic. At least he knew he wouldn't set them off. A homeland security officer boredly waved him through.

The library opened all around him, and a large seed of nostalgia settled heavily in his stomach. How many hours had he spent here with Evelyn, with Ainsley, with this nanny or that governess? This library had been his school prior to his escape. Much like the rose garden, the library had a main chamber which opened to other, smaller chambers, each of which was framed with tall, ornately carved columns. New signs indicated different reading rooms. The crystal dome let in the weak winter sunlight, which reflected tepidly onto the smooth wooden bookcases. Cheap, industrial black runners covered the parquet in the more trafficked areas.

Everywhere, people milled, casually browsing through the more common tomes, checking out items at a new-to-him circulation desk. He wandered instinctively towards the old card catalog, but found it had been moved or removed and replaced with a bank of public computers, most of which were taken. Ario wandered over to one, wondering if it might provide some assistance. A popup welcomed him to the palace, cautioned that all searches were monitored, and asked him to limit his browsing time to a half hour to accommodate others. Opening the internet browser brought him to the catalog.

Ario hadn't intended for his search to leave a trail; cards could always be replaced, after all. While the public computer might mask his browsing, surely a camera had spotted him. Catherine might suspect it was him if she somehow knew he was searching for information about heartlines. Would this library even have tomes about magic? Surely those must be heavily restricted and the users flagged. But, he supposed, because he'd already been caught, and she'd reminded him of the concept, then surely there would be no consequences for this.

His fingers fumbled over the keyboard, clumsy after months with little use. Evelyn would have forbidden Peony use of her emails and social media, and she herself changed domains frequently; Ario had no way of contacting her. He had some burner emails for some of Marko's people, but emailing them from a capitol computer could have unforeseen consequences.

Maybe he should just ask a librarian.

Ario cleared his internet history and went over to another new addition - a research desk just off the main chamber. A tired looking young woman with very pale skin, red hair, and heavy, dark-rimmed glasses typed away rapidly. "How can I help you?" she asked, without enthusiasm.

"I'm doing research for a paper–" He began in his best non-Land-fallan accent.

"For university?"

"Yes."

"You have a copy of your permit? Or did you put it in our portal?"

Those cursed permits. Peony used to bemoan whenever she had to submit one for a completely innocuous subject. Ario made a show of searching his pockets. "Oh dear... I must've..." He huffed. "I left my bag on the train. It must be in there."

She met his eyes. Hers were a dull green. "That's okay. What's the name?"

"Sorry?"

"The name. On the permit?"

He offered one of his many aliases–a generic, but believable, name. Hopefully there was someone with the same name who had used the library recently.

The librarian shook her head. "What university did you say you were from? Maybe you have an ID? Or was that also in your bag?" Her voice dripped with skepticism.

"It's been a simply terrible day," he said. "I'm from Night-bridge–the history department." A known, but not too prestigious, school in a heavily loyalist territory.

The librarian relaxed. "Maybe I can help you. What are you looking for?"

"My term paper is on pre-revolutionary propaganda. I was won-dering..."

She looked sheepish, but firmly shook her head. "Anything like that, I absolutely need your permit. If you want, I can help you fill one out now?"

Ario sighed heavily. "Let me contact my university. Maybe they can send it over."

"Sure. I'll be here until close."

Stupid. So much for that.

Defeated, he made his way over to the fiction section of the library and poured over the new releases. He supposed he would just have to ask Catherine or Xander, or sneak back here at night and try to use the librarian's terminal. Or just get to the damn archives.

Ario spent an unremarkable afternoon reading in one of the squashy window chairs, the words hardly reaching his brain as he turned page after page. Even most of the furniture had been changed for hardier, cheaper pieces that could stand up to higher levels of use.

He snuck out of the library when a particularly spirited gaggle of university students swept into this section of the library, and took a roundabout way back to his rooms. It was not at all surprising to see Xander there, patiently waiting.

At the sight of Ario, his lip curled into an unhappy sneer. "Another field trip?"

"Of a sorts."

"What happened to your hand?"

Ario pulled down his sweater sleeve, trying to conceal the bandages better. "What do you know of heartlines?" he asked instead.

"Me? Not terribly much, I'm afraid. I've been waiting to tell you what I've learned of the rebellion."

Ario squinted through the gloom. Xander was noticeably rumpled, his hair frizzy like Evelyn's when she got stressed, his black button up wrinkled. "Are you quite alright?"

"The head of the department for health and hominid services has *resigned*. He was caught harboring a friendly, and distributing information about the vaccine to said friendly. I should be at an emergency meeting now."

"Well, why aren't you?" Ario asked slowly. "Isn't this... good for us? If someone so high up is joining our side?"

"Well, he can't join our side. He's already been executed. It's all over the news."

Ario squeezed his eyes shut and sat on the sofa across from Xander.

"My brother is suspicious of me," Xander admitted.

"Xavier?"

"Xanthos."

"But why?"

Xander tugged on one of his braids. "He finds it suspicious that one of our top staffers walks away with vaccine information at the same time you have free range of the castle."

"But I've no communication devices. If they really wanted to, they could view all the security footage I've doubtless been in–"

"And I'm your only alibi. Xavier could very well volunteer information about your little adventure. I suspect he isn't because it amuses him."

Ario leaned against his knees and took a deep breath. Xander had started a fire in the fireplace, and the woodsmoke was heavy in his throat. "Your mother wouldn't believe that."

"Wouldn't she?"

"I spoke to her early this morning. It was... it's been difficult." He swallowed and pretended the ache in his throat was from the poorly ventilated fire. "I prayed last night." He told Xander everything that had happened. "She should not have been able to answer that prayer. Not without magic in my body."

Xander shot up and started to pace. "So it's hopeless, then."

"No. No, I don't think so."

"What are you supposed to *do*, Ario? Just let magic die?"

Realization lay around him silkily. The itching, aching panic dissolved. "No."

"Then what?"

He held up his injured hand. "I figure out a way to sever the bond."

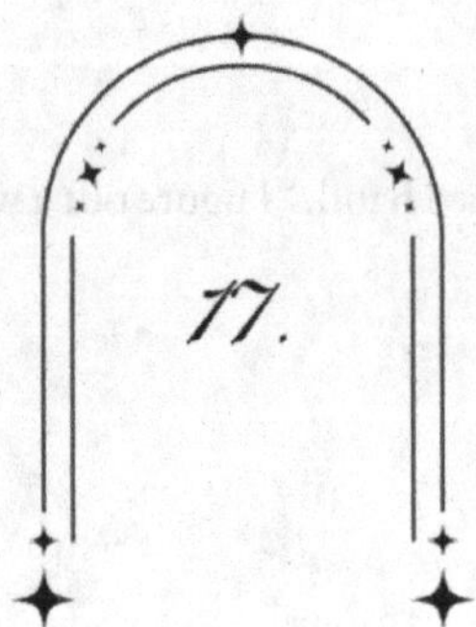

17.

X ander stared at him.

"It seems my bond to Her transcends magic. If I could only figure out some way to break the bond between Her and us..." Ario traced his finger lightly against the bandaged, and flinched at the pain.

"But you have no power," Xander said. "How is your will supposed to defy that of a Goddess?"

"There's a piece of Her within me. And in my... daughter. I've created pacts with others—that of my priestess and guard, and... well."

He trailed off before he let slip about Mara. "Those pacts can be broken. This must just be on a larger scale."

Xander slumped against the cushions.

"If I am able to be with or near my daughter, I might be able to utilize her bond to the Goddess by proxy."

"Wouldn't doing that hurt her?"

"I don't *know*," Ario moaned. "I couldn't... I couldn't do that to Peony."

Xander squinted. "The child's parent?"

"Her mother. Yes." He reached automatically with his uninjured hand for his throat, feeling the absence of the pendant. "But if it meant... saving the world, then..." He breathed out. "I don't know if I could do it." He tried to imagine himself... what, standing over her? Amalia's face was hazy in his mind. "I don't imagine the Goddess would take kindly to infant sacrifice. I just know the *power* I had when I was pregnant might have been enough to do this."

Xander wrinkled his nose. "I don't suppose another child of yours would have the same effect."

"Even if we had an additional nine months, I would rather die than go through that again. Besides, it's only the *Heir*, so even if we somehow harvested eggs and got a willing surrogate, it's moot. If I'd had siblings, they'd be no more powerful than Ainsley is." Ario swallowed. He felt that he was shaking. "There must be information about rituals somewhere that can help me. If I convince your mother I want to eliminate the Goddess, what do you think are the odds she would let me access arcane information to do so?"

Xander just shook his head repeatedly. "I don't know. She seems to favor you. It might be possible *if* that information actually wasn't destroyed like she said it was. Ario, this sounds like a long shot. Worse than our chances of successfully collapsing the government. *If* you are successful in severing the Goddess's bonds, and the miasma miraculously disappears, where would that leave the state of the planet? Isn't the notion that She is what allows life to exist?"

Ario pursed his lips. "Is this a roundabout way of telling me you believe in Her?"

Xander scowled. "It is hard to refute the evidence She's real, at this point. Especially if Mother believes this too. I wonder…" He tapped his fingers together, but fell silent.

Ario got up to lay another log on the fire. "What is it you're thinking?"

"Do we communicate that to the public?"

"The public mostly knows. That the world is dying, at least." The flames felt particularly hot against his wounded palm. What he wouldn't give for a healing salve. "Most of the resistance believes that magic can provide a solution—much like I did. Your mother thinks taking magic *away*—through murder and now through this vaccine—will starve the miasma."

"And what do you think?" Xander asked.

"That vaccine wouldn't rid the remaining magic in the earth. It would only buy time for the miasma to eat what's left. And then it may very well dissipate—but we'll all be dead. If I cut Her bond to the magic, weaken Her, we might have a chance to stop everything. Any political agenda would have to run in perfect counterpoint."

Xander paused, his brows furrowed. His hair was so pale that Ario saw the puckers in the skin of his face. "That could bolster our rebellion significantly. Even the most staunch fatalists still need to eat."

"The problem is that I need to know *how* to do this. I need arcane information."

"I guess you'll just have to persuade Mother," Xander commented. "Not that you intend to sever the bond... but perhaps you may find more information on how to effectively "starve" Her."

"Yes," Ario said. "Are you still able to get a message out for me?"

"With things so chaotic? I'm likely being monitored, but yes. That's part of the reason I came to see you." He reached into his pocket and took out a brightly colored birthday card. "Write what you need to on here. Who am I conveying it to?"

"The former high priestess."

Xander instructed him to leave the note under a particular candelabra in the old art gallery. After that, he swept out of the room, looking harried and uncomfortable.

Ario sat on the floor in front of the fire, using a hardcover novel as a makeshift writing desk. Evelyn had drilled a relatively complex cipher into him soon after their escape that he could use should they be separated. He'd hoped to never have to use it.

He first composed his message in plain language on a piece of scrap paper:

> *Dear Evelyn,*
>
> *This is the first time I've been able to secure communications. I am alive, but I am altered. Any rumors you may have heard about the vaccine are true; I have lost my magic. I desperately hope that you, Peony, Michael, and even Mara are keeping safe and well. Tell Peony I miss her dearly.*
>
> *Things are not what they seem at the castle. I have an ally in someone very high up. He has helped orchestrate some chaos and some smaller rebellions have been brewing. There are more mundanes on our side than you'd think.*

> *Even powerless, I sense that I may be able to do something about the miasma. I have received revelation from the Goddess even as I am now: the miasma is Her will and Her doing. I am so sorry.*
>
> *We must all work together. The tides of change are coming.*
>
> *All my love,*
>
> *Ario*

He ciphered the message and burned the original version, watching the flames leap. He wondered, briefly, *if* the message was even properly conveyed, would Mara be able to track him here? She'd been reliant on the smell of his magic. But being able to speak with her would make this a lot easier.

Later in the evening, Ario stole out of his rooms down towards the art gallery. The hallways were almost completely devoid of staff aside from the odd wraith sentinel. Little puffs of dust squished out of the thick carpets, bringing with it that metallic musty smell of miasma. He realized he'd grown used to it.

He found said candelabra with ease–a heavy, ornate, thoroughly ugly wrought iron *thing* from the pre-miasma era. Checking quickly to make sure he was out of sight of any cameras, he tucked the note under a suspiciously loose description placard and spent a few moments pretending to examine the artwork, as if he were merely bored. The paintings he remembered had been twisted and warped by memory. He walked past landscapes of the continent, far too bright in color, blushing maidens in fluffy gowns, swashbuckling scenes of war. Conspicuously, the royal portraits were missing.

He'd only had a handful himself; one with his parents as an infant, one with Ainsley after their assassination, and one alone at five (and he very distinctly remembered the starchy, itchy white dress he'd been forced into). That child–fat with childhood, with long lilac curls–felt as far removed from him as the moon.

Ario wandered back to his infernal rooms to think about what to say to Catherine.

A blustery, horrible winter storm overtook the capitol. Wind screeched through the courtyards and made the double-paned windows wobble. Ario watched the snow fall and tried to remember the last time it had been white, gentle, and puffy. He watched human servants attempt to clear paths through the courtyard most visible from this vantage point. The cold would pass, the snow would melt, leaving the ground feeling oddly squishy.

Where was Peony in this weather? He recalled winters spent with Evelyn holed up in whatever shelter they could find–caves, basements, cabins in the woods, houses if they were lucky–and hours spent too close together. And... their daughter? Was she warm? Looked after?

His stretch marks had faded to a sickly, hard-to-see pale brown, but he still caught sight of them in the mirror occasionally. For every thought about Amalia he had ten about Peony. If he were truly honest with himself, if it meant his daughter or the world, could he choose the world?

He hadn't held her much in the weeks prior to his trafficking. The more he tried to recall her face, the harder it became. She'd had a smell, he remembered that much, like oats and chai, regardless of what soaps Peony used on her.

Would he ever get to actually be a dad? He scarcely remembered his own father; shadows of pats on the head. His clothing had been confiscated when he was taken in, he knew, and had not yet been returned. Xander had done his intake. Why hadn't it occurred to him sooner? Surely nobody would see the harm in returning a piece of jewelry.

But Ario did not see Xander for several days, not even to remove the stitches; the nameless, stoic castle physician did so, arriving without announcement. The castle was closed to tourists because of the storm, and he wandered, trying to perhaps find a radio or television that could illuminate what was happening–even the regime's spin on what was happening. The storm had surely slowed vaccine distribution. But it would also have slowed any other riots.

Catherine summoned him one of these endless, snowy afternoons to her quarters. She did not bother with the pretense of tea and looked relatively undone, puffy and glassy-eyed. "Ario, I am sorry, it has been a chaotic time. I did not want you to feel forgotten." She gestured him to the settee where he'd had his last breakdown. "It is truly like herding cats."

"Has something happened?" he asked innocently.

"I forget you have no access to the news," she murmured. Her hair was lank, greasy, the bags under her eyes purple and pronounced. "Yes. Quite a lot has happened. The winter has been very rough on the people. I've been having to advise Xanthos on military maneuvers. He is so *green*. I knew I should have waited to confirm him–" She sighed and composed herself. "You do not need to worry."

Even in his sweater, and cardigan, the dank, raw chill was reaching Ario. He fought not to shiver. "I've been doing a great deal of thinking," he said. "I wonder if there's something in the grimoires, something that can help us expedite the starvation process. I may not have magic, but I can still interpret a spell book just fine."

Something flashed in her dark eyes. "Is that something you could look for? That you could do?"

Ario tried not to look excited. "Yes, of course. If they still exist."

"I never destroyed those books. I'd rather thought... I'd manage to get a way to use them."

He frowned. "You mean me."

She bobbed her head. The lamplight threw the wrinkles on her face into relief.

"Is there... any way to... *restore* my power?" His pulse thumped painfully in his ears. "So that maybe I could do *more*–?"

"Xavier is confident that, if you were to rebound, it would have happened by now. The vaccine–it uses the miasma, in a way. Fools your immune system into destroying the magic before it can be used. At least that's how I understand it. Science was never my strong suit." She shrugged demurely and pulled her dark shawl tighter around her shoulder. "The grimoires are in my personal archives. I'll have someone escort you."

Ario hesitated. "Xander?"

She pursed her lips. "Xander is waylaid at the moment."

"Is he ill?"

"No." She did not elaborate further.

Ario looked at his knees, feeling the blood rise in his face.

Catherine softened, her hands fidgeting in her lap. "You have developed a rapport, have you not?"

Time to play ball. "I suppose. He is the person I see most often, aside from you."

"May I confess something?"

Ario swallowed the taste of his heart. "Anything."

"Xander is wily. Strange. I don't understand him. My other sons are like open books. But Xander... always closed part of his heart, to me."

Lie bigger. "He always speaks of you warmly."

"He doesn't have much of a mind for government. That tariff was his idea, and look at the mess we're in." She spread her hands.

"Tariff?"

"Oh—you wouldn't know. Trade disputes. Boring!" She forced a laugh. "His labor is needed elsewhere, is all. I assure you my guards are discreet. Should you like to go now, they can take you."

"I know you are... very busy," he said. "I should give you the time back."

She clapped her hands smartly, twice. "Very well. Jude! Perseus! Please escort the prince to the archives."

The doors of her quarters opened and in came two wraiths, in decorative armor, slinky and indistinct. Ario swallowed bile.

"He is not to be bothered. Thank you." She offered a last simpering smile to Ario. "I look forward to your findings, prince."

He tried to smile back. It felt like a grimace. He was finally getting what he'd wanted for months, and the victory was soured with worry for Xander. *Waylaid* could mean dead. Or caught. Surely she wouldn't kill one of her children? As he trailed after the shadowy guards, Ario had a very cold realization. Much in the same way he'd thought about sacrificing Amalia for his plans, perhaps Catherine had thought about sacrificing Xander.

Catherine's archives were hidden in the bowels of the castle, behind two sets of interlocking steel doors. The wraiths saw him through past these doors, and then waited there, passive, for more orders.

Ario looked over his shoulder, then back to the creatures. "Are you truly as mindless as you seem?" he asked them. "I've met wraiths that seem to have a semblance of self. Do you remember anything?"

Their silvery eyes remained unblinking.

The harsh fluorescent light fell onto the new scar on his palm. "I wonder if the death of *my* magic resulted in a wraith," he mused out loud. "Though I doubt vanquishing it would return the power."

Neither of them reacted. Ario held up his hand, as if to coax them to touch back, but nothing happened. "Alright. Enough faffing about."

As he turned to the massive sets of stacks, he heard a soft *"wait."*

Tingling adrenaline flooded him. Trembling, Ario looked back towards his erstwhile guards. One had pulled away from the other, who remained perfectly still. "Can you understand me?" he asked it.

"In bits. And pieces. Through a... veil." The voice had no gender; it had hardly any *sound,* much like the wraiths he had seen in Lindenfell. "It is cold here."

"Do you remember your name?"

"I think... it started with an S."

"Does Catherine know you're sentient?"

The edges of its form shimmered; either in recognition, or in fear. "She does not hear when I speak. Nobody ever does. Except for you." Wisps of darkness flickered in front of its eyes.

If magic had been the conduit for the first time he heard them, it should reason that he should not be able to hear this being now. It seemed that the rules were bending. But to what degree, and why? Why would the Goddess provide an assist if She wanted death? "Where are you?"

"A place. A cold place."

"Like you're very distant from here?"

"Can you kill me?" it asked.

Ario exhaled. "I'm sorry. I don't have the means right now." A lump formed in his throat, and it tasted like copper. "Your... partner. Are they–"

"A husk."

The phenomena must be rare, then. "I see."

"I want to be *whole,*" it insisted, its form quivering. "I feel hotly smeared across the world."

"I have no power with which to free you," Ario said. "As soon as I find the means, S, you will rest." He lifted his palm again and offered it to the creature, who reciprocated. Ario expected the bite of its fog to hurt, as it always had before, but it merely felt like winter chill. "I promise."

"Hotly smeared." That was how it had felt when the Goddess was inside his body. Ario felt like enough of a shell of himself as it was–he tried to imagine what it must be like to not even have a corporal form, to forget himself, to hunger endlessly... They'd always treated wraiths as dangerous inconveniences, utterly unaware that they *could* retain some semblance of personhood. Or perhaps he simply had never been able to hear.

"I will be back soon," he told S.

S returned to its partner, and became still once again.

Right. The archives. Much like Xavier's laboratories, this place was stark, white, and very brutalist. The entrance opened to a wide aisle, with rows of stacks on either side spreading into what felt like oblivion; but then Ario noticed his own reflection, very small, in the distance. There was a mirror at the opposite end of this archive. Perhaps it was one of those one-way mirrors; he'd have to get close enough to hold a fingernail against it. Regardless, he had express permission to be here, so it did not matter who was watching him.

There had to be a catalog or finding aid here somewhere. Surely?

Ario strode down the sets of stacks. A flat, textured cream runner ran the whole way back, all the way to the mirrored walls. Unlike the dungeon, the air was stale here, and very dry. In the middle of the space, framing the stacks, were two large square columns; at the base of each were metal filing cabinets, a flat metal table, and a few uncomfortable chairs. A single desktop computer was on top of the left hand side cabinet, asleep.

In the piercing quiet of the archives, Ario's heart seemed unusually loud in his ears. The tomes he'd always wanted to read as a boy, and anything that could help him now, were all here at his easy disposal. So where to even begin?

He decided to check the computer and cabinets for a finding aid. The computer woke easily and had no password–why should it, when it was this protected? Only a few programs were available; an internet browser, basic office software, a remote desktop access, the file library, and the archive database.

The program was almost remedially simple–barely a step up from a searchable spreadsheet. He was momentarily dazzled by the organization of it all before venturing a single search for "heartlines." He had expected very few, if any, results to turn up, but was disappointed when the catalog gave him only two pieces of media anyway; a scholarly article from forty years ago, and a nonfiction book titled *The Modern Heart: Lines of Communication in this Day and Age.*

Alright. Well. Time to look for the proverbial needle in the haystack.

Ario was not sure how long he remained in the archives; there were no windows, and the computer clock remained on 00:00 AM for the duration of his search. He found a bathroom tucked into a far corner, and a kitchenette of sorts in another (plastered with signs saying to NOT BRING FOOD OR WATER INTO THE ARCHIVE) which provided him with water. Only hunger and exhaustion could put a stop to the search, and really, his appetite was still not *normal* on the account of the whole "being starved" business. Idly, he wondered if Xavier somehow had made a connection between magical starvation, or if he were just cruel. It was possible both options were true. Ario shuddered just thinking about it.

The mage in him yearned to burrow his nose in delicious books that would not serve any useful purpose, books he'd only heard vague reference to. He forced himself to focus, digging for titles that attempted to explain away the dispersion of the last miasma, as well as research on pacts and bonds between people. There was a common denominator to all of these: death.

Pacts and bonds broke upon the death of one or the other. The Goddess wanted death. But how to kill her without everyone else dying? Was that even possible? Were heartlines and bonds different? They had to be.

He left his first research session only when a migraine threatened behind his blind eye. Weary, somewhat faint, he followed S and the other wraith back to his quarters, keeping a dim recollection of how to find the archives again. Ario had intended on writing a summary of what he had (or hadn't) found, but exhaustion quickly claimed him.

For the next day, and several after that, Ario spent hours upon hours poring through the books, articles, scrolls, and writings of mages, priests and priestesses, and magic experts. While he did certainly find interesting things, most of it was not particularly useful to him and for this task. What had started with excitement had become a frustrating slog. Was there more that Catherine was hiding? It was possible, and probable. He wondered how much of her story about "just stumbling upon" Ilario's writings was true.

Ario still had not seen Xander, or Catherine, for that matter. Ario hoped that, wherever he was, he was safe, perhaps simply *busy*. On one of Ario's ventures into the castle, he checked the old candelabra, and while his original message was gone, there was no response in its place.

On one of these endless days, he was taking a study break and examining the vast mirror at the far end of the archive. He'd deduced it was not a one-way mirror, but a piece of architectural folly. He supposed it made sense to try and make the bland space appear larger, but the rest of the rooms were so simple it seemed odd that the designer would even care. Surely the same effect could have been accomplished with a smaller—though still large—mirror. Why did it run floor-to-ceiling? He trailed his fingers gently across the cool surface, catching sight of his scar, which looked particularly gruesome in this unflattering light.

Under his fingertips, he felt a faint sliver, a gap, in the mirror—what had otherwise been a single coherent piece. Ario crouched to look at it closer. Yes, there it was; a nearly invisible slim rectangle in the glass, vertical. He pressed against it. It did not feel like glass, this piece, but had the heft of metal. Along this rectangle, this *handle*, were two tiny dots a few centimeters apart, like something needed to be inserted into them.

Surely there must be paperclips in an archive?

A search for such materials proved useless, though he did find two mechanical pencils. Attempting to insert the leads into the divots did nothing. The more he toiled, the more he was certain this was the handle of a door hiding something. There were secret panels all over the castle; what was one more? The divots were not buttons that could be pressed, nor were they large enough to need a key. There must be some object that acted to unlock this door, small and inconspicuous—

Something like a wristwatch, perhaps. Ario mined pressing his wrist against the handle and found the divots lined up exactly to the center of his wrist.

Ainsley hadn't been delusional after all.

All the more crucial to get the watch. Could this hidden passage hold answers? Or was it just another mystery he could not solve?

He found out what happened to Xander the next morning, after forcing down some rubbery, suspiciously chewy eggs and soggy toast—in Xander's absence, an anonymous staff member left meals at his door at random and odd intervals. Ario was preparing himself to go back down to the archives when there was a knock at the main door of his rooms. Nobody ever knocked.

An unremarkable mundane young woman in servant's livery had an envelope in her hand. "Message for you," she said. She bobbed her head once, passed the envelope to him, and shut the door.

Ario looked at the missive. It was on fine official stationery, folded over with a glistening scarlet red seal. He went over to his desk and opened it. A piece of onionskin fell face-down onto the desk. As he reached for it, he read the main message:

> *Her Imperial Lady CATHERINE BEAUMONT WINDSOR*
> *requests your presence at*
> *HER ANNUAL BIRTHDAY BALL*
> *On TUESDAY, THE FIRST OF MARCH, 7pm*
> *in the imperial ballroom, CAPITOL PALACE, LANDFALL*
> *High Formal Attire Required*

His heart skipped a beat. Did Catherine really trust him enough to bring him in public like this? Surely not? Unless she was planning to expose him or otherwise use him during this event?

Before coming to any further conclusions, he picked up the piece of scrap that had fallen from the invite. Another cipher; and by then, he recognized Xander's handwriting. Ario breathed out, surprised by how relieved he was. He deciphered the message quickly.

> *I wanted to warn you before Mother sank in her claws. We need to discuss strategy about this. Am well enough. Sent your message. They'll know to meet you at the far docks, where the grocery ship-ments used to come in. My guess is that it will take at least three days for the message to arrive.*
>
> *Let's meet in the third landing down of the servant's passage from your rooms this afternoon, around the change of the guard.*
>
> *Destroy this.*

Ario ripped up the paper and flushed it down the toilet. Okay; he had three days before he could make contact with (he assumed) Mara. And not much terribly longer before the ball. Should he do this? Should he reveal himself to the public–on her side? Would that further complicate matters? Perhaps it would cause domestic relations to crumble all the more quickly. Or else it would just discourage any resistance efforts at all.

He watched the gray snow fall.

At the appointed time, Ario snuck down to the landing Xander indicated. He hunkered down in the shadows, wondering if he'd been set up, but before long he saw Xander's tall, lanky figure hobble into sight.

"Are you alright?" Ario asked. In the faint sconce light, he couldn't see much, but he saw enough to be concerned. Xander's hair was loose around his shoulders, and his face was puffy, as though he'd been severely ill.

"I'm well enough," he said hoarsely.

"I heard you were... waylaid."

He scoffed. "That's an interesting way of putting it. Come with me."

Ario followed down the stuffy passageway, remaining silent for a moment. The brisk pace he'd gotten used to had slowed considerably. "Are you ill?"

"I was."

"Your mother made it sound quite ominous. If you merely had the flu–"

"I'll explain," he said softly. "Quiet, prince."

They proceeded through the maze for a few minutes, into a section Ario did not recognize; based on the freshness of the air, the brighter lights, and the whitewash over stone, these must be newer passages.

At long last, Xander opened a small panel and helped Ario through; the entrance was quite narrow, despite their thinness. "Sorry about that," he said, when Ario flopped gracelessly onto thin, threadbare carpeting. "I had to add the panel myself, and carpentry isn't my strong suit."

Ario brushed dust off of his slacks and looked up. His hair was finally long enough again to cover his forehead. This room was nearly as spartan as his cell had been months ago, except perhaps a bit larger and less dingy. It was a neat square, with one large window opposite the door. In one corner was a double bed, made with a single pillow and a simple wool blanket. In the other was a chipped wooden writing desk with a laptop, books and papers stacked neatly beside it on top of a metal filing cabinet. Next to the desk was a radiator, and next to that was a narrow wooden wardrobe with drawers in the bottom. In the dead center of the room was a futon with a card table in front of it. The walls were painted a dull sage green, and it smelled of too much habitation. "Is this your room?"

"I could've had one of the nicer suites, if I truly desired," Xander commented. He hobbled over to a hot plate, which was over a black minifridge. He reached into a cabinet and pulled out an electric kettle. "I've no need for frippery. This was my room when I was still the mundane liaison. It serves me well enough."

There were hardly any lighting fixtures, Ario noted. Just a single lamp by the bedside and on the desk and a basic overhead fixture. Nothing on the walls, not even curtains for the windows. No book-cases or shelves for books. But judging by the wear of things—the chips on the legs of the bed, the sunken-in nature of some of the futon cushions, the crumpled-up papers in the metal wastebasket—it hadn't exactly been staged recently.

Xander returned from what must've been the bathroom and put the kettle on the hot plate. "There. Tea, at least."

In the brighter light, the carnage was clearer. His face was hollow, his skin nearly jaundiced, and he didn't quite meet Ario's eyes. Ario frowned. "Look at me," he said. "Look me in the eye."

Xander sighed heavily, and made eye contact. Ario's suspicions were confirmed; his eyes had that silvery glint Mara's had prior to her miasma removal.

He breathed out in a hiss, instinctively taking a step back.

"My allegiances have not changed," Xander insisted. "This was a compromise. A... show of good faith, to her."

"A threat, to you," Ario said.

"Yes."

"What does the enhancement... do?" Ario asked. "You have no power to begin with, nothing to enhance."

Wincing, he reached for a pair of mugs from the same cabinet. "The idea, on paper, was that Xavier needed a control group for the efficacy of the vaccine. Really, this is just another way for Mother to assert her will over me. My brothers took it too, of course."

"Can she... control you? Like issue commands?"

"If she has, she hasn't yet. Not to my knowledge." He set the kettle on the glowing hot plate. "All the more reason to hurry, Ario."

"I am *trying*." Ario debated withholding information, because if Xander was now *compromised* he might be obliged to spill information to his mother. But Mara, after receiving a *second* enhancement that somehow "didn't take," had still been able to tell him everything she knew. Then again, she had by then sworn loyalty to him... would trying to enter into a pact or deal with Xander, in both their states, and given the nature of the Goddess, be a terrible idea? "You said you did my intake. I was wearing two pieces of jewelry. What became of them?"

"They would be in a locker down in the labs, with anything else of value."

"I would like them. I need them, actually." Ario bit his lip, feeling the chapped and ragged skin. "I suppose I could just ask her. No harm in returning an uncharmed necklace and watch. The more I can do without sneaking around, the better."

The kettle burbled softly. "She's going to want you there, you know. At the ball. Both of us."

"...Yes."

"What do we want to do?" Xander plucked two tea bags out of a tin, breaking the stale, sad air with the scent of oranges and rooibos.

"It's probably not opportune to plan any sort of attack," he said. "It all depends whether she wants me to openly identify myself or not. I suppose I could simply *ask*. But if she *does* wish for me to out myself, there would be considerable public doubt. I am not female anymore, and I look significantly different, especially since the vaccine. And even if they believe it..." Ario took the offered mug. "Are these balls televised?"

Xander eased over to the couch and sat on the far end opposite Ario. "Yes, on the public stations."

"Don't you know hackers? Could they hijack the broadcast remotely? Send the rebellion a message?"

"They would need a security key. If I gave it over, I would either have to implicate myself or someone else. There aren't many keys, and believe me, *those* records are well-kept."

Ario swilled the tea bag around and around the mug. "What about a... manual, hijack?"

"That creates a whole other host of issues."

He shifted his weight on the cushions, feeling a spring press against his tailbone. "Well, we can puzzle it out further. Once I get into regular contact with the resistance, they can tell me what seems reasonable given the state of their current forces, and then we can plan from there. We have some weeks, it appears."

Xander was silent for a moment, twisting his tea bag around and around his mug. "The system is going to collapse sooner or later. Things are not going well for the common person. We can only hope that whatever comes next is better. Or at least survivable."

"Yes. Quite."

The next morning, Ario was summoned to Catherine's chambers. When he arrived, he found her in the study, standing on an improvised dais, a mostly-complete ballgown draped over her body. Some poor modiste was dutifully attending an unfinished hem.

"Ah–Ario. You'll have to excuse me double-dipping," she said. In the harsh winter light, she, too, looked sickly, not helped at all by the wine-red of the silk. Her face was puffy, and her eyes, though natural in color, were glassy. Her hair looked greasy, and was carelessly swept into a bun to be out of the way of the dress's neckline. "This was the only time I could see you. Go on, sit. There's a tea cart somewhere if you like."

Ario, thoroughly sick of tea at this point, went and sat on the nearest settee. The scent of raw silk brought back a flash of blurry memory–watching his mother in this same room get fitted for yet another gown she would wear once. She'd tried to coax some kind of excitement out of him ("What princess doesn't love dresses?"), and had been disappointed when he'd found his puzzle more interesting. "This looks like it's for an important occasion," he remarked.

"Bah–just the annual ball. My gown from last year is still perfectly serviceable, but my advisors insists it's bad optics."

"Why have the ball, then, if you don't enjoy it?"

"It's sort of a… reward, for the court, you understand. They all get to dress up and gossip and eat and drink too much. Things are tenuous enough as it is."

The staffer's face was still, impassive, as she moved around the skirt, placing pins. Ario noticed she was wearing earbuds. "…Is that so?" he asked.

"I won't lie. Things are not going well." She turned towards him, causing the skirt to flutter; the staffer tutted with displeasure and quickly pretended to cough, but resumed pinning. "How is your research going?"

"So far? Not so promising. I'm trying my best. Was anything… destroyed?" He bit the inside of his cheek. "Is there anything I should know that I don't?"

"I… cannot be certain," Catherine said. "*I* personally would not have overseen destruction of anything in that archive, even if it is legally contraband. That doesn't mean there wasn't any theft or destruction in the early days, before I had full control over who could access the castle and the spaces within it."

"…I see." He crossed his arms, feeling more acutely the rough wool of his sweater.

"That is not *entirely* why I asked to see you." Catherine cleared her throat, then coughed, a wet, rattly sound. "Bring me some tea, dear?"

Obediently, Ario looked for the tea cart and crossed over to it. An enamel teapot covered in roses steeped on a heater; he poured a cup of brackish green liquid into one of the matching cups and brought it to her.

"The damp air wreaks horror on my asthma," she explained, offering a sheepish smile. As she sipped, she continued, "I would very much like for *you* to attend the ball."

He feigned shock. "*Me?* But why?"

"I feel it would be beneficial to diplomatic relations. You surely didn't think I would keep you prisoner forever? You've been docile and shown good intentions. That should be rewarded."

Chagrin washed over him, and he hoped he wasn't blushing. "The people won't recognize me as the Heir," he said. "Not just because of the gender, but the vaccine caused me to lose any markers of magic anyway. They could think I'm an imposter. Besides, what could *I* do anyway?"

"You could beseech the people to lay down their arms, so we can come to a peaceful resolution, and work towards change together."

Ario scoffed; he could not help it. Catherine squinted, or glared, at him; he could not tell.

"Why do you react so?" She held out the empty cup for him to take. He did so.

"Magic users have no reason to trust you, or trust you suddenly want *peace*. Not since your administration has been killing them for over a decade. For all they know, it could be a deception. A total lie."

"You *know* why the magic has to die, Ario. I don't–*like*–the blood on my hands. But someone has to take the blame, so I do. Gladly. My soul will be tormented for eternity, but it will be worth it. If we'd had this vaccine years ago–" she sputtered. "I know the lives that might have been saved."

The staffer stood. "All done, madam," she said, oddly loudly. She reached up and plucked the earbuds out of her ears and held them out to Catherine.

Catherine offered a sweet smile and took them. "*Thank* you, dear. I will have my maid bring it down to you when I'm through here."

The girl bowed and left the room.

"Noise cancelling," Catherine explained. "You'd be surprised what would get around otherwise." She delicately stepped off the dais, and set the buds onto her desk. "My regime was born because your Queen refused to see reason and adapt to her populace. I will not fall so easily. I am not an unreasonable woman."

"*I* know that," Ario placated her. "It's just that the *people* have considerable trauma caused by your regime, and *my* presence alone, my endorsement, even, would not be enough. After all, they've no reason to trust *me* either. I hid for twelve years."

Her eyes flashed; he wondered if he'd given away too much. "What do you propose, then? What would *you* do?"

"What were you trying to accomplish before the miasma took hold?" he asked instead.

"I was fighting *for equity*. Do you even remember what it was like? Do you know what it was like for the common people?"

He did, but he remained silent, certain she was going to answer the question anyway.

Catherine reached up and pulled out a hairpin, her hair falling hesitantly to her shoulders. "The economy was in shambles. The debts and taxes imposed upon the cities were killing them. Healthcare was becoming inaccessible. Higher education was becoming inaccessible. *Food* was becoming inaccessible–unemployment was at an all time high. And with all her supposed *power* Chiara, then Ainsley, did *nothing* to fix it. *I* fixed it."

"Until now."

Pushing past him, she meandered towards the windows; the train of her gown dragged against the plush carpet. "That's what I need you for, Ario. I need you to stop the miasma to buy *time*. I need you to stand *with* me." She held out her hand. "Together we can earn their trust."

He did not believe this at all. "I'm not sure we can."

She sighed. "So *moral,* are we? Fine. I still want you there. I want you to see the court for yourself. Maybe then you'll understand. I must go get ready for my next meeting." She started towards her bedroom.

"Wait–"

She turned towards him, her face impassive.

"When I came here, I had a watch and a necklace. They were my father's. Could I have them back?"

"Sure. Fine. I don't care. Xavier or his staff would have access." She shut the door behind her with a sharp *snick.*

Had he messed it all up? Had he been too candid, and revealed his true feelings? Still, playing the game or not, Ario could not see a version of himself that readily agreed with the killings. She must know that. None of the rebellions holding any water would believe he'd suddenly switched sides. And he was sure there were no means of resolving this peacefully to end up as a unified front. Otherwise, they'd be there already.

Ario mulled over this as he made his way towards the labs. Coming here *purposefully* was no easier than it had been last time; he shuddered when he started seeing the cells with their colorful blocks next to the subject slots. More were empty, this time, than full. Were those people alive and free, just deadened? Or at the worst come to pass? He would probably never know with certainty.

Before too long he found a staffer in a white coat, and after they checked something on a tablet, they told Ario to wait where he was. A few moments later, they returned with a plastic bag containing his belongings. They took his finger prints and a retinal scan with the same tablet, and then resumed whatever they had been doing before.

He waited until he was in the relative privacy of his rooms before opening the bag. Items from the before times... how odd. His starched linen shirt, now slightly too large; the stretch pants he'd been forced to wear because nothing else fit; even his sneakers were here, still coated in a faint layer of sand. Ario held the shirt to his face, expecting it to smell of Peony or the baby or even sweat, but after so long in the lockers, it just smelled like sterile nothing.

The watch and the necklace were in a smaller, separate pouch with a sticker on it that read "certified charm-free" with a scribbled initial. Xander's handwriting. Small blessings, he supposed.

Ario took the pendant in his hands, feeling the cold silver chain. The pearlescent teal shimmered faintly in the lamplight. *I love you, I'm trying,* he intoned, wondering if Peony could somehow feel or sense him. He wondered how long it would take before her face, too, became blurry in his memory. He slipped the necklace on and tucked it beneath the collar of his sweater, feeling its coldness against his breastbone.

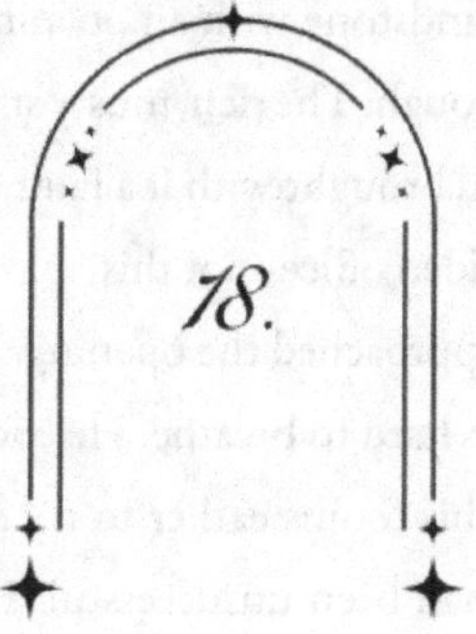

After his afternoon meal, Ario once again stole back down to the archives. He was unaccompanied by S or Perseus/Jude, but found that the doors opened for him anyway with ease. Perhaps some camera looked for his eyeprint. He strode towards the large mirror and found the secret handle quickly. His heart threatened to crush his ribs. With trembling fingers, he placed the watch's sapphires into the divots.

At first, nothing happened, and he wondered if he'd been led on a wild goose chase. But just as he was about to move the watch and sulk, he heard a loud, grinding *crunch* that rumbled the floor beneath his feet. A fine rain of dust fell from the ceiling. The *whole* mirror was pulling apart into the walls, liquefying into a glimmering silver sheet, revealing dark sandstone with an opening carved into it barely big enough to walk through. The rich, musty smell of pure earth broke the room's sterility and brought with it a faint, humid breeze.

He'd expected a hidden office–not this.

Swallowing, Ario approached the opening. The air had a pungent thickness to it that was hard to breathe. He had no flashlight, or even candle; he'd searched his rooms earlier to try and find something to bring with him, but had been unsuccessful. He was unsure of how the mirror knitted itself back together, or *if* it even did. He looked at the broken watch. The piece no longer kept time, but its face glowed subtly in the dark. It would have to do.

Ario stepped through the doorway, feeling like he'd been swallowed. The ground beneath him was raw, smoothened earth, sloping gently downwards. The smell of dirt became overpowering, the must of the miasma. The fine hairs on the back of his neck crawled. He wondered, briefly, if this was how Amalia felt when she was Named, in the dark, in the dirt.

Slowly, within the narrow passage, something began to glow a faint teal, almost exactly like the stone under his shirt. He squinted and was able to make out jagged edges of crystal. What *was* this place? What had his father known? Ainsley had alluded to the watch's importance in her first letter, which obviously indicated *this* place's importance. But if it was safe, important, why was his skin crawling? Why did every nerve itch?

Maybe he should turn back.

He took a moment to steel his will. This was too important to give up because *he was a little frightened.*

It was hard to tell how long he followed the path. Sometimes the path switched back, but he never saw any other doors or openings to continue through. As he passed, more crystals activated. This could be some mage's hideaway from years' past, or a secret escape route prior to the advent of the castle's passages.

Most glaring of all was the dead silence. He didn't even hear rats or bugs scurrying about, just his own increasingly harried breaths. Ario had spent too much time in tight spaces to be truly claustrophobic, but still, he swore he felt the press of the earth anyway—

Just as he was about to turn around and start his laborious climb upwards, the earth gave way abruptly to hard, human-carved stone. Earthen walls were replaced with milled stone and old-fashioned columns. At shoulder height, he saw a battery lantern hanging on a hook, jarringly modern in contrast with the primordial nature of the passage, but if Ainsley or Cyril had been down here within the last twenty years, it made sense. The lantern clicked on, its light wobbling unsteadily for a moment before brightening considerably.

The ground rumbled, a dull *roar* flooding the passage, and he dropped into a ball, feeling certain he was about to be crushed to death. But when no stone smacked him into oblivion, Ario slowly stood. "Hello?" he whispered.

A second roar shook the earth. A hot seed of dread rooted in his stomach, making him feel weak. He knew that noise. He knew that dread.

Ario was able to walk more quickly now that the stone was flat and even. The hallway opened into a large, round stone temple, primitive in its design, maybe about fifteen meters in diameter. Moldering frames had ragged tapestries, and any wooden pew had long since disintegrated. More, brighter crystals framed the room, making his lantern obsolete. Towards the front of the temple was a stone altar, an exposed piece of earth before it.

He approached the altar and inspected the blade. It was of modern make, slightly rusted but otherwise in good condition. He already knew what to do. He pricked his left thumb and let blood drip softly into the earth.

For the Ario of two years ago, this place would have inspired awe. An impossibly ancient and convenient temple of the Goddess, here under his feet all along; he was certain Evelyn did not know about it, or if she did, it was one of the secrets only someone of her station could keep. He would kneel and pray and bleed for the Goddess's favor, all the while thanking Her for letting him see something so blessed.

For the millionth time, he wished he had his magic. He could use it to learn *so much* about this place, and the last person to come through here. Ario pocketed the athame, figuring he, if anyone, had the right to take it. And it may very well come in useful. He licked his thumb to stop the bleeding.

"Am I supposed to pray?" he asked, feeling bitterness twist his words. "Is that what you would like?"

He wasn't expecting a response, but the ground rumbled again, causing the sickly crystals to shimmer. He stumbled, his feet suddenly sinking into the too-soft earth, his calves, his knees, and before he could fully comprehend what was happening he was pulled under.

He must've blacked out; the shock, to suddenly be lying on a cool, dry, pallet of blankets, fresh air swirling around him, was too much. Maybe there was gas, down here, causing hallucinations.

~~Hario.~~

He started, looking around frantically. Something was wrong with his vision, too sharp and too deep; he realized he had depth perception for the first time in years. He appeared to be on a sort of bed in a grassy field, a roiling sunrise setting on the horizon.

~~Dear beloved creature.~~

He had improved *vision*, but his mind could not make sense of what was in front of him. One instant, it had the appearance of a plump, long-haired woman; the next, an emaciated black bear; a wolf; a red-tailed hawk; and then face after face after face of women with violet-silver hair, of varying builds, then his grandmother and mother, until finally the face was his own, pre-vaccine, and then it became another young woman with Peony's eyes and nose and chin.

"Don't be frightened," said the girl.

"Amalia?" he gaped.

"Well, yes, and mostly no. Right now I'm the conduit."

He looked at her more closely. She looked to be about twenty, her hair long and curly, her body covered in a simple white shift. Was this who she would turn out to be?

"She wants to apologize, you know, for taking you over. She feels terrible." Her voice was low, pleasant. "But She can only do this here."

"What is this place?" he asked.

"There's a reason this castle is *here*," she said. "It's where She buried herself, to hide from the ceaseless watcher. It's where one of Us found Her, and bred with Her. It's where We were born."

"Earth," he murmured.

"Everything stems from here. The mountains, the rivers, all a shell to protect her."

"Why is She so frightened of the moon?" he asked.

The girl's face was stiff, impassive. She did not emote much, when she spoke. "Are you not frightened and enraged by what created you?" she asked. "Do you not wish to—have agency? To control your destiny, and not be forced to watch as your own creations die and die and die? Does it not get tiring?"

"I thought She wanted to die," Ario said.

~~I do.~~

He felt the weight of the meaning, even if the girl's mouth did not move to make words.

~~I wish to rest. To be at peace. I am so tired.~~

"But what about *us*?" he asked. "If you are tired of watching *us* die, why do all this?"

~~I have thought and thought and thought about that. You are flesh, you are doomed to die regardless. Why fight for survival?~~

He just stared, his mouth dry. "I want to live. I want my people to live."

~~But why? I do not understand.~~

"For hope. For joy. To be with others," he said slowly. "Every beautiful day, every happy memory."

~~Others.~~ Her tone became wistful.

"Maybe you shouldn't hide from the watcher. Maybe it's as lonely as you are. Maybe... maybe that's why it became controlling, because you hid from it. I know how it feels to be controlled by a force larger than me. When you made me carry the conduit." He had tried to forget the pregnancy the instant it was over, but he recalled the way Amalia felt when she squirmed and banged around inside him.

~~I thought it would be the final piece. Your power, your line. I gave away piece after piece of me away, and still, it was not enough to die. And then your piece came back. And Amalia's remained. And I realized it would be forever.~~

"The vaccine," he whispered.

~~He will torment me *forever*. Unless I die.~~

Ario had to sit in the weight of that for a moment. "If You don't think You can reconcile with Him, maybe there's something else I can do."

Her eyes lit up. ~~Please. Make it stop.~~

"I thought Your heartlines were tied with the planet itself. But... You're tied to Him. If You tell me how, I can break that bond and set You free."

She remained silent, still. ~~You have power.~~

"You keep saying that. *Catherine* keeps saying that. But I don't know what–"

The girl pointed wordlessly at his chest. ~~You have a soulbond. Breaking that might release enough power to do it. I can take the piece of me from the child and do the rest.~~

Horror closed around his heart. "B-but I couldn't."

~~You cannot dangle hope just to revoke it,~~ She hissed.

"It would hurt Peony. It might even *kill* us." His breath came fast and hot, the flavor of a fresh meadow disconcerting.

But the pain of two people over the deaths of millions of hominids, and billions of animals. It should be an easy choice. If they both managed to survive, Peony would never forgive him for destroying their bond. And what would it do to their poor daughter?

What was perhaps the hardest was that he had already chosen, and had already made up his mind, and the fact that he had been able to do so hurt.

Ario blinked tears out of his eyes. "What do I have to do?"

~~When she is here, I'll teach you the spell you'll need to break the bond.~~

"How long do I have?"

~~This can go on for months. But it will be helpful when *He* is least aware.~~

"...Meaning a new moon." So this was what despair felt like. He hadn't felt so when he'd lost his parents, or his home, or when he and Evelyn had been starving, or when She forced his body to betray him with that parasite, or when Xavier had him strapped to that table and raped his soul. It was heavy. Leaden. "...The next one is a few weeks. It'll... coincide with the ball." He scowled. "That was also Your doing, wasn't it?"

~~A few more weeks... I think I can do that.~~

His body crushed out a dark laugh. "Oh, *You* think You can do that, can You? At least say *thank* you. What becomes of us, then, when Your bond is severed?"

~~Corpses make flowers bloom,~~ she said.

And then he woke up on the floor of the temple, his head pounding and his vision halved.

For the next few days, Ario allowed himself to fall into the lushness of depression. He slept endlessly, though gained little rest. He stole a bottle of absinthe from one of the bars Catherine had to entertain staff in the middle of the night, drank half of it, and spent the next day so terribly hungover he might've believed he was in purgatory.

Purgatory didn't exist. Paradise didn't exist. Or at least they wouldn't when the Goddess was dead and he was either dead or irreversibly altered. Why him? Why couldn't he just be a normal guy and go to college and get married and have some *stupid* meaningless job and someone else could save the world, thank you very much–

He thought he would find satisfaction in breaking things, but after he smashed the delicate teapot he was sent for breakfast, the breaking just intensified the faultlines inside of him, and he gave up.

It would be so *easy* to give up, to just become Catherine's little pet while the world burned, yes-anding Xander's plans for a revolution. He could become a turncoat and save Peony and Amalia, but at the expense of *everything,* and at the end of the day, Ario would not be able to cope with the guilt of letting the world end. He'd made the choice, the deadline was approaching. He'd thought it would be easier.

On the bedraggled, neglected dock at the base of the palace, Ario waited. He did not have long before he was expected back, he knew. He had another note to hide if they didn't figure it out in time. Getting outside of the palace during one of the bitterest Februaries they had experienced yet had been a real trick. But Catherine trusted him, and *surely,* her precious, traumatized pet would do no wrong.

At sunset, he saw Mara approach, the glinting of her power barely visible against the tepid glow. There was no reason to guard this place, and there were no wards. She twisted into existence, her body poised for a fight, her long blue braid swinging perilously. Seeing the empty air, she looked around until she spotted him at last.

Mara searched his face. He saw her lack of recognition, at first. Then she straightened, and bowed, palms pressed together. "Your priestess believed you were leading me into a trap, prince. I figured you had better help than that."

"She was right to be wary." He stepped forward. He felt like he should touch her, but a hug was too personal and a handshake might offend. "You probably should have heeded her."

"Yet, here I am."

"It is *good* to see you. You look well. How–how is she?" It felt strange, to let his true feelings bleed onto his face.

"The child is well. Peony's a good mother."

"And Peony?"

"Misses you with a ferocity bordering on melodrama. Thinner, but unharmed. She said to tell you she loves you."

He breathed out with relief, the shard of his upcoming betrayal burrowing a bit deeper.

Mara looked down. "I can take you with me, you know."

He figured she'd make this offer, but that made it no easier to hear. "I can't. As much as I want to, I can't."

"Michael figured you had a plan. Do you?"

He nearly buckled, then. He nearly told her the terrible truth. "It is unconventional, but yes."

"How can I assist?"

"I need to be within reasonable vicinity of Amalia. To feed off of that bond."

Mara's face did not change, but he saw a faint glimmer of suspicion.

"I have *not* been compromised," he assured her. "It's *very* complicated, and I have *no* power, but I *need* a connection to the Goddess to do what needs to be done. And I don't exactly have one myself anymore."

"And here I was hoping that was a bad dye job," she remarked, gesturing to his hair. "What are you going to do, prince?"

He took a deep breath. "I am going to kill the Goddess."

Skepticism bled onto her face. "And how exactly do you intend to do that?"

"I have to sever heartlines. It will work. I *know* it will work."

Mara thought a moment. "What will it cost you?"

Ario nearly cracked then. "It's a steep price. I've already agreed to pay it. I... can't tell you." He cleared his throat, trying to budge the lump that had formed. "Catherine's annual ball is soon. I need her to be here by then."

She raised an eyebrow. "You expect me, a wanted and very visible fugitive, to bring your infant daughter across the country in winter so you can... use her power."

"I trust you, Mara. I know you can do it."

She sighed. "*I* know I can do it. The trouble will be getting Evelyn and Peony, you know, the girl's *mom,* to agree to it."

"All our lives depend on it. Tell them I have a plan and there's people here who can guarantee their safety. The best chance is to smuggle them in during events leading up to the ball."

She did not shiver, but he saw goosebumps forming on her exposed forearms.

"If you can pull this off, I'll consider your debt paid. You'll be free." Not to mention, the death of the Goddess would render their pact void anyway.

She scoffed. ""Free." Hardly. But it won't... *kill,* the baby, will it?"

"I don't think so. No."

""I don't think so" doesn't inspire a whole lot of confidence," she admitted. "But if you ask me, I have to do it."

Ario felt the ghost of a smile. "Have you actually developed *affection* for them, then?"

She smirked. "No, I am still a heartless bitch," she quipped. "That is perhaps the only thing trauma is good for–making friends out of enemies."

A harsh breeze cut through the docks, and she rubbed her arms.

"I should let you return to them," he said. "Give my love."

"How can I get in touch with you?"

"Have the resistance contact Microdot. They'll do the rest."

"Codenames. *Fancy,*" she remarked, then sobered. "Be careful, Ario. I have a vested interest in your wellbeing. ...So does your family."

"I'll do what I can," he said.

She nodded, bowed again, and disappeared in the direction she had arrived.

Time, his archnemesis in this accursed palace, suddenly seemed to be moving very quickly. Ario interacted with the world blurrily, wishing he had more absinthe. He knew he should be scheming and plotting his little heart out, but as it was, he found himself simply agreeing with Xander's ideas. Some king he was.

"You seem despondent, prince," Xander commented one evening they were able to steal together in Ario's rooms. "Have hope—we're getting stronger than ever before."

Oh, to only have to dwell on a revolution. The political situation had continued to devolve. Catherine had signed off on an executive order to dissolve the city-states' ability to self-govern, effective immediately, a move so *stupid* that Xander openly wondered why she would sabotage herself like that. Ordinarily this would make Ario's heart sing, because it only galvanized the cities to work together against her.

"I know what I must *do*," Ario said. "But I don't know what I must *do*."

"My prince, I don't understand," he said, stooping to turn the radiator's knob.

"I know how to stop the miasma."

Xander lurched to a stand. "And you didn't *lead* with that, perchance?"

"It will come at a great personal cost to myself. The decision has been made. That doesn't mean it will not hurt terribly."

Xander crossed his arms. "Kings have to make tough decisions."

"Yeah, well, it turns out tough decisions *are quite tough to make.*"

Xander sat back down on the settee. "Do you have a plan, then? And does Mother know?"

"She's been too distracted to meet with me, even over something like this." Which was easier to control: a slow, edging smolder or a grease fire? "I'll need your help more than ever, Xander. We'll have to leverage all the goodwill we have."

"Prince, you know I'll do my best, but *what* are you talking about?"

"Oh, just bringing an Heir, a siren, and a wanted fugitive into the castle undetected."

His eyes bulged. "Because that's so simple."

Ario stood and started to pace. "Well, the good news is that, with Peony, they all read as mundanes. Sirens–their magic *is* to block magic."

Xander tapped his fingers on the side table, rattling his cup of coffee. "I suppose... we might be able to fabricate their arrest, but then spirit them away before my brother gets his hands on them..."

"They have a very safe means of *getting* here. I guess..." It occurred to him; he needed to know *how* Mara could get from place to place. Did she have to know the location intimately, to teleport? Could he simply pass her a photo to the temple, and have her take them there? It would be unpleasant, but it would be safe, and relatively easy to smuggle down supplies... "I guess it's a matter of finding the right people to turn a blind eye."

Xander shook his head. "No good. She'll be using extra wraiths at every doorway."

"Then it's a good thing I know one." He described S. "Wouldn't it be simple enough to swap them with another wraith? Does your mother know the difference?"

"It's part of why the wraiths have armor... to keep track of them. They're numbered. I guess we'll have to persuade S to put on another set. That should be doable."

Xander stared into the middle distance for a moment, the silver in his eyes catching the lamplight. "And then what?"

"What do you mean?"

"After this is over, after the miasma is defeated. What do we do then? Mother will surely have put together that it's your doing. Do we keep–hiding your family down in that temple? Is that even humane?"

Ario picked at the sleeves of his sweater. All of his clothing was so similar—gray sweaters and black slacks, each just a bit too worn to be presentable. "That's where the plans have to overlap, in some way."

"Where we'll have to kill her," he said wearily, sagging onto his knees. Then, laughing darkly, "do we conspire a way to kill them all, while we're at it? Poison? Bombs? *Must* this all happen at the same time?"

"If I lied about the nature of the severing, she surely would want to be present as I do it. For obvious reasons, we can't let that happen. But she won't exactly buy that it *just went away*, not when the vaccine has been thwarted." A dim pounding started behind Ario's eyes. "I have to *think*. Do you suppose there's *any* way to isolate her and your brothers during the ball?"

"I'm sure you could probably get her on her own. She trusts you. But *they* would be difficult to overpower."

"And just killing her wouldn't necessarily mean the end of things as we know it." He tapped his fingers together. "And if we jail them? Or does Xavier know the dungeons too well?"

"He knows them *well*, but that doesn't mean he can trick a locked door. I know for a fact that neither of them will just blindly enter a cell if you ask them nicely."

After a few heartbeats, he felt the smooth edges of an idea, and grimaced. "I know how we might make it work."

Xander cocked his head, frowning. A fine scruff had started to bloom on his chin. "And what's that?"

"Catherine has been alluding to *what we can accomplish together*. What if I were to offer her that on a string? The government is actively collapsing. We could push her to dissolve parliament, and then once more autocratic power is established, then..."

"You kill her."

"Or we jail her. The way to the throne would be clear. Then I start allying with city states..."

Xander crossed his legs. "Dissolve parliament?"

"She dissolved city-state independent rule. She's desperate enough to do it."

"And *should* the public choose not to believe you're the long lost Heir?" He raised an eyebrow. "Why would the people want another autocrat?"

Ario sighed. "It's not going to *be* an absolute monarchy, Xander. That just paves the way for us to further dismantle the system."

"What will it be, then?" he asked bitterly. "Even if we get this far?"

"You say this as if I've not given it extensive thought." He brushed the hair out of his eyes. "We'll build a transitional constitutional monarchy, stabilize the kingdom, and then eventually, move towards total democracy."

"So simply?" he deadpanned.

"No. It won't be simple at all. It's going to take *forever*." Ario smiled despite himself. "But the severing will buy us time."

Xander pressed his hand to his forehead. "So... the plan is... get on her good side publicly, save the planet, and perform a coup?" He ticked them off on his fingers.

"Essentially, yes."

He laughed out loud, again. "This is the closest it's felt to plausible. And yet it's still a long shot."

"It's the only shot we have. We're running out of time."

Xander reached for a notebook and a pen. "All right. Then let's get started."

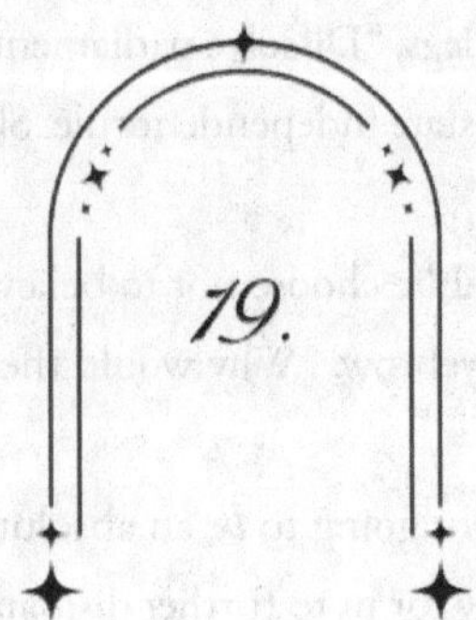

19.

The cashmere, even over a starched shirt, felt much too lush against his skin, and Ario fought not to shudder. The tailor ran a piece of chalk down his arm to adjust the suit's fit.

"You're going to look very handsome," Catherine said. She insisted that the fitting take place in her quarters, though she appeared to be writing quite laboriously on her laptop.

"I've never worn a suit," Ario said honestly. "Cotton would have been adequate."

"Nonsense. This is your debut. I want you to look your best. I... was wondering." She pulled her hair back into another messy knot.

"I was thinking about your hair color predicament. Your hair did not take dye before, did it?"

"...No." One of the tailor's pins pinched him, and he winced.

"I wonder if it may now? The colors stylists can create now, you have no idea. It's been largely a headache, but I wonder if we can... bring back your old look. It would sell your legacy better. Or—we could do a public DNA test, prove there's no shadow of a doubt..." What that guilt, he felt, at the excitement in her words?

"Whatever you think would be best," he mumbled.

"This is going to be so *helpful*, Ario, you have no idea. Right now especially we need to be providing a unified front. You're doing the right thing." She grinned. She must have worn lipstick at some point today, because it was smeared on her teeth. "How is your project coming?"

The raw maw of earth leading to the temple had sealed up when he'd left it, leaving behind just a trace of stale, musty air. The watch sat, innocuous, on his wrist. "...I'm working on it. Really."

Now that there was a set end, a set goal in sight, Ario found he was so full of conflicting emotions that he felt numb. An eagerness to begin, a hunger to set magic users free; a yearning to see Peony again, but utter leaden dread for the price he was going to have to pay. And if he survived, if they all survived, there would be more mess, more work, forever and ever and ever.

But there would be no more hiding. No more death.

He'd received a communication from Mara through Xander that they had agreed to make the move back towards the castle. Her missive had not shed any light on how Evelyn, Peony, or Michael *felt* about the situation, but that they trusted his judgement enough to come *anyway* said worlds. If this killed him, at least he'd be able to see them one more time. Based on event itineraries he and Xander had been able to weasel out of Catherine, it seemed that the best time to sneak them in would be the dead of night the evening before the ball. Should all go well, it would all be over the following evening. Of course, *he* may be over too. Ario encouraged the resistance through Xander to be ready for his signal; to do what they could to take advantage of the deteriorating situation.

It felt too real and not real at all. It felt unreal when Catherine's stylist stripped the color from his hair and dyed it an awkward approximation of his former color. It felt unreal when the suit was left for him in a garment bag, neatly pressed and beautiful, with a violet sash and a rose lapel pin. It felt unreal to persuade S to switch armor with a lower-floor wraith, and they were so eager to die they played along. Ario felt he was setting up a chessboard, and doubted the strength of his opening move.

All around the palace, preparations were being made. More banners were hung with Catherine's colors, and every surface was scrubbed clean and flooded with real and silk roses. The plants in the greenhouses were pruned, sprayed with dye to look more vibrant, and supplemented with more silk flowers. When the court and ambassadors started to pour in, Catherine asked Ario to lay low because "she wanted it to be a surprise."

He could see some of them from the vantage point of his window, passing through courtyards with maids and bell boys and assistants. People of all genders, middle-aged or older, almost entirely mundane (that he could see). These people looked ordinary talking on phones or taking offered champagne. They did not look like the harbingers of genocide. They did not look like the pit of vipers they were.

Anxiety soon replaced his sense of unreality. What if Mara got caught? He almost prayed—almost—figuring that this prayer, of any, might actually be answered. Ario found himself watching the clock as the appointed hour slowly began to arrive, light striping across his room before fading to ink black night. He drew on his black sweater, picked up his athame and flashlight, and entered the passages. He'd been down here a few more times since, mostly to spirit away supplies, but it grew no easier; those walls seemed to press and crawl. Was there enough air down here? Would they suffocate?

His pace quickened. After eight months, eight *months* of being the mask and playing games, finally he would see her again, and his family. Finally, something like hope loosened the tight muscles in his diaphragm, and he made his way to the temple. There were multiple sets of footprints in the dirt. They were here, they were really *here*–

But in this dark, still place, he *should* be able to hear them whispering, hear them talking. Everything was just *silent*. Were they asleep, exhausted from their journey? "Hello?" he hazarded calling.

"Oh, *hello*, Ilario. I'm so thankful you could join us."

He knew that voice, grating, the voice by his ear, jabbing him with needles. Ario's hand, gripping the torch, trembled, and he tried to consider his options, until a baby started to cry. Blindly, Ario ran forward into the temple, and the scene unfolded around him in the dull glow.

To his left, crumpled on the floor with palladium cuffs around her wrists, was Mara, unconscious and breathing shallowly, blood dripping from her hairline. Near her, Michael, in a similar state of unconsciousness, sprawled spread-eagled. On the right, cuffed in steel and splayed on the ground near the altar, was Evelyn. Her dark hair covered her face, and she breathed shallowly, so Ario could not tell if she was also unconscious, or simply feigning it.

In the center, impossible to avoid, were Xavier and Xanthos, dressed in their imperial blacks. Xavier, looking more smug than anything, held the squalling infant, and Xanthos, beatific with vindication, a long scratch down his face, was restraining a decidedly conscious Peony, a makeshift gag tied hurriedly around her mouth. She struggled against him, mumbling and moaning against her gag, but was evidently not strong enough to escape. Her eyes met Ario's, teal, beseeching, and yet so doubtful.

"You have nothing to say for yourself?" Xavier asked.

He swallowed, tasting must. "How did you know?"

"You fucking idiots *almost* got away with it," Xanthos said, jostling Peony; she stomped hard on his foot. In response, he threw her to the ground. "Bitch. We should have knocked her out too."

"Mother needs her awake, and preferably unharmed," Xavier said.

Peony tore away her gag. "Oh, *fuck* you." She started to get up, to reach for the baby, but Xanthos kicked her back down.

"Leave her out of this," Ario snapped. "She's done nothing."

"Nothing. Nothing?" Xanthos cackled. "Who do you think put up the biggest fight?"

Peony rolled to her feet. Slowly.

"Hands up, bitch. Don't fucking say anything," Xanthos snarled. He whipped something from his pocket; a syringe. "Or I'll dose the baby."

She glared at him, but obeyed. She was visibly dirty, dressed in too-large clothes, her long dark hair hacked to her shoulders.

"You were clever. I give you that," Xavier said. "Mother had no idea until I put the pieces together. It about broke her heart, with how much she trusted you. She would've given you the world on a string, you know. She almost did. But I knew, I just knew, something was off. And our dear brother was just lavishing so much attention on you. And honestly, I probably would have even let that slide, because at least it was getting interesting."

"Enough with the monologue. When can I get him?" Xanthos hissed.

"In a *moment,* brother. Our little prince at least deserves to hear the whole story. I really was only *truly* worried when you asked for that artifact back. See, we keep a log of these things. I've been at this castle a long time. I've seen your bloody father wearing it, and because all charmed crown objects were logged, I became enamored with it. I had a castle mage examine it before... well. They told me about this place, and were even generous enough to make a copy."

"That doesn't explain how you knew about everything else," Ario said.

"Do you know our enhancements can be used to track subjects?" Xavier asked instead. "I noticed my brother lingering in odd places other than your quarters'. I know about the candelabra, and the dock, and any other number of little hiding spots. I never messed with them, never had reason, but once Mother wanted me to keep an eye on him, I just had to take a closer look. I found some of his notes. Really? A simple *substitution* cipher? It took me and a computer fifteen minutes to break your little communiques. And *still,* I was not going to say anything. Until I heard you were bringing *them* here. Especially *her.*" Xavier nudged Mara with his foot. "You've ruined one of my prize subjects, and that, I cannot forgive."

"So now what?" Ario asked.

"You will be brought before Mother, and receive her judgment," Xavier said. "Your peers will be judged at the same trial. This one will be eliminated." Nodding towards Mara. "And your Heir will become ward of the state."

"You think I'll just let that happen?" Ario asked.

"Have you any choice? It's *over,* prince," Xanthos snapped. "Come along quietly, or I jab the baby."

Ario thought of the knife in his waistband. If he threw true at Xanthos's throat, that wouldn't stop Xavier from seizing the needle. "Alright," he said.

"Ario!" Peony cried.

"It'll be fine, Peony," he said. "Just go along with it."

"*That's* more like it. Hands behind your back." Xanthos clamped a pair of metal cuffs on his wrists, but did not search his person. "You, girl. Take the child, but do not leave my side." She obeyed, hatred in her eyes.

Ario would have to do this carefully. He drew in a deep breath and began working the blade out as the brothers escorted him and Peony from the temple.

Please help me, Goddess, he prayed.

The blade fell onto the dirt silently. He cast one last look over his shoulder and saw Evelyn looking through her bangs, down at the blade. At the same time, a wraith melted out of the shadows and started towards her. Ario felt its kiss and immediately knew it was S.

A blast of ice magic flattened them all to the ground, flooding the passage with the smell of ozone. Xavier swore. "Did you use the wrong cuffs, you moron?"

"There was only one palladium set, *you bastard*," the other brother hissed. Peony grasped Ario and pulled him back. Another wave of ice passed them harmlessly and soldered the brothers' limbs against the earth.

Peony helped him to his feet and tried to unlatch the cuffs, but they held firm. "Evelyn..." she murmured.

Ario looked from the squirming, swearing brothers towards the high priestess. She stood, side-by-side with S, her eyes glowing slightly with magic, the blade in her hand. With slow, regal steps, she made her way first towards the closest brother–Xanthos–and pressed her blade against his jugular.

"Oh, you fucking *cunt*," he spat at her. "You think you're winning?"

"Are there forces waiting for us?" she asked in a hoarse voice, like basements. "Upstairs?"

"Yes, of course," Xavier said dully.

"How many?" Ario asked.

"A dozen wraiths and half a dozen armed guards. And Mother."

"Traitor," Xanthos snapped at him.

Evelyn withdrew her blade. "They can't escape the ice. It won't melt. That'll buy us time. You. Can you help me again, with the cuffs?"

S approached Ario, their eyes glinting, and slipped the cuffs off with ease. Ario flexed his wrists.

"The Goddess must be on our side," she said, breathlessly. "Come. I can revive the others."

"Do you know if there's another exit?" he asked.

"Just death," Evelyn said cheerfully.

Peony regarded the two trapped brothers. Xavier had taken it stoically, lying silently and watching them like they were a tennis match. Xanthos writhed and kept spitting out slurs. Peony kicked him once in the side.

"Our odds aren't good," he said. "This is a dye job–I have no magic. Peony, I know you're not great at combat–"

"I haven't been *just* a mom these past months," she said. "Mara gave me some tips."

"And Michael has his military training, and we have our friend, here, for some reason," Evelyn said. "We can either fight, or try to flee... and there's nowhere to flee." She made her way towards the crumpled figures and began healing them. S removed Mara's cuffs.

Mara groaned and clutched her head. "The hell happened? All I remember is the flashbang–"

"I need you to help me fight." Evelyn took out a handkerchief and wiped away the blood. "We're in a predicament, but everyone's going to be fine."

Mara caught Ario's gaze and smiled. "Knew you didn't betray us."

Peony turned to Ario. He couldn't be sure, because of the dirt on her face, but he thought she might be blushing. "Hi."

"Hey. I'm... I'm so sorry..." He blinked tears out of his eyes. "I missed you so much."

She kissed his cheek, then his mouth, softly. "Take her. Okay?" Without waiting for a response, she eased the child into his arms.

This was no newborn. Amalia had heft, and there was an alertness in her eyes, her lavender curls sticking up every which way. She cringed away from Ario, resuming her cries.

"That's your dad, sweetie, mommy has to kick some ass," Peony said, pressing a kiss against her forehead.

She doesn't remember me, Ario thought, pain breaking through the shock. "I'll protect you."

The expression on Amalia's face was almost dubious, but she soon quieted. It felt... awkward, to hold her, his arms and body unused to such gestures. He was still rather bony. "Hi, you," he murmured. Would the Goddess "taking her piece" back hurt as much as the vaccine had hurt him? It could quite literally kill her.

Evelyn finished reviving the party. Michael just crossed over to Ario and squeezed his shoulder once. "We should go. There's no point waiting," he said.

"Our fate is in the Goddess's hands," Evelyn murmured.

It still took time to make the long journey up towards the guards. Peony walked near him, but her expression was wary, somber.

"I can't even imagine what this must have been like," he said. "I thought of you every day, if you were safe."

"We were... safe," she said. "We moved around a lot."

"Yeah. I remember how it used to be."

"I guess in a sense our baby got to see the world," she said wistfully. "Do you think Catherine will kill her, Ario?"

"No. I know she won't. She didn't kill me. Likely she won't even give her the vaccine." He sighed and looked down at Amalia and saw her watching him.

"She'll use her," Peony murmured.

"If the world even survives that long. Yes."

She frowned. "Did it hurt? The... vaccine?"

"It was the worst pain I ever felt," he admitted. "Worse than birth, and it lasted *weeks.* He... kept giving me more doses. It's not going to come back. Part of why I asked you to bring Amalia here. *If* we survive the next hour or so, I can fix everything."

Mara, ahead of them in the line, looked over her shoulder. "I can take you, prince. You and the child. I can't do more than two..."

"You will if it comes to that," Evelyn suggested. The neutrality of her tone indicated that they had built some rapport.

"No," Ario said. "No, it's going to end here. One way or another."

At long last, they saw the bright light of the archives. "Stay back, Ario," Michael said. "Do you have a weapon?"

"I only had the athame, and Evelyn needs it more," he said.

"It will have to do. Be ready. Maybe we can still negotiate some kind of peace."

Mara scoffed. "Do I get to fight, or not?"

In the distance, they heard a guard shout, "Come out with your hands up!"

Peony squeezed Ario's arm tightly, kissed him once, and kissed their daughter. "I love you," she whispered.

"I love you too," he said.

One by one, they re-entered the room. Ario braced himself for gunshots, but none came, and slowly, so terribly slowly, he could see the guards behind Michael and Mara. They had automatic weapons drawn, and behind them, wraiths boiling madly in the bright light.

At the center, though, there she was: Catherine, Catherine as he knew her, her face cold and hard, her eyes aflame with such *fury*. On his knees, in front of her, a dagger pressed to his throat, was Xander.

He looked like he'd been beaten; one eye was swollen closed and there was a streak of blood coming from his lips. His hands were bound behind his back and he seemed too dazed to even meet Ario's eyes.

"So," she said, any hint of sweetness or simpering gone. "This is how it is, is it? I *chose* to trust you, prince. I chose to show you mercy again and again. There was no reason for it to end this way. Conspiring with my own *son* is a new low. It takes a lot to surprise me. *Where* are my sons?"

"They are alive," Evelyn said. "We will return them to you safely if you show us no violence."

She did not move. Xander winced at the blade digging into his flesh. "I could kill you all now and be done with it."

"You could," Ario agreed. "But don't you need me?"

"I don't need *you* for anything," she spat. "Powerless, feckless, spineless, you're just a useless *snake*. But that." She gestured with her free hand towards the baby. "How *that* escaped detection is beyond me. I'll spare your lives if you hand over the infant."

"Never," Peony bit back, full of venom.

Catherine's head swiveled towards her. "Now *you,* my dear, *you* were a pleasant shock indeed. I didn't even know any of you were alive. How *has* the last decade treated you, Thalia?"

She went still with shock, her eyes wide and glimmering. "...What?"

"They kept records," she said. "The Queen insisted on it. Records of your bond... your bill of sale, you might as well call it. She amended the document, covered up your birth name with *another.* They took it from you. They took it *all* from you, dear. Your true form. Your first chosen name. You don't even have a choice of allegiance, bound to him like that like a chain."

"She's trying to psych you out. Don't let her," Mara hissed.

"I'll let you live. I'll even let you keep mothering the child, if you remain docile," Catherine said.

Mara snarled, an entirely lupine sound that set Ario's hair on end.

"What did he offer you, Samara?" she asked her. "Asylum? To a state that does not exist? To a throne of glass, if you will? You're no more free than you were before. Step aside, and we can reconsider. Let us *all* just take a breath."

"My *name* is Mara," she said through her teeth. "I am a sworn guard to the crown. You can go fuck yourself."

"This is all *very* touching. But let's see. There are..." she made a show of counting them. "Five combatants? Even your most powerful cannot stop *all* the bullets. Come quietly, or die, I don't care."

Amalia started to cry.

"Think about it. Do you really want the child to bear witness to this?" Catherine asked.

It occurred to him, suddenly, what to do.

"She's right," Ario said. "Let me through. Let's end this peacefully."

"Ario, *no,*" more than one of them hissed.

Ario took the hand of the person closest to him—Evelyn—and passed a message only she would understand.

T-R-U-S-T

"Let him go," she said hoarsely.

He pulled free of the group. Ario touched his breastbone, feeling the edge of his necklace. He brought it into the light. *Goddess, help me. I'm ready. We're all here.*

And he heard Her terrible voice: ~~by My hand, shatter the necklace. Draw the powder across your face and the child's face. Will something to break. You have to mean it.~~

He looked back at them once and squeezed the gem in his palm, feeling it crack and give more easily than something diamond-hard should. Peony gasped quietly. The sand felt too soft under his fingers. He drew a crescent on Amalia's forehead, then his own. "I'm sorry," he whispered. "I said it would end here."

With a ghastly grinding sound, the earth shifted under their feet. There was a moment of silence.

And then it all exploded.

That was how his mind rationalized it, anyway; bright piercing light and shrill, inhuman keening, alongside the human screaming. Before his vision went white, the wraiths vanished, and Xander swept Catherine's feet under her, causing her to topple amongst the chaos. A few guards attempted to use their firearms, but the bullets shattered midair into harmless powder. Mara, in her wolf form, tackled the guard closest to Catherine and tore out their throat. Xander, hands still bound, found the knife that had so recently been at his jugular before it could be swept away by the roiling earth. There was too much noise, too much chaos, and Ario's ears rang. Something was *happening,* something in his blood and bones, and it was all he could do to curve his body protectively over Amalia, who was thrashing and (silently) screaming. He looked over. Michael was crouched over an unconscious Peony, shielding her; Evelyn was on her knees praying like mad, shooting out spells between prayers. Before the pain hit him, he saw Xander struggling with Catherine on the ground. He raised the dagger and plunged it into her chest two, three times before a guard successfully dragged him away. He seemed to be sobbing. Mara hopped next at that guard and tore at Catherine's head, finishing anything Xander might not have been able to accomplish.

Everything seemed to vanish; to disappear, to be wreathed in that horrible mollifying light, the semblance of self he knew to be *Ario* violently rending itself from anything *Peony* and anything *Goddess* and anything *miasma* and just as it seemed the pain would be too much to bear, that he'd finally fall unconscious, it rose and peaked and rose and peaked and he was left clinging to his daughter as the world ended, or perhaps began.

~~Thank you~~, She said.

Part 999

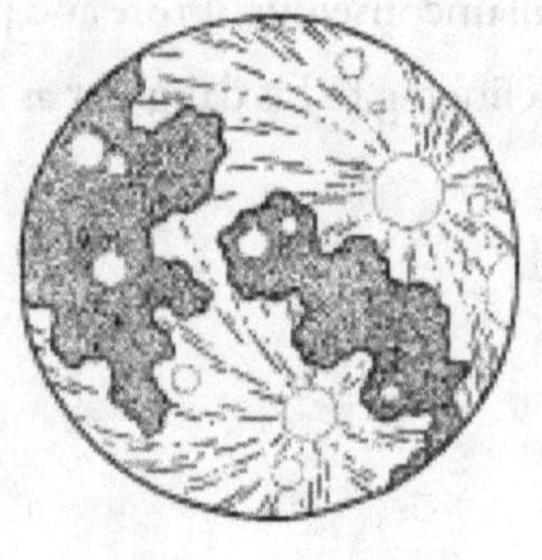

Denoument

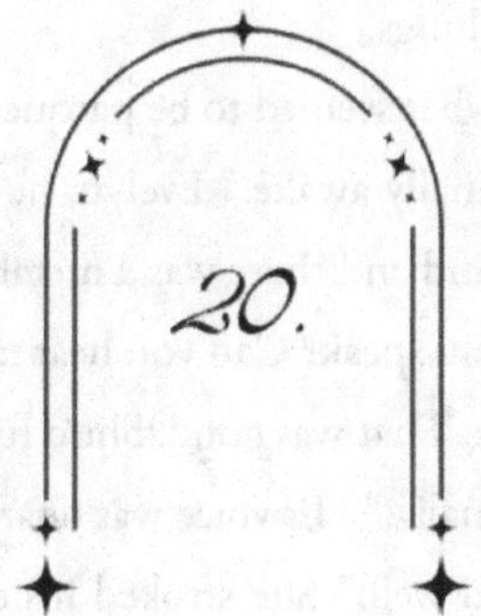

20.

He woke in darkness. Not night, but *darkness,* nothing visible in front of him. Was that it, then? Was this the great abyss?

And then he became aware that he had a body. And it *hurt.* The nerves burned, the muscles seized, the organs felt pulverized, the meat of him aching softly. Did it always *hurt,* being alive? Once the sensation of overwhelm came to pass, he felt he was on a soft, but narrow, bed, and warmth was kissing his hand. He chanced moving, pressing his hand farther into the invisible warmth, and it clicked.

The world was not bathed in darkness. What he felt was sunlight; he was blind. His next breath came hard and shrilly, and he felt every pinch as it entered his lungs.

Footsteps, against what seemed to be parquet. "Ario? *Ario?* Thank the Goddess, you're finally awake." Evelyn; he knew that voice anywhere. She took his hand and there was a metallic scratch against the floor. A chair? "Can you speak? Can you hear me, dear?"

So: Evelyn was alive. That was good. She'd fix this, get it all sorted, and then... "Peony. Amalia." His voice was hoarse to his ears.

"Are both alive and well." She stroked his cheek; he smelled the familiar herbs-and-ink of her skin and relaxed the faintest.

"What's *happening?*" he asked.

"What's the last you can remember?" Her voice had moved; he heard something liquid being poured into something else, and a glass was pressed against his lips. He drank it all down. There was something different about the water, something almost sweet, but he didn't think anything had been added to it.

"There was this... light, and an earthquake," he said haltingly.

"What did you do?" she asked. "I can make inferences, but... Ario, what did you *do*?"

"Is it bad?" he asked, his panic increasing. "Did I make it worse?"

"Well, no," she said. "Ario, whatever you did... the miasma's gone, and the wraiths. All of it."

"It worked." He laughed. "It really worked."

"Care to elaborate? You shouldn't have been able to do magic at all. It nearly killed you."

Ario took a deep breath. "She told me what to do Herself. We communed in that temple."

"Oh, praise be–"

"She needed to be freed of Her heartline to the moon." Which... that had disturbing implications all on its own. The moon had never felt *threatening* to him, but he supposed being stared at for millenia rather than eighty years or so would get a bit stifling. "I needed an ancestral piece of her–Amalia–and something powerful to sacrifice."

"...What did you sacrifice?" Evelyn adjusted the blankets on him slightly.

"My soulbond."

She sputtered. "Oh, Ario."

"I had to do it." He heard the hysteria in his voice more than felt it. "I *had* to, there was no other way–"

She pulled him up and into her arms. "My dear boy, my dear, precious, brave boy..."

In that moment, he was not king, but a sobbing, disjointed mess. What he felt was not *grief.* You could only grieve something you loved, hoped for. Everything he felt for her had been razed, leaving behind a deep hollow. How much more was he supposed to give up? His bodily autonomy, his magic, his religion, his *love*, and now his sight. What was left?

When he felt he could compose himself, he wiped his smarting eyes. "How is she?" he asked. "Does she seem affected, or..."

Evelyn sighed. "She's moody and depressed, but honestly, I thought that was a result of post-traumatic stress. We're all trying to cope with what happened that night."

"I swear I saw Xander and Mara kill Catherine..."

She cleared her throat. "Yes. They did. She is no more. Her sons have been successfully detained."

Ario leaned back against the sheets. "So who's in power? How long have I been out?"

She paused for a long time. "Resistance forces came to our defense once the word was out. A few people from her administration made stabs at taking the post, but the problem was that there wasn't much *military* to establish martial law. They had been sent across the country to deal with the riots, and once word started to spread, not many returned to their posts." Another, wetter throat clearing. Was she crying? "That leaves you. Xander has gathered a few folks he feels can be of use from the previous administration, and he's working with Ainsley as an interregnum. The public has not yet been officially made aware of Catherine's death. Or your existence, for that matter."

He took a deep breath. "We did it." It did not feel real. "Is it over? Is it really over?"

"Yes, you marvellous boy. You did it. Goddess *bless* us."

Ario struggled to sit up, his core muscles complaining. "She wanted to die, Evelyn."

"Catherine?"

"The Goddess. This was a compromise."

"She... cannot die, Ario." There was something scolding in her tone.

"But She wanted to. The miasma... it was Her attempt at suicide. I wonder if She's sleeping."

Evelyn didn't speak. Ario wished he could see her face. "I didn't want to believe your letter. You're certain?"

"I heard it directly from Her."

Another few beats of silence. "I'm sorry–" he began.

"I will contemplate this on my own time," she said, a wobble in her voice. "We need to focus on getting you well, if you're to take over."

"...About that. I'm sort of blind."

***

It became clear quickly there was no salvaging his vision. Evelyn, Maeve, and three separate resistance healers all tried, to no avail. Ario wasn't expecting success; magical wounds can only be undone using an equal amount of power as receiving the wound incurred, and while very competent, none of the healers were divine. He would simply have to adapt, like he was having to adapt to the chronic pain. It was nothing short of a miracle—possibly Her last—that Amalia had not been affected.

The problem was, when one was king, one needed to read and read *a lot*. It wasn't as though he had time to learn Braille. Evelyn devised a half-baked solution—a pair of glasses that would transmit the text into his mind—and it was through this lens that Ario became king.

Resistance members and regime-members that he did not quite trust helped him draft his first executive order. Xander, as the last free member of Catherine's family, ceded control of her administration to him, in writing. Ario re-established, with a single scribble, the monarchy, from his hospital bed.

In the coming days there was a flurry of people, coming in and out of his room, some of whom he knew, many he did not. Ainsley felt the need to join him and offer her "advice," which mostly consisted of pointing out who was genuinely a civil servant from her reign and who he should probably not re-appoint. Emergency elections for parliament had to be held, magic users freed, the worst of the offenders of the genocide arrested for trial, a justice system to be rebuilt. The press, freed from its restraints, churned out story after story after story about "what really happened" and misinformation, both positive and negative, spread like wildfire.

At some point there would be a coronation, an official introduction to the public, but it turns out *establishing the government* was a very difficult and time-consuming project, and things he understood not terribly much about, like the kingdom's budget, had to be delegated to people he wasn't even sure he could fully trust. These meetings, the endless tedium, exhausted him so fully he could do little more than sleep and work in those first awful days; he did not even have time to visit with Peony, or his daughter, to see what was happening. He could've–should've–*made* the time, but something in him dreaded the meeting.

He knew he felt terrible, on a logical level. He should be devastated, heartbroken, even. But what he felt towards her was a scary nothing, and he was reminded, again of the powers that be constantly messing with what he could do and feel. That did not make his heart feel any less withered. He could decide how he felt, now. They could pretend they'd never met, try this relationship for real. If she could ever find it in her to forgive him–and he wouldn't blame her if she couldn't.

He finally saw her about a week into his reign, when he was finally able to limp about a bit with a cane (to lean on, not to tap the ground with, not yet). He was getting better at sensing when people entered the room, and placing the sound of their footsteps. He heard Amalia giggle and coo.

"Um, hey." Her tone was mild, measured. "She, uh, really wanted to see you. So I figured I'd come by."

He eased over to the chair in his study, nearly missing it. "I'd be happy to see you, Amalia."

Peony came closer. She smelled nice–of course she must have access to such things again–but it did not evoke the rush of yearning it used to. "Hold out your arms?" Peony suggested, and he did, feeling the press of weight. Amalia let out a little squeal. She was wearing something silky. "There you go. There's daddy. She really missed you, I could feel it."

He made himself smile. "I missed you too, sweetie."

"She's, um, smiling. They said you can't see?"

He sighed and shook his head. "Nothing. Not even light. Evelyn hopes it *might* come back at least a little, but it never did with my right eye, so I'm not holding my breath."

"You were blind in your right eye?"

He felt, of all things, a flash of irritation. "Did I never tell you that story? ...Strange. Yes, on the night of the coup–the, ah, other one–I used too much magic. That's what too much magic does, just starts eating you right up."

"...I never noticed."

"Well, it wasn't terribly visible, no? My eyes look normal, but they don't work much at all. Do you want to sit? I've got a little time before Xander brings in the next one."

The scrape of a chair. He didn't know how she oriented herself. "Is it hard?"

"More inconvenient than anything, really. And the specs Evelyn made from me are not foolproof. I swear, they read out "incompetent" as "incontinent" and I had to wonder why toilet humor had found its way into my law."

"*Your* law." A wry laugh. "That's still weird."

"You're telling me." He brushed his daughter's head with his palm, lightly; her curls had been pulled into a very short ponytail. "Is her hair still–"

"Purple, yeah. We think she still has power. She reads off the charts. Yours is really black?"

"It will be, eventually. I'm keeping the silver for optics as I come out, but then I'll probably shave or dye it."

"You'd look so normal."

"Well, I *am* a mundane. Like it or not."

A very long pause. Ario shifted Amalia from one leg to the other. She gurgled and clapped her hands. "You don't have to be qu–" he began.

"What did you do to me?" She said it flatly, but there was a tremor to her voice.

"...Do to you?" he repeated.

"That night. The night the miasma dispersed, and you killed your goddess, or whatever. Something happened. What did you do?"

The next breath in hurt terribly. "She asked me for a sacrifice. I only had one thing powerful enough to give up."

She exhaled heavily. "I thought it was something like that." Two very heavy footsteps, and Amalia was snatched from him; the baby let out a cry in protest.

"Peony–"

"*No.* I am so *sick* of my fate being determined by people who think they know better. Well, the blinders are off, okay? You've got no love to guardrail this any more."

"You think I wanted this?" he shot back. "That I had to give up the only thing that ever made me happy–"

"Did I? Did we really?" She must've been in his face; he felt her breath and smelled more of that perfume. "Or were we just brainwashed into it?"

"What was I supposed to do?" he said. "Let the world end? Let everyone and everything die–*including* our daughter, might I add–"

"You *hated* her!" Peony yelled. "You called her a parasite."

His diplomacy training told him to de-escalate. "Leave my dysphoria out of this."

"What about *mine,* huh? You think it was easy watching you go through that?"

"You never said–"

"*You never asked.*"

Amalia made a confused noise.

"I'm sorry," he said, even as fury boiled within him. "Peony, I am so, so sorry I had to do this. I'm not expecting forgiveness."

"Then what *are* you expecting? Me to smile and be all dressed up at your side?"

"You don't *have* to do anything."

"Then what is there for me? I left behind Lindenfell for you, I became a mom for you, and now I don't even know that I want anything to do *with you*, but she's a *princess*, and that comes with strings. I could go home. But there's no home, there's no Rory, there's just *nothing*. You took *everything*."

"You say that like I liked it," he snapped. "You don't think it destroyed me too?"

"Sure doesn't seem like it."

He let out a frustrated grunt. Amalia started to cry.

Peony exhaled. "I'm sorry, sweetie, this isn't nice," she said, evidently to the baby. "Mommy's having big feelings." Then, to him, "I'm going."

"Wait–can I see her–"

"I guess. Whatever."

"Can we at least talk?"

"About what?"

He fell silent.

"Yeah. I thought so. Have Michael come get her when you want her. Not that it'll be often, I bet." More clacking footsteps, Amalia's cries echoing, and the slam of a door.

Ario pressed his face against his hands and did not move until he was summoned.

***

At the end of his first month in office, the kingdom was still in shambles. Despite wielding decidedly too much executive power, those employees of Catherine's who had been benign enough to retain their positions often decided to push back, tying up decrees in yet-existent judicial systems. Anti-magic sentiment was still very much present, and there were some protests against the new rule. A squad of 440s went rogue and took the capitol's post office hostage, almost killing a few federal workers and slowing much-needed shipments of supplies. Considering Ario only had a fraction of the military Catherine had had, he was forced to concede to their demands: deferred sentences of their war crimes. This was not received well by the public, who still saw Ario as shadowy, a fraud. Sacks of hate mail came in by the dozens, though, Xander noted, Ario did receive *less* than his mother had. Some hope.

Some of the city-states refused to meet with him, hastily establishing their own independence, and Ario had to admit he had nothing compelling to offer and much to ask for. The crown could not provide protection or steward trade deals or cut taxes—which he was horrified to learn how misdirected the wealth was. Tiny departments of her government had bloated budgets and crucial infrastructure was underfunded. Xander said it was like this by design.

"The problem is I cannot simply *undo* anything with the swish of a pen," Ario said hotly one (afternoon? evening? Lack of perceived daylight was hard to adjust to) meeting. "Like she seemed to have."

"Because you're not a dictator," Xander said. "Kindness is often more work."

"You're telling me," he muttered.

Ario heard Xander get up and walk across the room, possibly towards the window. He'd elected, for some reason, to heal naturally from the injuries he'd occurred the night of the Severing; several broken ribs, a bruised kidney, and a badly scratched cornea, and any number of bruises and cuts now invisible to Ario. Perhaps he saw it as penance.

"The important thing is that the people are safe, and the economy has yet to crash." The gentle tapping of a pen against a hard surface. "That, in and of itself, is more than I could've thought to ask for. The cities could've decided to drop deals they had with Catherine." His voice twisted slightly when he said her name. "What will become of me, when the dust is settled? I committed high treason."

Ario took a long drink from his water glass, and reached for the dreaded reading glasses. "You are also primarily the reason I'm king, and one of the only reasonable people I talk to on a daily basis. *If* it really matters to you, we can have any number of felonies put on paper. Or insist on house arrest."

"I only want to... fix what I broke," he said. "This is all because of me. *I* gave her what she needed to take over. And then I spent years doing *nothing*."

"It was collapsing anyway," Ario said gently. "My mother was a terrible queen, and Ainsley simply didn't have the skill or power to fix what was broken. There's still a lot of fatalist sentiment, which will scarcely go away. I'm hoping that at least the people will realize I bought us time."

"You saved the world, majesty," Xander pointed out.

"And my just reward is... paperwork." He turned his face towards the bills on the desk in front of him, hearing the glasses read off in their awkward, stilted voice. "Paperwork, a partner that hates me, and a traumatized daughter. Not to mention a disability. It *is* cruel, isn't it? Fate?"

"...She hasn't come 'round, then?" Ario heard footsteps, heavy glass clinking, liquid swilling, and smelled the sweet tang of whiskey. A glass was placed somewhere near his hand.

"She's only here because she has nowhere else to go," Ario admitted. He picked up the rocks glass and sipped. "If I were in her shoes, I would be even more furious."

"I take it that's why you also avoid the queen whenever you can."

Ario kicked back the rest of the drink and shuddered as it burned its way down. "You know better than I how complicated these familial relationships could be. Were it purely up to me, I would have nothing to do with her. But she has too much information I need. And... well. I'm a hypocrite, Xander."

"...Majesty?"

"I judge her for her choices, and yet, I've made terrible ones as well."

"You sacrificed something innate to you for the greater good. It sounds like... what she did to Peony was much grayer."

Ario waved dismissively, causing the glasses to sputter gibberish as they struggled to focus on the paper. "At the end of the day, the damage is done."

Xander slurped his own drink. "...Quite."

"How are you coping?"

"What do you mean?"

"With all this. You paid a price, too."

Xander laughed out loud. "The minute I decided to side with the resistance was the minute I lost them."

From the doorway came the distinct four-beat knock that Mara used. "Lindenfell's ambassador is here, Lord King," she said, and then a second later, sniffing, "Is that whiskey?"

"Send them in," Ario said, hastily reaching for the mints he kept in the top drawer.

***

True to her word, the next few times Ario requested to see Amalia, Peony refused to see him, instead having Michael or Mara or even Marko bring her to him with a very overprepared diaper bag that just screamed condescension for his parenting skills. Amalia no longer saw Ario as a stranger, but he did suspect she saw him more as a babysitter than a parental figure. She showed more enthusiasm for Mara (and playing horsey in her wolf form) than she did for him. If he somehow had time to worry about anything other than the state of the kingdom, he worried if they would ever develop a true bond. Not helped by the fact that he had no idea what to do with her. She grew bored of being read to (and, with the glasses, it was quite a process).When he felt well enough, he took her for walks outside in the clean spring air. It didn't help that he was still mentally mapping the castle. Mostly he found himself talking to her about... nothing much.

He turned his face in her direction. "I guess you'll eventually have more memories of this place than I will."

Amalia made a noise that might have been an agreement. Birds, migrating back now that the miasma had abated, filled the capitol city, and he heard them chirping.

"See the birdies?"

So it went. His status and the nature of his condition meant he couldn't really be left alone with her, not yet. Especially because she was showing more magic, including an uncanny ability to get out of her stroller. He hoped she wouldn't have to do this—to be queen—when she got older. His transitional plan was still sketchy and contingent on things going well. And the moon only knew how that would go.

One particularly rainy, raw March day, he received a communication from his new warden of the dungeons. They were processing the releases of magic users and subsequent reparations, and they had come onto one file that he might find of interest. Was he interested in pressing charges against Rory? They wanted to know.

The pre-Severing version of himself would demand penance for what she had done, but Ario knew Rory had gone through enough—the destruction of her own magic and loss of her home. He summoned her.

When Mara brought her up to his study, she was still in cuffs; Ario heard the clinking of the metal. "The prisoner is here, majesty."

Part of him was relieved he could not see her, her face. He held his own expression neutral. "Let her have a seat. Bring her some tea, if you wouldn't mind. I know how terribly drafty it is down there."

As she got closer, Ario caught a whiff of the cheap detergent and soap allowed prisoners. The soft squash of the pleather and her sharp intake of breath filled the space for a long moment, and finally he said, "I'm sorry it took us so long to get to your file. We're terribly understaffed."

From Rory, another tremulous breath. "I'm surprised you wanted to see me. Your highness. Er. Majesty. Sorry." Her voice was very hoarse. He heard the gentle clink as Mara must have passed her a china teacup.

"I've had to make some hard calls myself. But my reasoning is slightly more selfish." He knotted his hands, feeling the dryness of his skin. "I want you to see your cousin."

"I... I *can't*," she said quickly. "I can't face her. I'm sorry. I'm so sorry. I just wanted..."

"Peace, Rory."

"Are you going to kill me?" she whispered.

"Of course not," he said. "I'm not sure... I can just let you go, but you've already lost enough. I... I went through it too, you know. The vaccine. I'm so sorry."

"I'd heard rumors, but I didn't think it was true."

"I'm not ashamed of it." He cleared his throat. "Peony... she isn't doing well. I'm sure she'd love to see you again."

"How can she forgive me?" Rory asked. "After that?"

"She's... not quite happy with me right now." Understatement of the millenium. "She might find your actions a bit less disagreeable. Either way, that is for you to broach with her. You might find it cathartic."

A whisper. "I almost got her killed."

"But you ultimately didn't. I'm not telling you not to be guilty."

"...And if she wants nothing to do with me?"

"I'm afraid there's nothing I can do about that. But maybe she'll surprise you."

A dull laugh. "Maybe."

Ario thought for a moment. "Maybe you'd like to help me. My government. We could organize a sort of work-release. What did you study in university?"

"...Business."

"Always useful. I'm sure we could find something for you in the state or treasury departments." The component bits had been messily merged under Catherine, and now he was extricating them and expanding them. He was surprised that people were actually applying for all of the new roles, but considering how volatile things had been under her, they probably just needed the work. Now that he had some funds to reallocate, he could actually pay people. And once farmlands recovered, the cost of food and other goods would surely drop.

She fidgeted; he heard the clink of her cuffs. "If I work for you, I'll get let go?"

"Yes. Of course. I'm sure you could use the money. Mara?"

He heard her quick, light footsteps. "Yes, majesty?"

"Please remove Rory's bindings and see if Peony is willing to speak with her."

"Yes, majesty."

Ario would not learn for some time what happened, exactly, in the reunion, but Peony did evidently meet with her. He released Rory to a more comfortable room and saw she got to work; her supervisor reported she took to the job well.

The spring days wore on, endlessly, and it felt he would never leave his desk.

In his incredibly limited spare time, Ario undertook his own research project, especially as he became accustomed to his blindness. His reading glasses had been improved somewhat, to include access to maps of the castle, and although he could freely go where he wished (albeit with a guard), he treasured small hours stolen alone in the library and in the lower archives. Librarians and archivists were still cleaning up and restoring the mess of the Severing, but there was less damage than he'd feared–maybe because a lot of the tomes had protection spells cast on them. But he found little about the topic he desired. He would have to bite the bullet and ask Ainsley, who was obliged to see him several hours each week.

"Aunt?"

"Yes, dear?" After weeks of stable food, her voice was no longer so coarse.

Ario crossed his arms. "I need you to tell me more about Peony. Her people. The archives don't have much."

She set down her teacup. Accursed tea; he wished never to see it again. He'd learned to only pretend to drink when dignitaries met with him, lest he also be plagued with an overfull bladder amid the tedium. "I'm surprised she hasn't asked me."

"Well, rightfully, her trust in us has been challenged, if not shattered entirely." He cocked his head. "You negotiated the terms of the bond. Catherine claimed the crown cut her off from her the rest of her power, which you previously denied. Is this true?"

"We'd never do something so cruel."

"Could you swear that under oath?"

"Yes, Ario. It was probably caused by the miasma."

"Forgive me for finding it hard to believe she just *washed up on a beach* somewhere."

Ainsley made a displeased, indignant noise. "Some of them did run, you know."

"And you did not find it, at all, prudent to mention this, ever." His lip curled. "Do you know where the remainder are? We have to let her know and establish relations immediately."

"I don't know *where* they went. I guess you could put out an inquiry. Or command someone to go looking."

"Where's the treaty outlining the agreements of our bond?"

"Ario, I'm sure there's nothing you don't already know."

He spun in his chair and got up. "Catherine could. Catherine did."

A screech of chair on floor; Ainsley had gotten up too. "Catherine lied about many things, Ario."

"But fewer than I thought. She called Peony *Thalia*. Did you know she was trans, and simply never let on to Evelyn that all-important detail? Did you not think it fit to tell me?"

"When I saw you again, I seem to remember you being in a rather unreasonable state—"

Ario snorted. "So you knew. And you did nothing."

"What was I *supposed* to do?"

"Let me know. Let her know."

"And if you were captured, and it were interrogated out of you?"

"I *was* captured after all," he snapped, his voice rising. "What do you know about her, and her people?"

He heard Ainsley breathing tremulously for a few moments. Then, "she was the daughter of the chief. I didn't know that you were... that you would..." She stuttered. "Queer political matches were uncommon. But you were compatible, she could shield you. Your presence wasn't necessary for the bond to take hold."

"And who did the bonding?"

"Her father. The chief."

"So you were there? In the colonies?"

"On a sandbar nearby, but... yes."

"Did he survive?"

"I don't think so." Her voice was flat.

"Is there any way to rebuild the bond?"

"Only the officiant or someone of immense power could do that. Unless you chose to pairbond."

Unlikely. "Did she have family?"

"Two mothers and a handful of younger sisters."

Ario felt his blood pressure rising, heat flooding his face. "And you withheld this... why?"

"They're *dead*, Ario, it's not like she can see them."

"*Catherine's* regime functioned on lies. So did yours. But mine will not."

"So you'll break her heart again. For what?"

"She and my daughter deserve to know where they were from. You're *pathetic*," he bit out.

A long pause, and then, "I know."

He started pacing.

"I never *wanted* to be queen," Ainsley said. "I was content with my own personal pursuits, and as second born, I didn't have much magic. Our mother never bothered to give me much training in *diplomacy* or history or anything that would possibly help run a country, and then your mother got herself blown up and I had to try and fix the country she bankrupted. I told myself I was doing the best I could. You've–you've seen how much *work* it is, all of these little pieces you must balance just right. I don't have the mind for it."

"Maybe you never tried," Ario said. "Maybe if you had just believed."

A few ticks. Wind pressed against the windows of his study.

"Your mother said you were something, when you were born," Ainsley commented. "Something she couldn't understand. I wonder if she went through with it because only someone else could fix all this."

"She went through with it like I did: because she had no choice," he said. "And I *am* fixing it. But I refuse to fix it with more lies." He cleared his throat. "I'm going to prioritize resources to scope out the siren colonies. We should get a measure for how the ocean is coping, anyway."

"Whatever you say, Lord King."

"I am *very* busy. I would appreciate it if you took your leave."

Ainsley said no more, and her heels clacked on the parquet as she left.

Ario mustered his way through the end of the day–meetings with accountants, nominees for the new department of medicine and magic health services, and other career bureaucrats he knew were necessary but could scarcely tell their functions—all the while nursing a seed of dread. He was going to go to Peony's quarters and tell her what he'd learned. Hopefully she would understand it was an olive branch, of sorts. She, Evelyn, and Amalia were staying down in the nursery—a set of royal apartments that hadn't been used for their intended purpose in years. It had been generations since an Heir had more than two children, but Ario was staying in the Heir's quarters, and only Ainsley had the stomach to return to the queen's. While he couldn't really see what changes were being made to the castle, he enjoyed the differences in scent, texture; the brackish miasma had been replaced with cleaning products and something floral. Judging distance was still hard, making him grateful he had Michael with him. He heard people passing and their whispered conversations halted by acknowledgement of his presence, which still felt strange. Perhaps it always would.

A pair of guards were stationed at the door. He'd never met them when he was sighted, and they remained shadowy in his mind. "Lord King," one said. He really should know the names of the people who were guarding his daughter.

"As you were, please," he said. "Is Peony here?"

"She recently returned with the princess, majesty."

"Excellent. Might we see them?"

A low whisper, perhaps into an earpiece, then, "she said to tell you, and I quote, "unless you wish to clean up a diaper blowout, leave us alone.""

Ario was surprised to feel the beginning of a smile. "You can tell her I'd be more than happy to clean up, and that it's important."

Another small series of whispers, then, "Alright." The guard opened the door with a soft squeak.

The sullen voice came from somewhere to his left, and Ario heard Amalia squalling. "What do you want?" Peony asked.

The nursery certainly smelled like a child lived there–and not just because of the aforementioned mess. He smelled sunscreen and that particular tang of formula and something sweet. "I know you don't wish to see me, so I'll keep it brief. I've learned more about the sirens. I wished to tell you directly–because this game of telephone won't help either of us."

The click of the diaper bag's latch. "What did you learn?" Was that hope, edging into her voice?

He took a few hesitant steps into the space towards her voice. Ario only had the foggiest notion of what the space was like, and no idea at all for the configuration of furniture.

Amalia made a happy noise and clapped; was she pleased to see him?

"You had a family."

"Of course I had a family. I didn't come out of thin air." The rustle of fabric, probably as she dressed the baby. She stood, and he heard footsteps in the opposite direction. Amalia babbled.

"Your father was the chief," he said, slightly more loudly. "You had two mothers. And younger sisters."

For a moment, there was just silence, and he nearly asked Michael if she was still there. But then more hurried steps, running water at an unseen sink, a startled *whumpf* from Amalia as she was scooped up, and Ario could smell Peony's perfume in his face. "Sisters?" she asked.

"Two. I had my librarian check the census records for their names. The one just after you was Haukea, and the youngest was Keala." He felt his breath shuddering slightly. "My aunt doesn't think they survived."

He heard her breathe out, the same juddery sound. "*Two* moms?"

"Yes. I didn't know the sirens practiced polyamory. It would make sense for pairbonds to work in multiple directions. Why shouldn't they?" Ario felt a small hand slapping on his upper arm and held his out automatically. Peony's fingers, ice cold, brushed his as she acquiesced to Amalia's desire.

"The librarian. Did they say if the last daughter was named Thalia?"

"...Yes."

A gasp, then what might've been a laugh. Then, "They... let this happen?" she asked, very quietly.

Amalia pressed close to Ario's chest and let out a long sigh.

"They thought they were doing right by you, and your people," Ario said. "The crown promised them protection. We failed." *I failed.* "I'm organizing an expedition to see if there are any survivors or returning settlers."

"Let me go. Please," she said. "I have to know they're really gone. I have to see it for myself." Her voice was choked with tears.

"Of course. You don't even have to ask."

"What about the baby? I've never been away from her. If it's horrible I don't want her to see it. Not yet."

A voice from the far opposite end of the room answered, "I can look after her." More steps. He was starting to tell the difference in types of shoe apart; these had sensible rubber soles.

Ario started a little. "Evelyn. I didn't know you were here."

"I made the mistake of trying to nap," she said lightly. "It has been a pleasure being your advisor... but I wouldn't mind the break. It's hard to be a priestess for a force that doesn't exist. Don't you *dare* suggest recruiting an au pair." In and around the joke were metallic notes of pain. Ario had not pried about Evelyn's faith, if she had retained it, or if she were still in crisis. It had been hard enough losing his own, and she had been much more devout.

Amalia bounced slightly and laughed. "Eh! Eh!"

"Perhaps you both should go," Evelyn suggested.

"I could hardly leave my desk for potentially weeks," Ario began. "I've just barely been able to navigate the castle. I would be no use on a ship."

"I seem to recall we have these things called "cellular telephones" and "computers,"" Evelyn said lightly. "The royal fleet *used* to be able to handle telecommunications. I don't see how that would have changed."

He considered not saying it, but then spoke anyway. "I figure Peony doesn't want to spend time with me in an enclosed space. This is very personal. I would be a nuisance." He expected a hot and hardy agreement.

But Peony just exhaled. "No. You should come. You were the other half of the bond. It feels right."

"You could think about it," he offered.

"Da. Da!" Amalia insisted.

"I want to see this through," she said. "All the way. Don't make me say "please.""

Ario swallowed, feeling the lump in his throat. "I would never."

From near the doorway, Mara remarked, "so I guess we're going on a field trip."

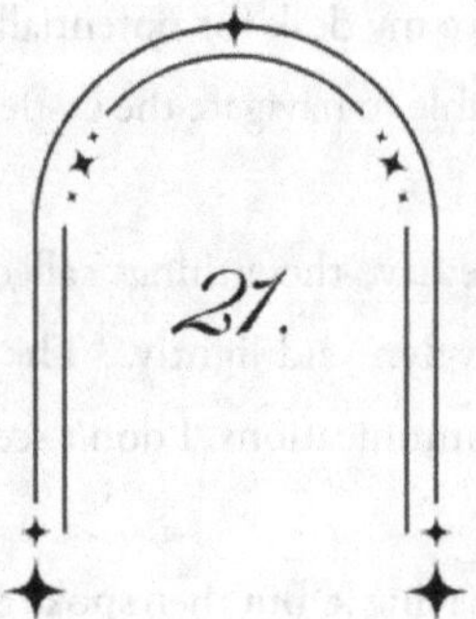

It turned out there was a lot of work to organize an expedition. Most of the sailors of Catherine's personal sailing vessel—the old royal ship—had deserted their post, so more had to be hired. They had to recruit marine biologists and specialist mages to study the effects of the lack-of-miasma on the ocean. Unsurprisingly, there were not exactly volunteers in his pool of bureaucrats to serve as diplomats if there *were* any living sirens down there. Ario could've commanded them, but he figured it would only make the situation more delicate. Peony stepped forward.

Yet all too soon the appointed day was coming, and they were saying goodbye to their daughter and boarding the ship, which had hastily been rechristened as the *Everglade*. While its engines were primarily solar and hydrogen powered, it also had sails, mostly for optics and occasionally to harness any particularly good wind. Ario only had vague memories of being on the boat as a very small child–after Chiara's death, he was no longer taken far from the palace–but apparently Catherine had changed a lot of the decor, leaving much of the royal quarters papered in "stomach medicine pink" according to Mara.

The sea air smelled clean and rich. They set off accompanied by two smaller research vessels from universities in other parts of the kingdom.

In years past, the sea would've been choppy at this point of year, but the limited snowfall had lessened the violence of the waves, which Ario was immensely grateful for. He was unsure if it was his lack of vision, or if he were this way naturally–gifted by an earth goddess and all–, but he was laid up for the better part of the first two days with terrible seasickness. Only once he'd heard from Evelyn that *of course* she'd laid aside medicine for that did he begin to feel better. Despite the tedium of his work remaining the same, the change of scenery alone was novel enough to lift the crushing dread he'd felt all this time.

Peony spent most of her time above deck, chatting with the researchers and sailors. Mara said she was learning knots and climbing some of the rigging. At Ario's horror, she commented, "she's been on baby patrol for almost a year. Let her play. There are like a dozen people who can heal on board."

It wouldn't take very long to reach the colonies, maybe a week if the weather held. At first, he took his meals in his quarters, which of course were right next to Peony's as the "consort". But then curiosity won out, and he joined the others in the galley. This, of course, dampened their spirits as they awkwardly pretended it was natural for royalty to be here (and that they openly supported him, as well), but it took approximately one conversation with the coarse first officer to fix that.

"Don't just sit there and stare, finish up and get back to work," he said in a very thick, gruff southern accent. Then, "don't pay them any mind, Mr. King, they just haven't been to work in a minute."

This charmed Ario immensely. "What *has* it been like, to be at sea all these years?"

A scoff. "We ain't been at sea. We go up and down the coast with supply shipments, always land in sight. You have no idea how suffocating that feels. I figure now what that gray goo is gone, done ruining our seas, we have to go back out."

"That must've impacted your livelihood." The ship was listing, slightly; Ario held fast to his tray.

"Impacted? More like destroyed. Those of us lucky enough to keep working still barely got by." He chewed loudly. "Not that I expect you to know what that's like. No offense."

"I've actually lived in poverty most of my life."

The officer guffawed. "And I'm queen of all the land."

"We'd probably be better off if you were," Ario said. "I'll say this: I never *could* quite enjoy the taste of pine bark. Gets in your teeth like you wouldn't believe."

"You really ain't messing with me," he said, with wonder.

"I would never."

The crew was more relaxed around him after that. When he could steal moments away from his laptop and spectacles, he tried to talk to them, to get their perspectives. In the evenings, after dark, they would gather either on the deck (if it weren't too cold and windy) or in the recreational area (if it were) to find ways to pass the time until lights out. Sometimes the sailors did silly little acts or played cards or sang along to a poorly-tuned guitar and an accordion that had apparently survived a great ordeal. And they drank: cheap beer or a clear spirit that made his eyes burn through scent alone. Ario largely abstained, but found the crew more amenable to his questions when they were just a bit drunk.

Someone slid onto the bench next to him. "You seem to be enjoying yourself," Mara commented.

"I find them very interesting," he said. "If you'd like to partake, I highly doubt anyone is going to hurt me."

She scuffed her foot along the floor. "No. Booze doesn't do much for me, not since Xavier."

"That's a shame."

"Not that I need a vice, you know." She laughed suddenly, a bright shock, then described a scene unfolding presently. "One of the graduate students lost a bet. Two of the sailors have them upside down over the keg. They're chugging... they're chugging..." A retch and a horrid *splat*. The sailors cheered. "You should probably intervene. Not very becoming of a royal vessel." The student started singing a very off key drinking song, and the others joined.

"Who do we have to impress out here?" Ario asked.

One high, clear, pristine voice stuck out amongst the others, and though he'd never heard Peony sing, he would've placed that voice anywhere.

"Why'd you stay?" Ario asked.

"Sorry?"

"I told you you would fulfill your debt if you were able to get everyone to the palace that night. You did, and besides, the Goddess is for all intents and purposes dead, rendering our deal null and void. You could've run away in all the chaos."

In a soft, almost melancholic voice, she countered, "where would I have gone? I have no family, no friends. If I went home, I doubt anyone would know me. The enhancements have made me look so beat to shit."

The drinking song morphed into another. "We're working on treatments, you know. For anyone affected by the miasma or the vaccine." That was one of Evelyn's primary duties.

As if he hadn't said this, she continued, "besides... it hasn't been half bad, working because I *want* to, not because I have to or am conscripted to. Are you going to make me say it?"

"That depends."

"I *like* you, majesty. I like Peony and I like the baby. I like feeling important and like I'm protecting something, not pursuing it."

Ario smiled, but turned his head down.

"Plus the benefits aren't bad. And... well. Maybe I want to be better. Maybe you were right, that night you were all crazy and didn't kill me like you should've."

He turned his head towards her. "Just know you *can* leave," he said. "I'm giving you the choice."

"I appreciate that, majesty."

"Ario. Please."

"You are perhaps the most unprofessional royal I've ever met." She made a startled noise. "Peony's brought out her mandolin. She's going towards the front of the room." The drinking song ended and whispering broke out. "Someone's offering her a chair..." The space had terrible acoustics; he shouldn't have heard the soft plucking as she tuned, but he did.

"I'm real happy to be here," Peony called out. "I want to say thank you to all of the people who are with us. You're bringing me home, and I didn't think that would happen. So. I wanted to play something for you. Don't worry; I'm not half bad."

Scattered drunken chuckles. She cleared her throat and started to play.

It was different than any song he'd heard from her throughout their brief period of happiness. The music was heavy, melancholic, weighty, weary through the lower tones and desperate within the higher, all heartbreak and chains until a sudden cloudbreak of hope struck, lightening the despair and giving something for the ear to cling to. The song became an odyssey, a labyrinth, struck through with pitfalls and missteps, arriving at a hard-won sense of joy.

At least I hope that's how it ends, he thought she said, over the sudden raucous cheering and requests for songs, which she was all too happy to oblige.

Ario blinked and felt wetness on his face. "I, um, need some air. Can you help me above deck?"

"...Certainly, majesty."

Up here, the wind was not quite so violent, but it was raw and cold, which suited his mood. Funny, how his high-quality wool coat did not protect him as much as shoddier plastic ones from years past. Or maybe he just wanted to be cold. Ario stood at the ship's bow, wondering what sight was ahead of him. Maybe at some point he would stop thinking about what he *might see*, and start thinking about what was really there.

"Peony's coming to you, majesty," Mara called from her place; she'd left enough space for him to feel alone, not so much anyone could sneak up on him.

"You spoiled the surprise," she said.

"You go ahead and startle someone standing right against a railing," Mara said lightly. "Majesties, shout if you need anything."

Ario heard her footsteps on the metal and felt the heat of her next to him; he caught the faintest whiff of that spirit. "You wanted to see me?" he asked.

"I just sort of... ended up here." She was slurring just slightly. "Real warm down there."

The breeze kicked up a bit. "Yes, the ventilation leaves a lot to be desired." Ario leaned against the railing. "You were excellent. As always."

"Mm, was nothing."

"I feel like... I've only ever seen you through your music."

"Well, you don't really *know* me," she said, though there was no harshness in her tone.

Ario sighed. "Be honest: how drunk are you?"

She chuckled. "What are you, a cop? Oh... wait... isn't the king like the ultimate cop?"

"I really hope not. No, I don't care if you're drinking, but I do want to talk to you with some degree of sincerity, and I don't want to do that if you're not all there."

"I'm sober enough to play, right?"

"...Touche." Ario tapped his fingers together. "What do you want, Peony? What can I do to make you happy?"

"That puts the work on me," she said softly.

He felt his brows raise. "You're... right. I'm sorry. I should..." He exhaled. "What we *were*... it took on this idealized notion in my head. But without the bond, we're just–"

"Strangers with a baby?" she offered.

"Well, yes. I could always count on having *you* at the end of the day. And now you hate me."

"I don't *hate* you."

"I didn't *want* to do it." The emotions he'd swallowed threatened to comeback out. "I didn't *want* to sacrifice our bond. I've given up everything again and again and I *hurt* you."

"I would've chosen the world too," Peony murmured. "Maybe I wouldn't have if we didn't have Amalia. There's a *world* there for our daughter now and not just slow starvation. But I..." She huffed. "It hurt. For days, it physically hurt. It still does if I think about it too hard. Doesn't it hurt?"

"Most of the time I feel numb," he admitted. "Even if I somehow had the power, and could fix it, would you even want that?"

"I don't *know*," she said. "If I was happy, it was because I was *made* to be happy the same way you were *made* to keep the pregnancy. Not my choice. I'm *miserable*, but at least I feel like I'm fully me, and not beholden to anyone."

His heartbeat was almost as loud as the waves. "Yes... that's it, isn't it?" Michael had likened it to an arranged marriage all those months ago. "What would it take for you to choose happiness?"

"What, with you?"

"Not necessarily. As mother of the Heir, you're afforded–"

She pressed a callused finger against his lips. "Stop being king. Just be Ario for a minute." The finger fell away. "What would *you* choose to be happy?"

Ario turned back out towards the sea. "Is it a nice night?"

"Hm?"

"The sea. What does it look like?"

"Uh... well. There's some clouds, but they're moving quick, with the wind. The water's all smooth and shiny, because the moon is almost full. You can see all these stars... it's been years since I've seen stars."

"...Thank you." He took a deep breath. "I want to make something lasting, something that the people control. A socialist democracy, where everyone is equal, and everyone can *be themselves* and survive. I don't want our daughter thrust into queendom, because all that would do is start the cycle over again." The breeze ruffled his hair. "I want a simple house somewhere nice, somewhere with a library and a park, maybe a car to take drives. We could go to the ocean. And you're there, we could be roommates, raise her together right. You could do your performing and I'll..." He tried to think of some conceivable career for himself. "I'll be doing something simple and unobtrusive that doesn't affect *anybody*. I want a stupidly simple life with you. And we'll have our friends and family over for dinners and go to movies and–"

She grasped him and pulled him into her arms. Her touch, after so long without it, was foreign, but their bodies did still fit together the same way.

***

The next morning, unprompted, she sat with him during breakfast. Perhaps she was hungover, because she kept sighing, but she was there nonetheless. He didn't want to say anything and spoil the moment. She was a butterfly perched on his finger.

He tried to think about how he felt. Sadness, sure. Rage at the heavens, of course. But there was something small and new and nameless, something not quite like *hope*, in and among the ashes. "Tell me what it was like," he said, over the eggs and terrible coffee.

"How do you mean?"

"All that time you were away. With her. We never did get to talk before–"

"It sucked. How was your time in the castle?"

"...It sucked."

She laughed then, and so did he. Over the next few days, between meetings and calls with Xander, her stories slowly started to unfold, the lost time beginning to crystallize itself into memory.

The happy pieces:

"...And that was *exactly* how Amalia discovered horsey."

"She snores–just a little. She sounds just like you when she sleeps."

"I don't know how he did it, we didn't have *anything*, but Michael managed to get me salted caramels for my birthday, and I ate them all and was *so* sick."

And less so:

"Mara and Evelyn were the *worst* to each other, in the beginning, but then Evelyn had that fall and got a concussion and Mara carried her back to where we were staying, and neither of them said a word, but after that, they stopped yelling."

"A man in a tunic followed me back from the store. He had a dog with him, and now I wonder if it was really an agent like Mara. Michael had to pretend to be my husband to get him to leave."

"She cried for you. In the beginning, she cried for you."

And his own: he told her the whole story, the twelve years of running, transitioning in the wild in secret, how he really felt during pregnancy (so forsaken and so *lost*), his torture at the hands of Xavier, finding trust in Xander, losing his faith. How overwhelmed he felt, now, as the very young king of a shambling and rotted nation.

These whispered moments wove together, creating something that, if anything, was at least *real*.

***

The morning they arrived at the approximate location of the colonies, it was bright and still but very cold for April even this far south; Ario felt the bite of sunlight. After a hurried breakfast, and a strategy meeting, they sent down a set of divers and a drivable camera. On the water's surface, there wasn't much indicating any civilization, nor were there any structures for very young infants. Ario and Peony took a dinghy across to the sandbar that Ainsley must have mentioned, and he planted a pole with the island's flag while she set up a small mortuary tablet. He couldn't see her expression, but he could *feel* the tension and grief that radiated off of her. She knelt at the tablet and sobbed, a guttural, bone-deep sound that made him ache for their child.

He could do little more than whisper a prayer: "Moon, please safeguard the souls of the dead, that they may rest peacefully."

She sniffled, utterly spent. "Moon?"

"If there's any divinity left, that's it," Ario said. "The Goddess's watcher... that has to mean something."

"I used to pray to the moon when I was a kid," she said. "I have these half-memories of these... temples. They were full of colorful glass, and the light would hit them just right–"

A voice came from past their boat: "Majesty–we've found something."

Back on the ship, they watched (or rather, someone described to him what the *others* were watching) the camera and divers as they found undeniable signs of life. At first, the land under the sea appeared to be razed into near oblivion, leaving behind little more than scattered stone ruins. But an anthropologist pointed out that some of the ruins looked *staged*, as though they were *pretending* to be destroyed so nobody would bother them. The divers proceeded cautiously, and when the camera tripped a set of traps, they had confirmation there were survivors, because a few came to examine the device.

Peony made a noise that was half-scream, half-cry, and gripped Ario's hand painfully tightly. Three figures; one male, one female, one indeterminate, all appearing of middle age, and they appeared, at first blush, to be in good enough health. They mumbled to each other in their language; Peony admitted she did not recognize the dialect, but they recognized the device as from the mainland.

"I have to *go*," she kept saying. "I have to go down there. I have to go." Ario tried to get her to choose between mundane oxygen or magical means of getting air, but she seemed not to fully understand, too dazed from seeing her kind. Twice she started into the waves, fully clothed, and someone had to drag her out before she drowned herself. Finally, she consented to be charmed and to wear a wetsuit, and slipped into the waves.

He'd hear it from her later, but watching it unfold in real time was miraculous. While the sirens were wary of the crown's divers, they recognized Peony for her bond necklace. Moreover, she was recognized for who she was; a princess come home.

Because the air charm did not last forever, the sirens agreed to come ashore to meet the new crown, though only because of its relation to Peony. Ario *felt* their collective joy, bright and intoxicating. Once he went ashore on the sandbar, Peony grasped his hand and dragged him over. "It's more than us," she hissed reverently. "There are almost a *hundred* survivors." She grasped his face, trailing seawater down his arms. "A *hundred*." She said something in the native language, which got a gruff-sounding response. "They still speak your language."

Truthfully, Ario had not been expecting to meet anyone. He did not know their etiquette or what they expected. He could not even look towards their eyes. "Hello," he began haltingly. "Nothing has brought me more joy than learning of your survival. The moon has granted us blessings today."

"Many blessings," said a feminine voice.

"My name is Ilario Credenzo. I am the... new king of Landfall."

There was some heated whispering in the siren language, with what sounded like assurances from Peony.

He felt the need to bow, so he did. "My mate's main goal has been finding her people. I am here to offer whatever may be beneficial to you—aid, supplies. We owe you reparations. I know that much."

"Why should we trust your goodwill?" another one said. The accent was smooth, pleasant, even if the tone of voice had some vitriol.

"I wouldn't trust me either," he said. "I wish to make things right for my mate, and for our child. You have been lost for so long. Things are different now. Better. Empty words, I know, until I prove myself." When his words were met with silence, he added, "If you wish to be left alone, we can abide by that as well."

"We will have to discuss it with our council," the first voice said. Then, in the native language, they asked something else, to which Peony replied with another question. "The... child. They are one of us?"

"She has fledgling scales," Ario said. "We won't know for sure for another three months, but it seems promising."

"And she is your princess?"

"...Yes."

A pause. "We will see if the council is willing to meet with you." There was more discussion in the siren tongue, then soft smacks of skin, possibly kisses on cheeks. "Blessings, Wei Thalia. We will not soon part." Then he heard them swim away.

Ario sank down to his knees, clutching the damp sand in his palms, and he felt Peony join him. "I can't believe this," he muttered.

She was crying. "Maybe some of my family survived. They *knew* me, who I was, before the miasma took my power..."

"I hope so. Oh, I really hope so."

But how to provide reparations for one of the worst disasters in history?

It became clear that this was a process that would take time. Ario would never fully heal the distrust that had grown between their two nations. The political match helped somewhat, but seemed strangely conditional on whether Amalia could change forms, which Peony pointed out was hypocritical because *she* couldn't, and they accepted her with open arms. The sirens—the council of seven elders that made most decisions, anyway—stated that they had had independence all these years and would remain their own sovereign nation, something he had assumed and had been more than prepared to support. They bristled at notions of trade, though because the miasma had been here like everywhere, they would be forced to take the supplies. Ario weighted all deals in their favor, but they refused money outright.

The chief, his wives, and one of their daughters had been killed or otherwise died, but Keala had survived and even had a baby of her own. She initially did not believe Peony was her lost sister, but when she saw her, the two collapsed in a pile and cried and cried and spoke so quickly they could barely get the words out.

After these long, wringing days, he and his team were able to engender enough favor with the sirens to recruit an ambassador, an apparently very young-looking girl named Maili with the pinkest tail Peony had ever seen. Having lived most of her life away from the mainland, she was infinitely charmed by mundane technologies and grilled foods. She would accompany them back and help develop favorable policy for her people. Keala and her child were returning as well for an extended visit with her sister.

The retinue started back towards the capitol. At least the weather had finally broken, leaving it warm enough on deck to forgo coats or jackets. Ario liked feeling the sea air on his face, but he found himself missing the palace, and the people there, most of all his daughter. Keala's son was about a year older than her and was all up in everything, babbling away; it was not uncommon to see his mother darting after him, muttering how being on board made him much *faster*.

On their penultimate night at sea, Ario lay alone in a hammock strung along the balcony of his quarters. Were he not so sick of his glasses, he would try to read an actual book. Instead, he swayed there and dwelled on the lack of stress, an unfamiliar sensation. Perhaps things had finally turned a corner and it would no longer be so hard. Or perhaps he was just getting a respite.

Gentle footsteps; he figured it might be the child. "Hello, little one," he said, though the boy did not understand much of mainland language yet.

~~It's you~~, said the voice, genderless and very old as though crusted over with salt.

Ario sat up, his heart flying into his throat. "I thought you were–"

~~She is. Yes.~~

"Then who are–*what* are you?"

It ignored him. ~~We disagreed, you know, about where our creations belonged. She wanted them in the light, on the earth, to feel what she couldn't. I wanted them safe below the water.~~

Sweat beaded along his brow. "Are you telling me you're the watcher?"

~~A curious experiment, after myriads upon myriads alone, with only each other. Could a speck of dust eventually wind up like us? The~~

~~dust became elements, became cells, then multicellular creatures, be-~~
~~came thinking meat that had to explain its existence, not capable of~~
~~seeing the world as it truly is, only catching it in gasps. We knew there~~
~~was no catching up for you. We gave you what you call *magic*, to see if~~
~~it would help.~~

Something cold, almost *stony*, brushed his cheek. He shuddered, and wanted to jerk away, but found he couldn't.

~~I told Her we should let you all alone, so we could be together again~~
~~at last. But She had grown tired by then. You let Her go. And after all~~
~~this time I had to learn to grieve. You: a walking, talking sack of raw~~
~~meat. And yet, I cannot hate you, because She loved you. Loved you~~
~~all, but you especially. So I must keep loving you.~~

"I'm not sorry," he said to the moon. "I had to save my people from Her."

~~I cannot conceptualize that. Giving up what is so solidly yours for~~
~~another.~~

"It's what people do."

~~Yes. I see that. My beloved and I will be together again eventually.~~
~~I will take care of you. Perhaps She will forgive me. Perhaps not. But~~
~~it is just Us.~~

That had wild cosmological and philosophical implications, so much that he felt dizzy. "Why did You come to see me?"

~~I wanted to see what She loved so much. The spoils of Her plan to~~
~~outwit me. I wanted to see it now that there has finally been a change,~~
~~after my whole existence.~~

He swallowed. "And what do You think?"

~~I feel relief. Something exists outside Us.~~

Ario blinked. "Was it very lonely?"

The stone texture brushed across his hands. ~~*Lonely.* A strange, alien~~
~~term. A human one.~~

"I take it you were, then."

~~You are—faint electricity dancing along neurons. And yet you understand existence better than I could after billions of years. You wonderful, clever creature. I will watch you, and try to learn from you. And maybe then She will return to me.~~

"...Maybe people understand existence better because it will end."

~~Is that the difference? Is that all?~~

"You're a celestial body. You tell me."

A rough, grinding, lapping sound that might be laughter.

Ario figured that if the god wanted to kill him, it would have done so already. "Is there... any way to get it back? My magic?"

~~You have been altered inexorably. Were I to try, you may not survive the process.~~

He exhaled. "I figured that might be the case."

~~You do not need it. Not anymore.~~

"I've already served my purpose and saved the day?"

~~Does anything have a purpose?~~ It countered. ~~I don't. She didn't. But you humans seem to have made up one anyway. Isn't that something? Perhaps I could too.~~

"Other than managing the tides? Sure."

~~I will keep watching. You have my blessing, child.~~

"Goodbye."

From somewhere below, there was a not-inconsiderable splash as it hit the water.

Epilogue

An Abdication

ome time has elapsed

Cashmere no longer felt alien to his skin, but it did not seem the most apropos choice given the summer heat. He still hated the stiffness, the formality, of meetings like this; that hadn't changed.

Ario glanced at the mirror. The glasses assured him everything was in order, the pins and frippery in place, hair not too rumpled. They would never truly replicate sight, but they did help. Right now they were indicating a swiftly-encroaching presence.

"Da-*dee*," Amalia whined. "Mommy's taking *forever*."

"I think, today of all days, we're allowed to be late." He turned and picked her up—soon she would be too big to do so—wrinkles be damned.

"I don't wanna go," she continued.

"Isn't it terrible? So boring?"

Amalia giggled. He chucked her under the chin.

"No more boring meetings for daddy," he said. "But you know it means lessons for you."

She sighed, world-weary.

The click of heels and the swish of skirts. "*Sorry.* I couldn't get the pins quite right."

"It's only right to hold up traffic just once more," he said. Ario offered Peony his free hand. "I'm sure you look beautiful—as always."

"I could be wearing a sack and you wouldn't know the difference," she teased.

"I would, actually. Sack cloth makes a terrible ruckus. *Speaking of*—is it terrible out there?"

A sigh. "Mara said the corridor is loaded. Something about documenting the occasion, or something."

Ario laughed. "One last show."

"One last show."

True to form, the noise started the instant they left the room; the clicking of cameras, hushed murmurs from journalists broadcasting. Ario set down Amalia, forced a smile, and made his way towards the executive chambers.

He did not need an aid to know when Xander joined him; he knew him by the sound of his breath, at this point, but it was helped when Amalia cried, "Xandy!"

"Great, now the world will know my embarrassing nickname," he muttered. "Hi, princess."

"There are worse things to be known as," Ario pointed out.

"The prime minister elect is already there, and keeps sighing and looking at their watch," Xander said to him quietly. "I, ah, do have a full docket of items for them today, with a hard stop at four to prepare for the ball—"

"*Sorry,*" Peony whispered again.

"I have *one* more day to be impressive and inconvenient, and I will use it," Ario said cheerfully. "Then we will be out of your hair, Xander."

"That's the part I dread," he admitted.

Down in the executive chambers—an impressive, old space paneled in rich dark woods and full of sculpted, raked benches—were more photographers, the judge, the prime minister elect, and a desk with a single piece of paper and a pen.

The prime minister, a tall, weedy person of mixed magical/mundane heritage, approached him, took a shallow bow, and then shook his hand. "Majesties."

This person was the most competent and well-meaning of the selected candidates, but that didn't make the formal exchange–after months and months of transitory work–any easier.

"I, erm, didn't realize you were bringing the princess," they said in their northern accent.

"Her mother has to sign for her, as she is a minor," Ario said. "And I just *wanted* to, you know?"

This made the peanut gallery chuckle.

"Shall we get started?" they asked.

Ario felt slightly unreal as he sat at that horrible desk for the last time. The judge announced the contents of the decree–the formal abolition of the monarchy, effective immediately–and he signed on the dotted line. Then Peony signed for Amalia, and Amalia insisted on also scribbling "her autograph" below that.

The whole process took maybe five minutes. There was not relief, not yet–he still had the ball to get through, and surely there would be more calls until the prime minister was truly confident in their role, but it was, definitively, over.

"Congratulations, minister," Ario said.

"Thank you, sir," they said. *Sir.* That felt weird, but was correct. "I will try to make you proud."

The judge had the minister recite a secular oath with their hand on the cover of the constitution. A handler turned to sweep them out. "Good luck," Ario mouthed in Xander's general direction, and the emotion on his face, according to his glasses, was "trepidation."

Back in the safety of his quarters, after helping a squirming Amalia out of her formal dress and into play clothes, Ario found Evelyn waiting, a bottle of old ritual wine sitting unopened on his (blank! clean!) desk.

"It's over, then?" she asked.

"Yes. Poor Xander."

She laughed brightly. "I should be furious you've destroyed my life's work."

"And yet?"

"And yet I couldn't be prouder." She came forward to embrace him. She'd recently cut her hair–which was now almost entirely white–and it tickled his cheek. "I am looking forward to my retirement."

"It's hardly *retirement*. You still have to help me train this child. Besides, the strides you made with treatments–"

She waved her hand dismissively. "Let me have the *illusion* of rest." She crossed over to the table and pulled the cork laboriously from the wine, then poured two glasses. "To the monarchy."

"And the Goddess."

The wine had vinegarized, which only suited the moment.

***

In their new home down the coast, close enough to the capitol for Ario to feasibly commute and for Peony to visit the colony, they planted roots. The crown–administration, he corrected himself–afforded him an allowance for all the work he'd done, and it wouldn't be forever, so they put it to use and built the two-story home, and an adjoining duplex for former staff, now family. Michael insisted Ario still needed a security detail and was probably right. At least now Ario could more easily insist on vacations.

Life became slow. Less frantic. Outside that bubble of stress, there would be traumas to cope with and to come to terms to, but he had the space to do so now, and to figure out just who Ario really was outside of the yokes he'd been destined to carry.

One evening that summer, he sat on a blanket on their section of beach as their daughter played in the waves. She was a siren, so there was no risk of drowning. Getting her to come in at the end of the day was the bigger issue.

"You're letting her go out pretty far," Peony said, startling him.

Ario cleared his throat. "Lesson done already?" She'd had a client.

"Did you fall asleep?"

"...No."

She tsk'ed.

"Hey, I'm blind, and she can't drown. It's fine."

She sighed heavily, but joined him in the sand. "I'm... glad she's not going to be a princess."

"I have a feeling she'd be a menace," Ario said. "Stubborn, impulsive–"

"Like someone I know," she cut in.

"...Too powerful for her own good. She doesn't get that she can't just do whatever she feels like."

Peony took his hand. "Ario. She's five."

"It always felt like a *burden* to me. I find it so bizarre that she sees it as the opposite."

"Well, she's had good people and a good world shaping around her. Of course she'd see it as a good thing, when her daddy saved the world."

Ario scoffed.

"It's true. That's how you'll go down in history books. People will probably always have a parasocial relationship with you."

"The problem is I don't know what to do *now*. You have your clients, Amalia has her lessons."

"Get a hobby. Several. You said you've been wanting to read that new series by your favorite author." She leaned against him. "For the moon's sake, just *rest*. It's okay."

"I don't know how," he admitted.

"Well, you can help get our house in order. It's a mess in there with all the boxes."

Ario chuckled a little.

She turned her head. "What's so funny?"

"It's here. That stupidly simple life we wanted."

"Isn't it great?"

He took a deep breath in, then out. "I guess it is."

A lot went of love and effort went into *Heartlines*. It feels like "self-publishing" is a little bit of a misnomer—I am grateful to be part of a thriving community of indie authors.

Firstly, I'd like to thank the Indie Author Revolution LLC, a wonderful group dedicated to supporting and uplifting indie authors, connecting them with artists, editors, narrators, and personal assistants. A.C. Toy, S.B. Ellie, Black Dahlia, Milli C. Vieira, A.E. Amaris, S. Pedigo, Erin M. Silva, Cypher C.—thank you for all you've done for independent artists. To join the revolution, you can visit their site at indieauthorrevolution.com.

Secondly, I'd like to thank my partner, Killian, for his unwavering support as I dove fully into this endeavor, and for listening to my rantings and ramblings. This definitely would've been a much rougher journey if not for his love.

Third, to all of the original readers of *Heartlines* from the super cringey, probably-problematic online version from five years ago, if not for your faith in my world and your love of these characters, I would not be here today, and I would not have so much faith in myself as a writer.

To my parents, thank you for your openness as I pivoted course, and for nurturing a lifelong love of reading and stories.

I'd love to give a special shoutout to my first editor Michelle—without you, I would be nothing close to the writer I am today. And also to my other lads Caitlin and August, who read earlier versions of this story.

The cover was created by Anna Graziosi, a wonderfully talented artist and one of my best and oldest friends. Her insight into the visual world of *Heartlines* is honestly super cool.

I would be remiss not to mention Alexandra Murphy, from the Martha's Vineyard Institute of Creative Writing. Alexandra helped shape the beginning of this novel into a more compelling story.

Lastly, thank you, dear reader, for getting this far. I genuinely hoped you enjoyed the story, and if you feel so moved, Goodreads and Amazon reviews do so much for indie authors.

I hope you consider continuing to follow me on my writing journey. I can be found on TikTok as @rachel.e.wilder, on Bluesky as @rachel-e-wilder, and on my website, rachelewilder.com, where I share special updates and some peeks at new projects. You may also find a free short story or two.

Rachel E. Wilder (they/them) is an indie author based in upstate New York. Rachel has been writing for nearly 20 years in all kinds of genres: fantasy, horror, sci-fi, literary/contemporary, magical realism. Having gotten their start writing *Danny Phantom* fanfiction, Rachel fell in love with language and storytelling and quickly branched out.

Rachel has an undergraduate degree in creative writing, and a master's in library science. In addition to writing fiction, they have experience writing grants, organizational copy, and academic papers. They are also a skilled developmental and copyeditor. When not writing, Rachel enjoys gaming, hiking, baking, and cooking.

Rachel lives at home with their partner Killian and their cat Xeno.

Rachel is a part of the Indie Author Revolution, LLC, an organization dedicated to supporting indie authors, artists, narrators, editors, and personal assistants. Find out more about the revolution at indieauthorrevolution.com.

To keep up with Rachel's work and progress, you can subscribe to their newsletter at rachelewilder.com, and follow them on TikTok at @rachel.e.wilder or on Bluesky at @rachel-e-wilder.bsky.social.